Angel on the Dead Tree

A first novel by L J Watson,
Undiscovered Authors Literary
Prize Winner.

Angel on the Dead Tree

By L J Watson

Cover Design, Text and Illustrations copyright © 2006 Linda Watson

Original Cover Design by Tom Bunning Design

First edition published in Great Britain in 2007
by Discovered Authors

The right of Linda Watson to be identified as the Author
of the Work has been asserted by her in accordance with
the Copyright, Designs and Patent Act 1988

A Discovered Authors Diamond

All rights reserved. No part of this publication may be reproduced, stored in a retrieval system, or transmitted, in any form or by any means without the prior written permission of the Author

All characters in this publication are fictitious and any resemblance to real persons, living or dead, is purely coincidental

ISBN 978-1-905108-33-6

Printed in the UK by BookForce

BookForce UK's policy is to use papers that are natural, renewable and recyclable products and made from wood grown in sustainable forests where ever possible

BookForce UK Ltd.
50 Albemarle Street
London W1S 4BD
www.bookforce.co.uk
www.discoveredauthors.co.uk

ACKNOWLEDGEMENTS

To Ian, Jane, Emma and Tamsin
for all their support
and to
Sue, my long-term reading partner

Prologue

June 1798

Claudio Farrigiani, Knight of St John of Jerusalem, Rhodes and Malta, stood on the rocky peninsular of Mount Sceberus and gazed moodily across the Grand Harbour to the frowning fortifications of Valletta. Malta slept in a sunlit silence.

Nine years he had spent here. Nine years in which his hopes, his dreams, his ideals, had drained from him like water seeping from a leaky well. The hot sun beat down on his head with an anger that mirrored his own.

How long ago it seemed that he had stepped ashore on this barren island of harsh limestone crags, a nineteen year old novitiate inspired by the images of knights and heroes, his head filled with the war cries of battle and a burning determination to take up his sword against the enemies of Christ. It had been his ambition since boyhood, when he had listened in fascination to the stories of the Knights.

And they were told with a special pride in his home-town of Amalfi, birthplace of those merchants who had travelled to Jerusalem to build a hospice which would be a place of rest and shelter for pilgrims to the Holy Land. Five centuries ago that had been, but out of the small seed of this original hospice had developed a giant tree: the Order of St John of Jerusalem, Rhodes and Malta.

Claudio sank down on a rock, despairingly. And now the tree was dying. Of that he was certain.

Here on the island of Malta, the death blow was about to be struck.

1

July 2004

Tom gazed around the busy airport terminal, aware of the first flutterings of unease. He could remember his father's words clearly: "You won't have to bother with luggage when you reach Gatwick, it'll be transferred automatically to the Malta plane. Go straight into the terminal and I'll meet you at the entrance to Waterstones."

So where was he? Tom had been waiting twenty minutes already, what if Dad didn't turn up? Should he continue to Malta? That was where his luggage was heading, where his relatives lived, even if he knew nothing about them.

He grinned to himself, remembering the phone call. How excited his Dad had sounded. 'I can't wait to show you Malta, it's full of history and if you get tired of the Knights there are plenty of beaches where you can swim and snorkel and windsurf. We'll have a marvellous holiday. I've got a big surprise waiting for you, something you couldn't possibly guess, and at last you'll be able to meet your Maltese relations.'

'Relations,' he'd mouthed at his mother, hovering by his side.

'What relations?' she mouthed back. 'Ask him.'

'I didn't know we had any relatives on Malta?' Tom queried obediently, feeling a sudden rush of interest, but his father was bringing the conversation to an abrupt end.

'See you at Gatwick. Waterstones, remember, just inside the entrance.'

So where was he? Dad must have been held up, Tom decided, but it's no big deal, there are two hours before the connecting flight. Feeling conspicuous standing there, he ventured further inside, joining the throng of people at a table covered with travel guides, and ferreting through them until he found one on Malta. May as well be prepared for what lay ahead.

Mission accomplished, Tom repositioned himself in the entrance. Still no sign of Dad and the flutterings of unease were beginning to crystallise into a hard knot in his stomach.

The sound of his own name being called broke into Tom's thoughts.

'Will Thomas Newton, travelling to Malta, report to the British Airways Desk.'

Stupidly, Tom suddenly felt self-conscious, under the scrutiny of countless pairs of inquisitive eyes that seemed to follow him as he moved out into the concourse. A pleasant young woman in a smart, blue uniform pointed him in the right direction.

'I'm Tom Newton...Thomas Newton...the tannoy said...'

'Passport?'

Tom delved into his rucksack. A cursory glance from a fraught-looking official and he was handed a brown envelope, his name marked clearly on the front.

'What's it about?'

'No idea. We were just asked to deliver it to you.' The official turned his attention to the next passenger, effectively dismissing Tom.

Sitting on one of the central benches he opened the envelope slowly, guessing that he wasn't going to enjoy the contents. *'Sorry about this,'* he read, *'but something's cropped up – that big surprise I've been planning - and I'm taking this evening's flight to Malta.'* Yesterday's date, Tom noted. So his Dad was there already. Fantastic! *'You're old enough to continue alone and I'll be waiting for you at the airport when you* arrive. I'm afraid I may be tied up for a few days, but I'll take you out to Haz Zahra first. You'll find plenty to do at the Villa Magrino. Sounds grand, doesn't it? Though it's actually a farm. They'll enjoy looking after you, I know. They, by the way, are Luigi and Francesca Farrigiani. Perhaps their son Ricardo will be there, you'll like him. See you soon, love Dad.'

Forty minutes later, Tom boarded the Malta plane with the feeling that he was getting quite experienced at this flying lark, nothing to it, his composure vanishing instantly when he found himself sitting next to an incredibly attractive girl with long, dark hair and honey-gold skin; in her late twenties at a guess- the kind who always threw him into an instant panic. She didn't help matters by smiling at him.

'Would you like the window seat?'

'I'm okay.' How surly, Tom rebuked himself, you could at least have thanked her.

'You'd be doing me a favour. I'm not fond of flying, I always feel happier in the aisle seat.'

'Alright then.' Tom cursed his bluntness. They'd have three hours together. Some conversation it would be if he couldn't manage to string together more than a few words. She was probably already regretting her friendliness. He could feel the familiar flush staining his cheeks a bright cherry-red.

'Ever been to Malta before?' she asked, once they'd changed places.

'No.'

'Then you're in for a treat, it's a fantastic place. I should know, I was born and brought up there.'

Tom relaxed as she chatted away about the beauties of the island and by the time they were airborne he'd rediscovered his voice, found himself, to his surprise, confessing to the fears haunting him about this unexpected holiday; fears that he'd tried hard not to admit even to himself.

'I am looking forward to visiting Malta, but Dad's pretty much a stranger,' he explained. 'I was only nine when he and Mum divorced and even when they were living together I didn't see much of him. It wasn't Dad's fault, his job took him all over the world. He's a historical researcher, you may have seen one of his television programmes. He's Joseph Newton. I'm Tom.'

'I don't get chance to watch much television, though I love history. I couldn't do anything else after growing up on Malta. Whichever way you turn, you're confronted by some aspect of the past. Didn't you ever get to travel with your father?'

'We went to Italy once, and to Greece when he was making a programme about the origins of the Olympic Games, but Dad had work to do and Mum and I were left pretty much on our own. Looking back, I think she minded more than I did. It can't have been a lot of fun for her because I wasn't old enough to be much of a companion.'

'Do you live with your mother?'

'I did. She married again, yesterday in fact, to an American. I think that's why Dad offered me this holiday, as a kind of consolation. After this, I'll stay with my grandparents in Manchester until I finish school. I'm going into the Sixth Form next term, exam results permitting.'

'Does your father know Malta?'

'Yes, though I didn't know that. Apparently we have some relatives there.' Tom opened the front pocket of the rucksack, extracting the note and reading, 'Luigi and Francesca Farrigiani. They have a son, Ricardo. They sound Italian, don't they?'

She laughed. 'Malta has an incredible variety of surnames. Comes from our history. We've been colonised so many times, and the Knights of St John were divided into eight languages, or tongues, which simply means the language they spoke. They were Italy, France, Provence, Auvergne, Castile, Aragon, Germany and England. They were all one Order but they lived in their own houses, called auberges. Have you heard of them?'

'Only the name,' Tom confessed. 'Dad mentioned them when he rang me about the holiday. Weren't they something to do with the Crusades?'

'Originally, yes. They were formed in Jerusalem by a group of merchants from Amalfi, under their leader Brother Gerard, and they built a hospice to give aid to the Crusaders and pilgrims flocking to the Holy Land. That was in the twelfth century. When the Knights were thrown out of Jerusalem they went to Cyprus, on to Rhodes, and finally to Malta. This was their last real home. I should imagine the Farrigianis are descended from one of the Italian Knights.' She laughed. 'They were supposed to have taken a vow of chastity, but towards the end of their stay on Malta things had become very lax. By the time Napoleon threw them off the island, many of the knights had fathered sons and daughters.'

Tom listened enthralled as she continued to fill him in on the history of her island, fascinated by its many invasions and sieges. He couldn't help thinking how well she'd get on with his father.

Their food arrived and they ate in silence. When the trays had been cleared away, Tom rested his head against the back of the seat, eyes closed, his mind a whirl of Turkish fleets and knights on horseback, their swords flashing in the sunlight. He woke to find the girl smiling down at him.

'Have a good dream?'

'Yes, Malta sounds great. I'd like to learn more about the

Knights.'

'Then you need to spend some time in Valletta. With every stride you take you'll be treading in the footsteps of the Knights: their ghosts haunt you at every turn. Whenever I'm down by the harbour, I can almost see an anxious knight scanning the horizon for a sight of Turkish invaders or for Napoleon's enormous fleet in those last dark days before the Order crumbled and the Knights were banished from the island.'

'Is Valletta near Haz Zahra?' Tom pulled his travel guide from the rucksack, opening it to the map on the front page.

'Haz Zahra's too small to be shown on a map this size, but it's somewhere around here.' Her finger hovered briefly around the middle of the map.

'Do you live near there?' Tom flushed. 'Sorry, I don't know your name, which is awful because you practically know my entire life story. I don't usually talk this much. Mum often says I'm going through my teenage grunting period.'

She flashed him a sympathetic smile. 'I'm Alice. . .Alice Rogerson. I live way over the other side of the island.' Noting his disappointment she added, 'But if I get any free time I'll look you up and show you some of my favourite haunts.'

'Do you live with your parents?' Tom thought it was about time he became the listener.

'Yes.'

'What do they do?'

'They're farmers, like your relations.'

'Have you any brothers and sisters?'

'A brother.' She hesitated and Tom felt awkward, suddenly realising it sounded like an interrogation. However, she flashed him another smile before continuing, 'He's called Ewen and he also wants to be a farmer. We'll be starting the descent soon, if you want to put your things away.'

Tom paid a visit to the toilet and then they both sat in silence as the plane swooped down towards a small, straw-coloured leaf floating on a jade-blue sea.

'Put your watch on two hours,' Alice reminded him as they hit the runway.

Six o'clock. Tom felt as though he'd been travelling forever. 'Will they speak English?' he asked suddenly. 'My relations?'

'Sure to, Maltese and English are our two official languages.'

The plane screeched to a halt. Malta. A whole month with Dad. A chill ran down Tom's spine, a prickling of the hairs on the back of his neck. What his grandmother called a ghost walking across his grave.

He followed Alice down the aisle and through a long covered tunnel to a carousel where luggage was gliding along a circular conveyer belt. Just when he was beginning to panic that his own suitcase must be lost, it appeared and he grabbed it thankfully, looking around for Alice. There was no sight of her and he felt a sudden rush of disappointment. He'd meant to introduce her to Dad. Too tired to want to do anything but get the meeting with his father over as quickly as possible, he made his way into the terminal.

Tom was totally and utterly fed up. This was beyond a joke. For the second time today, he'd been standing for half an hour waiting for a non-existent father. The other passengers from his flight had disappeared long ago. Wearily, he made his way to the British Airways desk.

'I wondered if you'd got a message for me? My name's Thomas Newton and my father was supposed to meet me half an hour ago.'

'Arrived from England have you?' Tom nodded. 'Half an hour's not very long. Maybe he's been delayed. Come and wait in the office and we'll put out a call.'

The room was small, a single table and two chairs, and it seemed even smaller by the time the clock had ticked away another twenty minutes. The walls appeared to be closing in around him and he found it a struggle to keep his eyes open. Anyone would think he'd had a hard day. Every few seconds he heard the wheezing hiss of the tannoy announcing: 'Will Joseph Newton, meeting his son Thomas, come to the British Airways Desk.'

The door opened and the official appeared. 'No luck yet, I'm afraid. I thought you might be thirsty.'

'Thanks.' Tom accepted the Coke gratefully.

'Hungry?'

Tom shook his head. 'I had some food on the plane.'

'Don't look so worried, people are late all the time. We'll find your father for you. You don't happen to know where he was staying?'

Tom cursed himself for not mentioning it straight away. 'We've got relations here, Luigi and Francesca Farrigiani, they live at the Villa Magrino in Haz Zahra.'

'No problem then, I'll give them a ring. If your father's not there, we'll send you out in a taxi.'

Tom sipped his Coke, wondering how he felt about meeting his relations alone. Whatever had happened to stop Dad turning up, he could at least have rung the airport and let him know.

When the door reopened, he knew immediately that something was wrong. He should have known that Dad wouldn't let him down like this. The official was accompanied by an older man, who sat down opposite Tom. 'You were supposed to meet your father here at the airport?'

'An hour ago. What's happened to him?'

'Tell us again about these relations.'

Tom repeated the information, wishing they'd hurry up and give him the bad news. Nothing could be worse than this dreadful uncertainty. 'Have you rung them?'

The man nodded. 'We rang the Villa Magrino and spoke to Luigi Farrigiani, but he says he's never heard of a Joseph or Thomas Newton. They have no English relations.'

It took a few moments for the words to actually make sense. When they did, Tom leapt to his feet, angrily. 'That's ridiculous! Why would Dad make it up?'

'You tell us. Sit down, there's no point in losing your temper. Now take a deep breath and just tell us exactly what your father said.'

'I can do better than that, I can show you.' Tom reached for his rucksack. 'Dad left a note for me at Gatwick so you can see I'm telling the truth.' Opening the front pocket, he stared in disbelief. His wallet lay there, together with the travel guide, but there was no brown envelope.

'Perhaps you placed it inside the rucksack,' the official said more kindly, noting Tom's distress.

'I never opened it on the plane, just this front pocket.' Tom checked anyway, knowing all the time it was useless; he had a clear picture in his mind of slotting the envelope between the guide book and his wallet.

'You took the envelope out on the plane?'

'To show to Alice.'

'Alice?'

'Alice Rogerson.'

'A friend?'

'Not really. I sat next to her.'

'Perhaps you dropped it.'

'No, I didn't! I put it back in this pocket, at the same time as the travel guide. Someone must have stolen it.' Even as the words tumbled from his mouth Tom realised how stupid they sounded. The officials must have thought they were dealing with a lunatic.

The elder one cleared his throat. 'Are you accusing this Alice Rogerson of stealing your envelope?'

'No, she was kind to me, and why would she want the note?'

'Why would anyone want it?'

Tom was silenced, too tired to think straight. Nothing made sense anymore.

'This Alice Rogerson, you say she was kind to you. Would she put you up for the night?'

'I don't know where she lives. I don't know anything, anymore. Not where my Dad is, why my relations say they're not my relations, why my note has vanished. . .'

The officials rose to their feet, the elder one patting Tom on the shoulder. 'The best course of action seems to be for us to ring the British Consulate. They'll probably ask us to put you in a taxi to Valletta.'

'What good will that do?' Tom asked, aware of his rudeness but beyond caring.

The official's patience was coming to an end. 'I presume you do want to trace your father? They are the people to help you. If they don't have any success, they'll see that you get back to England safely.'

Much good that will be, Tom thought, as they departed. Mum's on her way to America and my grandparents are touring Scotland. I've no idea how to get in touch with them. The realisation that he was on his own, in a foreign country, hit him like a physical blow. For the first time in his life he felt totally alone. Impulsively, he picked up his rucksack and sidled out into the terminal. There was no sign of the officials. He had a hazy idea in the back of his mind of questioning Luigi Farrigiani personally, there must have been some mistake, Dad couldn't have got it wrong, but how on earth was he to reach Haz Zahra? Best not to stand in one place for too long, and certainly not in front of the office door. As he began to move through the crowds, a welcome sign caught his eye: TAXI DESK. Hurrying over, he pulled the wallet from his rucksack. Thank goodness Mum had been generous with money. The queue seemed to move far too slowly. What would the officials do when they found him gone? He cast anxious glances left and right, expecting at any moment to hear his name called. The woman in front of him, thin and bony like a stick insect, appeared to be haggling for a price. Even when her transaction had been completed, she took what seemed ages to stow the money in her purse, glaring at Tom as he elbowed her aside.

'Could I have a taxi to the Villa Magrino in Haz Zahra?' Nothing could have been simpler. His destination was written on a slip of paper.

'Take this to the taxi rank outside and. . .' The man stared at the notes Tom was offering. 'Sorry, we only take Maltese currency.'

'I haven't had time to change any yet. Couldn't you. . .'

'Over there.'

Tom's eyes followed the pointing finger. On the far side of the terminal a sign read: EXCHANGE DESK. The trouble was, between him and his destination stood the two officials, gazing around in obvious bewilderment, the older one looking decidedly angry. As Tom watched, they began to move through the crowds towards him.

'I'll be back,' he hissed to the startled man at the desk and, keeping to the side of the terminal, slid into the nearest toilet.

Tom felt like a secret agent in a spy movie as he pulled his Manchester United shirt and cap from the rucksack, putting them on hurriedly. Spies always changed in toilets. His was not much of a disguise, but it was better than nothing. Studying himself in the mirror, he tucked his long, rather dishevelled hair under the cap, pulling it down to shade his eyes. It took courage to step out into the terminal. His mouth was dry and he thought longingly of the unfinished Coke on the office table. Sauntering forward, eyes firmly fixed on the Exchange Desk, he tried not to look suspicious. With £50 of Maltese currency in his wallet, he risked a dash to the taxi desk. Another long queue. He was never going to make it at this rate. With a confidence he didn't feel, he strode to the front of the line, aware of the angry mutterings behind him.

'My taxi slip.' The man stared at him with no remembrance and Tom suddenly recalled his disguise. Raising his cap, he offered his wallet of money. Easy.

Perhaps Tom relaxed too much. As he approached the automatic doors leading out to the taxi rank, they slid open and he came face to face with the two officials.

2

In the back of the taxi, Tom was still shuddering. How he'd kept his nerve was a miracle. The officials had stared straight at him with no sign of recognition. What on earth had possessed him to stop right in front of them?

'Taxi rank outside,' he'd asked.

'To the right,' the elder one answered curtly, brushing past.

The taxi driver had been all business, taking the slip, ushering Tom into the back seat, and setting off without uttering a word.

Now he turned slightly, asking, 'Holiday?'

'Yes.'

That was the end of their conversation. Tom stared out at the countryside, amazed that night hadn't yet fallen, though the sky was awash with the eerie purple sheen of twilight. He knew he should be devising a plan for when he reached Haz Zahra, but his brain had shut down. The adrenaline that had kept him functioning until now was draining away rapidly. His eyes registered hedged fields which appeared to be growing crops of giant clover and dusty roads and...

'Here we are, then.'

Tom woke with a start. How could he have fallen asleep? Staggering out of the taxi, he found himself facing a rectangular stone house which looked nothing like a farm. Before he could gather his wits, the taxi driver dropped his case beside him and drove off. Well, that was the end of his return journey. He'd intended asking the driver to wait until he'd spoken to Luigi Farrigiani. Tom had no idea what he was going to say. He clenched his fists nervously, feeling the sweat pooling in his palms. What a stupid situation this was. He couldn't believe he'd been so foolish as to get himself dumped in the middle of nowhere.

Above the doorway, an ornate spidery writing read: *INTERIORE VIDE*. Latin, he guessed. Probably some ancient family motto. With my present luck, Tom thought, it'll probably translate as, 'Beware of Strangers.' Come on, he told himself, stop prevaricating. Rapping sharply on the door, he took a step backwards at the echoing crescendo of noise, beads of sweat standing out on his forehead. For a few moments he thought there was going to be no answer. What then? This time there was no convenient taxi rank. In fact, there didn't seem to be any sign of life anywhere. Tom was suddenly aware of the strange darkness and the complete silence; no faintly glowing street lights or the comforting sound of passing traffic.

The door opened without warning to reveal a shadowy figure in the blackness of the hallway.

'Yes?'

'I'm Tom. . . Thomas Newton. . . my father Joseph said. . .'

The man stepped forward into the light, so that Tom saw a craggy face, brown and lined, under bushy grey hair.

'I told the airport official, I have never heard of Joseph or Thomas Newton, nor do I have any English relatives.'

Tom, to his shame, found tears streaming down his face.

He was in a large kitchen, the stone walls covered with racks from which hung pots and pans, bunches of dried herbs, and long strings of garlic. The room was dominated by an enormous, wooden table, well-scrubbed, surrounded by four wooden chairs. Tom sat on one of them, sipping gratefully at a steaming cup of tea.

Luigi and his wife, Francesca, were still standing, clearly ill at ease. Tom got the impression they were almost as nervous as he was. He supposed it wasn't every day they found a sobbing boy on their doorstep, claiming to be a long lost relative. He couldn't help feeling sorry for them.

'This is good, thanks.' Tom indicated his tea and tried a smile.

Francesca sank into the seat opposite, smiling in return. 'In an emergency, you English drink tea, yes?'

Tom nodded. 'My grandmother in Manchester thinks a cup of tea is the answer to any problem.'

There was an awkward silence. Luigi and Francesca were so clearly mystified by his claim, or they were excellent actors, which Tom doubted. They were in their late sixties, early seventies, both with the coarse, weather-brown complexions of people who have spent most of their time working outdoors. There was something strong and sturdy about them, something dependable, which he liked. It seemed impossible to think of them lying, even though that made his father the liar which, despite the unhappiness of the divorce, Tom didn't want to consider.

Luigi sat down next to him. 'I wish we could say something constructive but. . .' He spread his hands out on the table in a gesture of helplessness.

'What I can't understand,' Tom said, 'Is how Dad got hold of your names. He got all the information correct, including the Villa Magrino and the village Haz Zahra. He knew you lived on a farm. Why would he tell me we were relations if it wasn't true? And why wasn't he at the airport?'

The tears were ominously close again and Francesca took his hand. 'You have no idea where your father could have gone?'

Tom shook his head. 'I don't know anyone here.' Except Alice, he thought, wishing fervently that he'd taken her address. She'd never have left the airport so quickly if she'd known this was going to happen. 'Dad never mentioned Malta until a few weeks ago. I asked Mum but she was equally in the dark. His parents were already dead when she met him and he was an only child.'

Luigi frowned. 'What I can't understand is why the airport officials sent you out here.'

Tom flushed. 'They didn't send me, I ran away from them.'

'They don't know you're here?'

'No, they left me in the office while they went to ring the British Consulate. They'd have sent me back to England and I know Dad came to Malta.'

Luigi hurried from the kitchen and Francesca stared at Tom helplessly.

'I couldn't think what else to do,' he said miserably. 'I thought you must have made a mistake and if I could talk to you personally. . .'

They sat in silence until Luigi's return.

'I've told them you're safe and that we'll keep you here for the night.' He waved away Tom's thanks. 'It's the least we can do after you've made such an effort to reach us. They'd managed to get hold of someone at your Consulate, who is going to make enquiries about your father, so I've promised to run you into Valletta in the morning.'

'I really am grateful,' Tom stammered. 'I'm sorry for being such a nuisance.'

'Nonsense.' Francesca rose and took his cup. 'First you must eat and then I'll find you somewhere to sleep.'

Forty minutes later, Tom lay under the covers in a strange bed. In a strange room. In a strange country. No mother, no father, no grandparents to rely on. Just himself. Somehow that was a fitting end to a day in which nothing had been as expected. Through his tiredness one clear thought emerged: Tomorrow, whatever anyone else intended, he'd set about finding his father.

Breakfast was typically English: eggs, bacon, sausages and tomatoes and Tom tucked in gratefully. Somehow, the night-time anxieties didn't seem as bad when bright sunshine streamed through the open door and Francesca fussed over him as though he weren't the stranger who'd descended on them out of nowhere.

'I was thinking,' Tom said, 'Dad mentioned your son, Ricardo. Did he get that right, as well?'

The worried look crept back to Francesca's face. 'We have a son, Ricardo, yes. He lives in Valletta. He is a teacher.' She turned in obvious relief as Luigi entered. 'Tom's father also knew of Ricardo.'

Tom felt a ray of hope. 'If he's in Valletta, could we call and see him before we go to the Consulate? Perhaps it's Ricardo that Dad met and he gave him your names.'

'Ricardo is in Sicily,' Luigi said slowly, considering the idea. 'His wife and daughters are with him, they are on a school trip until next Friday.' Looking at Tom's disappointed face, he smiled gently. 'I'll see if I can get him on his mobile. Ricardo would not forgive us if we turned away his friend's son.'

Tom finished his toast with renewed enthusiasm, hoping that at last the puzzle would be solved. It was so clearly the obvious answer that he almost laughed for not thinking of it earlier, though it still didn't explain where his father was at this moment or why he'd said these people were his relations. Perhaps they were distant cousins, a link which his father had discovered and told Ricardo. Maybe they'd intended to surprise Luigi and Francesca with the news. He looked up hopefully as Luigi entered.

'I managed to get Ricardo before they set out on their day's excursion, but he hasn't heard of your father I'm afraid. Or of you.'

Tom stared silently at the whorls in the wooden table, blinking furiously. The last bite of toast stuck in his throat and he swallowed hard. He was a teenager for goodness sake, almost an adult, not some little kid who blabbed his eyes out at every disappointment.

Luigi sat down next to him. 'Ricardo says that perhaps we should keep you here until he returns next Friday. There must be an answer, if we can only figure it out, and he would like to try and help you.'

'How? If he's never heard of Dad what use can he be?'

'It's the best offer we can make for now,' Luigi apologised, 'but if you prefer I will drive you to the Consulate at Valletta as planned.'

'No,' Tom said hurriedly. 'They'd send me back to England and I know Dad came to Malta. This is where he'll expect to find me when he does turn up. I'd like to stay with you, thanks.'

'You're sure there is no one in England who will worry about you?'

'There's no-one left to worry.' Tom realised how pathetic that sounded and added hurriedly, 'Mum's in America and my grandparents are touring Scotland. I'll try not to be a bother.'

'It will be nice to have someone young to look after.' Francesca began gathering up the breakfast dishes.

Luigi stopped by the door. 'Perhaps you would like to borrow Ricardo's bike? Then you can explore the area. We can find you a map.'

'Thanks, I'd like that.'

'I could pack you up some food,' Francesca offered.

'No, if I'm hungry I'll buy something,' Tom said quickly, not wanting to be more of a burden than he already was. 'Mum gave me plenty of money.'

After collecting his wallet, he paused in the hallway. The kitchen door was shut but through it came the sound of raised voices. He couldn't distinguish the words, though it didn't take a genius to guess what Luigi and Francesca were arguing about. Was it stupid to just hang around Malta? What if his father never got in touch? Would he have to go through life never knowing what had happened to him?

Wearily, Tom leaned against a chest, his elbow dislodging a framed, sepia-tinted photograph. Picking it up, he smiled at a younger Luigi and Francesca, taken on their wedding day. How solemn they looked. Beside it was one of a young boy, dark-haired and smiling. A five year old Ricardo, Tom guessed. And here was one of Ricardo on his own wedding day. Behind this, almost hidden, was another of Luigi and Francesca standing proudly behind two teenage boys. The elder one was immediately recognisable as Ricardo. The younger? Tom felt his insides lurch and he swallowed hard. For a moment he could have sworn that he was looking at a photo of his father. Then reason asserted itself. Why did he think that? Easy enough, because Dad was foremost on his mind. He wanted to see him more than anything else in the world, even if he'd got to the stage of almost hating him.

This boy, with a wide grin that split his face, was nothing like his father. Dad hadn't been much of a one for smiling. Perhaps, when he was happy. . .

Tom's thoughts were cut short by a plump, rosy-faced woman who came bustling in, brandishing a duster and bringing with her a strong smell of furniture polish. She stopped short at the sight of him.

'I'm Tom Newton,' he explained. 'I'm staying here for a few days.'

She smiled broadly. 'I'm Carmel. I help in the house and my husband Luis works on the farm. Francesca will like having someone to fuss over; she's never got used to the fact that the boys have grown up and left home.'

'The boys?' Tom held out the photograph. 'Are these them?'

'Yes.' She took the photo, gazing at it fondly. 'Ricardo and Guiseppe, though most people called him Beppe.' She chuckled, a smile creasing her round face. 'What a rascal he was.'

'Where's Guiseppe now?'

'What are you doing with the photograph?' The kitchen door had opened and Tom jumped at the coldness in Luigi's voice as he almost snatched the photo from Carmel's hand. 'My son Guiseppe died when he was eighteen. That was over twenty years ago.'

Tom paused in the farmyard where a rusty bike was propped up against the wall. Not knowing which way to go, he just wanted to be as far away from here as possible. Give Luigi time to recover. There must have been something especially tragic about Guiseppe's death for it to have affected him that badly and so much for the fanciful notion that the boy had been his father. He'd died four years before Tom had been born. It had been a stupid notion from the start; talk about making a mystery out of a mystery. He'd better find somewhere to visit and get himself out of their presence for a while.

A small girl came racing round a corner of the stone barn, stopping dead at the sight of Tom. Carmel's daughter, he guessed, noting the rosy face.

'Hello, I'm Tom.'

'Lila.' She pointed a brown finger at herself.

'Perhaps you can help me? I'm looking for a place to explore.'

'Who you wish to see? We have nice people on Malta.'

'Not a person, a place. Somewhere interesting.'

'Francesca and Luigi very nice.'

'I know they are.'

'Ricardo very nice.'

'I haven't met him yet, but I'm sure he is.'

'Pietro very nice.'

Tom groaned inwardly. Who on earth was Pietro? Lila was clearly into a long list of her acquaintances.

'Alice very nice.'

'Alice?' He stared at her. 'Alice who?'

'Ewen very nice?'

Tom put up a hand to stop the flow. 'Is Ewen her brother?'

'He is very nice,' Lila said predictably.

'Are you talking about Alice and Ewen Rogerson?' she nodded. 'I want to see Alice Rogerson. Can you show me where she lives?'

Lila nodded even more vigorously. 'Villa Trevisan. You go Villa Trevisan. Alice is very nice.'

That was my impression, Tom thought, as he turned left on to the road. Yet now he was beginning to wonder. Alice had suddenly become another piece in the puzzle which had dogged him ever since he'd set foot on Malta. He'd told her about the Farrigianis, about Haz Zahra, why had she said she lived on the other side of the island? According to Lila, Mr and Mrs Rogerson, Alice and Ewen lived on the next farm. He stopped suddenly, blood rushing to his face. Suppose the answer was simple: she didn't want to see him again and thought if she told him how close she lived he'd be pestering her all the time. He flushed even more as he remembered how he'd prattled on about his parents' divorce and his worries at meeting Dad. She must have thought him a silly little boy. Tom pulled on to the grass verge, sitting down to think. No way was he going to embarrass himself by calling on her. It was obviously the last thing she'd wanted. Yet, Alice could at least vouch for the note, that his father had really given him the information about the Farrigianis and where they lived. They'd have to believe him, then. That was worth a bit of embarrassment, surely? It was getting to the stage where Tom was beginning to wonder if he'd imagined the whole thing.

Before he could change his mind, Tom grabbed his bike and pedalled furiously away, grinning as the bike creaked in protest. Sure enough, a dirt track identical with that at the Villa Magrino was signed: TREVISAN. The selfsame small fields and rubble walls fronted another rectangular stone farmhouse.

Don't stop to think, Tom warned himself, just knock. The door was opened by a young boy of about twelve, who looked surprised to see Tom standing there.

'Are you Ewen Rogerson?'

'Yes. Do I know you.?'

'I've come to see Alice.'

Ewen grinned. 'Should have guessed. Come in, she's upstairs.' Standing on the bottom step he bellowed, 'Alice! Someone to see you! A boy!' before disappearing towards the back of the house.

Now that the moment had arrived, all Tom wanted to do was run. Why hadn't he just gone back to England and saved himself all this humiliation.

Footsteps sounded overhead.

'Hello!'

Reluctantly, Tom raised his head to stare in disbelief at Alice Rogerson. She was about his own age, perhaps even younger, and she was absolutely nothing like the girl on the plane.

3

'I'm sorry for troubling you,' Tom stammered. 'I thought you were someone else. I won't take up any more of your time.' He turned to go, anxious to escape as quickly as possible. What a ridiculous situation he'd got himself into.

'You can't leave it there!' the strange girl laughed. 'I'd never sleep tonight for curiosity. I'm Alice Rogerson, who did you think I was?'

'Another Alice Rogerson,' he stuttered, feeling a complete fool. He was so embarrassed he wanted the ground to open up and swallow him.

'You mean there are two of us?' She raised her eyebrows questioningly. 'We're the only Rogersons in Haz Zahra; or I thought we were. Where did this other Alice spring from?'

Tom shook his head, helplessly. 'It's a long story, too complicated to. . . Look, I'd better go, I'm sorry that. . .'

'You can't just walk out after telling me that I've got a namesake. I'm not doing anything in particular and you look a bit hot and bothered, so how about I offer you a drink and you entertain me with this long and complicated tale?'

Without waiting for an answer, she ushered Tom through to the kitchen, opening the fridge and taking out a large jug. 'Home-made lemonade suit you?'

He found himself nodding silently when all he really wanted was to put as much distance between them as possible. He watched as she poured the lemonade into two glasses. This new Alice, as well as being much younger than the one on the plane, was a complete contrast. Smaller than Tom, she had light brown hair, glittering with strands of autumn-red, fastened back in a long plait, and incredible blue eyes.

'Now, I want to know the full details.'

As she turned to him, the kitchen door opened and an older woman entered, stopping in surprise at the sight of Tom. 'I didn't know you had a visitor, Alice.'

'Mum, this is. . .' Her eyes cast an appeal for help.

'Tom Newton,' he said, stepping forward quickly and holding out his hand.

'Nice to meet you, Tom. Where did you and Alice. . .?'

'We were just going to sit in the orchard,' Alice interrupted, thrusting a glass of lemonade in Tom's direction and, before he could draw breath, whisking him out of the kitchen. 'Sorry about that,' she chuckled, 'but Mum was about to ask where and when we'd met. It'd have looked a bit strange to say in the hallway thirty seconds ago.'

In the orchard, Alice sat down on an old tree stump and looked up at him expectantly. 'Well?' Tom took a deep breath and launched into his story.

'So when Lila mentioned Alice Rogerson,' he ended, 'I presumed it was the girl on the plane and I couldn't understand why she'd said she lived on the other side of the island.'

Alice frowned. 'And now you think it was another Alice Rogerson?'

'Well, it wasn't you.'

She grinned. 'It definitely wasn't me.'

'In some ways it's a relief. I liked her and I didn't want to believe she'd told me a pack of lies.'

'Drink your lemonade,' Alice told him and glancing down Tom found that his glass was still full.

He took a quick gulp before asking:'You're not convinced about her, are you?'

'I'm quite ready to believe there's more than one Alice Rogerson on Malta, though you must admit it's a bit of a coincidence that she happened to sit next to you on the plane and not only had the same name as the girl on the farm next to where you were heading, but her parents were also farmers and like me she had a brother called Ewen.' She paused for breath. 'Seems a bit unlikely, don't you think?'

'What's the alternative? Why would she pretend to be you?'

'Haven't a clue. Though if she deliberately impersonated me, she must know my family and presumably I know her. What did she look like?'

'In her late twenties. About my size. Long dark hair. Tanned.'

'Might be anybody,' Alice admitted. 'We're all tanned on Malta, comes with the climate. Sorry, no one springs to mind.'

'I've got a secret feeling that I'll probably never know,' Tom confessed. 'After I've seen Ricardo on Friday, I'll go back to England and wait for Dad to get in touch.'

'You said he mentioned a surprise waiting for you on Malta? A big surprise that you'd never guess. This couldn't be it, I suppose? A little puzzle to test you?' She grinned. 'Find the Dad!'

'It's not funny.'

Alice flushed. 'Sorry. I wasn't thinking.'

'Dad's a rather serious person, he's definitely not the kind to indulge in practical jokes.' Even as he spoke, an unsettling flicker of memory surfaced from his subconscious: his ninth birthday, the last one before the divorce. He'd not known that at the time, of course, though his father must have done. He'd tried to make the birthday as memorable as possible.

'What is it?' Alice asked. 'You've drifted away.'

'It was you mentioning puzzles,' Tom said slowly. 'I was remembering my ninth birthday. Dad set me a series of puzzles to find my present, like a treasure hunt. It took me all over the house. In each hiding place was a small lead knight. The final clue was a fortress.'

'What did the knights look like?'

Tom shrugged. 'I haven't played with them for years. They must still be in my bedroom somewhere, probably at the back of a cupboard, unless Mum gave them away. They were in different colours, that's all I can remember.'

'Bet they were the Knights of St John,' Alice said triumphantly. 'Each of the nationalities had their own colour scheme. That gives you a connection with Malta.'

'Not much of one, though it might explain why I was so interested when the girl on the plane told me some of their history.'

'And it establishes that your father liked puzzles.'

'There's a wealth of difference between devising a kid's game and leaving me stranded in a foreign country. He'd never do that.'

'I guess not.'

Tom finished his lemonade, setting the glass down at his side. 'I might as well do some exploring while I'm here. Got any suggestions? I daren't ask Lila again, she'll only send me off to see another of her friends.'

Alice stared at him incredulously. 'You're giving up on the puzzle? You're admitting defeat before you've even started to work it out?'

'I haven't much choice, have I? I've run out of ideas, not that I had many in the first place. I didn't think any further than finding my way to Haz Zahra and it's not as if I had any clues. Every time I think I might be getting somewhere, like hearing an Alice Rogerson lived on the next farm, or finding the photograph, it turns out to be a dead end.'

'You really thought the photo was your father?'

'Just for a minute I did, probably because I had Dad so much on my mind. Now I can see how ridiculous it was.'

'I've been thinking about that.' Alice looked at him seriously. 'There's something odd about the whole situation.'

'You're telling me.'

'No, it's odder than you realise. For a start, I've lived in Haz Zahra all my life. I can't count the number of times I've been over to the Villa Magrino, especially when Ricardo's there with his daughters, they're friends of mine, yet I've never heard of Giuseppe Farrigiani. I always thought Ricardo was an only child.'

'Giuseppe died before you were born.'

'But you'd think they'd at least mention him now and then. They've kept him well hidden, and it's even stranger than you realise. Your father's called Joseph?'

'Usually shortened to Joe.'

'Well, Giuseppe is the Italian form of Joseph.' Tom stared at her. 'Giuseppe and Joseph. Another coincidence? It looks as though your father could be Giuseppe Farrigiani.'

'No he couldn't, Giuseppe's dead.'

'We've only got Luigi's word for that,' Alice countered.

'Luigi wouldn't lie, would he? Not about the death of his son.'

'Someone's lying to you, got to be. Your father says they're your relatives; they claim they're not but they've suddenly got a son I've never heard of and he's got the same name as your Dad. I think it's worth trying to find out something about Giuseppe Farrigiani.'

'How do we do that?'

'Dad must know, he and Ricardo are great friends, they went to school together in Mdina. He'd know if Ricardo had a brother.'

'Could we ask him?'

'We could but I've a better idea. How did you get here?'

'Ricardo's bike. Luigi said I could borrow it for the week.'

'Then I'll collect mine and we'll cycle into Haz Zahra. It's so hot I could do with an ice cream.'

'I'd rather find out about my father,' Tom protested. 'I can't really believe he's Giuseppe Farrigiani, but at least I'd be doing something constructive.'

'Don't worry, that's what I intend to do. We'll visit Marco's cafe; he's a great friend of both Ricardo and Dad and he's a fantastic talker. He never stops. If anyone's going to spill the beans about Giuseppe, it'll be Marco Petroni.'

As the girl on the plane had said, Haz Zahra was a small village, though dwarfed by an enormous church. In front of this, the village green was circled by picnic benches and shady trees.

'It's our festa next weekend,' Alice told him as they cycled past. 'That's like your fetes in England, though ours are centred round the church. Religion's very important here. We're supposed to be one of the oldest Christian peoples in the world, ever since St Paul was shipwrecked on the island and converted us.'

'Is your church dedicated to him?'

'No, ours is the Church of St John. He's really important on Malta because of the Knights. Their first hospice in Jerusalem was supposed to have been built on the site where the angel announced the coming of John the Baptist. I don't know if it's true but it makes a good story and that's why the Order took his name.'

There was much coming and going at the church.

'The women are cleaning our treasures and relics,' Alice explained. 'They'll be on display during the festa. It's a fun packed weekend, with a fete and a band concert on Saturday, followed by a procession on Sunday in which our statue of the saint is carried through the streets. The whole thing ends with a huge bonfire. Do you think you'll still be here next weekend?'

'If Dad turns up, yes. He promised me a month's holiday. I hope he does, I like the sound of your festa. Other than that, it depends on Ricardo when he gets back from Sicily on Friday, though I can't see what help he can be if he's never heard of Dad. Perhaps we'll learn something about Giuseppe from Marco.'

They propped their bikes against the cafe wall. At the other side of the doorway, three elderly men sat on a bench, brown-faced, white-haired, in check shirts and v-necked jumpers. They made Tom perspire just to look at them.

'Is it always this hot?' he asked as they entered the café.

'In summer, yes. We get very little rain, which is why the roads are always so dusty.' She lowered her voice. 'Let me lead the conversation. I know how to get Marco talking.' She chuckled. 'I should do, I've had plenty of practice. Ewen and I sometimes play a game to see which of us can keep him talking the longest.'

Tom thought that Marco Petroni looked as though he spent far too much time eating his own ice-cream. Everything about him was round, from his cylindrical figure enveloped in a striped apron, to the glowing orb of his face. He beamed broadly at the sight of Alice.

'How's your Dad?'

'Fine, thanks. I've brought Tom to see you, he's from England. I told him you made the best ice cream on Malta.'

It was impossible for Marco's smile to get any wider without cracking his face. Collecting two long glasses, he began to fill them with scoops of various coloured ice creams, talking all the while.

'I should be an expert by now. My father used to run the café and his father before that. We've got Italian blood in our veins and the Italians know the secret of making ice-cream. James would always insist on stopping off here after school. Liked ice-cream as much as Alice does.'

'James is my Dad,' she confirmed, taking the glass and tucking in eagerly. 'What about Ricardo? Was he an ice cream fanatic?'

'They both were.' Marco leaned on the counter, watching Tom. 'Good?'

'Very good,' Tom agreed.

'You are here on holiday?'

Tom nodded, his mouth full of delicious coldness.

'He's staying at the Villa Magrino,' Alice added.

'You are related to Luigi and Francesca?'

'Distantly,' Tom mumbled, remembering Alice's instructions. He couldn't help wondering what Marco would think if he said he might be their grandson.

'He hasn't met Ricardo yet, he's on a school trip to Italy,' Alice said. 'I told him what good friends you, Dad and Ricardo were during your school days.'

'Still are,' Marco declared, 'and always will be, even if we don't see each other as much as we'd like now Ricardo's moved to Valletta and your Dad's always so busy on the farm. What a team we used to be; we went everywhere together, just the three of us, except when Beppe and Tommasso tagged along.' He chuckled. 'Which wasn't often, thank goodness, they were usually too busy hunting the Farrigiani treasure. Not that they ever came close to finding it, but that didn't seem to dampen their enthusiasm.'

'What treasure?' Alice asked, but Tom was even quicker off the mark.

'Beppe? Do you mean Giuseppe Farrigiani?'

'I remember one time,' Marco continued, seemingly unaware of both interruptions, 'when we took tents and went off for a week. Cycled from one end of the island to the other. Mind, I was much thinner in those days.' He patted his ample stomach. 'We cooked all our own food and most nights we took our sleeping bags outside the tent and slept under the stars. We really ought to do it again some day, though I'd need a much stronger bike.'

'Is Giuseppe dead?' Tom persisted, ignoring Alice's warning frown.

Marco looked suddenly flustered. 'Why ask me? If you want to know about Beppe, Luigi is the person to talk to.'

'What's the big deal? Surely you can tell us if he's dead? Was it a long time ago?'

Marco's smile changed to a scowl. 'For a newcomer you ask too many questions. You should know better than to meddle in old tragedies, especially ones which don't concern you. Either of you.'

'I only want to know if. . .'

Marco moved away to the far side of the counter, busying himself with a group of customers. Tom's ice cream lost all taste.

'Finish it,' Alice advised him quietly, 'or Marco will be even madder.'

They sat for a while, glasses empty, but Marco made no further move in their direction. They might have been invisible for all the notice he took of them.

'We may as well go,' Alice said, pulling a face. 'It's obvious we're not going to learn anything else just now.'

Outside, she rounded on Tom. 'What on earth were you thinking about badgering him with all those questions? I told you to leave the talking to me!'

'It's my father who's missing!' he stormed back. 'I've a right to ask questions. It's just a game to you but. . .' He faltered under her hurt gaze. 'I wasn't asking for much, just to know if Giuseppe's dead.'

Collecting their bikes, they rode in silence, Tom inwardly cursing his stupidity. There was some mystery about Giuseppe, that much was obvious from Marco's response, but he was no nearer to knowing if

Giuseppe was dead or if he could possibly be connected with his father. One thing was certain, he couldn't ask Luigi, not after his reaction to the photograph that morning.

They reached the track leading down to Alice's farm. She stopped and turned to him. 'Sorry I was cross, I know it must be awful for you. I can't imagine what it must be like to lose your father, especially when you're stuck here on your own in a foreign country. Do you still want some help?'

'Such as?' Tom flushed at his rudeness, unable to shake off the depression settling around him like a black cloud. 'Fat lot of use Marco was. I've come to a dead end. I don't know why I expected anything else.'

'Not quite,' Alice said patiently. 'He did give us one clue; three even. Giuseppe had a close friend called Tommasso, they spent their time hunting for treasure - you said your father organised that treasure hunt for your birthday – so that's another link between them, and you notice Marco didn't confirm Giuseppe's death.'

Tom grinned in spite of himself. 'I don't think much to your second clue; all young boys go treasure seeking, I did myself, even without Dad's help.'

'Okay, maybe the treasure's not important, but we could try and trace this Tommasso. He ought to be able to tell us about his friend. Perhaps, if Giuseppe Farrigiani became Joseph Newton, then he named you after his friend Tommasso.'

Tom was sceptical. 'Finding him's going to be virtually impossible. We've no idea of his surname and how many people on Malta are called Tommasso?'

'Quite a lot,' Alice admitted, 'but we've got two courses of action. I can try to get Dad talking about his school days and you. . .' She paused,

'Yes?'

'If you're still interested...?'

'Alright! Sorry for my grumpiness, it's just I've had my hopes knocked down so many times since I left England. I can't believe that this time yesterday I still thought Dad would be waiting for me at the airport.'

'I know,' Alice said quietly. 'I shouldn't tease you. Well, when you get back to the Villa Magrino, see if you can make an excuse to go to the attic.'

'Why?'

'I've not gone mad, don't worry. I'm presuming Giuseppe and Tommasso went to the same school as Ricardo, Marco and Dad.'

'Yes, but what does the attic have to do with it?'

'When he was at school, each year Dad came back with a class photograph which had all their names on the back. My grandparents have a whole collection. A couple of years ago I went with my Dad to the Villa Magrino, Ricardo was staying with his two daughters, and Francesca sent us up to the attic. She said she had a trunk of old dresses we could use to make costumes for the festa. We had to root through several trunks before we found them and one we tried was filled with old school photographs. If you can find one of Giuseppe, it might have Tommasso's full name on the back. That should give us something to work from. It's worth a try. I'll see what I can get out of my Dad and we'll meet tomorrow to compare notes.'

Tom rode back to the Villa Magrino with a lighter heart, at last feeling as though he'd got an ally. How he was going to approach the problem of the attic he shelved for a moment. Carmel, her husband and Lila were just leaving and he waved to them cheerfully, realising he wouldn't mind being a member of this family. Putting Ricardo's bike in the shed, he entered the kitchen. There was no sign of Francesca but Luigi sat at the table. He rose, glaring at Tom.

'Why have you been asking questions about my son, Giuseppe?' Tom stared in dismay. Marco had clearly rung him. 'We are sorry for you, Francesca and I, but you have no right dragging up memories that are painful to us both. What did you think you were doing?'

'I was just curious.' Tom realised how lame that sounded.

'Curious?' Luigi's temper threatened to erupt.

'I saw the photograph and Alice had never heard of Giuseppe.' Tom faltered in dismay. Why was he dragging Alice into this?

'Her father will not be happy when he hears from Marco.' Tom felt worse than ever. What a mess this was turning into. 'If you wish to stay with us until Ricardo returns, I do not want to hear another mention of my younger son. Is that understood?'

Tom nodded miserably.

It was an awkward evening meal. Francesca's eyes were red, a visual reminder to Tom of how much he had upset them. As soon as they'd finished eating, he escaped to the refuge of his bedroom. Despondent he might be, yet it didn't stop him grasping the fact that, at the end of his corridor, narrow steps spiralled up to what was clearly the attic. Forget it, he told himself sternly, you've done enough damage for one day. It was a stupid idea, anyway.

However much he wished it, Tom soon realised that sleep was not going to be an option. His mind raced with images: Dad on their visit to Greece, showing him an ancient temple - the girl on the plane, smiling at him - two small boys treasure hunting, across what appeared to be fields of clover - Alice throwing back her plait and scolding him for being defeatist. The sky gradually darkened to an inky blackness, lit by brilliant streaks of moonlight. Tom got out of bed, creeping to the window and holding up his watch so that it caught the moon's rays. 2am. Was his father out there somewhere? In trouble? Should he have told the police? The British consul knew Dad was missing and they were trying to trace him. Wasn't that enough? What more could he be expected to do? He thought of Alice, of what she would say to him in the morning, and made up his mind.

Opening the bedroom door quietly, he stood listening. Complete silence. Tiptoeing into the corridor, he hesitated. It was very dark, shame he had no torch. One step. Another. He felt his way along, fingers sliding against the wall. Looking up, the stairs twisted and turned, ascending into an impenetrable blackness. He inched his way upwards, pausing and holding his breath as one of the steps gave a loud creak. What on earth could he possibly say if Luigi came out and caught him? He had no excuse whatever for what he was about to do. Waiting a full minute, he resumed his climb until his head came to rest against a trap door. Pushing it up as gently as possible he scrambled into the attic, closing it behind him.

He was in a large space lit by the moon shining through an overhead window; all around him, dusky shadows flickered in the gloom. Wherever you are, Dad, he thought, I hope you appreciate what I'm putting myself through. Alice was right, the whole centre area was a mass of trunks; the one with the photographs was the fourth he tried. Crouching beside it in the dust, he started to lift them out, one at a time, searching the names on the back. Ricardo Farrigiani, sandwiched between James Rogerson and Marco Petroni - Ricardo Farrigiani - Ricardo Farrigiani. He carried on regardless, scrutinising every photo. Ricardo Farrigiani -Ricardo Farrigiani. Tom began to despair. Had they thrown away all reference to their younger son? Ricardo Farrigiani - Ricardo Farrigiani. He came to the last one - Ricardo Farrigiani. Another avenue closed to him. Tom wondered why he'd expected anything else. Dad, the girl on the plane, they'd both assured him he'd love Malta. Well, he was beginning to feel only a deadly hatred for it.

Sitting alone in the dark attic, surrounded by shadows, he felt tears pricking his eyes and brushed them away angrily. All the misery of the divorce-and there'd been plenty of that-he'd managed to cope with. Uncertainty, he was finding, was a far harder cross to bear. And now he was even questioning the existence of his own father. Was the man he'd known for sixteen years as Joseph Newton really nothing but an impostor, hiding his true identity from his own wife and son? If that was the case, what dreadful crime had his father committed to be disowned by his own parents?

Wearily, Tom replaced the photos in the trunk. Standing to leave, he saw the imprint of his footsteps on the dusty floor. If Luigi or Francesca came up here they'd know at once that he'd been ferreting around. Too tired to care, he tiptoed down the narrow stairs. He had just reached the landing when there was a quiet cough. Panic fluttered in his chest. He held his breath and listened; in the corridor, footsteps. Tom shivered, yet sweat trickled down his back. A sudden shaft of moonlight streamed through the landing window, illuminating Luigi's face with a ghostly pallor. It looked strained and despondent, deep lines etched into chalky whiteness, and Tom imagined he could almost reach out and touch his unhappiness, caused because old wounds had been reopened; a buried misery had come bubbling to the surface. He found himself hoping fervently that his father wouldn't turn out to be Giuseppe Farrigiani.

Luigi made his way slowly downstairs without once glancing in Tom's direction. As soon as he was out of sight Tom made a dash for the bedroom, flinging himself into bed and pulling the covers tightly round him. Lying tense and still, the thought struck him that Luigi genuinely believed that his son was dead. If Dad was Giuseppe, had he run away from home? Disappeared and never let his parents know he was alive?

Then reason reasserted itself. Dad would never be that cruel. Somewhere, deep inside, Tom clung to the memory of the quiet, gentle father he'd known. The image of the grinning schoolboy rose in his mind and he relaxed, the tension draining from him, suddenly glad that there was no way that the boy in the photograph could have grown up to become his father.

4

Tom woke instantly. What had roused him? Despite the stillness, he knew someone was in the room. Cautiously he removed the blanket, eyes straining through the darkness. Was that a shadow over by the window? Muscles tightened as the figure lurched towards him. He wanted to move, to roll away from the encroaching menace, yet every limb was paralysed as though he were chained to the bed. Blinding light stabbed his eyes, the pain like hot needles piercing his eyeballs.

Opening his mouth to scream, a hand clamped down, cutting off his supply of air and generating instant panic.

'Don't make a sound!'

The torch moved back to highlight the face of his father. Tom froze. Had his memory been playing tricks? The once gentle face was suffused with anger, the eyes harsh and unfeeling.

'What are you doing here?' his father hissed. 'Why didn't you go back to England? You're going to ruin everything.'

'I didn't know what had happened to you,' Tom whispered. 'I only wanted to help.'

'Help?' The eyes widened, glittering with a hint of madness. 'Help?'

To Tom's horror his father began to laugh, peal after peal of wild, hysterical laughter.

'Stop it!' Tom begged. 'Stop it! Please, stop it!'

Bolting upright, his eyes opened to bright sunshine, a continuous tolling of bells filling the air with sound. Slowly, the details of the bedroom swam into focus.

Staggering to the bathroom, he splashed cold water on his burning face, heaving painful gasps as he tried to control his breathing, his legs shaking as though he'd completed a marathon. This was the first nightmare. He'd had bad dreams occasionally, same as everyone else he supposed, but nothing like this. He rubbed his eyes, realising how tired he was. Goodness knows what time he'd fallen asleep. The face in the mirror was almost that of a stranger, pale and exhausted, with dark shadows under the eyes. His father probably wouldn't recognise him, not even if they came face to face, which was becoming more and more unlikely. Back in his room, Tom eyed the bed. His watch told him it wasn't yet 8 o'clock; surely he could rest for an hour? Yet memories of his nightmare lingered too vividly for him to risk another ordeal. He could still taste the fear in his mouth, metallic, bitter and nauseous.

He dressed slowly, putting off the moment when he would have to face Luigi. How long had he sat alone downstairs, his mind filled with recollections of his lost son? Or his *dead* son? Tom no longer knew which was the more likely. He felt as though he were seeing through a fog where nothing was clear, still not quite believing what was happening to him. Was his nightmare-father telling him something that deep down he really knew? That he should have allowed himself to be sent back to England instead of becoming embroiled in a mystery that was not of his making? Perhaps it was time to tell Luigi he was going home.

The kitchen was empty but filled with the smell of freshly baked bread. A loaf lay on the table, next to a single sheet of paper.

'*Gone to Mass*,' Tom read. '*Help yourself to breakfast. Lunch will be at 1 o'clock.*'

He wasn't really hungry but he knew Francesca well enough already to realise she'd be offended if he didn't eat. He cut himself a piece of the crusty bread, nibbling it as he stood in the open doorway. Despite the early hour, the air was heavy and he moved to sit on an old barrel in a patch of shade, wondering what Alice was doing. Probably gone to church with her parents, she'd said they were hot on religion in Malta.

An image came to his mind, startlingly clear, of his father sitting next to him in a large church. How young had he been? It was certainly well before the divorce. He could recall long, narrow windows; a radiant kaleidoscope of stained glass. The cloying smell of incense. The soaring voices of the choir. They'd gone every Sunday, he now remembered with surprise, just him and Dad; Mum had never accompanied them. After the divorce, there'd been no more church and the memory had faded until now. In his mind, Tom watched his father turn his head and smile at him. You couldn't call it a grin exactly, though perhaps when. . .

Impulsively, Tom went into the hallway, picking up each photograph in turn. The one with Giuseppe was missing. Had Luigi hidden it? Thrown it away? Was that what he was doing in the midnight hours?

The bells ceased with a startling suddenness, leaving a tingling in the air. Mass must be starting. Tom stood in the hallway, undecided, fingers tapping nervously against the wooden chest and wondering if he dare risk another visit to the attic. Perhaps Giuseppe's photographs were all stored in another trunk. He glanced at his watch. If he allowed himself half an hour there was plenty of time to be back downstairs when Luigi and Francesca returned. Before he could talk himself out of it, he hurried for the attic.

In the light of day the spooky atmosphere had vanished and Tom looked around with interest. Apart from the trunks, there was all the residue of a boy's childhood years: an old rocking horse, its paint chipped and faded - a purple car with one headlight missing - a box of wooden railway tracks. Had they all belonged to Ricardo or were some of them Giuseppe's? Tom bet that Francesca was the one reluctant to throw anything away. Conscious of the time, he began to rummage through the trunks. One was clearly a dressing-up box, full of a variety of costumes. Another contained school projects, all embellished with the name Ricardo Farrigiani. It was as though his younger brother Giuseppe had never existed. Tom admitted defeat, closing the lids and making for the trapdoor. He nearly missed the small, very battered wooden box almost hidden behind the pedal car. It looked ancient but well-loved, covered with faded stickers. Tom lifted it out carefully, his heart sinking as he saw the combination lock guarding its secrets. He sank down, back resting against the wall, the chest on his lap. He'd had one like it as a kid, another birthday present from his father. Was that also a coincidence? He recalled the excitement as Dad showed him how to key in the combination of numbers. They'd used Tom's birthday. It was worth a try. With trembling fingers, Tom inserted his father's birth date, hearing the familiar click of the lock opening. Inside the lid was the inscription:

To Beppe on his 12th birthday
From Tommasso and the Lorenzo Family

Well, that was one problem solved: Giuseppe's treasure-hunting partner was called Tommasso Lorenzo. Now all he and Alice had to do was find him. Tom's watch warned him that he'd had more than his allotted half hour. He wondered if he dare take the box down to his bedroom. Better not, if it was discovered Luigi would be more than angry; he'd quite likely throw him out of the house. Tom fingered the treasures: a bag of shiny marbles, a stone containing the imprint of a fossil, a photograph of two young boys; both dark-haired and smiling. One was immediately recognisable as Giuseppe; the other, rounder faced, must be Tommasso. There was a collection of hand-painted figures, each unique. Knights, Tom realised. Were these the Knights of St John? As far as he could remember, they were ominously similar to his own collection. At the bottom of the box was a small envelope. In place of an address was written:

THE FARRIGIANI TREASURE

Taking the envelope and the photograph, Tom hurried back to his bedroom. Opening the envelope he drew out a single sheet, clearly torn from a school exercise book and began to read.

Description and location of the treasure
bequeathed to my descendants by
Claudio Farrigiani
Knight of St John of Jerusalem, Rhodes and Malta

Tom clutched the paper fiercely with trembling fingers. Underneath the inscription was what looked like a short poem.

Age fades, observe aright.
Hill beckons.
Alight ashore at cavernous
Steepness auguring
Heavenly summit.
Angel adorns dead tree.

Tom leaned back against the pillows, his mind a whirl of images: he was climbing a large hill, upwards and upwards, towards a dead tree where an angel, with outstretched wings, perched on the topmost bough.

Tom became aware of the knocking just in time. Thrusting the paper and photograph under the covers he called, 'Come in.'

The door opened to reveal Luigi. 'We wondered where you were.'

'I was tired,' Tom said awkwardly. 'I didn't sleep too well last night.' Just the wrong thing to say, he thought, remembering Luigi's own sleeplessness.

'Francesca has made some coffee.'

'I'll come down, then.' Tom stood up. 'I'm fine now.' He tried a smile, relieved when the smile was returned.

Francesca was bustling round the kitchen. 'Coffee?' she asked.

'Yes, please. The bread was good. Do you bake your own?'

'Every morning. Of course we don't eat as much now there are just the two of us. It's nice to have a young mouth to feed again.'

Tom wondered if she shared her husband's view of their younger son. It was difficult to tell. He couldn't imagine Francesca staying angry with anyone.

'We saw Alice in church,' she told him. 'I'm glad you've found a friend so quickly. They're a nice family, the Rogersons. James has always been one of Ricardo's best friends. Alice says you're welcome to go round there this afternoon.'

'I'd like that, if it's OK with you.'

She smiled. 'Best to keep yourself occupied while you're waiting for news of your father. Isn't that right, Luigi?'

He merely nodded. 'I've got jobs to do, I'll be back for lunch.'

Tom didn't think it would be tactful to offer his help. Instead, he sat outside in a patch of sun, trying to organise his thoughts and wishing he'd brought down the riddle. In a moment's panic, he imagined Francesca deciding to make his bed.

Dashing upstairs, he rescued the riddle and photograph, stuffing them in his pocket and longing for the moment when he could set off for the Villa Trevisan.

Alice's face flushed with excitement as Tom finished reading the riddle. They were once more sitting in the orchard, a jug of lemonade positioned strategically between them.

'So who said the treasure wasn't important?' she crowed.

Tom grinned. 'I was thinking more along the lines of gold bars or precious jewels, like a story book adventure, but this treasure is. . .' He hesitated, guessing, 'something to do with an angel? That's the image I got from reading the riddle.'

Alice took the paper from him, staring at it intently and to Tom's amusement chewing the end of her long plait. 'It's a bit obscure but you're right, there's nothing that it can be other than the angel and presumably we find it hidden in a dead tree.'

'At the summit of a hill,' Tom concluded. 'When you say "we", does that mean you're willing to come treasure hunting?'

'I'd love to, though I haven't a clue where to start. You really think this links with your father?'

Tom shrugged. 'I can't make up my mind. It seems too fantastic to be true but the whole situation is unbelievable. While Francesca was cooking lunch I was weighing up the coincidences. They're certainly mounting: Dad's name is the English version of Giuseppe, Dad bought me some knights just like the ones Giuseppe had as a boy, they both clearly enjoyed treasure hunts. Dad said I would meet my relations and gave their names as Luigi and Francesca Farrigiani. That's too much to ignore, surely?'

'Far too much. Though how your father's disappearance links to the treasure I don't know.'

'Neither do I.' Tom felt his spirits sinking. 'It seems stupid to be considering looking for long-lost treasure when Dad's missing, but at the moment the treasure's all we've got that seems to be a link with Giuseppe and somehow Giuseppe seems to be connected with Dad. I can't think of any other course of action.'

'Then it's a good job you've joined forces with me,' Alice said smugly.

'You've got an idea?'

'We need to make a trip to Mdina.'

'Mdina?'

'Used to be the ancient capital of Malta and it's a not-to-be-missed tourist attraction.'

'I'm not in the mood for sight-seeing.'

She flushed. 'Sorry, that wasn't much of a joke, but we do need to go there because it's the home of Giuseppe's childhood friend, Tommasso Lorenzo. Steady!' She caught the jug of lemonade as Tom sent it flying in his excitement.

'You know him?'

'Not personally, I wish I did, but I know of him. So do most of the people on Malta, it'd be hard not to! The Lorenzo family are one of the most influential on the island, part of the ancient aristocracy, and they're never out of the news. The father, he's called Taddeus, supports stacks of charities and his wife is always being filmed with different celebrities. They've got two sons, Tommasso and Alphonso. I don't know where they live exactly, except that it's somewhere in Mdina. As Tommasso was Giuseppe's friend then Dad could probably tell us but I daren't ask him, not after the telling off I got last night.'

'Luigi was furious, he made me feel awful. Sorry for dragging you into trouble.'

'You didn't drag me, I offered, and at least we know from Dad's and Marco's reactions that there's some mystery about Giuseppe.

Neither of them confirmed his death, which suggests it's Luigi who's the liar.'

Tom felt himself unaccountably troubled at the thought.

'It does look,' Alice continued, 'as though Giuseppe might be your father.'

Tom took the photograph from his rucksack, handing it over to her. 'I can't be certain; Giuseppe's about twelve here and Dad's thirty-nine.'

She took a closer look at the photo. 'There's nothing obviously mysterious about him, is there? He seems to be enjoying life, look at that grin.'

'That's what's making it difficult; all my memories of Dad are of a serious person. It's awful, I know, but I can't remember him smiling very much. I'm more convinced by the fact that Dad's birth date opened the lock on Giuseppe's box. The likelihood of them both having the same birthday is too unbelievable, surely?'

'Far too unbelievable. It would answer a lot of questions if he is Giuseppe,' Alice said slowly. 'He'd obviously know about the Farrigianis if they're his parents and he clearly meant to take you to see them.'

'So why didn't he turn up at the airport?' However hard he tried to push it away, Tom could not forget the hurt of his abandonment.

'Something must have happened to stop him. Do you think he could have solved the riddle after all this time? Remember Marco said that Giuseppe and Tommasso never came close to finding the treasure. Maybe your Dad had a sudden brainwave and flew out here to collect it, that could be the surprise he hinted at, and got into difficulties, leaving you stranded.'

Tom's excitement faded. 'That means if we can't solve the riddle we'll never find Dad.'

'Not unless he enlisted help from his old treasure-seeking partner, Tommasso Lorenzo. Finding him's worth a try, surely? Giuseppe might even be staying with him in Mdina. I don't know why he'd go there rather than home to Haz Zahra, unless there was an amazing quarrel between him and his parents, which I suppose there must have been for Luigi to go around telling people that he's dead. Tomorrow, first thing, we'll take a trip to Mdina.'

Tom hesitated, wondering if he really wanted to discover the truth. It seemed impossible that his father could be anyone other than Joseph Newton. If he did turn out to be Giuseppe Farrigiani, it opened up a whole new set of questions and he wasn't sure he was ready to face them. 'We don't know where Tommasso lives,' he said lamely. 'Somewhere in Mdina won't get us very far.'

'We can ask, we've got tongues in our heads. You're being defeatist again. Can you suggest anything better?'

'No.' Tom rose. 'How do we get there? Cycle?'

'Could do, but it's a bit hilly. Wait till you see Mdina, it's perched on top of a steep crag.'

'You mean it's on the summit?'

Alice's eyes widened. 'You're thinking of the riddle? It could be, though I haven't noticed many dead trees in Mdina. Not that I was looking for them. If we cycle to Attard, we can catch a bus. They run fairly regularly.'

'I wish we could go right this minute.' Tom grimaced. 'I hate the feeling of waiting for something to happen and it's even worse now I think Dad might be stranded somewhere. What if the *alight ashore* means that the summit is the top of a cliff? Dad could have fallen and be lying injured.'

'Sunday afternoon's not the best time for visiting Mdina, everything will have shut down.' Alice leapt to her feet suddenly, startling Tom. 'I know what we can do, though. Grab your bike.'

She was almost out of the orchard before Tom had risen and he sprinted after her. 'Where are we going?'

'To the village.'

'Not to Marco's again? I couldn't face that.'

'No fear, Dad would kill me.'

'Where, then?'

'You'll see when we get there.'

They had just collected their bikes when Mrs Rogerson came into the farmyard. 'Where are you two off to?'

'I'm going to show Tom round the village.'

'Pity you didn't decide that five minutes ago, you could have gone down in the car with Dad. He's visiting Marco.'

After they'd waved goodbye, Tom glanced curiously at Alice. 'She didn't seem cross. Does she know about us questioning Marco yesterday?'

'Must do.' Alice pulled a face. 'She and Dad don't keep secrets from each other, as I know to my cost. In fact, I think her words were a warning.'

'About what?'

Alice smiled. 'If you knew her as well as I do, you'd have realised that what she actually said was, "Your Dad's at Marco's so don't even think of pestering him again." We'll have to make sure we go nowhere near the café.'

It didn't take long for Tom to realise that Alice's description yesterday of the dusty roads had been more than accurate. After only a few minutes, his nose and throat felt like sandpaper and sweat ran down his face. The brilliance of the sun had leached all colour from the landscape.

Arriving at the village, she led Tom down a hedged lane that twisted and turned towards the back of the church. Propping their bikes against the stone wall, Alice looked expectantly at Tom. 'Understand now?'

'No.'

'The graveyard,' she explained, 'where all the Farrigianis are buried. The place to find Giuseppe, if he's dead.'

They climbed over the wall and into a grassy wilderness, dotted with flowers and old headstones. Tom's heart sank. There seemed to be hundreds of them.

'This way.' Alice pointed to the right. 'The Farrigianis have been here such a long time that they've got their own plot.' She ushered him to a shady corner overlooked by two tall trees, indicating a marble tablet. 'We don't even need to search the tombstones; they've done the work for us.'

The writing was faint and spidery, but clearly legible. At the top was the motto: *INTERIORA VIDE.*

Alice screwed up her face. 'My Latin's not brilliant.'

Tom grinned. 'Mine's non-existent.'

'Sounds as though it must be something to do with inside.'

'Look within.'

They spun round to face an elderly woman, all in black, the bunch of flowers she clutched vivid against her drabness. 'Look within,' she reiterated. 'The Farrigiani motto.' She left as abruptly as she had arrived.

'Mrs Gomes,' Alice explained. 'She visits the family graves every Sunday. They've been on the island for generations, like the Farrigianis.'

'Strange motto. It's written up above the front door of the Villa Magrino, I noticed it when I arrived. Makes more sense there than here, though. How can you look within a tablet of stone?'

His eyes widened as he viewed the list of names on the marble tablet. 'See there? The first name? He was real, not simply a fantasy of Giuseppe's.'

'*CLAUDIO FARRIGIANI 1799-1851,*' Alice read aloud. 'I wish he could tell us the meaning of his riddle.'

Together they traced the Farrigiani family down through the centuries until they came to the final name: *ISABELLA FARRIGIANI 1902-1972.*

She must have been Luigi's mother,' Alice whispered. 'When did he say his son died?'

'Twenty years ago.'

'Then where's his name? He's certainly not buried here.' She turned to Tom, eyes shining. 'Looks as though you were right, after all. Giuseppe Farrigiani could be very much alive. Now, all we've got to do is find him.'

June 1798

Night was approaching in a sea-washed purple haze before Claudio Farrigiani could bestir himself to move. He stood reluctantly, eyes still scanning the silent sea. How long would it remain empty? How long before the beast came stalking through the swelling breakers to destroy all that he held most dear?

'There you are. I thought I'd find you here.'

A smile came to Claudio's lips at the sound of the voice that had become as familiar to him as his own. He turned slowly. 'Paolo, what are you after now? Am I to have no peace?'

'You've been missing all afternoon. I need some company.'

The Knight facing him looked far younger than his twenty-eight years. Small, thin and with a triangular face burned brown by the Maltese sun, Paolo da Messina seemed to be in perpetual motion. He reminded Claudio of a restless sprite.

'Why me? What have you done with Gianni?'

'He's also gone missing and Tullio is scribbling away as usual. I think he must be writing an epic. Sorry, I'm afraid it's got to be you.'

Together they walked along the water's edge where fishermen beached their boats and sorted through the day's catch. The normality of the scene tugged at Claudio's heart. These simple folk, who took no interest in the world outside their own small island, had no idea of the fate which might befall them.

He looked down at the smaller Knight by his side. 'Am I permitted to ask where we are going?'

'Ramon has invited us to eat with them.'

Claudio groaned. The Auberge de Castile was a hotbed of unrest at any time. What hare-brained scheme were they cooking up now? He contented himself with saying, 'Another evening of talk, then.'

'And what would we be doing if we stayed at home? Talk. Nothing but talk. That's all we ever do these days.' Paolo's face crumpled in an uncharacteristic look of despair as he asked quietly, 'It's going to be bad, isn't it?'

Claudio gazed up at the scarlet flag of the Order flying high above Fort St Angelo and could find no words of comfort for his friend. Putting a gentle hand on his shoulder he said softly, 'Come, let's see what the Spanish have on offer for us this evening.'

Yet as they made their way up the steep track and through the stout gate into Valletta, Claudio Farrigiani's thoughts sailed over the fortifications and out across the dusty plain to the small village of Haz Zahra, which had become his second home on Malta.

His reverie was cut short by the sight of a familiar figure racing towards him.

'Come!' Tullio Falcone grabbed his arm, urging him forwards.

'Not again.' Claudio began to groan in mock anger, stopping short at the expression on the Knight's face. 'Tullio? What's happened?'

'It's Gianni, what did you expect? Who else would be so stupid as to get into an argument with the French at such a time?'

'What about?' Even as he spoke, Claudio could guess the answer.

'He said that Possielgue is a French spy, that he is not here visiting his cousin as he and the French claim, but is reporting back to France on the state of our defences.'

Claudio sighed. It was what they all thought, though not exactly a wise thing to say when the Knights from the three French Langues greatly outnumbered those from the other nations.

'Jacques Villaret has challenged him to a duel.' Tullio's eyes were wide with a mixture of fear and excitement. 'How could he be so stupid? Gianni will slaughter him.'

There was no need for Claudio to ask their destination. Knights and Maltese alike were streaming through the centre of Valletta towards a narrow alley alongside the Auberge de Provence. Pushing through the gathering crowd, Claudio was brought to an abrupt stop by the alarming sight of one of his closest friends.

Gianni Correr was built on a mammoth scale with broad shoulders and hair as bright as the Maltese sun. Rather than an Italian, he resembled an ancient Viking, with a berserker's hot temper to match his appearance. Sword dancing and crazed grin splitting his face, he was launching a full scale assault on his unfortunate challenger. Jacques Villaret, more talented with tongue than with sword, was striving to maintain his dignity whilst beating a strategic retreat.

As Claudio watched in horror, the Frenchman stumbled, falling to one knee.

Gianni gave a whooping cry of triumph.

'Now!' Claudio hissed at his companions, leaping before the startled conqueror. 'Gianni! That's enough! No more.'

He almost smiled at the sight of his friends clinging to the giant's arms, Paolo's feet barely grazing the floor. Gianni shrugged them off with contemptuous ease, but the French spectators had come to their senses: Jacques Villaret was well hidden in their midst.

Another French Knight stepped forward. Nicolas Portanier had joined the Order on the same day as Claudio and Paolo. Until now, that had been a strong bond between them.

'Take your friend home, Claudio. He's nothing but a savage.'

At the coldness in his eyes, Claudio knew without a shadow of a doubt that the Order of St John was not merely threatened from without: the *brotherhood was splintering from within.*

By the time they were approaching the Auberge d'Italie, Gianni had become a contrite, melancholy figure.

'You take him inside,' Claudio told the others. 'I'll join you in a few minutes.'

Gianni's face flushed scarlet. 'You still mad at me?'

'No.' Claudio smiled gently. 'I've just got something to do.'

A few minutes later he slipped into the hushed stillness of the Cathedral, sinking down into a pew, eyes fixed on the marble altar. Above it, hung the wonderful painting of St John in Heaven, by Mattia Preti. Raising his head, Claudio marvelled once again at the scenes from the life of John the Baptist which Preti had painted on the stone vault of the Cathedral. It had taken him five years to complete. No wonder the artist had been rewarded by acceptance into the Order.

Here in the Cathedral, erected as a tribute to the patron saint of their Order, Claudio felt surrounded by its treasures: the silver candlesticks on the altar, the statues, the paintings, the illuminated choral books, the crucifixes, the tombs of the Grand Masters, all bore witness to its great legacy. Above all, the Cathedral was home to their most precious relic, the hand of John the Baptist. What would happen to these treasures in the weeks to come?

Thoughts of the relic sent him spinning into the past, to the sun-drenched Italian coast of Amalfi and an old fisherman who delighted a young boy with tales from long ago; tales that had been handed down through the centuries from the merchants who had carried the early pilgrims to the Holy land. Claudio smiled at the memory.

It was the story of the first Crusade that had risen in his mind. Early summer. 1097. Antioch had fallen to the Crusaders but they in turn were besieged by a large Turkish army.

With little food remaining, morale was low, many of the Crusaders believing that the end was nigh. Then, the miracle occurred. Right there in Antioch the Holy Lance that pierced the side of Jesus was discovered. All at once, the Crusaders felt that Christ himself was by their side. Such faith it gave them, such a feeling of invincibility, that they stormed out of Antioch and against overwhelming odds defeated the might of the Turkish army.

Could the Knights of Malta hope for a similar miracle?

A figure slid into the pew at his side.

'Is Gianni settled?'

Paolo grinned. 'In bed and snoring like a baby. Tullio's watching over him. He's scribbling away again.' He waited expectantly and then pulled a face. 'Aren't you going to ask me what he's writing?'

'I asked you earlier. You said you didn't know.'

'Now I do And it's something you'd never guess.. He's writing about us.'

'Us?'

'About you, me, Gianni and the rest of the Italian Knights.'

'Whatever for?'

'He says that sometime, in the distant future, someone might be interested in the Italian Knights of St John and how we spent our last days on Malta.'

5

The following morning, they left their bikes at the home of one of Alice's school friends in Attard. The bus trundled through an open countryside of terraced fields broken by windbreaks and rubble walls. Alongside the road flourished a strange plant with broad, pedal - shaped leaves.

'Prickly pear,' Alice told him, seeing Tom's puzzled expression. 'It grows all over Malta because it doesn't need much rain. I've found Alice Rogerson for you, by the way.'

Tom stared. 'Why didn't you tell me straight away?'

'Because it hasn't done us any good. Last night I was trying to make sense of the situation and it dawned on me that we were ignoring the mystery girl on the plane. She must fit in somewhere. I searched through the telephone directories and the only Alice Rogerson I found lives in Valletta.'

'Did you get her address?'

'I did better than that, I rang her.'

'And?'

'She's 72 and has never been to England.'

'Perhaps she's got a daughter or a niece who's named after her.'

'I asked that. There are no other Alices in her family.'

Tom refused to be beaten. 'Perhaps the entry in the directory isn't in Alice's name, but in her father's. She said she lived with her parents when she's here.'

'That occurred to me. I rang the two Rogersons in Mdina, thought I may as well start where we're headed today, and asked for Alice. Both told me I'd got the wrong number. They didn't have any Alices in their families. Sorry.'

'Thanks for trying, anyway. I had forgotten about her, though you're right she must be playing some role in this mystery. It's awful because I really liked her, but I'm convinced now that she stole my note. I can't think of any other way it could have disappeared. And I can't even begin to guess why she'd want it.'

'The only reason I can think of is that she wanted to make things awkward for you.'

'She certainly did that.'

'If you'd had the note from your father then everyone would have believed you immediately.'

'That means she must be on the opposite side to Dad.' Tom felt uneasy at the thought. If that was the case, why had she been so kind to him? 'I wish we could find out who she is? There might be some simple explanation we haven't thought of.'

'Don't worry, I haven't given up. I'll continue my efforts tonight and we'll find her even if I have to telephone every Rogerson on Malta. Trouble is, I daren't make too many calls at one time, I don't want Dad to find out. Can I look at the riddle again?'

After that they journeyed in silence, each lost in their own thoughts, Tom trying to come to terms with the disturbing fact that he might not be the son of Joseph Newton, but the son of Giuseppe Farrigiani, descended from an Italian knight. What did that make him? A mixture of Maltese and Italian? He suddenly felt very English. Perhaps he wasn't even Tom Newton, but Tommasso Farrigiani.

'What's in a name?' he quoted softly.

Alice looked up, startled. 'What?'

Tom gave a sheepish grin. 'I was quoting Shakespeare, not something I do very often, don't worry. I was wondering who I was, Tom Newton or Tommasso Farrigiani.'

'Does it make a difference?'

'That's what I was trying to work out.'

'And?'

'And I haven't got an answer; not yet anyway. It needs some serious study. I almost feel as though I've been dispossessed of my identity and left in limbo. As if someone has picked me up, turned me round and dumped me pointing in the opposite direction. Tom Newton is a Manchester schoolboy who likes football and leads a simple life. There's nothing mysterious about him. Now I've got to come to terms with the possibility that I may be Tommasso Farrigiani and how ever many times I say the name it doesn't sound like me. Even if it turns out to be true, I don't think I'll ever be comfortable as anyone but Tom Newton. What about you? Solved the riddle?'

'No, it's a complete muddle. The *alight ashore* sounds as though we've got to approach the location by boat, which isn't easy when we're boatless, though I have got a friend whose father owns a boatyard so I could sound her out about borrowing one. Maybe you were right and the *hill that beckons* is a cliff which can only be reached by boat and if we climb it we'll find a dead tree on top and an angel.'

'It can't be a real angel, can it? They don't exist.'

She laughed. 'I'm sure some people think they do. Perhaps it's a painting of an angel; the churches on Malta are full of them.'

Tom was sceptical. 'How could you hide a painting in a tree? Especially a dead tree. There wouldn't be any leaves to conceal it.'

'Then what about a painting of an angel on a dead tree?' Alice argued. 'Hidden on the summit of a hill.'

'It'd be pretty visible.'

'Depends on the size of the painting.' Alice was reluctant to relinquish her idea. 'Perhaps it's one of those tiny icons; a lot of those are to do with angels. Some of the hills round here are very stony, the icon could be hidden in a crevice under a rock. That wouldn't be easy to discover.'

'It would be impossible to discover,' Tom said gloomily, 'unless you knew exactly where to look.'

'Presumably that's what the riddle tells us.'

'It says the summit's a heavenly one. I don't suppose Malta's got an Angel Cliff?'

'Not that I know of'

'What about another name for an angel?'

Alice grinned. 'You mean like Cherub Hill?'

'Sounds stupid, doesn't it?'

'It's worth thinking about but we'll have to leave it for later. Here's Mdina, home of the Lorenzo family. Let's see what help Tommasso can be.'

They were travelling up a steep road towards an imposing walled town without, to Tom's disappointment, a dead tree in sight.

The bus station was situated outside the City Gate. 'Visitors have to park their cars here,' Alice told him, 'which is why Mdina is known as the ''Silent City'', though with all the tourists at this time of year it's anything but quiet.'

They crossed the bridge over the moat and entered through the Main Gate. The tall stone buildings cast deep shadows into the narrow streets and Tom welcomed the coolness. He was already beginning to sweat uncomfortably.

Immediately to their right, Alice pointed out the Mdina Dungeons. 'We went there once on a school trip, it's pretty gruesome, all waxworks of people being tortured, with a soundtrack of screaming and groaning and choking, plus the most ghastly chopping noises.'

'Sounds fun!'

'If you want to go in there, you go alone.'

'I'll leave it for another day.' When this whole mess has been sorted out, Tom thought optimistically. Some part of him still held on to the hope that all of this, everything since being stranded at the airport, would turn out to be a simple mistake. No mystery involved, just a straightforward misunderstanding. 'What's our next move?'

'There's not much point just wandering around, I suggest we find a café with someone as talkative as Marco and see if we can learn where Tommasso lives.'

They settled on a tea-garden, situated up against the walls, and Alice ordered mqaret, little fried pastries stuffed with chopped, spiced dates, and glasses of Kinnie.

'What on earth's Kinnie?'

'One of our most popular drinks. You'll like it, I promise.'

Their waitress was young and plumply cheerful. As she set down the tray, Alice took a deep breath. 'I'm doing a school project on the old houses of Mdina, can you suggest a good place to start?'

She looked doubtful for a moment before a smile creased her face. 'You need to speak to Vincent, he is writing a book about the history of Mdina.'

'Where can we find him?' Tom began, but she was signalling wildly across the garden to a frail, gaunt-faced man serving coffee to two elderly ladies. He was the most unlikely looking waiter they'd ever seen.

Tom took a sip of his drink. It was well-chilled and he found the bitter-orange taste refreshing. 'You're right, this is good.' He tucked eagerly into a pastry. 'And so is this. It's a bit like our Christmas mince pies.'

On the waiter's arrival, Alice repeated her request.

Adjusting his wire-framed glasses, he sat beside them. 'I can give you a full list. Do you have paper and pencil ready?'

Flustered, Alice said, 'No, sorry.'

'You won't get very far in your project without writing materials. You will need to make notes, do sketches. . .'

'I'm going to buy a new pad before we start,' Alice broke in, quickly. 'My old project book was full.'

He sighed fussily, pulling a notebook from his pocket and a silver pen from the inside of his jacket. 'You'll need a map of Mdina.'

'In my guide book,' Tom said promptly, fishing in his rucksack.

The waiter cleared his throat and began, somewhat pedantically, 'You mustn't miss the Palazzo Falzon, on Triq Villegaignon, dating from 1495. When the Knights of St John first arrived on Malta, it was used by Grand Master De L'Isle Adam. Note its magnificent mediaeval windows.'

Alice dutifully began to scribble down the information on the sheet of paper he had provided.

'Further along is the Casa Inguanez, the ancient seat of Malta's oldest aristocratic family, who have lived there since the fourteenth century. It dates back to 1350 and has been in the family's hands ever since. Continue on and you will see the Casa Testeferrata. . .'

Alice was leaning forward, a rapt expression on her face which was, to Tom's way of thinking, rather exaggerated. They were going to be here all day at this rate. Suppressing his impatience, he allowed his mind to wander back to a time when life had been simple and uncomplicated; even the traumatic events of the divorce had been nothing compared to the sheer sense of frustration and wretchedness he now felt. What he hated to acknowledge was that he'd become scared of the answers they might uncover. If his father turned out to be Giuseppe, why had he hurt Luigi and Francesca so badly that they preferred to think of him as dead? Perhaps it would be better to remain in ignorance.

Forcing his attention to the present, he found that Vincent was guiding them along the Triq San Pawl.

'Before you reach the Cathedral you'll come to the Casa Peralta, home of the Lorenzo family.' Alice shot Tom a triumphant smile. 'Not that you'll be able to see much,' he admitted, 'The house is set far back behind enormous gates, but do take note of the exquisite door knocker shaped like a sea horse.'

'Thanks very much!' Alice stood abruptly, surprising Vincent. 'We won't have time to see any more. We're grateful for your help.'

'Perhaps you will come back another day to finish your project?'

'If we do, we'll certainly call on you before we start,' Alice promised.

Having secured their escape, she pulled a rueful face. 'I do hope you realise that since I met you I've become an accomplished liar.' She laughed away Tom's apologies. 'I almost feel as though we ought to visit these other houses first. Don't worry.' She held up a hand to forestall Tom's protest. 'I wasn't going to suggest that, but maybe I'll come and do it one day just to salve my conscience.'

Following the map, they arrived at the Triq San Pawl without difficulty. There was no mistaking the ornately decorated gates of the Casa Peralta, even without the distinguishing door knocker.

Having reached their destination, Alice's composure vanished. 'I'm not sure about this anymore. Dare we knock? They're really famous, it seems such a cheek. Dad would kill me if he knew what we intended.'

'It was your idea. We're not going to do anything wrong, I'll just ask Tommasso if he's seen Giuseppe recently.'

'Giuseppe's dead. Or supposed to be. That's not a very diplomatic opening question.'

'Alright, I'll simply say I want to know about Giuseppe Farrigiani and watch his reaction.' Tom relented at the sight of her worried face. 'Look, there's no need for you to be involved. Go and sit by the cathedral and I'll collect you when I'm finished.'

'No, this was my idea, as you so rightly pointed out. I've come so far, I can't back out now.'

As though to reinforce her decision, she rapped sharply with the knocker. They waited several minutes without anyone appearing, Alice fidgeting nervously and Tom prowling restlessly up and down.

He stopped suddenly. 'Do you think the knocker could be just for decoration? There's a bell-pull here, one of those old-fashioned ones.' Seizing it, he gave a tug. They heard nothing, yet within seconds the shadowy figure of a man appeared on the other side of the gates.

'Yes?'

Tom cleared his throat. 'We've come to see Tommasso Lorenzo.'

'Have you an appointment?'

'No, but it's important that. . .'

'Then phone for an appointment.' The figure moved away before Tom could utter another word.

Alice looked relieved. 'We should have thought of that. They're so rich they probably get stacks of nuisance calls. They're not going to open the gate to just anybody and especially not to a couple of kids.'

'I'm not giving in so easily.' Tom kicked the gate angrily and Alice glanced round, alarmed.

'You'll get us arrested if you do that. Let's go and see if we can find the phone number.'

'No.' Tom peered through the bars, releasing some of his pent-up frustration by giving them another kick. 'Even if we did manage to discover the number it'd probably be weeks before they'd give us an appointment. This is the fourth day Dad's been missing, anything could have happened to him. I'm not going to wait any longer.'

He gave the bell-pull a tug, then another. Alice punched his shoulder. 'Tom, you're not doing any good, we'll only get the same answer as last time and if we make nuisances of ourselves they'll never give us an appointment.'

'Then I'll keep ringing until they let me in. They'll get fed up, eventually.'

He reached for the bell-pull as the man reappeared at the gate.

'No need for that. I gave you your answer and nothing's changed.'

'It's important,' Tom pleaded. 'All we need are a few minutes with Tommasso Lorenzo.'

'Important! That's what they all say. If you knew how many people come begging for favours you'd understand why we don't let anyone in without an appointment.'

'Will you take Tommasso Lorenzo a message?' Tom interrupted. 'Say I've come to see him about Giuseppe Farrigiani.'

There was a moments silence. 'Wait there!' he said finally, moving away.

'The magic name,' Alice murmured. 'Even the gate man seems to have heard of Giuseppe. Strange how his name always seems to provoke a reaction.'

'Which suggests that he's not dead,' Tom said hopefully.

Or there's some mystery about his death, Alice mused, keeping the thought to herself. Clearly Tom was in a volatile frame of mind, not that she could blame him. She tried to imagine her own father missing but the idea seemed ludicrous: he was such a sensible, ordinary, down to earth farmer, far removed from the mysterious, romantic figure that Giuseppe had become in her imagination.

Without warning, the gates opened silently. The shadowy man was now revealed as short and stocky, with a squashed face like a crumpled paper bag. His expression was hardly welcoming.

'Straight along the drive to the door!' he commanded. 'You'll be met.'

Vincent had been right, the house was certainly set well back, the pathway twisting and turning through colourful flower beds dotted with ornate sculptures. It was like a miniature palace, Tom decided, with its turrets and battlements, its balconies and elaborately decorated stonework, indicating a family of great wealth.

'I'll leave the talking to you, this time,' Alice whispered, 'though I shouldn't start by asking if Giuseppe's dead. Let Tommasso tell us what he knows before we give anything away.'

They climbed an impressive flight of marble steps to a large doorway. The crest over the entrance echoed the sea horse on the knocker. The man waiting there was clearly a servant, his black uniform hanging loosely on a skeleton frame. He had a thin, sallow, emaciated face and dark eyes that regarded them suspiciously as he ushered them inside without a word, closing the huge door with an ominous bang.

Alice felt a sudden rush of fear, as though their escape route had been denied them. She couldn't believe this was actually happening. The Lorenzo family wasn't the kind you simply dropped in on for a chat. She knew that well enough, even if Tom didn't. He marched forward purposefully, a determined expression on his face; she followed warily, wondering whatever she'd let herself in for and praying that her father would never find out.

They were shown into a magnificent drawing room, all golds and blues glowing in sunshine streaming through French windows. Old paintings, many of them clearly family ancestors, dotted the walls. The servant left them standing awkwardly in the centre of the room, unsure of whether they dare sit down.

'I told you they were rich,' Alice muttered. 'I bet each of those paintings is worth a fortune. Probably more than Dad earns in a whole year. I really don't think this was one of my better ideas.'

'Do you think these refreshments are for us?' Tom pointed out a table by the window, surrounded by four chairs, on which sat a pitcher of lemonade and a plate of fancy biscuits.

'Better wait until it's offered, though it looks as though Tommasso's prepared to be friendly, thank goodness.'

At the sound of footsteps they turned eagerly to the doorway. Tom's first thought was that, despite the trendy clothes, Tommasso Lorenzo had not aged as well as his own father, at the same time remembering it was four years since he'd seen him. Perhaps Dad had also developed a paunch and tried to disguise it with a wide belt round his hips. He hoped not.

At least Tommasso was smiling, though there was no recognition in his eyes as they gave their names. 'Do sit down.' he said cheerfully, indicating the window table.

Tom noted that, despite Tommasso's friendliness, Alice looked positively terrified. He felt guilty at dragging her into this situation, wishing he'd insisted that she remain outside. Not that he fancied facing Tommasso alone. Remembering Alice's advice, he remained silent; let Tommasso make the first move.

'Lemonade?'

Tom nodded and he poured them each a glassful, pushing the biscuits across the table.

'I hear you made a bit of a nuisance of yourselves at the gate.' Tom flushed but said nothing. Alice stared at the carpet. 'I must admit you've got me intrigued. What can you possibly have to tell me about my old friend Beppe?'

Tom thought for a moment, wondering where to start. 'It's not exactly what we can tell you, but what we hope that you. . .'

There was a discreet knock at the door and Tommasso frowned in annoyance. 'Come in!'

It was the skeleton servant, hovering in the doorway. Tommasso joined him, his displeasure evident, the length of the drawing room making it impossible to hear their muted whispers. Tom gave Alice what he hoped was a reassuring smile and took a biscuit, offering her the plate. She shook her head.

Tommasso turned to them. 'I'm afraid I'm going to have to answer a phone call, will you excuse me for a few minutes? Do help yourself to refreshments. I'll try not to be too long.'

As the door closed behind him, Alice jumped to her feet. 'Are you sure this Tommasso Lorenzo is the right one?'

'You're not suggesting there are two of them?'

'There are two Alice Rogersons!'

'And you were the one who said that was too much of a coincidence. Tommasso does know Giuseppe, he called him his old friend Beppe. What's your problem?'

'Tommasso was Giuseppe's friend and Giuseppe was Ricardo's younger brother. This Tommasso is older than Ricardo. Years older by the look of it.'

Her doubts struck a chord with Tom's own misgivings, but before he could respond a figure appeared through the French windows. At Alice's startled gasp, he placed a warning finger to his lips, beckoning them outside.

Alice moved towards him, Tom catching her arm. 'No! We're not going anywhere! We came here to see. . .'

'Hurry!' the newcomer whispered. 'I'll explain when I get you safely away.'

'You'll explain now or we don't go anywhere!' Tom could feel his anger spiralling out of control. 'I'm fed up of being messed around.'

'Keep your voice down. If you don't follow me this minute you'll be putting Giuseppe Farrigiani in grave danger.'

Tom's heart leapt. 'Giuseppe's alive? Where is he?'

They all tensed at the sound of footsteps in the corridor.

'Come!' The man vanished onto the terrace, Alice hurrying after him. Tom followed reluctantly.

They were hustled through another large garden, all trees and flowers, bronze statues and fountains, to a small gate in the surrounding stone wall. The man unlocked it quickly, pushing Tom and Alice through.

Tom put his hand on the gate, preventing it from shutting. 'You said you'd explain.'

The man hesitated. 'Go to Peppino's Café, it's on Triq I-Imhazen, near San Pietro Bastion. I'll meet you there in twenty minutes.'

Tom was still unsatisfied. 'But we didn't come here to meet you, whoever you are, we need to see Tommasso Lorenzo.'

'I am Tommasso Lorenzo, you fool!' the man hissed at them, closing the gate in their faces.

6

An hour later Tom's patience finally came to an end. He slammed down his coffee cup, nearly smashing the saucer.

'I'm not waiting any longer! I'm going straight back to the house and this time I'll demand some answers.'

Alice looked at him wearily. 'Don't be stupid!'

'Why not? That's how everybody treats me. As though I'm a stupid idiot. No one tells me the truth, not the girl on the plane, not Dad, not Luigi or Marco or Tommasso - whichever one of them was Tommasso - we can't even be certain about that.'

'It was the second one,' Alice said quietly. 'He was the right age and I recognised him from the photograph you found in Giuseppe's box.'

'That was taken over twenty years ago!' Tom snarled. 'You couldn't possibly tell.'

'I don't care,' Alice said stubbornly. 'His face hasn't changed that much and he was the right age. The first one who spoke to us was far too old.'

Tom delved into the rucksack, pulling out the photograph. After studying it, he apologised sullenly. 'So who was the first man? Why did the servant take us straight to him if he's not Tommasso Lorenzo?'

'We don't know who he is, which is why it would be idiotic to go racing back in there without finding out. We have discovered that Giuseppe's alive and if he is your father, if he's in trouble, we could be making matters worse. You heard Tommasso say we'd be putting him in danger.'

'So, what do we do? Sit here for the rest of the day? It's obvious that Tommasso had no intention of meeting us; his promise was probably just a ploy to get us away from the Lorenzo house. Something's going on there and if it involves Dad I can't sit around doing nothing.'

'I think it'd be best if we went home. We're out of our depth here and you never know, there might be news from the Consulate.'

'You don't believe that! If they were going to find Dad, they'd have done so by now. I bet they're not even interested. Tommasso was our one chance to learn what's happened to Dad and now we've blown it.'

'I don't know what else to suggest,' Alice said miserably. 'I suppose we could turn our attention to the riddle, see if we can find the treasure and trace your Dad that way.'

'We don't even know if the treasure has anything to do with Dad's disappearance. We don't even know if it's still there. It could have been found long before Giuseppe and Tommasso started searching. Let's have one more coffee?' Tom begged. 'If Tommasso hasn't turned up by the time we've drunk them we'll go back to Haz Zahra, I promise.'

They were just finishing when Tommasso arrived, sinking into a chair at their table. He looked exhausted.

Alice took pity on him. 'Shall I get you a coffee?'

'I haven't time. Sorry to keep you waiting, I half expected you'd have gone by now.'

'You mean you hoped we'd have gone,' Tom said curtly. 'What kept you?'

'I had to help my brother and the servants search the house and grounds for you; it would have looked suspicious if I hadn't. I've got my wife and son to consider, we all live at the Casa Peralta. As you can imagine, your disappearance caused quite a stir.'

'Was that your brother?' Alice asked. 'The one we met first?'

'Yes, that was Alphonso. Did he say he was me?'

'Not exactly,' Tom confessed, 'we just presumed he was because we'd asked to see Tommasso Lorenzo and the servant took us straight to him. Why is your brother interested in Giuseppe?'

'We're all interested in Giuseppe,' Tommasso said quietly. 'What do you know about him?'

Tom frowned. 'We're the ones asking the questions.'

'I haven't got long.' Tommasso glanced round nervously. 'They'll soon come to the conclusion that you're no longer at the Casa Peralta. You need to get out of Mdina as quickly as possible.'

'We will after you've told us about Giuseppe,' Alice promised.

'What do you want to know?'

Tom decided that the time for diplomacy was past. 'Giuseppe's not dead, is he?'

'No, he's not dead. He's very much alive, a fact that worries many people.'

'Then why does his father say that he is?'

Tommasso sighed. 'It's very simple, there's no mystery about that. Giuseppe is no longer a member of the Farrigiani family. As far as Luigi is concerned, his second son is dead to them.'

'Why?'

'How much do you know?'

Very little, Tom thought, though he wasn't about to admit that. 'We know you and Giuseppe were school friends, we've got a photo of the two of you together, and that you spent your time searching for the Farrigiani treasure.'

'What a waste of time that was,' Tommasso said wearily. 'We never even got close, though we thought we had once. Beppe was my best friend. We met for the first time at the age of five. When we were kids the treasure hunt seemed exciting, as though we were living in a story book, and we used to pretend we were knights, like Claudio Farrigiani. I always envied Beppe having such a fantastic ancestor. We spent years trying to find the landscape in the riddle. You know about that?' Tom nodded. 'Talk about looking for a needle in a haystack. We must have climbed every hill on Malta and searched every summit. One summer holiday we borrowed a boat and sailed all round the island.'

'Looking for a place to *alight ashore*?' Alice guessed.

'Yes. We'd decided that the *cavernous steepness* must be a cliff. Trouble was there were so many of them. Malta's an island, for god's sake, it's practically surrounded by cliffs. I even got to wondering if Claudio Farrigiani had made the whole thing up as a joke.'

'What was the treasure supposed to be?' Alice asked. 'I thought it might be a painting of an angel on a dead tree, but why would Claudio need to hide it?'

'Perhaps he stole it,' Tom said grimly.

Tommasso laughed. 'Hardly likely, he was a Knight of St John, very honourable, they were. They certainly didn't go in for stealing. As to the treasure, your guess is as good as mine. Beppe thought it must be one of the Order's priceless relics that Claudio rescued from the clutches of Napoleon, when he ransacked the island and the knights were forced out of Malta. Claudio would have known it was unlikely they'd ever be allowed to return, so he left the clue for his ancestors, hoping that one day they'd recover the treasure. Shame he made the riddle so difficult.'

'The treasure must be really valuable, mustn't it?' Alice asked.

There was a sudden wariness in Tommasso's eyes though he answered easily enough. 'I suppose it must be, but Beppe always insisted its value couldn't be reckoned in terms of money. What was important was its historical significance. He regarded it as part of his family heritage.'

'Did he ever give up the search?'

'By the time we were sixteen my enthusiasm had waned, though by then Beppe had become obsessed. We didn't see as much of each other, he spent all his time researching the Knights of St John, looking for a reference to Claudio Farrigiani.'

'Did he find one?' Tom asked eagerly.

'He did indeed. We both did, actually. It was one of the times he'd persuaded me to join him. We discovered that an old book in the Bibliotheca – that's the library in Valletta – was about the Italian Knights and their last days on the island. Beppe pestered them with requests to see it, but he was always refused. Trouble was, Beppe wasn't one to give up easily. If you know him, you'll realise that.'

He gave up on me and Mum easily enough, Tom thought sourly. 'What did he do?'

'Enlisted my help, wanted me to persuade my father to ask for him, but he wasn't interested. In fact, he was pretty mad that Beppe had involved me again. Like Luigi, my father thought that Beppe was becoming paranoid in his desire to find the treasure. Luigi did his best to convince Beppe it was time to drop the whole thing. They quarrelled violently and Beppe left home to stay with Ricardo in Valletta. Ricardo had just started his first teaching job.'

'What happened, then?'

'Not so fast.' Tommasso leaned back in his chair. 'I've been doing all the talking so far. It's about time you told me who you are and why you want to know the story. All this happened in the distant past. Why the sudden interest?' He turned to Alice. 'I recognise you, you're Alice Rogerson, James's daughter. I used to know your father well, he spent a lot of time at the Villa Magrino with Ricardo. Beppe and I used to tag along after them when we weren't treasure hunting. He sometimes calls to see us when he's in Mdina. He showed me a photo not long ago, one of you and Ewen. He's very proud of you both.'

It was Alice's turn to look amazed. 'Dad never said he knew you.'

'He wouldn't, he's the quiet sort is James. Marco was the talkative one of that trio. Beppe and I used to have fun seeing who could get him talking the longest.'

'Ewen and I still do that.'

Tommasso gave a nervous chuckle, glancing towards Tom. 'So who's your friend and why his interest in Beppe?'

Watching Tommasso closely, Tom said, 'I'm Thomas Newton and I think that Giuseppe Farrigiani may be my father.'

He was unprepared for Tommasso's guffaw of laughter. 'Where on earth did you get that notion? It's one of the funniest things I've heard for a long time. Beppe's son! How old are you?'

'Sixteen. What difference does that make?'

'All the difference in the world, believe me. I'm sorry to disappoint you, but there's no way you could be Beppe's son.'

Tom was silenced, feeling the now familiar crush of disappointment. So much for that idea. He was about to stand and leave when Alice caught his arm.

'Wait. Tommasso might be just another liar to add to our collection. Seems to me we're surrounded by liars. First Luigi said Giuseppe's dead; now Tommasso says he isn't.' She turned to the now angry Tommasso. 'How do you know that Tom's not Giuseppe's son? You can't make a claim like that without giving us a reason. What happened to Giuseppe after he quarrelled with Luigi and left home?'

For the first time, Tommasso looked uncomfortable. 'That's a part of the story best not repeated. I don't know how you've become involved in this but it's in your best interests to forget about Beppe and take yourselves home.'

'Don't think you can fob us off like that. You may as well tell us,' Alice insisted. 'We're determined to find out. We could always ask your brother, he seemed far keener than you to speak to us.' The idea clearly alarmed Tommasso and he scowled fiercely. 'I mean it,' Alice said steadily, refusing to back down. 'Tell us or we'll go straight back to the Casa Peralta, only this time we'll ask for Alphonso.'

Tommasso scowled even more. 'Well, I did warn you. Don't blame me if you don't like what you hear. You want the gory details, you can have them. One evening the library was broken into, the book that Beppe wanted to see was stolen and a night security guard was knocked unconscious. He died later in hospital.'

Alice was reduced to the same silence as Tom, her fantasies about the romantic Giuseppe shattered with one blow. No wonder Luigi refused to acknowledge his younger son. For someone as honest as Luigi, it must be appalling to have a murderer in the family. She stared at Tommasso, trying to get her thoughts in order. He still hadn't told them everything, she was sure of that. If this happened a long time ago, why should their visit to the Casa Peralta put Giuseppe in danger? Why were she and Tom being hunted by Alphonso? None of that had been explained.

As she was trying to frame a question a young man burst through the café doorway, hurrying to their table. Bending down to Tommasso he whispered, 'They've begun to search the town.'

Tommasso stood abruptly. 'You must leave quickly, get out of Mdina. It's for your own good, believe me. Where are you staying?'

'At the Villa Magrino,' Tom said sullenly.

The answer clearly worried Tommasso. 'Not a wise choice,' he murmured, ushering them to the back door of the café. 'Is that how you heard about Beppe? I thought Luigi had erased all traces of him. That's what he threatened to do.'

'Why the secrecy?' Alice demanded. 'There's an awful lot you haven't told us. Tom and I weren't even born when all this happened so why should we be in danger? We haven't got anything to do with what happened.'

'I'll contact you as soon as possible,' Tommasso promised, 'and give you the rest of the story. Until then just stay out of sight and don't interfere. You'll cause a lot of trouble for a lot of people if you don't. Now, I must go.'

'What happened to Giuseppe?' Tom asked suddenly.

'Still thinking he might be your father?' Tommasso laughed. 'You're certainly stubborn, I'll give you that. You really want to know?'

Tom hoped his confident nod belied his growing fears.

'Giuseppe was the obvious suspect. The only suspect. No one else had ever shown an interest in the book; he had no alibi for that night and his scarf was found at the library, under the body of the security guard. Conclusive evidence. He was tried and convicted of theft and murder, and sentenced to twenty years in prison. Is that enough for you?'

Alice could think of nothing to say as they made their way back to the bus station. What a horrible day this had turned out to be. Tom was sunk in despair, oblivious to his surroundings, and she wisely left him alone, guiding him through the mass of tourists and keeping a sharp eye out for anyone taking a suspicious interest in them.

Once they were safely on the bus travelling back to Attard, she made an attempt to rouse him from his lethargy.

'I know you're disappointed he can't be your father, but there's still a mystery about Giuseppe. Tommasso accused us of putting him in danger so presumably he's out of prison. He's probably just been released if all this happened twenty years ago, which could be why Luigi is so edgy.'

'Why should I care?' Tom growled. 'Giuseppe's nothing to do with me, thank goodness. I wouldn't want a murderer for a father. Dad was twenty three when I was born in England. He'd married my mother the year before, also in England, and before that he'd done three years at Manchester University. All that time, Giuseppe Farrigiani was in a Maltese prison. It was stupid to even think he could be my father.'

Alice frowned. 'I still think there's too much similarity between the names Joseph and Giuseppe.'

'Don't start that again. Think how many Josephs there are in England and how many Giuseppes in Malta and Italy. It's not that much of a coincidence.'

'Okay, I accept that he's not your father, but he could be connected with his disappearance. Your Dad invited you out to Malta, said that you were going to stay with your relations at the Villa Magrino and. . .'

'No he didn't,' Tom muttered unhappily.

'But you said. . .'

'I know what I said, but I think I may have made a big mistake. I wish I'd still got the note, it's hard to remember the exact words, but I think that they were that Dad would be tied up for a few days and that Luigi and Francesca would look after me. The note didn't mention relatives, that came earlier in a phone call and I put two and two together and made five. The relations bit may have been just a ploy by Dad to allay Mum's fears. She wouldn't be happy if he dumped me on strangers.'

'You're not thinking straight,' Alice scolded. 'Luigi and Francesca couldn't have been strangers to your father, could they? Or he wouldn't have known their names or where they live.'

'He said I'd like Ricardo,' Tom remembered. 'That was definitely in the note.'

'Which means that either Luigi's lying when he says he doesn't know Joseph Newton, or he knows him by another name.'

'Whatever that is, it isn't Giuseppe Farrigiani. You heard Tommasso. Giuseppe was in a Maltese prison when I was born in England. There's no way he and Dad could be the same person.'

'So what's the link between them? There has to be one, they share the same birth date, remember. What about if Giuseppe had a twin brother. . .?'

'Now you are getting into the realms of fantasy!' Alice winced at the scorn in his voice. 'What are you suggesting? That Luigi not only managed to lose one son, he also mislaid his twin brother?'

'Then how do you account for the fact that your Dad's birth date opened Giuseppe's box? It's a bit spooky don't you think?'

'It's a coincidence, I admit that, but I don't think it's too far-fetched. In my tutor group at school there are only twenty five of us, but one of the girls shares my birthday. Out of the population in England there must be thousands who were born on the same day as Giuseppe.'

Alice didn't look convinced. 'I'm sure there are but not thousands who've come to Malta and directed their son to the Villa Magrino where Giuseppe used to live. I admit the twin brother idea is not very likely so what about your father and Giuseppe becoming friends? That's possible. You said your Dad did historical television programmes. Could he have been researching one about the Order of St John? I'm sure the knights he gave you that birthday belonged to the Order and they certainly seem to be at the heart of the mystery. What if he met Giuseppe and enlisted his help?'

'Giuseppe's been in prison for twenty years.'

'He'll have been released by now. It's quite possible that they met and what if your father had some information about Claudio Farrigiani which solved the riddle for Giuseppe and what if Giuseppe said his parents would look after you while they both. . .?'

Tom had come to the end of his tether. 'If. . .if!' he stormed. 'I'm sick of the word. We don't know anything for certain and I don't want to know. Not any longer. If Dad did go off with Giuseppe the least he could have done was met me first, or left another note explaining what was happening. He owed me that much. Any father who cared for his son at all would never abandon him to fend for himself in a foreign country. It's about time I went back to England and forgot the whole sorry mess.'

Alice gave up the fight and they travelled the rest of the way in silence, collecting their bikes and riding towards Haz Zahra with neither of them uttering another word.

When they reached the track leading down to Alice's farm, Tom roused himself sufficiently to thank her. 'You're the only person who's tried to help. Sorry I've been a poor companion.'

'Don't make any decisions tonight,' Alice begged. 'I'll come over to the Villa Magrino in the morning, when you've had a chance to sleep on it. See how you feel then.'

'I won't have changed my mind. I feel awful about the way I've barged into Luigi and Francesca's lives. They must have spent years trying to put the past behind them and then I drag all their misery out into the open.'

'It's not your fault, your Dad has put you in an impossible situation. I don't see what else you could have done.'

'I could have gone straight back to England. That's what I'll do tomorrow. If Dad ever wants me, let him do the searching for a change.'

June 1789

Claudio Farrigiani heard the singing voices echoing from the stone church at Haz Zahra. Mass was not yet over. He moved round and into the graveyard, sitting in the long grass dotted with white flowers, back resting comfortably against the wall, legs stretched out in front of him. Above, the sky was a cloudless blue alive with birdsong.

This was one of his favourite places.

He closed his eyes.

She joined him quietly. 'You were asleep?'

'Not really. I was thinking how peaceful it is here. It would be a good place to be buried.'

7

At 6am, Alice finally admitted that further sleep was an impossibility. She'd woken half an hour earlier from a weird, surrealist dream in which she and Tom were being pursued around the island by avenging angels and knights brandishing huge swords.

Propping herself up against the pillows, she closed her eyes, random thoughts cascading through her mind until she began to feel dizzy. There was some connection between Giuseppe and Tom's father, there had to be, only the unanswered questions seemed to be multiplying the harder she searched. If she didn't find an answer that satisfied Tom he'd go back to England and she knew she didn't want that.

Start from the beginning, she told herself. Think logically: Tom's father chose Malta for a holiday. Why? He said Tom had relations here, even if he didn't specify the Farrigianis. So somewhere on Malta, Tom and his Dad have relations. That's a definite. Perhaps his Dad visited them for holidays when he was a boy. Perhaps he even met Giuseppe and Tommasso, he must be about the same age, and went treasure hunting with them. That might have been the beginning of his love for history and why he bought Tom a set of knights. If he'd been researching the Order of St John, possibly for a television programme, and come across a reference to Claudio Farrigiani, it would be natural for him to contact Giuseppe. Even if it was before Giuseppe was released, they must have allowed him letters in prison. Maybe when Giuseppe got out, Tom's Dad arranged to meet him on Malta and decided to bring Tom for a holiday. Perhaps he and Giuseppe went to collect the treasure, that could have been the big surprise Tom's father hinted at, and something went wrong, leaving Tom stranded at the airport. That made sense, surely? Where did she go from here?

Her thoughts came to a stumbling halt. She was creating a whole new set of unanswerable questions. If she was right so far, why had his father kept these relations a secret from Tom and his mother? And if he'd been a boyhood friend of Giuseppe, why had Luigi and Francesca never heard of him? It's that *if* word again, she thought miserably. The only thing that's not in doubt is that Tom's father has disappeared, and somehow he seems to be connected with Giuseppe Farrigiani and a long lost treasure. Perhaps that's where we should be concentrating.

According to Tommasso, Giuseppe believed the treasure was something Claudio Farrigiani rescued from Napoleon when he ransacked Malta. Well, that could be anything. The Cathedral of St John was full of treasures. She remembered the dark Chapel of the Holy Relics, containing a wooden figure of St John the Baptist which the Knights had brought from Rhodes.

Her memory moved forward to a school visit to the Cathedral Museum with its vast array of silver, its beautifully illuminated manuscripts, and the Order's most precious relic: the hand of John the Baptist. At least, that had been saved from Napoleon.

She sat up, stretching. At the back of her mind something was puzzling her, but however hard she tried, she couldn't pinpoint the cause. Something to do with Claudio Farrigiani, that much she knew.

Dressing quickly, she hurried down to a kitchen already smelling of freshly baked bread.

Her mother smiled. 'You're up early. Got plans for today?'

'Not really.' Alice thought of Tom. He wouldn't go back to England, surely? 'I couldn't sleep, I thought I'd get some fresh air before breakfast.'

'Don't be too long, your Dad's already started the farm jobs. He's going into Valletta later this morning, you and Tom should hitch a lift. He ought to see something of the Knights' City while he's here.'

Alice nodded vaguely. In a few hours, Tom might be on a plane heading for England. She was surprised at how much the thought hurt her. Would he let her know if his father ever got in touch?

Collecting her bike, she cycled along the dusty lane to the village, deliberately emptying her mind and revelling in the peace of a summer's morning. The cloudless blue sky gave promise of another fine day.

Fifteen minutes later, without any calculated planning, she found herself standing in the graveyard gazing up at the Farrigiani monument. Her eyes lingered on the name *Claudio Farrigiani*.

Tommasso was wrong about one thing. Claudio had either never left Malta or he must have returned, if he was buried here. Was that what had been troubling her? If he didn't leave then there was no reason for him to hide the treasure and, if he came back, why on earth hadn't he collected the treasure himself? Saved them all this bother.

'Do you realise,' she said aloud, 'what a lot of fuss you've caused? I just hope the treasure, whatever it might be, is worth all this misery.' Then her eyes widened. So that was what had been puzzling her.

Hurrying round to the front of the church, she found the villagers were just leaving from early Mass. Waiting until the last one had shaken hands with the priest, she dashed forward.

'Alice.' His grave, narrow face broke into a smile. 'I don't usually see you this early.'

'I wanted to ask you a question. You know all about the Knights of St John, don't you?'

'Well, not everything,' he said, hiding a grin. 'But perhaps enough to answer one question, if it's not a hard one.'

'When did Napoleon invade Malta?'

'That's easy and it's a date you should have etched on your memory as it led to the end of Malta's association with the Knights.'

'Yes, but when was that?'

'Napoleon's fleet arrived here on June 9th, 1798. Do you want all the details?'

'I'd love to hear them but could I come back another time and bring a friend? He's interested in the Knights.'

'With pleasure. That would be Tom, would it?' Alice flushed and he grinned at her. 'You ought to know by now that in a village this small news travels fast. I'll look forward to seeing the pair of you. Is that all for now?'

'One last question,' Alice begged. 'After his arrival, when did the Knights have to leave Malta?'

'Napoleon must have been an energetic sort of person, he certainly didn't waste much time. Three days after he set foot in Valletta, the Grand Master and his Knights, apart from a few of the French ones, were banished from the island. They never returned. Does that answer your question?'

'Yes, thanks,' Alice said, refraining from admitting that all it did was add to the confusion. The date on the monument had stated clearly: *Claudio Farrigiani 1799-1851*. He had been born the year after the Knights left Malta.

Surprisingly, Tom found that Luigi and Francesca were as reluctant as Alice to see him return to England. He thought they'd have been delighted to see the back of him.

Alice arrived while they were having breakfast and lost no time in tackling Tom.

'Do you still intend to go home today?'

Tom shrugged. 'I really can't see any point in staying.'

'Dad's going into Valletta this morning,' she said quietly. 'We can deliver you to the British Consul or I can introduce you to the City of the Knights. Your choice.'

Francesca put a gentle hand on his shoulder. 'In a few days Ricardo will be back. He is very clever, I'm sure he'll be able to think of something. If you go back to England now, we will never know what happens to you. Always it will be a mystery. We will be left with the worry that we should have done more to help. We would like you to stay, wouldn't we Luigi?'

'It's Tom's decision,' her husband reminded her, but smiling at Tom as he spoke.

Tom gazed around the now familiar kitchen, wishing he could have been a part of this family. That was another disappointment; they'd have made good grandparents. In just a few days he'd grown amazingly fond of them. It must have been a nightmare when their younger son was convicted of murder and Tom knew that he was responsible for reviving those painful memories. Better to go back to England as he'd planned and let them get on with their lives. Though if Giuseppe was out of prison and involved in another mystery, that was unlikely. How could two such kind and honest people have a thief and murderer for a son?

He looked at Luigi and Francesca, at Alice sitting there so calmly but regarding him with a strange expression he found difficult to read.

'I'm really grateful to you all,' he stammered, 'but I've made up my mind. If Alice's father will drop me at the Consulate, I'll get the next flight back to England.'

Tom stood awkwardly in the farmyard, suitcase at his feet, clutching his rucksack.

'I'll give you a lift to Trevisan,' Luigi said quietly. 'You can't bike with the suitcase.' He turned to his wife. 'I'll just be a few minutes, I'll come straight back.'

She nodded and Tom was horrified to see the tears in her eyes. She gave him a quick hug and disappeared into the kitchen. Stupidly, Tom felt the tears welling up in his own eyes. Whatever was happening to him? The sooner he got the goodbyes over the better, before he disgraced himself.

Alice seemed to sense his discomfort. 'I'll ride back,' she said cheerfully, 'and warn Dad you're on the way. See you in ten minutes.'

They caught up with Alice halfway down the dusty track leading to the road. She was standing on the grass verge deep in conversation with a tall man in a blue uniform. A policeman? Tom's heart skipped a beat. Surely he wouldn't be smiling like that if he'd brought bad news?

Leaning through the window, Tom stammered, 'Have you come about Dad?'

'If you're Thomas Newton, which I reckon you must be, then yes I have.'

A few minutes later, they were all back in the kitchen, the policeman drinking a large cup of coffee and, to Tom's annoyance, discussing the forthcoming festa. Alice caught Tom's eye and smiled sympathetically before leaning forward to ask, 'What about Tom's father? Is there any news?'

'Yes and no.' The policeman took a long gulp of coffee and Tom felt like screaming. 'I'm afraid we've not found him, which I'm sure is not what you wanted to hear. Still, we have made some progress. We've confirmed that Joseph Newton arrived here on Malta last Thursday, the evening flight from Gatwick, the day before you showed up.'

Tom nodded. 'That's what he told me in his note.'

'We managed to get a photograph of him from a television

company. We showed it round at the airport and several people remember seeing him. He took a taxi to Valletta. We've spoken to the taxi driver and he dropped him at the main bus station; that's the last sighting we have of him. We've been through the records at the airport and spoken to the ferries but there's no trace of his having left the island, which does suggest that he's still here. You're sure he made no mention of where he'd be going, or what he'd be doing?'

'The note just said that he'd meet me at the airport and bring me to the Villa Magrino. That he had something to do which would occupy him for a few days.'

'Then it's obviously taking longer than he expected. No cause to worry.'

'But why didn't he meet me at the airport?'

'Got held up I should imagine. Knew you were a bright lad and you'd find your way out here.'

'That doesn't make sense. Luigi and Francesca had never heard of me or Dad. They certainly weren't expecting me.'

'That is a puzzle, I'll admit, though I'm sure it will be solved when your father turns up. There'll probably be a very simple explanation that none of us have thought of. The thing is,' the policeman confided, 'the Consul thinks that you ought to let your mother know what's happening. In your father's absence, she's responsible for you.'

'No,' Tom said forcefully. 'I'm not going to spoil her honeymoon. I'm quite safe here, Luigi and Francesca are looking after me. I'll ring her after I've seen Ricardo on Friday, and if he can't help and I still haven't heard from Dad I'll go back to England. Then, I won't be your problem anymore.'

When the policeman had gone, Tom grinned sheepishly at the other three. 'It looks as if you're stuck with me for a bit longer.'

He was rewarded by Francesca's beam of pleasure.

Alice leapt to her feet. 'Come on, then, I promised Dad we wouldn't be long. Grab your bike.'

They cycled down the track to the road.

'I'm glad you decided to stay,' Alice said tentatively, unsure of Tom's reaction. There was a distinctly moody look on his face.

'I've decided to enjoy myself for a few days, as much as I can. Not much point leaving Malta without exploring the City of the Knights, but no more mysteries. I'm not going to do anything that would upset Luigi and Francesca. They've got enough worries without me adding to them.'

'Can I just tell you one strange thing?' She hurried on before he could respond in the negative. 'Something was puzzling me yesterday, niggling away in the back of my mind, and this morning I went back to the graveyard.'

Tom remained silent.

'Don't you want to know what I found out?'

'Not particularly, but you're going to tell me anyway.'

'Remember Tommasso said that Beppe thought the treasure had been rescued from Napoleon's clutches by Claudio Farrigiani? Well, that's impossible because according to the tablet in the graveyard he was born a year after the Knights were expelled from Malta.'

'So Beppe was wrong. What's strange about that?'

Alice gazed at him in exasperation. 'You don't see it, do you? If Claudio Farrigiani was born here in 1799, then he couldn't have been a Knight of St John.'

'But he said he was, on the riddle he left about the treasure.' Tom looked interested for the first time. 'Who was he, then? Another liar?'

'It's a mystery,' Alice said shortly. 'And you don't like mysteries, so it doesn't matter, does it? Race you to Trevisan.'

As she sprinted away Tom yelled, 'Wait a minute!'

'What now?' Alice looked at him coldly as he hurried to join her.

'When you said the Knights never returned to Malta, did you mean individually or as the Order of St John?'

She frowned. 'I don't know. I ought to, we've done their history often enough at school, but we always seemed to end with them being banished from the island. I haven't a clue what happened after that. Why? Do you think Claudio Farrigiani could have been a Knight much later, somewhere else, and then come to Malta bringing the treasure with him?'

'Why would he do that?'

'It doesn't make much sense,' Alice admitted, 'and it doesn't answer the question of why he needed to hide it and leave the riddle.'

Tom felt the gloom descending on him once more. 'Best forget about the whole thing. Look at the trouble it got Giuseppe into, not to mention the trouble it's already got us into with Luigi and your Dad and Marco.'

Alice shrugged. 'We'd better get on, Dad won't wait forever.'

As the farm came into sight Tom asked, 'What have you told your parents about me?'

'Just the basic facts, that you came out to have a holiday with your Dad and he's disappeared. I haven't mentioned anything about Giuseppe.'

'Nothing to mention.' Tom pulled a face. 'I made a complete idiot of myself, conjured up a mystery where none existed. Let's face it, Dad vanished from my life for the first time when I was nine years old, why shouldn't he do it again? I've survived this long without him. If Dad wants to get in touch that's up to him. I'm not going to worry anymore. He can get on with his own life and I'll get on with mine.'

Alice wisely held her tongue.

Tom liked Mr Rogerson on sight. He was brown-haired, with the same red strands as Alice, and a pleasant, good-humoured face.

'Sorry to hear about your father,' he greeted him and then, to Tom's relief, avoided the subject. They spent the rest of the journey to Valletta discussing the preparations for the village festa.

'The lights decorating the outside of the church go up tomorrow.' Mr Rogerson grinned at Tom. 'You'll probably be called on to help, it's a job for the men.'

'I'd like that.'

'Alice,' he continued, eyes twinkling, 'should be spending the day helping her mother with the baking, but you probably know her well enough by now to realise she never does what's expected of her.'

'Not my fault,' she said calmly. 'You know Mum insists on having the kitchen to herself. I'd be getting under her feet all day. I'm much better at putting up decorations and building the bonfire.'

'Remember when you look round their city today that we owe thanks to the Knights for our festas.'

'I didn't know that.'

Mr Rogerson groaned theatrically, rolling his eyes at his daughter. 'Don't they teach you anything at school these days?'

'Plenty, too much sometimes, but I didn't know the Knights were connected with our festas.'

'Before they arrived here, this island was just an insignificant little rock. I can't imagine they thought much of Malta when they saw it for the first time. Don't forget they'd come from Rhodes, which was a fertile island with wooded slopes and vineyards and lush valleys. Malta, with its harsh landscape of rocks and crags, very few trees or grass and hardly any running water, must have seemed like the end of the world to them.'

'Why did they come, then?' Tom asked.

'They'd nowhere else to go. The only thing that pleased them about Malta was what we now call the Grand Harbour. When we get to Valletta, make Alice take you to the Upper Barrakka Gardens, there's a magnificent view right over the harbour and you'll see why the Knights were so delighted.'

'I'll take him with pleasure, I love it up there, but where do the festas come into all this?'

'I was just coming to that, don't be so impatient. The Knights brought wealth and honour to the island, particularly after the Great Siege when they were hailed as the saviours of Europe. Suddenly, Malta became one of the most famous places in the Mediterranean and the wealth extended to the villages. The Order encouraged churches to be built, ours at Haz Zahra being one of them. The Knights were great ones for celebrations and processions, and the villages started competing with each other as to who could provide the most spectacular festivities.'

'I bet Haz Zahra won,' Alice said loyally.

Her father grinned. 'As all this was long before our time, we'll never know, but Tom will be able to judge our present festa this weekend.'

When they reached the suburbs of the town, Alice told her father to drop them in the centre of Floriana.

'Are you sure? I can take you up to Valletta Bus Terminal, I've got plenty of time.'

'It'd be nicer to walk up there,' Alice decided, with an innocent expression which Tom immediately distrusted. It was the face she'd adopted for the waiter in Mdina.

He left them by the Wignacourt Water Tower, promising to pick them up from the Valletta Bus Terminal at half-past four.

'Do you need some money for lunch?'

'My treat,' Tom said quickly. 'A thank you for the sightseeing tour.'

As the car pulled away, he turned to Alice. 'Your father may believe the story of wanting a walk, but I don't. What are you planning, now?'

She flushed. 'I thought while we were here we could pay a visit to the library.'

'And ask to see the book that mentions Claudio Farrigiani?' She flinched at the sarcasm in his tone. 'I'm sure they'll be fighting each other for the pleasure of showing us. Just like they were with Giuseppe.'

'Don't be stupid!' she snapped. 'That book was stolen and Tommasso didn't mention anything about it being found. Anyway, I wasn't meaning the Bibliotheca, that's in Valletta, but the Central Library here in Floriana.'

'Why would we want to go there?'

'We can use the microfiche to look up back numbers of the newspaper and find the reports of Giuseppe's trial.'

'You can't let it rest, can you?' Tom growled. 'How many times do I have to tell you I'm no longer interested in Giuseppe Farrigiani.'

'Why not? I know he can't be your father, I've accepted that, but he could be connected with his disappearance. Luigi, Francesca and Ricardo don't know your Dad, which makes it likely that the one who did was Giuseppe. And,' Alice pressed on before Tom could open his mouth to retaliate, 'surely we should check Tommasso's story before believing him? I thought you'd have learned by now not to take anything on trust. There's a lot Tommasso didn't tell us, such as that strange episode with Alphonso and why he was hunting us. That doesn't make sense, we're hardly a danger to anyone. We might find that Tommasso's whole story about the murder was a pack of lies.'

'He wouldn't lie, he's Giuseppe's friend,' Tom protested.

'He was his friend, a long time ago. He could be his enemy by now for all we know.'

Tom gave in, less than graciously, but Alice was prudent enough to hold her tongue and keep her exasperation to herself though she wondered, not for the first time, how long she was going to be able to stand Tom's moods without losing her temper. He wasn't proving to be the easiest friend in the world.

They were both too preoccupied to notice the man in the blue shirt watching them intently from across the street.

The library was crowded but a friendly young woman found them a spare microfiche.

'Need any help?'

'No thanks,' Alice said hurriedly. 'I've used one at school many times.'

Tom leaned back in his chair and watched her efforts with a feigned lack of interest as she scrolled back through the years to the announcement of the robbery. The paper had given a full report. The details of the trial, the final verdict and conviction were exactly as Tommasso had described.

'Satisfied?' Tom sneered. 'Every word he told us was true. Giuseppe's a thief and a murderer and even if he is connected with Dad I don't want to be involved. I'd have done better to go to the Consulate as I planned before you and Francesca talked me out of it. Now I'm stuck here on Malta till the weekend.'

'The decision to stay was yours,' she retorted, continuing to scroll forwards.

'What are you doing, now?'

'Looking for any reaction to the trial. There may have been a follow-up piece.'

Tom's patience snapped. 'No! That's enough. I hate Giuseppe Farrigiani for what he put Luigi and Francesca through. He can rot in prison, for all I care.'

His hand, which had been about to switch off the machine, froze in mid-air as the word *APPEAL* flashed across the screen. He sank back in his chair, silenced. They read, with bated breath, of how Taddeus Lorenzo, father of Giuseppe's best friend Tommasso, had used his enormous wealth to finance the appeal, hiring a top Maltese lawyer. Giuseppe had been acquitted after serving six months in prison.

The final mention, a few weeks after the acquittal, was restricted to a single sentence.

According to his best friend, Tommasso Lorenzo, Giuseppe Farrigiani has left the island to make a new life for himself abroad, vowing never to return to Malta.

'What do you bet,' Alice asked, eyes shining and all her crossness forgotten, 'that Giuseppe Farrigiani went to England, ended up in Manchester, changed his name to Joseph Newton, married a local girl and had a son named Tom?'

June 1798

'What will happen to us if we have to leave Malta?' Paolo da Messina crumbled his bread nervously into tiny fragments, staring at it miserably. 'Where will we go?'

Claudio Farrigiani and his companions were in the courtyard of the auberge, breaking their morning fast. It was a strained, silent meal, each

Knight lost in his own thoughts, until Paolo voiced the question that was in every mind.

There was a long pause before Claudio said hesitantly, 'Russia, probably. We know the Tsar has offered protection to the Order.'

'Russia!' Gianni exploded. 'It snows in Russia. We can't go there, it's far too cold.'

'I don't know why that should cause you worry, you have enough fat to keep you warm.'

They all turned to the amused voice from the archway. Ferdinando Rosato was a Knight of long standing, an old-timer as Paulo jokingly called him, which was why for the last few months he had been in charge of the small garrison at Mdina. He strode into the room and tore off a chunk of bread, before easing himself down into a chair.

Tullio eyed him anxiously. 'Is something wrong in Mdina?'

'Nothing that isn't also wrong throughout Malta.' He groaned, stretching out his legs. 'My body doesn't take too kindly to riding these days. I had to set off before dawn to make it in time.' He pulled a frowning face, glared at them and poured himself a tankard of wine.

'In time for what?' Paolo dared to ask.

'I'm seeing the Grand Master in an hour's time, to discover what preparations are being made for the defence of Mdina.'

Gianni gave a bitter laugh. 'You don't need to see the Grand Master for that. There are no plans to defend Mdina, or Valletta, or anywhere else on Malta.'

'We're all being alarmist,' Tullio added, 'seeing a threat where no threat exists. That's what Von Hompesch says and he's Grand Master so he should know.'

'Is that right?' Ferdinando Rosato raised bushy eyebrows and said mockingly, 'I suppose that's why I had a deputation from the nobles of Mdina yesterday who all seemed to believe the danger from France was *imminent. They demanded to know what I was going to do to protect them.'*

'I hope you told them to go back into their big houses and lock their big gates,' Paolo sneered.

A vague hint of a smile creased Ferdinando's face, though Claudio noted the glint in his eye. 'As a matter of fact I did tell them that, yes, though in slightly more diplomatic terms.'

'They're an arrogant bunch of patronising aristocrats and they've never liked us since we set foot on this island.'

'You remember it well?'

Paolo flushed and Claudio rushed to his friend's defence. 'Paolo's right, you know that, they've always resented the Knights, but in a way it's understandable. Before the Order arrived, the nobles had ruled here for centuries. They were naturally bitter at all the privileges they lost.'

'Well, arrogant or not, they have a right to our protection which is something I can't manage with a garrison of four Knights and a handful of Maltese militia.' Rising to his feet, Ferdinando tore off another chunk of bread, adding, 'I have a feeling I'm going to need all my strength. Anyone going to walk me along to see the Grand Master?'

'How much longer is he going to be?' Paolo shifted restlessly on the steps leading up to the entrance of the Grand Master's Palace. 'It can't take forever for the Council to decide how many Knights to send to Mdina.'

He climbed upwards to the stout wooden doors as they burst open, sending him sprawling backwards. Ferdinando Rosato paid no heed to the young Knight sprawling at his feet, stepping over him and striding away, his customary jovial face black as a thundercloud.

Following him were the leading figures of the Spanish and Portuguese Langues, looking equally angry.

Claudio gestured to the still recumbent Paolo. Gianni hoisted him to his feet and the four companions set off in pursuit.

Space in the Auberge d'Italie was hard to come by. Pushing through the throng, filling tankards from a flagon of wine, Claudio Farrigiani dreaded what he was about to hear.

Ferdinando Rosato took a huge gulp of wine and looked around. 'Well, for those who weren't present in the council, we are now on our own. Totally on our own. I know he is my Grand Master, but Von Hompesch is a fool.'

There was an intake of breath from the gathered knights.

'Napoleon,' he continued, undaunted by the reaction, 'apparently has his sights set on Egypt, to counter the British influence in the Mediterranean. He has no interest whatsoever in the small island of Malta.'

'Not even,' a burly Portuguese added, 'though we have the largest harbour around, which would be a boon to the English fleet, and that Malta lies on his invasion path. Ferdinando is right, Von Hompesch is a fool, but Napoleon certainly isn't. He will be well aware of the strategic importance of Malta.'

'Even if we wished to make preparations for defence,' Ferdinando continued bitterly, 'we would be unable to do all that is required. According to Von Hompesch, the Order is in dire financial straits.'

'And why is that?' Tullio broke in angrily. 'It's because the French Assembly has annexed all our property in France. And after Napoleon's victory in Italy we also lost that wealth. No wonder the treasury is bare.' He looked round helplessly. 'What are we to do?'

Ferdinando Rosato rose wearily. 'You must do what you can. Me, I ride back to Mdina to see what I can achieve with four Knights. And I can tell you now, it won't be much.' He gave a bitter laugh. 'All we can hope is that Von Hompesch is right and we are wrong.'

As he left the room, he placed a hand on Claudio's shoulder. 'Walk with me to the stables.'

They strolled in silence through the stifling streets, each lost in thought.

Ferdinando glanced with affection at his young companion. 'I've become fond of your little band. Look after them, won't you?'

'Me?' Claudio mocked. 'You're asking me to look after Gianni?'

'Paolo's just a kid, despite his twenty-eight years, and Tullio either has his head in a book or is writing one. As for Gianni, you know yourself he hasn't got the sense he was born with.'

'I'll do my best,' Claudio promised.

'Something troubling you? Beyond the obvious, that is?'

Claudio flushed. 'I didn't like the way you talked about Von Hompesch. Whatever we may think, he is our Grand Master and we've all sworn an oath of allegiance to him.'

'I know, it was wrong of me. Blame my hot temper.' He looked at Claudio gravely. 'It doesn't alter the situation, though. Maybe we should obey his orders and carry on as usual, but I believe this is one time that we cannot hide behind our duty to the Order. It is a time that each one of us needs to stand up and be counted. We must all take what action we deem necessary.'

Claudio nodded and, as they passed the cathedral of St John, he suddenly knew what he was going to do.

8

After leaving the library, Tom and Alice walked up into Valletta, collecting some pastries and taking them into the Upper Barrakka Gardens to sit on a bench overlooking the harbour. Tom didn't have the strength to obey Mr Rogerson and admire the magnificent view. He looked incredibly pale, as though all energy had been drained from him.

'Are you alright? Alice asked anxiously.

'I feel sort of empty.' He grinned suddenly. 'And it's not a lack of food, though these pastries are much appreciated. I like Maltese food, it's got a bite to it. What's in these?'

'Ricotta cheese, mostly, with a bit of seasoning that gives it the bite. So if it's not hunger that's causing you to look all pale and wan, what's troubling you?'

'My insides feel as though they're spinning round and round. I guess it's because yesterday I'd convinced myself that Giuseppe was my father, then I was equally sure he wasn't, and now today it looks as though he might be. My brain can't cope with all these sudden changes.'

'I know how you feel. It's like wandering through a maze with so many unexpected forks in the path, most of them leading to dead ends, and not a signpost in sight.'

'Perhaps not, but I'm going to be positive from now on.' He smiled ruefully at Alice. 'No more grumpy moods or bad temper, I promise.'

'That'll make a change.'

'I know I've been a bit of a pessimist, you must have got really fed up with me at times, but now I can see a way forward. Thanks to you, we can start with the fact that it's possible my father isn't Joseph Newton, as I've always thought, but Giuseppe Farrigiani. Even the surname seems to be significant, now.'

'Newton? How do you work that out?'

'Dad's a historian, don't forget. Whenever we went on car journeys he used to point out the meanings of place names. *Ton* I remember was Old English for a village or a settlement.'

'And your father was settling in a new place. Newton. New place. That's clever.'

'We can also understand why it looked as though Luigi was lying when he said he didn't know him. He obviously wasn't aware that Dad had ended up in England or that he'd changed his name.'

'And why your Dad never mentioned any Maltese relations to you and your Mum,' Alice added. 'Because of the quarrel with his family. Is that all we know for definite? It doesn't seem much, not for all the effort we've put in.'

'At least it gives us something to work from, though where we go from here I don't know.'

Alice screwed up her face in concentration. 'Trouble with these forks in the path,' she declared, 'is that as soon as we start to travel down one we lose sight of what we learned from the others. There are so many loose ends, like the girl on the plane. We haven't got any further with her but she must fit into the puzzle somewhere, and why on earth did she say she was me?'

'We'll just have to hope she surfaces sometime. Other than that, I don't see any way of finding out her identity. Why do you think my Dad decided to come back to Malta after all this time? Do you think it could be connected with the treasure? That's what got him into trouble in the first place. I'm sure he must have finally solved the riddle.'

'I take it we're accepting that he didn't steal the book and murder the security guard?'

'Dad wouldn't kill anyone. Why? Is that important?'

'It could be. Remember Giuseppe's scarf was found under the guard, which means that if he wasn't the culprit then someone must have framed him.' She shivered. 'Somewhere in this mystery there's a murderer who's never been caught. Someone who knew all about the riddle and the book Giuseppe wanted to see. What if solving the riddle led to Giuseppe discovering who committed the crime? The murderer wouldn't want Giuseppe around and that would put him in the danger Tommasso mentioned.'

'The danger which seemed to involve his brother, Alphonso. Look how he pretended to be Tommasso and had men out hunting us.'

'That's according to Tommasso,' Alice pointed out, 'and do we know if he can be trusted. We didn't see anyone searching for us, he could have made the whole thing up to frighten us off. Don't forget, Tommasso told you that Giuseppe couldn't be your father; he never mentioned the appeal. He's already proved himself a liar.'

'Who can we trust?'

She hesitated and then said tentatively, 'Perhaps we should go to the police?'

'And tell them what? You heard the policeman this morning, they don't believe anything's happened to Dad. They just think he's got business somewhere and he'll turn up when he's ready. They'd think I was a nutter if I started babbling on about hidden treasure, especially if I tried to implicate the Lorenzo family.'

'Okay, the police are out so what about telling everything to Luigi and Francesca? Giuseppe is their son, surely they've a right to be told?'

'I'd rather wait until we've got definite proof. It'd be awful to raise their hopes and then find we were wrong. And while they don't know anything they can't be in the danger Tommasso mentioned.'

'Then we'll tackle it ourselves,' Alice said, with a confidence she didn't really feel. 'I suppose we need to do some serious thinking about the riddle.'

'We don't know that Dad's worked out the answer. I can't think of any other reason for him coming out here, but it seems unlikely somehow when he and Tommasso searched all those years without getting anywhere.'

'Your Dad's a historian now, an expert. When he was looking for the treasure before, he was only a kid like us. And if he has solved it, then that's where he'll have gone. We'll find him wherever the treasure is.' She glanced at her watch. 'We've got a couple of hours before we have to be at the Bus Terminal. How about taking a look at the Grand Master's Palace?'

'Will that help?'

'I don't know, but it wouldn't hurt to learn more about the Knights, would it? We've got to start somewhere and you are descended from one, don't forget.'

They turned into Republic Square, bordered by open-air cafes. Tom felt himself surrounded by people, families, couples and individuals. They were all doing normal things: drinking coffee, taking photographs, studying guide books, gazing up at impressive buildings, laughing and chattering without a care in the world. Tom envied them their cheerfulness, finding it hard to sustain his feeling of optimism. Come on, he told himself, you only made the decision to be positive a few minutes ago. Don't spoil it already.

'Do you believe in pay back time?' he asked suddenly.

'What?'

'Last term, when I seemed to be doing nothing but revise or exams, I complained to Mum that life was boring and nothing exciting ever happened to me. I'll never grumble about that again. I just wondered if life was paying me back.'

'If it is, it's certainly succeeding, but you're coping remarkably well considering. I'd have fallen apart long before now.'

Tom doubted that. There was a resilience about Alice that made her equal to any situation. 'Where's the Grand Master's Palace?'

'It's down the end of the square,' Alice told him, 'but I thought the building on the right might interest you. It's the Bibliotheca.'

'Where the book that mentioned Claudio Farrigiani was kept?'

'And where the robbery took place. Want to have a look?'

They gazed at the plaque on the wall, stating that the Bibliotheca had been completed in 1796, the last building of importance erected in Valletta by the Order of St John. It housed, they read, '. . .*a collection of old books, mediaeval manuscripts and the archives of the Sovereign Military and Hospitaller Order of St John of Jerusalem, Rhodes and Malta.*'

'I wonder what happened to the book that was stolen?'

Alice frowned. 'I should think the thief's still got it, whoever he is.'

'He isn't Dad.'

'I know, I believe you. What I hadn't thought of, though, is if a book in here mentioned Claudio Farrigiani then he must have been a Knight of St John, mustn't he?'

'Even though his dates don't make sense?' Tom thought for a moment. 'When was the memorial tablet erected in the graveyard?'

'Haven't a clue. Why?'

'Perhaps it was put up long after Claudio's death and they got the dates wrong.'

'Could be, I suppose, but hardly likely. Shall we take a look in the Grand Master's Palace?'

'Will they be able to tell us what happened after the Knights left Malta? That's one thing we should check.'

'I don't know, but we can ask.'

In the foyer, a middle-aged lady took their money. 'Do you want a guided tour?'

'We haven't time,' Alice said. 'This is just a flying visit. What we do need to learn is what happened to the Knights after they were banished from Malta by Napoleon.'

'I'm afraid we concentrate on the time they spent here on the island. Is it their full history after Malta you want or would a brief outline do?'

'Anything would be a help,' Alice assured her. 'Tom is descended from one of the Italian Knights and he'd like to know what happened to him.'

'Grand Master Von Hompesch made his way to Trieste with a few of the Knights. Most of the others, including the Italian ones, ended up in Russia, St Petersburg to be exact, and sought the protection of the Emperor Paul. They even offered him the title of Grand Master but the Pope refused to ratify it because the Emperor wasn't a Catholic and he was married.

'Malta was taken over by the English, who drove out the French, and I think arrangements were being made for the Knights to return there when war broke out between England and France once more and scuppered that idea. They never did come back.

'I'm not sure about the next few years, though they must have been uncertain ones, until they finally made their headquarters at the Palazza di Malta in Rome. The Order rebuilt itself as a religious and charitable organisation. Its main concern today is not in defending the faith against the enemies of Christ, but in providing hospitals and medical supplies for regions that are suffering from poverty or war.' She smiled at them apologetically. 'And that's about the extent of my knowledge.'

'Thanks anyway, you've been a great help. . .I had to say that,' Alice protested as they made their way towards the armoury. 'I know she didn't tell us anything that makes sense of Claudio Farrigiani.'

'She did, actually. She confirmed that my idea of Claudio being born after the Knights left Malta makes no sense at all. He'd have ended up in Russia or Rome and he wouldn't have had any connection with Malta. I'm sure the dates on the memorial tablet must be wrong.'

'I guess they must be,' Alice agreed, without much conviction.

The Armoury was two huge vault-like rooms filled with weapons and suits of armour.

'Some of these belonged to the Grand Masters,' Alice said, pointing out the breastplate worn by La Valette. 'He was one of the best.'

'Is Valletta named after him?'

'Yes. He was the Grand Master here during The Great Siege and when it ended he began constructing new fortifications which became the City of Valletta.'

'When was that?'

'1565.' Alice laughed. 'That's a date that every child on Malta learns from a very early age.'

'Like our 1066.'

'The Battle of Hastings. Don't look so amazed, we do English history as well.'

'Do you think Claudio Farrigiani had a sword like this?' Tom pointed to a steel blade with an ornately decorated handle.

'I should imagine so. Swords are something I associate with knights. Like the Knights of the Round Table, they were always having sword fights.'

'What do you think he looked like?'

'Claudio Farrigiani? Well, he's Italian. They're dark aren't they?'

'All of them?'

'Perhaps not, but that's how I picture them. Ever since you found his riddle I've thought of him as looking like Ricardo.'

'I've never met Ricardo.'

Alice considered for a moment. 'He's tall and quite slim, with crinkly black hair that flops over his forehead, and very brown eyes.'

Tom was intrigued. 'You could have been describing Dad.'

'They've probably both inherited their colouring from some Italian gene. Aren't they passed down in families for centuries?' She looked at him critically. 'You've got the brown eyes, even if you missed out on the hair.'

'My Mum's fair and my grandmother used to be. She's grey now. That's obviously my English gene. All this here around me is my Italian heritage. What I don't understand,' Tom said, gazing at the sword, 'is why all the weapons? Look at them. As well as swords they had crossbows and muskets and pistols and canons. I thought they were supposed to be a religious order? They named themselves after John the Baptist and he was hardly a warrior, was he? The girl on the plane said they were formed to treat sick pilgrims.'

'That was right at the start. When the attacks on the pilgrims and Crusaders got worse, the Order decided that weapons were needed to defend Jerusalem. I think it was the Pope who gave them his approval to become a military organisation. They certainly did a lot of fighting. Come on, I'll show you the frieze of The Great Siege, it's in the Supreme Council Hall. I know that happened centuries before Claudio Farrigiani was here on the island, but I suppose it's part of Claudio's heritage.'

A group of sightseers were in the middle of a guided tour and Tom and Alice wedged themselves at the back, Tom gazing in awe at the large tapestry divided into a series of elaborately detailed scenes.

'This panel,' the guide was saying, 'depicts the siege of Fort St Elmo, the small fort guarding the entrance to the two harbours. It was staffed by sixty Knights, backed up by a few hundred Maltese, and they faced the might of the Ottoman Empire. Mustafa Pasha, the Turkish senior officer, was confident that St Elmo would fall within five days. The sixty Knights of St Elmo have become part of legend. They fought heroically against the weight of the Turkish artillery for 31 days. When the enemy began to breach the walls, the Knights used lances and swords and scimitars in what proved to be deadly battles. One by one the Knights were killed, but no thought of surrender crossed their minds. With the end in sight, the Chaplain gave the remaining Knights the Holy Communion and they hid their sacred objects, the treasures of the Order, before burning the chapel. Then they began to ring the bell, the signal to Grand Master Valette and the Knights across the harbour that St Elmo was about to fall. Having committed their souls to God, the St Elmo Knights set about their final hand-to-hand encounter with the enemy. They fought to the death. There were no Christian survivors. The Turks lost over eight thousand men.'

'Was the treasure ever recovered?'

The guide looked startled at the interruption and Tom flushed as every eye turned in his direction.

'I really don't know. I've never been asked that question before.'

'If there weren't any survivors,' Tom persisted, 'then no one would know where the treasure had been hidden, would they?'

'I suppose not.'

'If it'd been found, wouldn't that have been recorded somewhere?'

The guide began to look annoyed. 'If you want answers you'll have to find a historian. I'm only the guide here. Now, this next panel...'

'I was going to ask him what the treasure was,' Tom protested as

Alice led him into a small courtyard.

'You weren't being fair to him. He has his job to do and we hadn't even paid for the tour.'

'Have we time to visit Fort St Elmo?'

'Not today, it's on the very tip of the peninsula and we have to meet Dad at four thirty. Are you thinking that the treasure they hid could be Claudio's?'

'It's the only treasure we've heard of so far.'

'But it was hidden long before Claudio Farrigiani arrived on Malta.'

'We don't know his dates. You agreed that the memorial in the graveyard may have got them wrong.'

'I agreed that they might be out by a few years, but two hundred years is stretching it a bit.'

Seeing Tom's dejected face, she sank down on to a low wall, pulling him down to sit beside her. 'Let's have a look at the riddle, see if we can find any clue to Fort St Elmo.'

Tom pulled the envelope from his pocket. '*Alight ashore* would make sense if the fort's on the coast.'

Alice nodded. 'I'll give you that, but what about the heavenly summit, the dead tree and the angel?'

'The guide mentioned a chapel. That's heavenly.' Tom paused. 'You're not convinced, are you?'

'I'm beginning to wonder,' Alice said slowly, 'whether we should be taking the words so literally.'

'How do you mean?'

'Words often have more than one meaning, don't they?'

'Such as?'

'*Alight* for a start. We assumed it meant getting off a boat, but if you *alight* on something doesn't it also simply mean that you find it?

And *ashore* could just be on land rather than on the sea.'

'Find on land. That doesn't help much. I know Malta's only a small island compared to some, but there's still rather a lot of land to search.'

'You do give up easily,' Alice grumbled. 'What about the next bit?'

'The *cavernous steepness*. That contradicts itself, caves are underground, they go down not up, and this one leads to a summit.'

'It could be a cave in the side of a hill, with a tunnel leading to the top.'

'And the hill has a heavenly name?' Tom grinned suddenly, his good humour restored. 'I thought we'd discarded Cherub Hill?'

'We were just thinking of angels then, but heavenly could be. . .' She faltered. '. . .Paradise, or Celestial Hill or. . .'

'Heavenly can also mean fantastic,' Tom broke in. 'Or terrific or. .'

'I don't think it did in Claudio Farrigiani's day, but it could simply be the heavens, like the sun, moon, stars, planets. We need a detailed map of the island.'

'What about the auguring bit? An augur's a tool, I've used one in woodwork at school. It bores into the wood.'

It was Alice's turn to grin. 'That's an auger, with an "e". This is augur with a "u". It's something to do with predicting the future, I think. Prophesying, like the witch did when she told Macbeth he was going to be king.'

Tom grimaced. 'This is getting us nowhere. I still think Fort St Elmo's our best bet.'

'It'll have to wait for another day, we have to meet Dad in. . .' Alice glanced at her watch and shot up. 'Come on, we've just got time.'

'Do you know Alice in Wonderland?' Tom asked as he dashed after her.

'Yes, why?'

'You remind me of the Red Queen. She was always telling Alice to "Come on!" Where are we going?'

'Here.' Alice pulled up in another small courtyard. 'And just for your information, the Red Queen was Looking Glass not Wonderland.' She pointed up at a stone wall with a large clock at the top. 'The Pinto Clock. Named after another Grand Master. Can you see the four dials? They show the time, the day, the month and the phases of the moon.'

'Impressive.'

'That's not the best bit, watch.'

Precisely at 4 o'clock, the hours were struck very loudly by four bronze figures wielding what looked like sledge hammers.

'Well?' Alice demanded.

'Very impressive. Now I suppose you're going to say "Come on!" again?'

'Afraid so. Dad won't be too happy if we're late.'

As they wandered back through a long corridor full of suits of armour Tom asked, 'What about tomorrow? Any chance of visiting Fort St Elmo?'

'You can, I can't, though. You heard Dad, it's the day the whole village turns out to prepare for the festa. I couldn't get out of it, even if I wanted to.'

'Then, I'll stay and help; I'd like that. Tomorrow, for one day, we'll forget about the mystery and concentrate on enjoying ourselves.'

They left the Grand Master's palace at a run, oblivious to a man, in a bright blue shirt, who leant against a side wall watching them curiously.

As they disappeared into the crowds, he took out a mobile phone and began dialling.

9

Tom lay in bed watching the early light of dawn fill the small rectangular window. For the first time since arriving on Malta he'd slept soundly; no weird dreams of angels or nightmares about his father.

Not that my situation's any better, he told himself. In some ways it's even more complicated, but today there'll be no mysteries, I promised Alice, and although they don't know it yet I've become part of the village. If Alice and I are right, this is the house where Dad grew up and spent eighteen years of his life. Perhaps I'm even sleeping in his bed.

He wished he could do as Alice had suggested and confide in Luigi and Francesca, tell them he could be their grandson, though he knew that would be unfair. They'd insist on tackling Alphonso and Tommasso, putting themselves in danger.

Ricardo, he thought suddenly. Only two days now until Ricardo returns. He's Dad's brother, the person he went to for help after his quarrel with Luigi. I'll tell Ricardo the full story, he'll know what we should do next. It was a relief to realise that at last he'd have an adult on his side that he knew he could trust. That settled, he prepared himself to enjoy the day.

Hurriedly washing and dressing, he dashed down to the kitchen.

'Just bread and cold meats today,' Francesca apologised. 'I've a lot of baking to do for the festa.'

'Like Alice's mother.' Tom laughed. 'Alice says she hates anyone in her kitchen at such times.'

'We all do, so eat up and take yourself off. Have you got any plans for today?'

'I'm going into the village to see what jobs come my way. Mr Rogerson said something about putting lights up on the church.'

Francesca looked pleased. 'You can go down with Luigi, he's taking our trestle tables on the cart. Run and tell him to wait for you.'

When he returned to the kitchen she had made him a large sandwich and he took it gratefully. 'Luigi will be going down again later so I'll send you some lunch,' she promised.

'Not if you're busy.'

'I'll have plenty of pasties and apple cakes ready by then. I'm sure I can spare a couple. We can't have you starving away.'

'I'll look forward to them. No Carmel today?'

'She has her own baking to attend to and Luis will be already in the village.'

Tom took his sandwich and joined Luigi, who was just heaving the last wooden trestle on to a cart containing a large urn, two kettles, several jugs and a string of coloured flags. A sturdy brown pony was harnessed to the shafts.

'We look like tinkers,' Tom exclaimed in delight, clambering up to sit beside Luigi.

'We like to preserve the old ways on such occasions. Cars are all very well for general use but this is preferable.'

'Very preferable,' Tom agreed. 'No noise, no petrol fumes and a much better view.'

They travelled in a friendly silence: Luigi was a man of few words and Tom realised how shattered he must have been by the quarrel with his son. Perhaps Ricardo would tell him on Friday and put him out of his misery. All I need is to get Dad back, Tom thought, and I'll become part of a happy family. As well as new grandparents, when Ricardo returns I'll have an uncle, an aunt and two cousins. Not bad for someone who's always been short on relations.

Haz Zahra was crowded. They pulled up beside the village green, Tom helping to unload the cart before Luigi set off back to the farm.

'See you later.' He waved and Tom felt a rush of pleasure; a real sense of belonging. This was going to be a good day.

'There you are.' Alice came rushing over, long plait flying wildly out behind her. 'I thought you'd never get here. Everything okay?'

'Fine. This is a mystery-free day remember.'

'Dad's at the church, let's go and give him a hand.'

Ladders had been placed along its façade and a group of men were unravelling strings of lights, Mr Rogerson working beside a chattering Marco. Tom held back, unsure of his reception.

'Got a head for heights?' Marco called, catching sight of him. The incident in the café seemed to have been forgotten for the moment.

'Yes,' Tom said automatically, hoping it was true.

'Then take this ladder. Up you go.'

Alice, to her annoyance, was stationed at its base. She pulled a gruesome face up at Tom and he was thankful to see that, despite her antics, she was keeping a firm grip on the ladder.

He found himself perched at the top of the church, Alice's father to one side and a boy slightly older than himself on the other.

'I'm Pietro,' he announced, smiling. Lila's friend, Tom wondered, remembering Carmel's daughter and her long list of acquaintances. 'When the lights reach you,' Pietro explained, 'Loop them round that hook and pass them along to Mr Rogerson.'

Tom felt rather precarious, especially when he had to stretch out full length to reach them, but the others were chatting and laughing as they worked. After each successful mission, they moved a few steps down the ladder to await the next set of lights.

'It must look spectacular when they're switched on,' Tom declared.

'When does that happen?'

'Later this afternoon and it is spectacular. I've seen it every year for as long as I can remember but it still sends shivers down my spine. Here you are.' Pietro handed him another twine. 'The whole village turns out to watch.'

They repeated the process countless times and Tom's arms were aching by the time they reached ground level.

'I should have a rest for a while,' Mr Rogerson advised. 'You're looking rather hot. You get the full glare of the sun up there.'

'I'm roasting,' Tom confessed. 'I can feel my skin sizzling as though I'm my own personal barbecue. I don't think I've been anything but hot since I set foot on Malta.'

'You are a bit pink.' Alice gazed at his flushed face. 'We're so used to the sun that it doesn't worry us, but visitors have to be careful. Let's get a drink and then I'll show you the inside of the church, it's cool enough in there.'

Tables had been set around the grass and Tom took a glass of lemonade gratefully. It was wonderfully cold.

'What's happening over there?'

'Bandstand for Saturday's concert. Dad plays in the band and so does Marco. This afternoon we'll start building the bonfire. That's lit on Sunday night, to finish the festa with a bang.' She grinned. 'A very big bang.'

'Fireworks?' Tom guessed.

'Lots of them. Finished your drink? Then let's get you into the shade for a while before you start burning.'

For a small village, Haz Zahra had an impressive church, the wooden pews and pillars richly carved and washed by a warm glow of crimson light.

'From our Rose Window,' Alice whispered, pointing upwards.

'People come from all over Malta to see it.'

'It's beautiful,' Tom agreed.

Each petal-shaped section was a ruby mosaic of tiny glass segments from delicate pink to blushing scarlet, forming in the centre the figure of a stern looking man. Around him were what appeared to be a series of biblical scenes.

'John the Baptist,' Alice explained.

Tom's eyes wandered down to a triangular niche below the window. 'What's that?'

'You mean the chalice?'

'No, to its right.'

'A statue, why?'

'It looks like an angel.'

Her eyes widened. 'The riddle! I never thought of that. It's far more likely that the treasure is a statue of an angel rather than a painting. I've seen some wonderful ones in Valletta, covered with jewels, which would fit Tommasso's description of it as a priceless relic. Though we're still left with the problem of the dead tree. How on earth do you hide a statue in a dead tree?'

'Maybe there's a hollow between the branches into which it's been wedged. It shouldn't be impossible to find a summit with a dead tree on top.'

'We can't start looking today.' Alice glanced at her watch. 'I'm hungry, perhaps people are thinking about lunch.'

Tom followed her slowly through the doorway, his mind trying to conjure up a phrase he remembered from an R.E. lesson: something to do with the Great Tree of the Angelic World. That was another thing that would have to wait for later.

Groups of picnickers dotted the grass. Mr Rogerson signalled to Tom.

'Hope you're hungry. You've just missed Luigi but he left this hamper for you with enough food to feed the entire village judging from the weight of it. You'd better get Alice to help you.'

Even with the two of them tucking in eagerly, they barely made a dint in its contents.

'Don't worry, it'll do for later,' Alice assured him. 'We've still got a long day ahead. Come on, we'll dump the hamper inside the church, it'll stay cool in there and be quite safe.'

Mission accomplished, they were joined by the young people of the village, the building of the bonfire being their allotted task. Pietro seemed to have designated himself as organiser and Tom recognised Ewen, in the middle of a group of boys, dragging an enormous log.

'Dead tree,' Tom murmured, pointing. 'Maybe it's just a log we're looking for, that's been hollowed out and the statue stuffed inside. Shame that on our mystery-free day we suddenly can't get away from angels and dead trees.'

He moved forward to help Ewen and his gang, who were struggling to heave their prize on to the already assembled timber.

'Thanks,' Ewen gasped. 'That was heavy. I recognise you, you're Tom, Alice's new boyfriend.'

Tom flushed bright scarlet.

'Ewen!' Alice shot him a furious scowl. 'I should carry on before I thump you.'

Her brother moved away chuckling, not noticeably alarmed by the threat.

Alice eyed Tom's hot face with amusement. 'Don't take any notice of Ewen, he's a complete horror, but most boys of twelve are, aren't they?'

'No. . .yes. . .' To Tom's horror his stammer had returned and he felt an utter fool. 'Sorry, it's just. . . what with everything that's been happening I'd not thought of you as a girl.'

It was Alice's turn to flush though Tom noted, to his dismay, the angry glint in her eyes. How could he have said anything so stupid?

'I didn't mean that like it sounded,' he muttered lamely.

'Glad to hear it! What did you think I was if I'm not a girl?'

'I didn't mean you weren't a girl, I just. . .'

'Perhaps you'd better leave it before you make matters worse.'

'No, I've offended you and. . . it's just for the last few years I've not been at ease with girls,' Tom confessed. 'Especially not with pretty ones. You should have seen the way the girl on the plane threw me into a spin. Mum says it's a phase I'm going through. I never know what to say and I end up silent or stuttering nonsense, but with you it's been different. You've been easy to talk to. It might not sound like it but I'm paying you a compliment.'

'Message understood.' She smiled sweetly. 'I hope you're not going to go all self-conscious now the penny's dropped. I'd miss your witty conversation.'

Alice moved away and Tom grinned as he hurried after her. So like a girl, he thought, she has to have the last word.

They helped to erect the bonfire in a companionable silence, the effort needed discouraging speech, and Tom couldn't help thinking that a new dimension had been added to their relationship. Why hadn't he noticed how pretty she was? Did that make a difference? Not really, he decided, he valued her friendship and loyalty before anything else, though honesty compelled him to admit that her beauty was a definite bonus.

Towards the end of the afternoon, starving once more, they returned churchwards to rescue the food hamper.

'I'll get it.' By now Tom welcomed any opportunity to escape the burning sun.

Inside the church was a damp coolness, the noise outside silenced by the thick stone walls.

Picking up the hamper, Tom gazed once more at the Rose Window, below which nestled the small statue of an angel. It was a simple, crudely carved figure, yet his imagination decked it with sparkling jewels. If they could only find the hill with the dead tree...

'Are you going to stand there all day?' Alice regarded him impatiently. 'I'm so hungry my stomach's making horrific gurgling sounds.'

Laughing, Tom approached the entrance, moving back involuntarily as Alice came to a standstill.

'What's the...?'

She gave him a sudden shove, sending him sprawling so that the hamper went flying from his grasp, before closing the door hurriedly.

'Come on!' Grabbing his hand she pulled him into the side aisle, huddling behind a wooden pillar.

'What...?'

'Ssssh!'

Tom realised that her hand, still clutching his, was trembling violently. What on earth had frightened her so badly?

A shaft of light crept into the church; the door was opening slowly. Alice hauled Tom to his knees. Crouching low, he heard the tread of heavy footsteps, catching a glimpse of dark trousered legs and black shoes through a gap in the pews. Passing, they headed further into the church towards the altar.

Cautiously Alice stood, inching her and Tom backwards and into a small, curtained cubicle: the confessional, Tom realised.

'Who is it?' he whispered.

'The man who let us into the Casa Peralta and took us to Alphonso when we asked for Tommasso.'

'The one who looked like a skeleton?'

She nodded. 'I didn't recognise the other person, but there's no mistaking Alphonso's servant.'

'Do you think they're searching for us?'

'Can you think of any other reason why they should be in Haz Zahra? We can't let ourselves be caught, Tommasso said that would be putting Giuseppe in danger.'

'We don't know anything that would be of use to them. I haven't a clue where Dad is.'

'They obviously think you do.'

'It's not as if. . .'

Tom paused. The footsteps were returning, ominously close. Alice gave a gasp and he squeezed her hand tightly as the men stopped outside their hiding place. He could see the outlined silhouette as one of the men leaned backwards.

'No sign of them anywhere.' The voice was clipped and harsh. 'Alphonso was sure they'd be here today.'

'Why's he got us searching for a couple of brats?'

'The girl's not important, it's the boy he wants. Apparently he's just discovered who he is.'

'So who is he?'

You think Alphonso'd tell me that? All I know is that the kid barged into the Casa Peralta bleating about Giuseppe Farrigiani and then ran off before Alphonso could question him.'

There was a short laugh. 'Not a healthy thing to do under the circumstances.'

'Exactly.'

'So what do we do now?'

'There's not much point hanging around here, we're far too noticeable.'

'Go back and report, then? Alphonso won't be pleased. I'll let you tell him we were unsuccessful.'

'Maybe we should take a look at the Villa Magrino.'

They moved away and Alice let out a long sigh, suddenly aware that she'd been holding her breath.

They waited until the church door banged shut before emerging into the cool dimness of the church. Tom stood motionless, mind reeling.

'We've certainly aroused their attention,' Alice said shakily. 'What do you think would have happened if they'd caught us?'

'They'd have questioned us about Giuseppe. Not that we could tell them anything. At least it means they don't know where Dad is either. What about when they get to the Villa Magrino?' Tom's head was pounding. 'I've got to warn Luigi and Francesca. They don't know anything about what's been happening.'

'Hang on a minute!' He was brought up short by Alice's words. 'We haven't any transport. The men must have a car if they came from Mdina.'

'I've got to get to the Villa Magrino somehow. Do you know anyone with a bike I can borrow? What about Ewen?'

'He came in the car with me and Dad. We can ask Pietro, I don't know how he got here. Or we can ask Marco if we can phone from the café. That's probably the best bet.'

The problem was solved as they emerged into the daylight and saw a crowd gathering outside the church. Standing next to Alice's parents were Luigi and Francesca, waving at them madly.

Tom beamed before looking round anxiously. 'Any sign of those men?'

'They'll have gone,' Alice assured him. 'They'd stand out too easily, this is a village occasion. I should imagine they're well on their way to the Villa Magrino, which they'll find deserted. Hopefully, they'll abandon the search. At least we've now got proof that Tommasso was telling the truth about Alphonso hunting us.'

'We wondered where you'd got to,' Francesca said as they joined the adults.

'Went to collect the hamper from the church. You must have thought I'd been starving for months by the amount you packed.'

She gave him a teasing smile. 'You didn't make a very good job of collecting it.'

Tom reddened, realising the hamper was lying abandoned in the church doorway. Did everyone think the same as Ewen? That he and Alice…? He felt his face flushing even more.

Alice herself was more than equal to the occasion. 'We got led astray by the Rose Window,' she said airily.

They all nodded, appreciatively.

'Our church's claim to fame,' Luigi responded proudly, 'Created in the fifteenth century by Angelo Ricconte. It depicts the story of John the Baptist.'

A tall, burly man strode up, clapping Tom on the shoulder. 'Want to do us a favour, lad? It was your first time decorating the church, so we'd like you to do the honours by switching on the lights.'

As Tom stood ready, Luigi and Francesca on one side of him and Alice on the other, he wished fervently that his father could be there to see him. How many times, he wondered, had Dad watched the switch-on, Luigi's hand on his shoulder as it now rested firmly on Tom's. He stole a look at Luigi's face, full of a quiet pride, suddenly aware that there had been a subtle change in their relationship. He treats me like a grandson, he thought. Has he grasped who I am? Despite the dangers it involved, it was time he talked to Luigi, told him everything he knew.

At the signal, Tom rammed down the plunger and the church became a glittering silver spectacular. Aloft on the steeple, a set of lights which Tom had so far missed blazed into a shimmering angel soaring high above the church.

'The angel?' Tom asked softly.

'Archangel Gabriel,' Luigi said, 'who announced the coming of John the Baptist.'

Tom had little chance to talk privately with Alice. Together with the other young people they'd picnicked on the grass, sharing whatever food remained, Tom's hamper proving most popular. As the sky slowly darkened the church lights gained in brilliance, the whole scene overtopped by the lofty angel. The adults had returned home to the tasks awaiting them, Pietro offering to see that Tom and Alice arrived back safely. They were now in Marco's café, finishing the evening with ice creams.

As Pietro became involved in a heated argument with a group of friends, Alice leaned over to Tom. 'I know what you're thinking. Our task's narrowed to a search for a statue of the Angel Gabriel. I should have thought of that, the number of times I've heard the story of John the Baptist and the Knights who took his name. The Angel Gabriel must have been very important to Claudio Farrigiani.'

'Could it be anything to do with the one above the church? It's certainly high up and you couldn't have a more heavenly summit than the top of a church.'

Alice frowned. 'I don't see how it could be the right one, the lights are put up every year and they wouldn't have been there when Claudio Farrigiani devised the riddle.'

'I suppose not.' Tom sighed. 'If it was that easy, Dad would have thought of it when he was a boy.'

Alice giggled. 'Bet he did. Can't you see him and Tommasso scaling the steeple? No wonder they were so unpopular with Luigi.'

'Have you noticed anything different about the way Luigi treats me?'

Alice stared at him thoughtfully. 'You've become close, anyone can see that. I keep forgetting he doesn't know you're his grandson.'

'I think he's guessed. I'm going to talk to him and Francesca when I get back to the farm.'

'I thought you'd decided that would be putting them in danger?'

'They're already at risk, you heard Alphonso's men planning to go the Villa Magrino. It's just lucky we were all in the village at the time. I need to warn them about what's happening.'

'I wish I could come with you. I'll be awake all night wondering how they take the news.'

'I'll come round first thing in the morning,' Tom promised. 'Tomorrow we'll begin our search for a statue of the Angel Gabriel.'

Pietro dropped him at the end of the lane. Tom walked slowly through the darkness, his mind teasing at the knotty problem of how to sound out Luigi and Francesca. Simply to say, 'Have you realised I'm your grandson?' seemed too blunt an approach.

Entering the kitchen, only Luigi greeted him. 'Francesca's exhausted with all that baking, she's taken herself off to bed. She knew you wouldn't mind.'

Probably best if I talk to Luigi alone, Tom thought, but Luigi was already heading for the doorway. 'I'll join her, now you're back safely. Put the lights out when you're ready to come up.' He stopped as though sensing Tom's disappointment and smiled at him gently. 'Don't worry, I know it's time we had a talk, but it's very late. You must be tired, I know I am. Tomorrow will be better, when we've all had a good night's sleep. You will tell me all about your father and. . .'

'You will tell me about your younger son,' Tom dared to add.

Luigi nodded gravely, turning to the doorway. Then he glanced back at Tom and winked. 'By the way, there's a message for you. You're to ring Alice.'

Tom stood listening to the dialling tone, wondering what on earth Alice wanted now. She was certainly a fireball of energy.

'Is that you, Tom?'

'Of course it's me, who else would be ringing you at this time of night? What's so important it couldn't wait until morning?'

'How did Luigi and Francesca take your news?'

'We're having a talk in the morning. Francesca was so tired she'd gone to bed. Is that all you wanted?'

'No, I know where we have to go tomorrow and it's not Fort St Elmo. It's so obvious I can't believe I never thought of it.'

'Thought of what?'

'Well, I wouldn't really, even though I've passed there several times, but I didn't know its name, see? Not until I was looking at the large map in our hallway, to find if there were any places connected with angels, which there weren't, though I did find Paradise Bay but then I thought that's not very old so it probably wasn't called that in Claudio Farrigiani's day, and just when I was about to give up Ewen told me. He went there last term on a school trip, see.'

'No, I don't see! What did Ewen tell you?' Tom asked when he managed to get in a word. 'Look, Alice, just take a deep breath and tell me slowly what you're talking about.'

'St John's Cliff,' she said triumphantly. 'Isn't it obvious? We have to go to St John's Cliff and climb the Gabriel Tower.'

June 1798

Claudio Farrigiani led his sweating horse into the stable and made for the end stall.

'Don't think you can come creeping in here unnoticed.' Paolo da Messina's head popped up from the adjoining stall.

'Paolo, you shouldn't scare people like that, and I wasn't creeping. What are you doing?'

'Checking the horses. When the invasion starts, they'll be needed for the scouts.'

Claudio nodded, noticing that they were all now using the word 'when' rather than 'if'. Taking a handful of straw he began to rub down his horse. 'Where are the others?'

'Inspecting the fortifications at Floriana, that's where we've been assigned to, and trying to organise the militia into workable groups. Tullio says it's a hopeless task but Gianni seems to be enjoying himself.' He looked keenly at Claudio. 'Where have you been? And don't say Haz Zahra, you've been much further than that judging by the state of your horse.'

Claudio hesitated. 'I rode up to the north of the island.'

'Why?'

Claudio leaned over the side of the stall and with a teasing gesture placed a finger to Paolo's nose. 'Secrets, little man.'

Paolo shook his head angrily. 'I don't know what's got into you. You've been strange for the last two days, ever since Ferdinando went back to Messina. And you've caught Tullio's disease. I've seen you scribbling away even more furiously than he does. Are you writing a book?'

Claudio grinned. 'Not a book, exactly. You could call it more of a poem.'

He laughed aloud at the incredulous expression on his friend's face.

10

Next morning, it was nearly ten o'clock by the time Tom managed to leave the Villa Magrino. Francesca had insisted on cooking a full English breakfast to make up for Tom's lack of food the day before and then there were the festa preparations to be rehashed in minute detail. They all agreed that Tom's switching on of the lights had been accomplished with masterly precision.

Luigi was clumping in and out of the kitchen, a quiet smile on his face. 'Tonight,' he whispered to Tom, laying a hand on his shoulder as he passed. Tom nodded. Hopefully, if Alice was right about the Gabriel Tower, he'd be able to give Luigi some definite news about his son.

Luigi watched him wheel out the rusty bike. 'What are you doing today?'

'Exploring,' Tom said truthfully. 'Alice said something about going to visit the Gabriel Tower.'

'You'll enjoy that. It was built by the Knights centuries ago. How are you getting there? You'll never bike all that distance. It's right up in the north of the island.'

'Perhaps we're going on the bus,' Tom suggested, with memories of their trip to Mdina.

'Doubt it, buses don't run that far.'

'I'm sure Alice has sorted out some travelling arrangements. It was her idea.'

Luigi nodded. 'She's a forceful young lady, takes after her mother.'

Alice was waiting impatiently in the open doorway of the Villa Trevisan. 'You've been ages, I was beginning to think you'd overslept. Put your bike round the back, you won't be needing it. Pietro should be here at any moment.'

'Pietro?'

'We needed transport. There's no other way to get to the Gabriel Tower. I rang him first thing this morning.'

Tom was horrified. 'You didn't tell him about Dad or the treasure?'

'No, of course I didn't. I said I wanted to take you out for the day, show you some more of Malta, and did he want to join us with his car. I didn't even mention Gabriel's Tower, it'll be just another place on our itinerary. Don't worry, I thought it all out when I was too excited to sleep last night. What do you think of my idea?'

'It makes sense but I'm trying not to hope for too much. I can't stand many more disappointments. What do we do with Pietro while we're climbing the tower?'

She sighed. 'Stop creating problems. You're being positive, don't forget. We'll think of something. Perhaps I'll keep him talking at the bottom while you go treasure hunting. Have you told Luigi and Francesca?'

'We're having a long talk tonight, though I'm sure Luigi knows who I am.'

A horn sent them racing round to the front of the house where Pietro was just getting out of his car.

'Your transport, Miss Rogerson.'

He bowed low to Alice who turned a bright red. Tom was delighted to see her embarrassment.

'Sure you didn't mind me ringing you?' she asked. 'You're the only friend we fancied spending the day with,' she continued earnestly, spoiling it by adding, 'who's got a car.'

Pietro grinned at Tom, and at Alice's father who had appeared from the house, contenting himself with asking, 'Where do you want to go?'

Tom left it to Alice, having no idea of the whereabouts of the Gabriel Tower, other than it was somewhere to the north.

'I thought we could go to Busskett Gardens for a picnic as it's the only forest we've got on the island and it was laid out by the Knights of St John. Tom's interested in their history.' She paused, as if expecting a protest.

'No problem so far,' Pietro said easily. 'Especially if your Mum's providing the picnic. Go on.'

'Then we could drive to Dingli Cliffs, along the coast and home via the Blue Grotto. I'd like Tom to see something of the north of the island. Is that too far?'

'Not at all. It'll be a good test for the car.' Pietro patted it lovingly.

'Your first?' Mr Rogerson queried.

'Does it show?'

'Yes, but don't worry; a first car's always special.'

Mrs Rogerson joined them, carrying the picnic hamper. Pietro took it from her, stowing it in the boot. 'I'm beginning to feel hungry already.'

'Won't you both stay for a meal when you get back?'

'I have to be home by seven,' Pietro said regretfully, 'otherwise I'd stay with pleasure. I promised to babysit my brother and sister.'

'I'd love to stay,' Tom assured her, 'but I'll have to let Francesca know.'

'I'll ring her during the day.'

'Please give a message that I won't be late back,' Tom said anxiously, thinking of his talk with Luigi and all that he might have to tell him.

'Will do. Off you go now and enjoy yourselves.'

They drove westwards, Tom finding it less than enjoyable. There were so many questions he wanted to ask Alice. Was the tower the kind of place where his father might be hiding? Was there anywhere that Claudio Farrigiani might have concealed the treasure? And what about the dead tree? The effort of holding his tongue gave him a queer pain beneath his ribs.

Alice, as if sensing his discomfort, left him alone and chatted away to Pietro, the two of them recalling moments at previous village festas. At any other time Tom would have been interested. Now all he wanted was for the next few hours to fast-forward to the moment he stood beneath the Gabriel Tower; everything between that and the present was a needlessly painful interim.

Lines from the riddle, which he now knew by heart, surfaced in his mind:

> *Alight ashore at cavernous*
> *Steepness auguring*
> *Heavenly summit.*

Auguring, he thought, Alice said that means predicting or prophesying, which is exactly what Gabriel did in announcing the coming of John the Baptist, and what could be a more heavenly summit than a tower dedicated to an angel? With the end of the riddle in sight, Tom found it difficult to keep his patience in check. In a few hours, would this whole sorry mess be over? The treasure was not important in itself, all he wanted was to know that the father he loved, despite everything, was safe.

They made their first stop at noon, wandering through the Busskett gardens and enjoying the shade from its wide variety of trees: pine and oak were familiar to Tom but his senses were roused at the sight and smell of orange, lemon and mulberry; so different from England.

Pietro grinned at him. 'You look like a bloodhound, sniffing like that.'

'Sorry, but you must admit the smell is terrific.'

'Busskett is from the Italian *boschetto*,' Alice told him. 'Meaning little wood. You should see the place at weekends; day trippers flock here for the most lavish picnics.'

'It's even more crowded at the end of June,' Pietro assured them. 'I came last year for the Festival of L-Imnarja. Puts our village festivities to shame. It was a huge party, thousands of people, with singing and dancing and lots of eating. Rabbit stew, mostly. Very tasty it was. We left about midnight and the fun was still going on. I wouldn't be surprised if half the people spent the the whole night in the gardens. Thought I'd try it sometime.'

They settled under an orange tree to eat the picnic. Mrs Rogerson seemed to have the same idea about food as Francesca and Pietro whistled appreciatively at the packed contents. 'This is incredible, wish I could eat like this every day.'

Tom did his best wondering if, when normal life resumed, he'd rediscover his appetite. Despite the excellence of Mrs Rogerson's cooking, the food seemed tasteless. He forced himself to eat, aware that he was responding automatically to Pietro's questions about England, his mind functioning on another level, stuck somewhere inside the maze of secrets posed by his father's disappearance.

At last even Pietro's appetite was satisfied. 'Fancy visiting the Verdala Palace?' he asked as they packed away the huge amount of food still left. 'If you're interested in the Knights, it was built for one of their Grand Masters. I can't remember which one, but they're sure to have guide books.'

Tom stood awkwardly. No way did he want to waste time when they were so close to the hoped for solution. Would it seem churlish to refuse?

'We'd probably have to queue and it's far too hot,' Alice said quickly. 'Tom's not used to our climate, he wilts very quickly. Let's make for the coast, there's sure to be a breeze up on the cliffs.' Before Pietro could question her decision, she gestured to the hamper. 'You two take that to the car and I'll fetch ice creams.' She shot off quickly.

'The cliffs it is then.' Pietro stooped to pick up the hamper, grinning at Tom. 'Does she order you around all the time?'

'Pretty much,' Tom admitted. 'Luigi says she takes after her mother.'

Pietro laughed. 'Don't let her mother hear you say that, though I must admit that Luigi's got a point. They both tend to take charge.'

'I don't mind, though,' Tom said quickly, thinking of all the times he would have given up the search for his father if Alice hadn't almost bullied him into continuing.

They were passing through a lemon grove on the way to the car when a call halted them in their tracks.

'Pietro! I thought it was you.'

Spinning round, Tom saw a young man about Pietro's age running towards them. He was dark and slim with a friendly, smiling face.

'Carlo!' Pietro put down the hamper. 'What are you doing here? The last I heard you were working in Mdina?'

'I am. I've got a few days holiday and I came out here with some friends.'

Pietro turned to Tom. 'Carlo and I were at school together. I haven't seen him in over a year, not since I started university.'

'We've plenty of news to catch up on. Are you hanging around here for long? I wouldn't mind a change of company, the friends I came with are decidedly boring.'

For an awful moment Tom thought their plans were about to come crashing to a standstill, but Pietro shook his head regretfully. 'Just leaving, I'm afraid.' Tom heaved a sigh of relief. Pietro hesitated a second, perhaps hoping that Tom would suggest they stay, before adding, 'Look, why don't you come with us, we're driving along to the coast to the Blue Grotto and then back to Haz Zahra? Stay the night at my place, I'm babysitting so we'll have plenty of time to exchange news. I'll run you back to Mdina in the morning,'

'I'd like that, if it's alright with everyone.' Carlo glanced at Tom.

'Fine,' Tom muttered, though it was the last thing in the world he wanted. Whatever would Alice say? When they reached the tower getting rid of Pietro would be difficult enough without adding Carlo into the equation. Perhaps they might sit outside talking while he and Alice explored. Having Carlo along, he decided, could work to their advantage after all.

Alice chose that moment to return with the ice creams. She held them clumsily, oblivious to the milky liquid streaming through her fingers. Tom almost enjoyed the look of consternation on her face; not often anyone caught Alice on the wrong foot.

Stepping forward, Tom relieved her of the cones. 'This is Carlo, he's a friend of Pietro's. He's coming with us for the rest of the day.'

'Would you like me to go back and get you an ice-cream?' she asked Carlo, with a marked lack of enthusiasm.

'No thanks, I'd better find my friends and let them know I'm deserting them. I'll see you in the car park.'

Alice strode along between Pietro and Tom, a bemused expression on her face. Tom wished he could tell her his idea that Pietro and Carlo might keep each other company, leaving him and Alice the freedom to explore.

They stowed the hamper in the boot of the car. Seeing Carlo approaching, Tom ushered Alice hurriedly into the back seat, whispering, 'It's okay, there's no need to get so hot and bothered. They'll probably keep each other occupied while we search the tower.'

'You haven't realised, have you?' She turned a stony face to his. 'Carlo was the other man in the church, the one with Alphonso's servant. The ones that were hunting us yesterday. How did he know we were here?'

Tom and Alice were both silent on the way to the coast, though Pietro and Carlo more than made up for their lack of conversation. Tom listened to them exchanging schoolboy memories, wondering desperately how he and Alice were going to deal with the situation. If Alice hadn't recognised Carlo then... but Tom's mind shied away from such a dangerous scenario. At least they had the advantage of knowing he was the enemy. Dare they risk visiting Gabriel's Tower? They could be leading Alphonso straight to his father.

At Dingli Cliffs the land fell away spectacularly to the intense blue of the sea, the headland itself composed of huge, jagged boulders. Below them, the rocks were alive with sea birds. Above, the sky was a cotton-wool white. Alice had been correct about the breeze, which was welcome after the sticky heat of the gardens. On any other occasion, it would have been the perfect spot for a lazy afternoon. Pietro sat sunning himself on a rock, Tom and Alice taking a perverse pleasure in wandering around separately, showing a keen interest in exploring every rock and crevice. Let Carlo think they were searching for the treasure. It was clear that he was unsure which of them to shadow, though Tom caught the occasional gleam in his eye which suggested he was aware of the game they were playing. Alice tired of the subterfuge before Tom, suggesting they continue with the journey.

A potholed tarmac road ran along the top of the cliffs and Pietro winced as his precious car bounced up and down over the ruts in the track. 'We won't have any suspension left at this rate.'

Alice had recovered her nerve and chatted away to Tom, apparently without a care in the world. He just hoped she'd thought of a plan, his own mind being a hopeless blank. 'We're just approaching Ta'Zuta which is the highest point on the island,' Alice commented in the tones of a tour guide, 'and then we come to St John's Cliff.'

They turned right, almost as though about to drive out to sea, and Tom saw ahead a tall, narrow stone tower perched on the very edge of the cliff, set in a wilderness of sun-baked rock. Despite the heat, Tom felt suddenly cold.

'Gabriel's Tower!' Pietro exclaimed. 'I'd forgotten that was here. It was built as a watch tower for the Knights, if I remember rightly. Something to do with Turkish raiding parties. They used to have a bonfire ready and if they sighted the enemy they lit a beacon as a warning signal.'

Bonfire, Tom thought. Dead trees and the angel tower rising from its base. The riddle was coming together at last.

'Can we stop?' Alice asked eagerly.

'With pleasure, I want to check whether the car's survived the battering.'

They piled out, Pietro studying it anxiously. 'Seems fine,' he said with relief. 'I suppose you youngsters want to climb up there?'

'Might as well.' Tom tried to be nonchalant, though his heart was beating rapidly. 'There should be a good view from the top.'

'Count me out.' Pietro grinned. 'I'd rather take another peek into the food hamper. Don't be too long if you want to see the Blue Grotto, if I'm not back by seven o'clock my parents will kill me.' He began unloading the hamper from the boot.

Alice smiled at Carlo. 'There's stacks of food left, do help yourself. Mum's a fantastic cook and she'll expect to see it empty when we return.'

'I had a good lunch, thanks. I think I'll climb up with you and maybe work up an appetite for later.'

Tom's heart sank. What were they supposed to do now? Not much point in going up at all if they had Carlo in tow. He glanced at Alice, seeking inspiration.

She took Tom's hand, squeezing hard as if in reassurance that all would be well, and tugged him over to the tower. 'You lead the way.'

She slotted herself in behind him, Carlo bringing up the rear. Pietro settled himself on a rock, already tucking into a ham roll. 'I think you're all quite mad but give me a wave from the top.'

Inside, the steep stone steps wound round like a helter-skelter and there was something claustrophobic about the grey walls enclosing them. Tom climbed slowly, hopes of discovering anything worthwhile almost gone. Surely his father wouldn't choose to hide in a place without an escape route? But what could they do if the treasure was there? Neither he nor Alice would stand a chance against Carlo.

About halfway up he came to a rectangular window space. Pausing, he leant out to exclaim, 'It's an awfully long way down. I can see Pietro, he looks like a little lego man from up here.'

Alice's fierce grimace sent him climbing once more. She stopped by the window. Tom had reached the next bend when a strangled cry came from behind. Swinging round, he saw Alice slumped across the steps, clutching her head.

'I shouldn't have looked down!' she wailed in uncharacteristic Alice fashion. 'I've gone all dizzy.'

'It's probably vertigo.' Carlo gazed anxiously at the way she was blocking his passage upwards. 'You'll be alright in a minute. Sit here until Tom and I get back down.'

To Tom's dismay he began to clamber over her, but Alice was more than equal to the situation. Her wails increased in volume and gasping and sobbing she clutched Carlo's arm fiercely. 'Take me down, please.'

'Wouldn't you rather Tom. . .?'

'Please! I think I'm going to be sick.'

The startling choking sounds made this seem ominously imminent. Her grip on his arm tightened and Carlo had no option but to obey. Staggering under her weight he began to manoeuvre reluctantly back down the stairs. Tom could see that Alice was going as slowly as possible. It was up to him now. He sped upwards, round and round, legs aching badly by the time he emerged into a small circular room with a huge window space overlooking the sea. Discouraged, he gazed round at the total emptiness. No father. No treasure. All that effort for nothing.

'Abandon hope all ye who enter here,' he muttered, at the same time cursing himself for his pessimism. Forcing himself to look more carefully, he noticed a deep ledge running round the room several metres above head height. A series of leaps proved too quickly that it contained nothing but layers of dust. Leaning by the window, Tom watched Carlo carry out Alice. She'd played her part well enough, given him every chance. Carlo thrust her at Pietro and turned back to the tower. That was that then. Might as well start making his way down.

Heavenly summit

The words from the riddle came unbidden into his mind. Raising his head, Tom saw that the ceiling was cone-shaped and in the very centre was a circular block of wood; probably used to hang a lantern, he reasoned, when the tower was manned by the Knights. Above this was a small, triangular dark space. Far too high to reach, Tom thought despondently, even if it did contain something, which wasn't very likely. And Carlo was already on the way up. Time seemed to stand still. Tom found himself staring at the large window space; at its narrow ledge. Brain ticking over. Dropping his rucksack he climbed carefully on to the sill, forcing his eyes from the vertical drop at his feet. One slip and he'd be plummeting earthwards, to bounce off the rocks and continue his lonely fall to the sea. He'd be dead long before he reached there. Inch by inch, he managed to turn around. The drop was now at his back, but no less visible: his mind held the imprint, sharp and clear.

Even now he couldn't see into the triangular space. The sound of pounding feet galvanised him into action. He launched himself out and upwards. The fingers of his left hand grazed the wood, losing their grasp; his right hand swept the space above for just a second before he crashed to the floor. Lying winded, tears of despair in his eyes, he saw that at the very edge of the circular wood now rested a small, rectangular box. Slowly, agonisingly slowly, it tilted and toppled into his lap.

11

Carlo burst into the tower room to find Tom crouched over his rucksack.

'I'm just checking to see if I'd got my binoculars,' Tom said, praying the strain in his voice was not evident.

'Any luck?'

Tom shook his head. Had that been a loaded question? Did Carlo suspect he'd found something? He felt panic welling up as Carlo approached. If it came to a tussle between them he was bound to lose.

Instead, Carlo moved past him and over to the window, gazing across the sea to the hazy blue line of the horizon. 'What a view! You can see for miles. It's so easy to imagine a Knight standing here on this very spot, scanning the sea for Turkish raiders.'

Perhaps his name was Claudio Farrigiani, Tom thought, clutching his rucksack. And when he had treasure to hide he remembered this lonely spot. Or was he getting the dates wrong again? According to Tommasso, Dad had thought Napoleon and the French were the enemy, not the Turks.

'Have you noticed that island?' Tom reluctantly joined Carlo at the window, following his pointing finger to a tiny smudge on the water. 'It's Filfa, a nature reserve. Unfortunately you can't land there because important colonies of sea birds use it as a breeding ground. It's also home to a unique species of lizard. I'd love to go there.'

Tom agreed, which confused him. Carlo was the enemy, he wasn't supposed to share his interests.

'Your girlfriend's alright, by the way.'

Tom didn't bother to contradict Carlo's assumption about his relationship with Alice. 'I can see her from here,' he said, as if to excuse his lack of concern. 'I'm going down now.'

Carlo followed close behind. At any moment Tom expected him to reach out and grab his rucksack. Surely he must suspect something. If Carlo turned nasty, how much help could they expect from Pietro? Had Carlo already summoned the rest of Alphonso's men? Perhaps they were waiting to intercept them and take the treasure. He and Alice needed to get back to the safety of the Villa Trevisan as quickly as possible.

Alice, sitting beside Pietro on the rock, eyed Tom keenly. 'Well, was it worth the climb?'

Tom nodded. 'Definitely.'

Her face brightened. 'Good.'

'Marvellous view,' Carlo added. 'Anyone up there would have been able to spot Turkish raiders long before they reached the coast.'

'I wish I'd seen it,' Alice said mournfully. 'I didn't realise I had such a poor head for heights.'

'Just remember in future.' Pietro picked up the hamper and began to stow it back in the boot. 'Where to now?'

Tom held his breath. All he wanted was to get to safety and open the box nestling at the bottom of his rucksack.

As if she could read his mind, Alice had an immediate relapse. 'I still don't feel too good, all sicky inside, do you think we could go straight back?'

'No problem.' Pietro was gazing curiously at Alice. He probably knew her very well, Tom thought. Did he realise this was all pretence? He hoped Pietro wouldn't share his suspicions with Carlo, the last thing they wanted was for him to suspect that their quest had ended at the tower.

Time for him to get in on the act; he couldn't leave it all to Alice, though he was sure his acting skills were not a patch on hers. 'Sure you're not fit for the Blue Grotto?' he asked petulantly. 'You know I fancied seeing that particularly, even if we can't approach it by boat as we wanted.' He hoped there was enough regret in his voice and that Carlo took the hint that there was treasure still to be found.

Alice stood, one hand clutched to her middle. 'I'll try,' she said, smiling bravely, staggering slightly as she stepped forwards.

Pietro put out a hand to steady her. 'You're in no fit state to go anywhere.' Frowning at Tom he said, 'There'll be plenty of other opportunities to visit the grotto.'

Tom gave in sullenly, following Alice into the back of the car and regretting that Pietro must now think him a spoiled kid. Keeping up the masquerade, Alice rested her head against the window and, to all intents and purposes, slept for the rest of the journey. Tom sat quietly beside her, hugging his rucksack.

Alice roused as they pulled into the farmyard, a large van preventing them from parking in front of the house.

'They've come to collect Mum's baking for the festa,' she explained. 'They go round all the outlying farms.' Climbing out of the car, she turned to Pietro. 'Thanks for taking us out. I'm sorry I was such a nuisance.'

'Not your fault, it could happen to anyone. I'm just surprised that you've reached the age of sixteen without knowing you suffer from vertigo.'

Tom added his thanks, less than graciously. Let Carlo believe he was still angry at not visiting the grotto. It would give him something to report back to Alphonso and hopefully send them on a wild goose chase. Tom enjoyed the thought.

Pietro joined them telling Carlo, 'Won't be a minute, I'll just make sure this invalid gets in safely and say my goodbyes to her parents.'

Mrs Rogerson was just handing over a last tray covered with biscuits. When the man had gone she greeted them with a smile. 'You're back early. I wasn't expecting you this soon.'

'My fault!' Alice said quickly. 'You're never going to believe this but I had an attack of vertigo inside Gabriel's Tower. I came over all dizzy and sick. Not like me, is it?'

'Not like you at all,' her mother said dryly. 'Sure you're not sickening for something?'

'I'm fine now, honestly.' To divert her mother's attention she pointed to the table. 'Those biscuits smell delicious. Are they for us?'

'They are if you feel up to eating.' Alice flushed, thankful when her mother's attention turned to Pietro. 'Would you like to take some back for your family?'

'I'd love to, especially if they're as good as your picnic. I can feed them to my brother and sister tonight, keep them quiet while I babysit.'

She began to fill a large basket, issuing commands as she worked. 'Alice take your things to the bedroom. Tom can put his rucksack in the cloakroom.'

It was a small, cramped room, pegs lining one wall. As Tom was hanging up his rucksack, he gazed out of the small window. Outside in the farmyard, Alice's father leant into the car, deep in conversation with Carlo. As Tom watched, they both broke into laughter, clearly sharing a joke. Don't be stupid, Tom told himself, he's only being polite. That's the kind of man he is. He probably met him at the Casa Peralta when he was visiting Tommasso. Stop trying to create another mystery.

Tom had returned to the kitchen when Mr Rogerson entered from the front of the house, assuring his wife, 'Your precious baking is stored away safely.' He smiled at Pietro. 'Have a good day?'

'Yes. thanks. The car survived and I met an old school friend I haven't seen for over a year. He's come back to spend the night with me.'

They all accompanied Pietro and his basket of biscuits to the car. With growing despair Tom watched the introductions being made, noting how Mr Rogerson and Carlo shook hands and greeted each other as though they were complete strangers. No sign of the former camaraderie between them now. If he couldn't trust Alice's father, who could he trust?

'Tea in twenty minutes,' Mrs Rogerson announced as they watched the car disappearing down the track. She returned to the kitchen, her husband heading for the barn.

'Shall we go to the orchard?' Alice asked. 'I know you found something.'

For a moment Tom was tempted to deny his discovery, but suspecting Alice was not an option: she'd proved her loyalty over and over again. Her performance at the tower had been brilliant. Without her acting skills, they wouldn't now be in possession of the box.

'I'll fetch my rucksack.'

Slipping into the cloakroom, he managed to avoid Mrs Rogerson and soon he and Alice were sitting in their favourite spot under a huge apple tree. Again Tom hesitated, but Alice was fired up with excitement. No trace now of the wan figure at the tower.

'Go on! Don't keep me in suspense. What did you find?'

He drew out the box, explaining how he'd found it at the summit of the tower.

'It's very small,' Alice said critically. 'It must be a very tiny statue.'

'The one in the church isn't much bigger.'

Tom studied the box. The lid had been sealed round with what looked like candle wax and he used his nails to scrape it away. He didn't like to admit that the box felt ominously light, as though it were empty.

Lifting the lid with trembling fingers, his worst fears were realised: the box contained nothing but a folded piece of paper.

'Read it, then,' Alice urged. 'Go on, Tom, it could tell us where to collect the treasure.

He straightened it out and they both gazed eagerly at the words.

If you're a Farrigiani then congratulations on having got this far in your search for

the treasure. We've taken the original but left you a copy.
Keep hunting. We mean to.
Beppe and Tommo

Underneath were four lines of verse.

Starless shadowy years.
Creation counts as reckoned.
Minutes enduring into days,
Everlasting seconds.

They gazed at each other blankly. Back to square one.

'I spoke too soon about not being able to take any more disappointments,' Tom said bitterly. 'We're no nearer the treasure than we were at the start of the week.'

'We're one riddle nearer.'

'What good has that done us?'

'We might be able to solve the new riddle much quicker now we've had some practice. It sounds like something to do with time, look at the years and days and minutes and seconds. It could be a clock.'

'Clocks don't measure the years.'

'Some might. How about the Pinto Clock, that doesn't just show the time it has the day, the month and the phases of the moon. And it would have been there in Claudio Farrigiani's day because Grand Master Pinto was much earlier than Napoleon. We could go back to the Grand Master's Palace and take a closer look. You never know, it might have the years marked on it somewhere.'

'How are we supposed to reach the clock? Fly?'

'Come on, Tom, don't tell me you're not intrigued by all this. Claudio Farrigiani thought the treasure was so priceless that he didn't want it to depend on just one clue. I know it's frustrating when we thought we'd solved the riddle, but in some ways this second one makes it extra special.' She looked at him anxiously. 'Don't get all depressed again. You'll be able to show the riddle to Luigi and Francesca when you talk to them tonight. They might have some good ideas.'

'I think it might be best if I went straight back there now.'

She stared at him suspiciously. 'Is something else troubling you, besides the riddle?'

'No,' Tom lied. 'Why should it be?'

She shrugged. 'You went all moody again even before we found the box didn't contain the statue. You ought to stay for tea, you'll upset Mum if you don't.'

'Okay.' Tom agreed. 'But afterwards I'll go straight back to the Villa Magrino.'

It was an awkward meal. Tom could think of little to say and Alice was clearly losing patience with him. Her parents regarded the pair of them with puzzled expressions, probably wondering if they'd quarrelled. Alice's mood was not helped by her mother's constant references to her vertigo at the tower. Tom could see how uncomfortable she was at having to lie.

Mr Rogerson covered the silence with more information about the Knights which, at any other time, Tom would have found fascinating. 'It's amazing the way they've left their legacy here on Malta. I'd forgotten about the Gabriel Tower, but there are others scattered around the coast, and then of course there are the people like the Farrigianis. They're incredibly lucky that they can trace their ancestry to an Italian Knight.' He smiled at Tom. 'You might think they are simple farmers, but the Farrigianis are actually descended from the nobility of Europe.'

Tom found his voice at last. 'How do you work that out?'

'Not anyone could become a Knight, you know. They had to be of noble birth from both parents and they had to be able to trace their nobility back at least four generations. In fact, the Knights were the sons of the greatest families in Europe.'

Tom could think of nothing to say. It was all getting to be too much. He was still trying to adjust to the fact that he could be a mixture of English, Maltese and Italian, without having to cope with the idea of having noble blood. It was a relief when he could escape from the table.

'What about tomorrow?' Alice asked coldly as Tom collected his bike.

'I honestly don't know.' Tom sighed. 'I'm not trying to be difficult, really I'm not. I can see you're cross with me.'

'I just wish you wouldn't give in so easily. You said you were going to be positive from now on and at the first hurdle you've collapsed.'

Tom could think of nothing to say.

'Will you let me know how you get on with Luigi and Francesca?'

'I'll ring you first thing,' he promised. 'And I'll try and be in a better mood by then.'

Tom rode home slowly, his mind buzzing with frustration. It was no consolation to know he'd been on the same track as Giuseppe and Tommasso. That had been over twenty years ago. Where was his father now? He'd been so sure the mystery would be solved at the tower and all he and Alice had for their troubles was another meaningless riddle. Eating into his misery was the problem of Mr Rogerson. He'd pretended not to know Carlo. During tea he'd commented, 'Pietro's friend seems a nice person.' Shame he wasn't as good at acting as his daughter. The words sounded so false that even Mrs Rogerson had gazed at him curiously. He was there this morning, Tom thought, when Alice outlined our itinerary. He's the only one who could have phoned Carlo and told him where to find us. He knows the Lorenzo family, Tommasso said that he visited them. That makes it likely he also knows Alphonso. He couldn't possibly tell Alice his suspicions, he knew how much she loved her father. So where did they go from here? He'd long ago given up expecting his father to suddenly turn up safe and sound, as the police so obviously thought. Best to leave everything to Luigi, and to Ricardo when he got home. It's beyond me, Tom decided, from now on I'll let the adults take charge.

He had reached the front of the house before becoming aware that the usual welcoming lights were missing. Surely they hadn't gone to bed already? Luigi had promised that tonight they'd have the talk that, Tom realised, they should have had days ago.

The back of the farmhouse was equally dark and Tom resigned himself to another disappointment. He should be used to them by now. He turned the doorknob quietly, determined not to wake them, applying slightly more force until it dawned on him that the door was locked. Before he could gather his wits an arm snaked round his body, another covering his mouth. Struggling frantically he jammed his elbow backwards, hearing a grunt of pain. Squirming and kicking, Tom worked his lips apart and bit down hard.

'Christ!' The hand flew off his mouth.

Then a blow on the side of his head sent him spinning into darkness.

12

The worst headache he'd ever known dragged Tom unwillingly back to consciousness, seeming to be lodged somewhere in the top of his skull. His tongue felt swollen and tender where he'd bitten it. His eyes were closed and he was reluctant to open them. Thinking was a problem, his thoughts muzzy as though he'd been drugged, a constant hum buzzing through his brain. A few seconds of pure bewilderment preceded the sudden memory of an arm snaking out of the darkness and he nearly gave way to panic, gritting his teeth to stop the scream emerging from his throat. The shock of what had happened hit him anew and his stomach clenched painfully. He had never been so frightened.

His returning senses recognised the throbbing of an engine. He was travelling in a car, stretched out flat on what was presumably the back seat, his hands fastened together across his chest so that the bindings cut painfully into his wrists. He risked opening his eyes; the darkness was shot with intermittent flares of light that burned his eyeballs, making him blink rapidly. Tears streamed down his cheeks. Trying to sit up, he discovered that the straps tethered him securely to the seat, his view restricted to a rectangle of black sky through the car window. How long had he been lying here? Not in a million years had Tom ever imagined himself in such a situation. With a great effort he twisted sideways, a wave of nausea rushing into his throat, and saw the backs of two heads, a dark jacket and a bright blue shirt. It was impossible to identify them from this angle but the men must belong to Alphonso.

Panic set in once more as he recalled the dark, deserted farmhouse. What had happened to Luigi and Francesca? Were they also prisoners? So much for his decision to warn them. He'd been nothing but trouble from the moment he set foot on their doorstep. And the worst thing was, they had no idea about what had been happening. Had Alice suffered the same fate? Probably not, if her father was involved with the Lorenzo family. The thought added to his pain. This was the moment he should wake up and find himself safely back in England. Yet England was in the past; ancient history. This was Malta and he realised with horror that the thrill of a treasure hunt had obscured the fact that at the heart of the mystery was a murderer who had already killed once. A murderer who had never been caught. Tom shivered at the thought that he might be about to become the second victim, assuming that Luigi and Francesca were still alive. What if they'd died without ever realising that their younger son had returned to Malta? Tears rained down his face and he was unable to raise a hand to brush them away. Dad, he prayed, wherever you are please show yourself and end this nightmare. No treasure could be worth what you're putting us all through.

Tom felt the car slowing down, coming to a halt. He tensed, closing his eyes quickly. Let them believe he was still unconscious. If he was going to escape his only hope was to take them unawares, and he had to escape. He had to find some way of helping Luigi and Francesca. The door opened. He felt the straps being released and hands dragged him roughly from the car. Without thinking, his eyes shot open and he began to struggle.

'Let me go! Get off me!'

'Keep quiet,' a voice warned from behind him. 'I don't want to have to hit you again.'

Tom was picked up and carried into a tall, narrow house and put down in a dimly-lit hallway. The driver, the one in the blue shirt, nodded at Tom's captor and left, closing the door behind him. He heard the ominous click of the lock. He was well and truly trapped.

'I'm going to cut the bindings round your feet and hands. Try anything stupid and I'll knock you out again. Your choice.'

No choice at all, Tom thought miserably. His captor was a bear-like man with huge shoulders and a large head covered by black stubble. Not someone to tussle with unless you were an idiot. He stood quietly while his hands and feet were released from their bindings.

'What are you going to do with me?'

The man ignored the question. 'Upstairs!' He clapped a hand to the back of Tom's neck, propelling him up two flights of stairs. Tom's ankles ached where they'd been bound and his legs felt strangely heavy. Stumbling, he was jerked roughly to his feet.

Opening a door on the second landing, his captor pushed him into a large room.

'Wait here and don't even think about trying to escape. The place is well guarded.'

For a prison it was quite luxurious, a dark green carpet covering the floor, the walls a pale yellow adorned with paintings; expensive, judging by their gilt frames, but anything Alphonso owned was likely to be expensive. A comfortable couch and two easy chairs were set before an unlit fire and heavy curtains were drawn across a window. Tom drew them back with the absurd expectation that he might find a fire escape leading down from the window. No such luck! All he saw was his own image staring back at him, wild and dishevelled. Really must get my hair cut sometime, he thought. He almost grinned at the stupidity of the notion; he'd far more pressing matters to attend to. How on earth was he going to escape? Turning out the light, the night sprang into focus. Tom could make out a deserted street with a stretch of tall houses facing him. No way of identifying where he was.

The light blazed on with a suddenness that startled him. Tommasso Lorenzo stood in the doorway. Tom felt a moment's relief before his anger came rushing back.

'Shut the curtains,' Tommasso said pleasantly. Noting Tom's stormy face he added. 'Please.'

Tom did as asked before stepping forward angrily. 'What do you think you're playing at?'

'It's no game, I assure you.'

'No? I've been kidnapped, knocked unconscious. . .'

'That wasn't meant to happen. It's your own fault. If you'd just cooperated we'd have brought you here peacefully.'

'I didn't get much choice, did I?' Tom gave a bitter laugh. 'How on earth was I supposed to cooperate with a hand round my mouth and. . .?'

'You started struggling and yelling. We didn't know who was around; it was necessary to get you away as quickly and quietly as possible, for your own sake.'

'Why?'

Tommasso sighed. 'Because you refused to heed my advice. If you had, then none of this would have been necessary. I told you days ago to stay out of sight and not to interfere. I warned you of the consequences but you've been worming your way into a nasty situation, making things worse at every turn.'

Tom's anger boiled over. 'I wouldn't have interfered if I'd been told the truth. It's not my fault you're a liar. And what have you done with Luigi and Francesca?'

'They're quite safe, they've been hidden away for their own good.'

'Where?'

'It's best you don't know.'

Tom scowled. 'Who says? You? Can you give me one good reason why I should believe you? Nearly everything you've told me so far has been wrong, why should I start believing you now? Why did you say

Giuseppe couldn't be my Dad? I know he was acquitted and that he went abroad to start a new life. Don't try and deny it, we read the truth in the newspaper cuttings.'

'So that's what you were doing in the library. I did wonder.'

'You were having us watched?' Tom suddenly remembered the car driver in the blue shirt. It was a very distinctive blue. 'One of the men who kidnapped me was in the Upper Barrakka gardens the other day, when Alice and I were having lunch. How long had he been following us? What's so important about me?'

'You're as stubborn as your father, that's what.'

Tom stared at him. 'You admit it, then? Giuseppe Farrigiani is my father?'

'Of course he is.' Tommasso moved impatiently to a chair. 'I recognised you as soon as I set eyes on you, despite the fair hair, though I had an advantage in that I knew of your existence, which is more than Luigi did.'

He shouldn't be surprised, Tom realised, but the confirmation hit him hard. There was no longer any pretending that this had nothing to do with him, no longer any pretending that at any minute Dad would walk in through the door and the nightmare would be over. Or that he would ring and ask what all the fuss was about. The Joseph Newton he'd known and loved had been nothing but an impostor.

'Why did you lie to me?'

'Because at this moment, to be Giuseppe's son is a distinct liability. Look, sit down. I can see I'm going to have to fill you in on some of the details.'

'All the details,' Tom insisted, sitting on the couch. 'I don't want to be fobbed off with any half-truths this time.'

Tommasso gave a twisted smile. 'The whole truth and nothing but the truth; is that what you want?'

'What's wrong with that?'

'Nothing, except the truth isn't always so easy. It's difficult to know how to start.'

'That's easy. You can start by telling me where Dad is.'

'I've no idea.' Tom rose angrily. 'Sit down, I'm telling you the truth. I wish I did know. It's imperative I find him before. . . before others do.' He hesitated. 'I take it you've not managed to track him down?'

Tom remained silent. He still didn't know whether to believe Tommasso.

'I'll take that as a no. Look, if we're going to work together, you'll have to start trusting me.'

'I would trust you if I thought you were telling the truth. You can start by telling me the full story. I want to know everything about Dad.'

'I'll have to go back over twenty years.'

'I'm listening,' Tom said quietly.

Tommasso leaned back against the cushions, a wistful look on his face. 'I told you Beppe and I were friends. He was my best friend, which is why I've removed Luigi and Francesca from the scene. Beppe would want that.'

'He didn't mind hurting them once,' Tom said bitterly. 'How could he go off to England without letting them know where he was? He didn't even tell them they'd got a grandson. That doesn't show much concern, does it? I can't believe Dad would be so cruel.'

'Don't judge him too quickly, you've no idea how difficult things were. Not just for Beppe but for all of us.'

'So tell me.'

Tom saw that Tommasso's eyes were not really seeing him; they were focused somewhere above his head, gazing back into the past.

'Everything I told you about when we were kids and the events leading up to the robbery were true. You can't imagine how hard it was for me to sit through Beppe's trial, listening to all the people brought forward by the prosecution to prove that he had been obsessed by finding the treasure. The staff at the Bibliotheca told how he'd plagued them to see the book. Trouble was, they were all speaking the truth, except they didn't know Beppe like I did. The outcome was a foregone conclusion, especially with the evidence of the scarf, but I always knew he was innocent. Beppe wasn't a thief and he had a horror of violence. He would never have killed the security guard and if it had been an accident he'd have been the first to sound the alarm.'

Tom nodded. 'What about the scarf? How did it get there?'

'Beppe hadn't worn that scarf for years, he wasn't a scarf sort of person, and anyway it was a warm evening. If I hadn't already known, the presence of the scarf would have convinced me of his innocence. It was so obviously a set-up.'

'Didn't you tell them that?'

'Of course I did, but I was a lone voice. Who would have believed me after all the evidence they'd amassed against him?'

'What about his parents?' Tom asked awkwardly, wondering if he really wanted the answer. He'd grown fond of Luigi and Francesca. In some ways he knew them far better than his father. Certainly far better than the person his father had turned out to be.

'Luigi took the stand and said he couldn't believe his son would ever commit murder, but he was in a difficult position. Everyone knew that he'd quarrelled with Beppe, warning him that one day his fixation with the treasure would lead him into trouble; that Beppe had walked out and gone to live with Ricardo. Luigi's such a truthful person, he couldn't deny that. The prosecution gave him a really hard time.'

'It must have been awful for him.' Tom thought of the gentle, proud Luigi and felt tears gathering at the back of his eyelids.

'Especially,' Tommasso continued, 'as after the acquittal Beppe refused to have anything to do with his family. As you know, he left immediately for England without even saying goodbye. It broke Francesca's heart, which is why Luigi was so angry that he removed all traces of Beppe from the house and refused to speak of his younger son. If anyone did ask, he said that as far as the Farrigiani family were concerned Beppe was dead.'

'Why was Dad acquitted?'

'Because I pestered my father, told him over and over again that Beppe was innocent, until he got fed up and agreed to finance the appeal. He hired a top lawyer who proved that all the evidence against Beppe was circumstantial.'

'Did you keep in touch after Dad left Malta?'

'For a time. Neither of us were much for letter writing but I knew he'd changed his name to Joseph Newton.'

'You never told Luigi and Francesca?'

'If Beppe had wanted them to know he'd have told them himself. He didn't even correspond with Ricardo, he was determined to break away from his old life. He swore he'd never come back to Malta. I heard from him when he married and again when you were born. He named you after me, a childhood pact we once made. My son is called Giuseppe. After that, when he began to travel, there were fewer letters – mostly postcards – though he did write at the time of the divorce. Beppe was very shaken by it; he hated losing you, though he knew it was better you lived with your mother.'

Tom flushed. 'That's not what it looked like. I saw him twice in seven years.'

'You have to realise what it was like for Beppe. I don't think he ever recovered from the trial and the six months in prison. I was horrified when he came out; he was broken in body and spirit, not at all like my boyhood friend who had been so full of life. It was like meeting a shadow of who he'd once been. Like Luigi, he's a proud man and he loves his country. Although he'd been acquitted he knew that many people on Malta still thought him guilty and that it was only my father's name and money that had secured his release. He couldn't get away from Malta quickly enough, yet even in England he was unable to settle. He threw himself heart and soul into his job as a way of coping with the situation and it cost him his family.'

Tom was silent for a moment. 'That should have been the end of the story, shouldn't it? I can understand why Dad never mentioned Malta to Mum or me, but what happened to make him change his mind about returning here. It was Dad who suggested the holiday and he gave me the names of Luigi and Francesca so he must have been going to take me to see them.'

It was Tommasso's turn to pause. 'Believe me, it would be best all round if you went straight back to England and left me to deal with the situation.'

Tom stared at him incredulously. 'You must be joking. I'm going nowhere until I know the full story and I've seen Dad. You're still holding something back from me, I can tell.'

'I suppose you've a right to know. You must promise never to repeat what I tell you to anyone.'

'Alright,' Tom said impatiently, thinking that Alice wasn't anyone. If he ever saw her again, she deserved to learn the truth. 'Why did Dad bring me out here?'

'Because he thought that together you could collect the Farrigiani treasure and he could make his peace with his parents by introducing them to their grandson.'

'He'd solved the riddle after all this time?'

'Yes.'

'What was the treasure and where was it hidden? Alice and I got nowhere. We'd just found the message and the second riddle that you and Dad left at the Gabriel Tower.'

'You did well for the short time you've been here. It took us years to get that far. Still, I suppose we were much younger than you when we started the search. We never got any further and I still have no idea; Giuseppe refused to divulge the information. After all this time, he intends to collect the treasure himself. All he said was that we should have paid more attention to Claudio Farrigiani instead of dashing madly about the island.'

'Why didn't he turn up at the airport?'

Tommasso glared at him in exasperation. 'Will you let me tell the story my way? You're jumping ahead too quickly.'

Tom bit back a fierce retort. It wouldn't do to anger Tommasso at this stage. 'Go on, I'll be as silent as I can.'

'You remember your promise?'

'I'm not in a position to tell anyone. I don't think I'm going anywhere in the near future, am I?'

Tommasso twisted his hands nervously. 'You can't appreciate how difficult this is for me. We can fast-forward the story to a few months ago. I hadn't heard from Beppe for years and I rarely thought about him, though I did on that day. It was my son's fifteenth birthday.' Born a year after me, Tom thought, I wonder if I'll ever get to meet him. 'We were having a party at the Casa Peralta and I organised a treasure hunt. Beppe had once written about one he organised for you.'

'My ninth birthday. I got a fort and a set of knights.'

'I pinched Beppe's idea and hid presents all over the house. I explored up the large chimney in the drawing room, it's never lit, in the hope there might be a ledge on which I could conceal a present. I got more than I bargained for; someone had beaten me to it. Hidden there was the book that had been stolen all those years ago from the Bibliotheca.'

Tom gasped. 'What did you do?'

'Took it to my father, he's head of the family. I could tell immediately that he wasn't surprised by my find.'

'He knew it was there?'

'After some prevaricating, he told me the truth and this is what I find difficult to tell. The reason father financed the acquittal was not out of love for me, as I'd always imagined, but to ease his conscience: he'd discovered that Alphonso and some of his friends had been responsible for the crime in the library. Alphonso has always been greedy for money, wanting far more than father has ever doled out. He imagined the Farrigiani treasure would make his fortune and give him the independence he's always craved.'

Tom stared at him angrily. 'Your father knew it was Alphonso and he let Dad take the blame?'

'No he didn't!' Tommasso said furiously. 'He didn't find out until after the trial.'

'He could have told the truth, then.'

'You don't understand.' Tommasso spread his hands helplessly. 'The family name means everything to my father. We have a reputation to uphold as part of the old nobility.'

'Nothing noble about shielding a murderer!' Tom taunted.

Tommasso smashed his fist down on the arm of the chair. 'My brother did not kill the security guard; it was one of his friends.'

'So that makes it alright?'

Tommasso stood abruptly. 'I'll finish this when you're in a mood to listen.'

'No.' Tom leaned forward. 'I know it must be hard for you. I still don't understand how Dad become involved again.'

Tommasso sat down reluctantly. 'That was my fault and I'm wondering now if I did the right thing. I sent Beppe the book, disobeying my father's instructions. He'd told me to replace it in its hiding place but I felt that after all he'd been through Beppe deserved to see the book.'

'Did you tell Dad about Alphonso?'

'No, just that I'd found the book in the house, but I'm sure he guessed. Beppe never liked Alphonso and I'm afraid the feeling was mutual. I was always sad about that because I got on so well with Ricardo. Three weeks ago Beppe rang me, very excited, to say that the book had been invaluable and he'd solved the riddle, that the treasure had been under our noses all the time, and he was coming to Malta and bringing you with him. He said he couldn't wait to introduce me to his son and his parents would be thrilled to meet their grandson. I was so glad. After all this time he sounded his old self again. I suddenly realised how much I'd missed him.'

About the time he rang me with news of the holiday, Tom realised. No wonder he was thrilled. 'What happened next? Why didn't it go as planned? Why did Dad come out a day early and leave me stranded at the airport?'

'Alphonso discovered that the book was missing. I've no idea how but he got wind of Beppe's intention to come to Malta. He suspected me, of course, though I denied any involvement; I claimed I hadn't heard from Beppe for years. I'm sure he didn't believe me. Alphonso was worried naturally that with the loss of the book and Beppe's imminent arrival the truth of the theft and murder would be revealed. I think there's also a secret hope that he could still come into possession of the Farrigiani treasure. My father doesn't know it but Alphonso has got himself seriously into debt.'

'What did he do?'

'Held a secret meeting here at the Casa Peralta with his old friends. Don't forget they would also be implicated in the robbery and murder if the truth ever got out. Father was away so Alphonso thought he was quite safe, but a servant who is loyal to me managed to overhear some of their conversation. I was horrified when I realised that Alphonso knew the date and time that Beppe was arriving and they planned to be at the airport to meet him.'

Tom looked baffled. 'Where were they? No one stopped me at the airport. They couldn't have failed to hear the tannoy asking for Joseph Newton to meet his son in the British Airways Office. Why did they leave me alone?'

'What they didn't know was that Beppe had changed his name or that he'd had a son. At that stage you were unknown to them.'

'Why did Dad let me travel alone? Didn't he know I'd be walking into danger?'

'This is where it gets confusing and I haven't got all the answers. I didn't find out about Alphonso until the day before you were due to travel. I rang Beppe immediately and he said he'd come out that afternoon, collect the treasure and hand it straight to the authorities. That would put an end to Alphonso's plans. I arranged to meet him at Ricardo's house in Valletta. Ricardo is away, I don't think Beppe realised that, though he may still have a key. I waited a long time outside, yet Beppe never turned up. I checked with the airport and he arrived here safely. After that he seems to have vanished into thin air.'

'Do you think Alphonso's holding him?'

'I did at first, naturally, but he and his friends are still searching for Beppe. And for you, too, of course, after you came storming into the Casa Peralta shouting Giuseppe's name. I'm sure by now they'll have discovered your identity.'

'They have,' Tom admitted, recalling the scene in the church and Carlo's sudden appearance at the Busskett Gardens. 'I nearly ruined everything, didn't I?'

'You certainly didn't help the situation, which is why I got you away from the Casa Peralta so quickly. Unfortunately you asked for me, reinforcing my brother's suspicions that I'm involved. The servant who showed you into the house is one of Alphonso's men. I was just coming out of my room when I heard him tell Alphonso of your arrival. I rang a friend and asked him to call the house saying he had an urgent message for Alphonso, then I dashed round to the French windows ready to spirit you away. Since your disappearance, Alphonso has been watching me like a hawk which is why I've been unable to approach you. Instead, I had one of my own men keep an eye on you.'

'The man in the blue shirt?'

Tommasso nodded. 'When I heard this afternoon that Alphonso was planning to seize you, I stationed men at the Villa Magrino. It was hard, I couldn't tell them the full story, but I persuaded Luigi and Francesca to go into hiding. They made me promise to take good care of you, which I have been trying to do for days, though you haven't made it easy.'

'What about Alice?'

'She'll be alright,' Tommasso assured him. 'You've no need to worry about her.'

Was that because her father was in league with Alphonso? Somehow Tom couldn't bring himself to ask. 'What happens now?'

'My main priority is to find Beppe before Alphonso does. I have an advantage in that Beppe was my closest friend and I still have places to search that are known to only him and me.'

'Can I come with you?'

'That would do more harm than good. I can hardly dodge

Alphonso with you in tow. I want you to stay here and keep out of sight until I find Beppe. When I do, I promise to take you straight to your father.'

June 1798

Claudio Farrigiani surveyed the fortifications of Floriana with a sinking heart. They had been erected over a hundred years ago and since then little had been done to maintain them. How, in what might be only a few weeks, possibly days, even hours, could they possibly make them sturdy enough to withstand a French assault? It was a hopeless task. Napoleon was known to have some of the best troops in Europe.

From where he stood he could see Gianni, much happier now he had an active job to do, organising his troop of Maltese militia into a chain line along which were passed huge chunks of stone to block the gaps. Too many gaps, Claudio thought, though that did not appear to deter Gianni. He was laughing and joking as they worked and Claudio marvelled at the enthusiasm and discipline he managed to instil into the men around him. He smiled to himself. If only we had an army of Giannis, then anything might be possible. Claudio had given up any hopes of a miracle.

Von Hompesch had refused to issue any orders for defence, leaving the Knights to organise themselves. Some were better at it than others. Gianni Correr was one of the best.

The sounds of sawing and hammering accompanied the Maltese carpenters' building of wooden platforms to provide walkway frameworks against the stone walls. Carts rumbled through the gateway, laden with foodstuffs needed to sustain a siege He knew that in the smithy the fires burned brightly as swords were sharpened.

Despite his efforts to concentrate on the task in hand, Claudio's mind wandered to the place from which it was rarely absent. On the way back from Gabriel's Tower he had visited Haz Zahra, in an attempt to persuade Maria and her parents to take shelter within the fortifications of Valletta. Her father had scoffed at the idea, insisting that should the French arrive the villagers would lock themselves inside their church. It was sturdy enough to withstand any siege.

Claudio prayed he was right. It was more important than ever that Maria remain safe. They had managed only a few moments together, just long enough for her to tell him that she was carrying his child.

Since then, Claudio had tried in vain to push from his mind the thought that perhaps, whatever happened to the other Knights, he could remain on Malta. Become a farmer. Become a father. Watch his children grow up on this island, followed by his grandchildren and great grandchildren until the day came for him to take his rest in the small graveyard beside the church.

It was a dream, he knew that, but a dream that sustained him during these troubled days.

The sound of a heavy cart broke into his reverie. The wheels were clanking over the cracked summer soil, throwing up clouds of dust and clods of earth. The black horse that pulled it had become a smoky grey.

The militia who had been pushing the cart split away to reveal Paolo and Tullio. Claudio hastened to join them. One look at their faces and he knew that all was not well.

'Have you seen what we've been given?' Paolo's voice was shrill in disbelief, as he pointed to two rusty canons perched on the cart. 'They haven't been fired against an enemy for about a hundred and fifty years. And do you know what the Commander at Fort St Angelo told us? "Do the best you can with them." I thought he was joking, but he was deadly serious.'

'That's not all,' Tullio said gloomily. 'We've collected what muskets and rifles they could spare us, but most of the shot is defective and the

powder rotten. How are we supposed to provide any line of defence?'

Claudio gazed at his friends and could find no answer. It was not the time to remind them that the Knights using these weapons had never faced an enemy in battle. With the finest weapons in the world at their disposal they would be facing an uphill task; as it was, their situation seemed hopeless.

13

By 9 o'clock Alice was tired of waiting by the phone. Luigi and Francesca were early risers, they had to be to survive in farming as she knew to her cost, and Tom was surely up by now. Okay, so finding the second riddle had depressed him, spinning him back into the moody sullenness she had grown to hate, but they'd still got a clue to follow. That was better than nothing. Something to do with time, she was sure, it had to be. It would be worth taking a look at the clocks in Valletta, even if Tom had been so scornful about her suggestion of the Pinto Clock. Maybe that was something they could do today. Tom would probably recover his spirits if they planned a course of action.

Her mother swept through the hallway towards the kitchen.

'Are you going to sit there much longer?'

'I'm waiting for a phone call from Tom. He promised to ring first thing.'

'Maybe Luigi's given him some jobs to do. With the festa starting tomorrow he and Francesca will be rushed off their feet. Like I am.' She looked in exasperation at her daughter. 'Why don't you bike over there and offer some help?'

'I'll give it another few minutes.'

Alice watched her mother retreat into the kitchen and sighed. At any other time she'd have cycled over without hesitation, but today was different. By now, Luigi and Francesca would know that Tom was their grandson. She wondered how they'd taken the news. Were they excited or upset that after all this time their youngest son had returned to Malta and become embroiled in another mystery? This was a family occasion, she couldn't just barge in on them without an invitation. It wouldn't do any harm to phone, though, would it? Before she could talk herself out of it, she picked up the receiver and dialled through to the Villa Magrino. The ringing tone echoed on and on until the answer phone cut in. Well, that was a first. Where was everybody? A sudden shiver ran down her back. Something was wrong. Unable to stand the suspense any longer, Alice grabbed her bike and set off for the Villa Magrino.

Tom prowled restlessly around the room, unable to settle in one spot for more than a few minutes. Was this how his father had felt? Forever wanting to be somewhere that he wasn't? His mind returned to the divorce, to the unhappiness that had invaded the house. Why didn't he tell us? We could have helped. He felt a spurt of anger at the memory of his mother's face, pale and drawn and full of a misery that could have been cured so easily if his father had just admitted the truth. If he had they'd still be together and this last week would never have happened.

Although Tom knew that the sensible course of action was to stay out of sight, he couldn't help feeling like a prisoner; that the important action was passing him by. It wouldn't be so bad if he had company, but Tommasso had left early that morning, after an attempt to be reassuring.

'Don't expect me back before tonight, though perhaps I'll have some good news by then.'

Tom glanced at his watch: 10 o'clock. Between now and evening stretched an interminable spell of sheer boredom. I can't stay here all day, he thought desperately, I'll be a nervous wreck by the time Tommasso returns. His prowling led him to the window. Remembering Tommasso's injunction he kept well back, staring at the houses opposite. They were further away than he'd thought last night, the darkness deceiving his judgement of the distance. Looking down, he realised the street was actually a small square, with a statue in the centre. His heart leapt. He knew where he was. That was the bust of Grand Master Manoel Vilhena, Alice had pointed it out on their journey through Floriana. The Central Library was just round the corner. Not that knowing the location of his hideaway was any help. He moved back from the window. What would Alice be doing at this moment? He wished he'd thought to ask Tommasso how he'd covered their absence. Carmel and Luis would have arrived at the Villa Magrino by now and he'd bet anything that Alice had cycled over. She wouldn't wait by the phone for long, not Alice, she'd ring him up and when there was no answer she'd take matters into her own hands. Suppose she called the police? They'd be sure to start a search for him and all Tommasso's plans could be ruined. Stop it! he told himself sternly. There's nothing you can do, it's up to Tommasso now.

Restlessness got the better of him. Time to explore. Maybe he could find a book to read, take his mind off the dangers that could be happening elsewhere. The house was empty, Tommasso had told him that before leaving, apart from his burly friend from yesterday who had been left on guard. Tom opened the door quietly, tiptoeing to the landing and looking down.

At the Villa Magrino Alice stared round the empty kitchen, the lack of familiar cooking smells disconcerting her. The back door had been open so where was everybody? A horrifying thought struck her: had Luigi managed to solve the second riddle? Was that where they were now, collecting the treasure? Tom wouldn't be so mean, she decided hurriedly. He'd have included me, I know he would. Even if they didn't want me with them he'd have phoned to let me know what was happening.

Footsteps overhead reassured her and she made for the stairs to find Carmel descending. She smiled broadly at the sight of Alice.

'I didn't expect to see you this morning, not now Tom's gone away.'

'Gone away?' Alice looked at her blankly.

'Didn't he tell you? I was sure he would, with you two being such good friends.'

'Where's he gone?'

'I don't know, only that they'll be away for a few days. Luigi and Francesca decided it was time Tom saw some more of Malta before he returns to England.'

'Luigi and Francesca have gone as well?' Alice stared at her in disbelief. This was ridiculous. Tom wouldn't have gone without phoning her first and tomorrow was the start of the festa. Luigi and Francesca wouldn't miss the occasion for anything, it was the highlight of the village year. They'd also want their grandson to experience his first festa.

'When did they tell you they were going?'

'It must have been a sudden decision. They said nothing when Luis and I were leaving yesterday. They must have fixed their plans with Tom last night because this morning we found a note under our door asking me to clean as usual and for Luis to take care of the farm.'

'Didn't it give any indication of when they'd be back?'

Carmel shook her head. 'No, just as I told you, that they'd be away for a few days. If they ring, shall I tell Tom that you were here?'

Alice nodded, knowing somehow that they wouldn't ring. In a daze, she collected her bike and set off home.

The hallway was deserted but Tom could hear a television blaring out; a film by the sound of it, violent certainly judging by the shouts and screams. He hadn't been told to stay upstairs, not specifically, though he knew that was what Tommasso expected, and he didn't fancy another encounter with his captor. The left side of his head was still distinctly painful.

Cautiously, Tom began to descend the stairs, the carpet muffling his footsteps, until he reached the landing. The front door was bolted and presumably locked, not that he intended going anywhere. That was the problem, he had nowhere to go. He wished he knew where Tommasso had hidden Luigi and Francesca.

The back of the house was a huge kitchen. Plenty of food, Tom noted, though he'd never felt less hungry. Still, it was good to know he wouldn't starve.

Returning to the hallway he tried another door, finding himself in a bright lounge furnished simply but comfortably with easy chairs and a long sofa, liberally covered in vivid cushions. Bookshelves lined the walls. Between two chairs stood a low table, holding a single book: "The City of the Knights." Had Tommasso been doing his own research? Tom sank back against the cushions on the sofa, turning the pages, his interest quickening. Dad had told Tommasso that they should have paid more attention to Claudio Farrigiani. What better place to start than the Knights' own city? At least he was doing something useful.

'*Valletta,*' he read, '*was built as a fortress. The first buildings to be erected were the auberges; these were the headquarters of the different ethnic groups into which the Knights were divided.*'

He studied the imposing façade of the Auberge de Castile et Leon, once the home of the Spanish and Portuguese Knights, which now housed the offices of the Maltese Prime Minister. Turning the page, his heart leapt at the words: '*Auberge d'Italie, on the Triq-il-Merkanti.*' Claudio Farrigiani would have lived here once, that is if he had really been a Knight of St John. Alice's discovery that the Knight had been banished from the island the year before his birth made even that seem doubtful and they'd learned nothing at the Grand Master's Palace to suggest he could have been born somewhere else before returning to Malta.

Tom put the book aside, discouraged. This was futile, the whole thing could be nothing more than a joke cooked up by one of his father's ancestors. He could easily imagine someone seeing Claudio's name at the head of the memorial and thinking it would be funny to devise a riddle for his children. He probably never imagined it would continue to be handed down through the centuries, or that it would eventually lead to murder. His father had probably just embarked on another wild goose chase and the consequences this time could be even worse, especially if Alphonso found him. He couldn't bring himself to think about what would happen if his father ended up in Alphonso's clutches.

The voice from the girl on the plane surfaced in his mind. He'd almost forgotten about her with everything that had been happening. What had she said? Something about a vow of chastity that the Knights were supposed to have taken, though towards the end of their stay on Malta, things had become rather lax. He heard her words clearly: '*Many of the Knights fathered sons and daughters.*'

That's it, Tom thought in excitement. Perhaps it's true after all. The Claudio who's buried in the churchyard could be the son of the first Claudio Farrigiani, the Knight of St John. That would make the dates right and he would have been on Malta when Napoleon invaded and began ransacking Valletta. He could easily have rescued some treasure and because he couldn't hand it over to a son who hadn't yet been born, he hid it and left a set of clues. Tom wished he could tell Alice, realising how much he was missing her. She'd never lost faith in the treasure, despite his waverings. She'd cheered him up and kept him on track every time he became too depressed to continue. He might have doubts about her father, but Tom knew that Alice was completely loyal.

He pulled out the second riddle from where it was stuffed in his pocket.

Starless shadowy years.
Creation counts as reckoned.
Minutes enduring into days,
Everlasting seconds.

Something to do with time, Alice had guessed, perhaps a clock. Tom flushed as he remembered the scorn he'd poured on that idea when it did seem the logical answer. Yet the first riddle had been anything but obvious until they'd solved the connection between the Knights, John the Baptist, the Angel Gabriel and the dead tree. Should they be looking for another connection?

Tom rested his head on a cushion and shut his eyes, thinking furiously. Forget clocks for the moment. Think of time in general. Time. . . past, present and future. . . Old Father Time. . . pass the time. . . time after time. . . time flies. . . timetable. . . doing time. . . He shuddered, opening his eyes quickly. His father's spell in prison wasn't something he wished to remember. This was getting him nowhere. He scrutinised the riddle once more. What was all that about shadows and creation? More than ever he wished Alice was with him. Did starless mean a dark night or bright sunshine? Probably the sunshine if it caused shadows. As for the creation, well first there was light, that fit, and then. . . Tom's thoughts went blank.

Picking up the book he sought inspiration from the photo of the Auberge d'Italie. Below, was a picture of a small courtyard, a mass of wonderful green foliage flecked with a rainbow of flowers, and in the centre a. . .

Tom shot to his feet. He couldn't waste the day here now. Remembering a telephone he had spotted in the hall, he shut the book and crept quietly from the room.

'For goodness sake, Alice, find something to do.' Mrs Rogerson eyed her daughter with exasperation. 'I take it from the fact that you've returned so soon that you're minus Tom's company today?' Alice shrugged. 'You haven't quarrelled have you?'

'No, of course we haven't.'

'You didn't seem on very good terms during tea last night.'

'We were both tired, that's all.'

'So why haven't you arranged anything to do today? You haven't spent a day apart since you met. You're not still suffering from your vertigo sickness are you?'

Alice reddened, well aware that her mother knew she'd been lying. 'No I'm not and we haven't arranged anything because Tom wasn't at the Villa Magrino.'

'Then there's no excuse for moping about. I've got plenty of jobs you can be getting on with here. There's your bed to make for a start.'

Alice pulled a face at her mother's retreating back. Although she didn't expect it to ring, she found herself unable to move far from the telephone, caught in a state of helpless indecision. Had something happened to Tom or could the note possibly be genuine? Perhaps they'd decided that the mystery was something that must be tackled as a family and they didn't want any outside help. She couldn't really believe that, but she had to admit it was a possibility.

Her father entered the hallway. 'I hear you're not doing anything with Tom today?'

'Don't you start on me as well.'

'He wasn't at the Villa Magrino?' She shook her head. 'Where's he gone?'

'I haven't a clue. Despite what you and Mum seem to think he doesn't tell me every move he's going to make.'

'You know what I told you?'

'Yes,' she stormed, 'I know what you told me and I have been trying but it's not always easy.'

'I didn't think it would be, it's just that sometimes. . .'

'Spare me the lecture; I'm going to make my bed. Mum's orders.'

'After that, if you want a ride out I've got to go into Valletta. I know it won't be the same on your own, but it'd be better than sulking round here.'

'I'm not sulking.'

'You could have fooled me. Anyway, the offer's there if you fancy a change of scenery.'

'I'll probably go into the village in a little while, see if everything's ready for tomorrow.'

In her bedroom, Alice sat down on the unmade bed. Why had everything gone so suddenly wrong? What was she supposed to do now? Should she try and solve the second riddle on her own? It won't be the same without Tom, she thought despondently, and I haven't got a copy. All she could remember was something about minutes and seconds. Not much point checking the clocks in Valletta if she didn't know what she was looking for. Perhaps a ride to the village was a good idea. At least it would clear her head.

She had just collected her bike from the shed when she heard her mother's voice. Guiltily, she thought of the still unmade bed.

'Alice!'

Clambering on to her bike, she pedalled across the farmyard at full speed. The bed could wait for later.

'Alice! Telephone! It's Tom.'

She flung her bike to the ground, sprinting into the hallway and grabbing the receiver.

'Tom?' She looked pointedly at her mother who retreated into the kitchen, closing the door tactfully behind her. 'Tom, where are you? 'You'll have to speak up, I can hardly hear you.'

'I can't shout,' Tom whispered. 'You'll have to listen carefully.'

'What's happened? I went to the Villa Magrino this morning and Carmel said you'd all gone away. That wasn't true, was it? I didn't think anything would make Luigi and Francesca miss the festa and I knew you would have rung me if you could and. . .'

'Alice, just shut up and let me talk. I've only got a few minutes, he might come out at any time.'

'Who might?

'The man guarding me.' He filled her in quickly on the details of his capture. 'Tommasso has his own plans but he's not coming back until tonight and I've solved the second clue. At least, I think I have.'

'Where does it lead?' Alice's voice was shrill with excitement and Tom rubbed his ear, wincing. The last thing he wanted to do was explain over the phone. What if she told her father where she was going?

'Tom? Are you still there? What are you going to do?'

'Sneak out of here for a few hours and check it out myself. I'd like your company. Can you meet me in Valletta?'

'I can be there in about an hour, Dad's offered me a lift. How are you going to get out of the house?'

'Through the kitchen window. I've been exploring and I should be able to squeeze through. Look Alice, I must go. My guard's watching a film at the moment, but it could end at any time now and he might decide to keep me company. Go to the Upper Barrakka Gardens, where we sat the other day. I should be able to find my way there and I'll see you there in an hour.'

Putting down the phone, Alice dashed to the kitchen. 'Where's Dad? I need him.'

Her mother turned from the sink. 'He left for Valletta about five minutes ago.'

'But he promised me a lift.'

'Which you refused, I gather.'

'He couldn't even be bothered to see if I'd changed my mind?'

'Alice, what's got into you today?'

'You wouldn't understand.'

Slamming the door, she raced into the yard, her mother following.

'You can't bike to Valletta.'

'I can try,' Alice insisted stubbornly. 'It's important. Or maybe I can bike to Attard and get a bus to Valletta.'

'Alice, stop a minute and think this out sensibly.'

'I haven't time.'

'Tom's there I suppose?'

Alice ignored the comment. 'I don't know when I'll be back. Expect me when you see me.' She waved and set off at a perilous speed.

Tom negotiated the window with ease, shutting it carefully behind him. He didn't like to think what Tommasso would say if he could see him, yet felt better now that he was doing something positive. What would the second riddle reveal? Hopefully, not simply another clue. No, he thought excitedly, it's far more likely that Claudio Farrigiani hid the treasure in his own home. That could be what Dad meant when he told Tommasso they should have paid the Knight more attention.

Another thought struck him. Perhaps that was where his father had gone when he arrived on Malta. He could even be hiding there, Tom reasoned, if he knew Alphonso was searching for him. He wouldn't dare go to the Villa Magrino in case it put Luigi and Francesca in danger and that's probably why he couldn't risk coming to the airport to meet me. If I find him, Tom decided, I'll take him straight to Tommasso's.

He made his way through Floriana by the back streets, keeping an alert watch for signs of pursuit. It wouldn't do to be caught by Alphonso when he was so near the conclusion of the mystery. In his present mood, everyone he passed looked suspicious, which is stupid, he decided, because Carlo appeared pleasant and friendly at first sight. I really liked him. And then there was the girl on the plane, who was still a mystery, despite Alice's attempts to trace her. It's only in films that villains look like villains.

Reaching the Valletta Bus terminal, he mingled with the crowds, suddenly aware that he had no idea which way to go. There was not much point in arriving at the Upper Barrakka Gardens before Alice, so he might as well try and find the Triq-il-Merkanti, even if he only looked at the Auberge d'Italie from the outside.

Passing through the City Gates he halted in a busy square. People looked at him curiously as he hovered uncertainly, wondering if he dare draw attention to himself by asking directions. Was his fear written on his face? He felt that it must be, radiating out to touch all who passed.

Next to Tom, a young couple were just settling a toddler into a pushchair. Plucking up the courage to approach them Tom asked:

'Could you tell me how to get to the Triq-il-Merkanti?'

'Sorry.' The woman gave him an apologetic smile. 'It's our first day here. We're just going to look for a bookshop, see if we can buy a map. Are you on your own? You're welcome to join us.'

'Thanks, but I haven't got much time.'

Tom excused himself and edged away quickly. He should have realised they were tourists. What he needed was someone who lived here, though they weren't exactly easy to spot in the throng of sightseers. Perhaps it would be better to wait until Alice arrived, though that would mean wandering aimlessly around Valletta for forty minutes which was not exactly a sensible option. A lone man stood a few feet away, his back to Tom. It was worth a try. If he turns out to be another tourist, Tom decided, I'll go straight up to the gardens and wait there.

'Excuse me. . .'

The man turned and Tom found himself staring up into the astonished face of Alphonso's skeleton servant.

June 1798

They were sitting in the courtyard, soaking up the sun and taking a welcome break from the hopelessness of the task facing them. Even Gianni had lost heart when the gaps in the fortifications seemed to increase as fast as he plugged them up.

'I planted that rose bush.' Paolo pointed to a magnificent specimen with large, blood-red blooms. 'I'm glad we've stayed long enough for me to see it flower.'

Claudio's eyes were fixed on the sundial, a secret smile on his face, his thoughts spinning forward into the future.

Tullio scribbled furiously, gazing round at his friends as he wrote. Paolo leaned over his shoulder, reading, 'Claudio Farrigiani is the dreamer of the group.'

Tullio put a hand over the page. 'I've told you before, I'll let you read it when it's finished.'

'And when will that be?'

He shrugged. 'I have no control over the events to come.'

'And what will you do with it when it is finished?' Paolo persisted.

'It depends on what happens to us,' Tullio said. 'If Napoleon takes the island, which seems more and more likely, he'll probably banish us from Malta. If that happens, I've decided to hide my book in the auberge. Someone might find it one day and be interested in who we are and what's happening to us.'

At that moment, bells started to ring, increasing in volume until it seemed that every bell in Valletta was tolling out a warning. Racing from the courtyard, they joined the throng of Knights, militia and citizens of Valletta all racing to the fortifications facing the sea.

There on the horizon, coming steadily towards them, was a mighty fleet of ships.

14

Attard had never seemed so far. I do this journey every day to school, Alice thought, but today it seems twice as long. She tried to take her mind off the road ahead and the steadily increasing ache in her legs, by anticipating her arrival. What should she do with her bike? Would there be time to take it to her friend's house or should she risk chaining it to the bus shelter. Her chain was in her saddlebag. It should be safe enough. She deliberately turned her mind from what her father would say if it was stolen. She'd face that problem if it ever arose. At the moment her priority was to meet Tom in Valletta. Dad would understand.

With Attard in sight, she renewed her speed. Thank goodness the bus shelter was on this side of town. She could see it in the distance, a small rectangular box, with one woman waiting. She'd have preferred there to be a queue indicating that a bus was due. Pedalling up, the first thing she saw was a bus disappearing into the distance.

She turned to the sole occupant of the shelter. 'Where was that going?'

'Valletta.'

'Damn!'

The woman stared at her coldly. 'I gather you were hoping to catch it, but disappointment's no excuse for bad language.'

Alice flushed. 'I'm sorry, but it's really important I get to Valletta quickly. Do you know when the next bus is due?'

'There's a timetable on the side of the shelter.'

Alice hurried round, running her finger down the schedule. She hadn't realised there were so many buses to so many places. She was so tired that the numbers blurred in front of her eyes and she wondered if she was about to disgrace herself by crying.

The woman looked at her more sympathetically. 'There's no point in getting upset, that won't solve anything. There's nothing you can do about it but wait for the next bus. Move aside and let me look for you.' Alice stood back. 'Here we are, there's another bus in an hour and a half. Have you got somewhere you can go in Attard, you're going to have a long wait.'

'I can't possibly wait that long!'

'What else can you do?'

Alice picked up her bike, reluctantly. 'This might not get me there very quickly, but it'll be faster than waiting for the bus.'

Tom ran like a madman, not stopping to breathe or even to think; all he had on his mind was escape. Was he being followed? Where were the rest of Alphonso's men? He didn't dare look back. He was vaguely aware of the startled faces of tourists as he thundered past, expecting at any moment to feel a hand on his shoulder.

This part of Valletta was a warren of narrow streets and unexpectedly steep steps. Tom felt as though he were negotiating a fairground roller coaster. He was halfway up one particularly steep flight when a figure appeared at the top, a black silhouette against the sun, unrecognisable but Tom wasn't taking any chances. He scuttled back down, almost losing his footing, and veered left even deeper into the maze. If only he could breathe properly. Gasps wracked his chest, intensifying the stabbing stitch in his side. Had he run far enough? Slowing down, he listened fearfully over the wheezing of his breath: no running footsteps; no yells for him to stop. The only person in the street was an old lady walking her dog who stared at him curiously as they passed. Tom forced himself to walk on slowly, trying to regain control of his breathing, completely lost. The Auberge d'Italie would have to wait for later, after he'd met Alice, that was supposing he managed to find his way to the Upper Barrakka Gardens. At the moment, even that seemed unlikely. Perhaps he'd better send Alice straight home. He couldn't risk her falling into Alphonso's clutches. I've done it again, Tom thought miserably, dragging her into danger. She won't like it but I'll send her straight back to Haz Zahra. He was so deep in thought that he failed to register the man who had turned the corner and was racing towards him.

Alice pedalled furiously, knowing that time was against her. Would Tom wait? It was going to take far more than forty minutes to reach Valletta. Secretly, she was beginning to wonder whether she would make Valletta at all. Her legs had never ached so badly and sweat was streaming down her face to blend with the dust being churned up by her wheels. Putting up a hand to wipe her eyes she lost concentration for a second. Her front wheel hit a stone and she was catapulted over the handlebars to land in a sprawling heap on the road. Alice struggled to her feet, rubbing her knee. Her hand came away dotted with blood. Tears ran down her face, not from pain, that she could cope with, but from sheer frustration. She nearly howled like a kid at the sight of her front wheel, buckled out of all recognition. In temper, she picked up the bike and hurled it into the ditch. What now? She wasn't even halfway to Valletta. When she didn't arrive in the Upper Barrakka Gardens, Tom would go and seek out the second clue on his own. Why hadn't she insisted he tell her where it led when they were on the phone. At least she'd have known where to find him. I'm a failure, she told herself fiercely. I've ruined everything.

The hand on his shoulder came as no surprise. Squirming in its grasp, Tom eyed his captor. Why was it that all Alphonso's men, apart from Carlo and the Skeleton, appeared to be built on a gigantic scale? Well, he wouldn't be taken so easily this time. Wriggling and twisting, Tom struggled to break free. He wasn't going to let this happen.

'Stop that or you're going to get hurt.'

'Get off me!'

As he lashed out again, Tom fought for breath and began yelling at the top of his voice. 'Help! Somebody help me!'

'Shut up!'

The man's hand clamped round his mouth, cutting off Tom's air supply with a force that made his head spin. Remembering the last time this had happened, outside the Villa Magrino, Tom made a vain attempt to open his mouth to bite the offending hand, finding it an impossibility. The pressure was too strong. His lungs were beginning to burn painfully and he was horribly afraid he was going to lose consciousness. He felt himself being dragged along the street, half on, half off the ground. Tom let himself go limp, taking the man by surprise, and dropping like a sack to the floor.

'Get up!'

'Make me,' Tom gasped.

He was yanked so roughly to his feet that he lost his balance, sending them both staggering. They crashed to the floor together, Tom on top. Scrambling to his feet, he took the opportunity to break free, but he had only managed a few strides when a hand grasped the back of his T-shirt, slamming him into the wall. His forehead connected painfully with the hard stone and for a moment everything around him lost focus.

The man clasped him in a tight bear hug, squeezing the breath from his lungs, and taking out a mobile phone he uttered a few sentences in an unintelligible language.

'Now,' he said, replacing the phone, 'we wait.'

'I don't know who you think I am,' Tom protested, 'Or what you think I know, but I don't know anything.'

'We'll see about that.'

Tom was just gathering the strength for another struggle when a car screeched to a halt beside them. Reinforcements? Tom's heart sank. Why had he disobeyed Tommasso? I never learn, he thought desperately. I just stagger from one mistake to the next. I'm no help to Dad at all.

The driver's door opened and a man stepped out. A policeman. Tom couldn't believe his luck.

'What's going on here?' He stared suspiciously at them both.

His captor released Tom from the bear hug, still keeping a tight grip on his arm. 'Nothing for you to worry about. The boy ran away after a stupid argument with his father. We've been searching for him for days and he needs a little persuasion to return home.'

'I didn't,' Tom panted, trying to draw breath into his lungs. 'I've never seen him before in my life. I was just walking along here and he grabbed me.'

'Don't start lying again.' His captor gave him another shake before turning to the policeman. 'If you must know, he stole some money which is why he doesn't want to go back to face them. I'm a friend of the family and I promised his father that. . .'

'I haven't stolen anything,' Tom shouted. 'He attacked me and bashed my head against the wall. Look!'

The policeman eyed the graze on Tom's forehead. 'What's the boy's name?'

For the first time, his captor looked flustered.

'If you're a friend of the family you surely know his name?'

'Of course I know his name. He's Ben Hardy and his father is waiting anxiously for news of him. He's been very worried as you can imagine.'

'I've never heard of Ben Hardy!' Tom gasped. 'My name is. . .'

'Yes?' the policeman queried.

Tom was stumped. Neither Tom Newton or Tom Farrigiani seemed a wise thing to say in front of Alphonso's man. He thought of Alice. 'My name's Ewen,' he said faintly, and then more firmly, 'Ewen Rogerson.'

'I think we'd better sort this out at the station.'

As the policeman opened the back door of the car, Tom's captor gave him a final shake and sprinted down the street.

The policeman watched him go, a bemused smile on his face. 'Seems like you were telling the truth after all.'

Tom nodded. 'Thanks for helping me. I'm fine now.'

'I'd still like you to come to the station. You need to make a formal complaint.'

'I'd rather not. He didn't really hurt me.' Tom wondered how on earth he was going to get out of this situation. 'I'm meeting a friend and I don't want to be late.'

'I'm sure he'll wait. Or is it a she?' Tom flushed. 'It won't take long. We'll just take a statement and confirm your identity.'

Wonderful, Tom thought, as he stepped into the back of the police car. How on earth do I prove I'm Ewen Rogerson?

At the station, he was shown into a small interview room. A few minutes later, another man joined him, sitting down across the table and smiling pleasantly.

'I'm Sergeant Green. I've heard what happened, Ewen. It must have been frightening?'

'It was at the time but I'm fine now, honestly.'

'Your head not troubling you?'

'It's only a graze.'

'You've no idea why he attacked you?'

'No.' I'm getting as good at lying as Alice, Tom thought miserably.

'And you say your name's Ewen Rogerson?'

Tom crossed his fingers under the table and nodded.

'Address?'

'Trevisan. It's a farm at Haz Zahra.'

To Tom's horror, he took down a directory, proceeded to leaf through it, and then picked up the receiver of the telephone on the table.

'What are you doing?'

'I believe you, don't worry, but I have to check with your parents. Alright?'

'Fine.' Tom swallowed hard, praying that no one answered the phone. No such luck.

'Mrs Rogerson? This is Sergeant Green at Valletta Police Station. There's nothing to worry about but I've got Ewen with me. He's fine, it's just that he's had a nasty encounter with someone who was probably trying to rob him. I need you to confirm your son's identity. I'll let you speak to him.' He handed the phone to Tom, whispering, 'Want a drink?'

'Please.'

When he had gone, Tom put the receiver to his ear.

'I know that's not Ewen,' Mrs Rogerson was saying, 'because I can see him from where I'm standing. Who is that?'

'It's me, Tom.'

'Tom! What on earth are you doing in a police station pretending to be Ewen?'

'I can't explain now, it would take too long. Please, Mrs Rogerson, would you do me a very big favour and say I'm Ewen, or they'll keep me at the station and it's really important that I'm somewhere else.'

'Is Alice with you?'

'No, I'm meeting her in a few minutes.'

'I shouldn't bank on it. Look, Tom. . .'

'He's coming back,' Tom said desperately. 'Please say I'm Ewen. I'll explain everything when I see you, I promise.'

'Finished?' Sergeant Green took the receiver. 'Mrs Rogerson? Have you had a word with your son?' Tom held his breath, wishing he could hear her side of the conversation. 'Yes, I can do that with pleasure. Sorry to have troubled you.' He put down the phone. 'And sorry to you, too, Ewen. I didn't really doubt you but I have to follow regulations.'

Tom breathed a sigh of relief. 'That's alright, I understand. Can I go now?'

'Not quite yet. Apparently your father's in Valletta and your mother's arranging for him to pick you up.'

Tom didn't know what to believe. Had Dad been found? How did Mrs Rogerson know? And was Dad really on his way to collect him?

Next moment, his hopes were dashed. The sergeant picked up the phone and made another call. 'Jim? A Mr Rogerson will be arriving shortly, can you send him to Interview Room 3? Thanks.'

He picked up Tom's cup. 'Your mother says it won't take him long to get here.' He handed him a pen and a sheet of paper. 'Do you think you could fill in the time by writing a description of the man who attacked you?'

'Sure, no problem.'

Tom watched him depart with the cup and then leapt to his feet. Having gone through all this, there was no way he could cope with Mr Rogerson. Thank goodness the room was at ground level. Luckily for Tom, the window opened on to a deserted side street. To his right led back to the warren of narrow streets. To his left was a busy main road, but Tom did not like the sight of the man standing at the corner gazing down at him.

As nonchalantly as possible, Tom set off to his right. He'd gone a few metres when a second figure appeared, this time from the other direction. Veering sideways, Tom sprinted along a narrow, dirt track into a courtyard. Scrambling over a crumbling wall, he cast round wildly for any hiding place. An arched passageway between tall houses offered the only possibility of refuge, its blackness swallowing the daylight. From its safety Tom paused to listen, holding his breath as footsteps moved towards him, only to pause a few feet away. Don't come any further, he begged silently. Just go away. Leave me alone. He could almost sense someone standing there, waiting. Backing cautiously into the depths of the passage, he collided with a rubbish bin which wobbled precariously before the lid went crashing to the ground with a metallic clang. The light from the street was cut off completely as a dark shape moved towards him. Abandoning any attempt at stealth, Tom kicked the bin, its contents cascading over the cobbles. Turning, he fled through the darkness, hearing a muttered oath as his pursuer slithered his way over rotting food and cans. Suddenly, Tom emerged into the brightness of a crowded market square. He had never been so glad to see such a mass of people. Dodging and diving through the stalls, he crouched down and pretended to be studying a box of shoes. After staying low for as long as possible, he rose cautiously, looking around. No one seemed remotely interested in him. A nearby stand, covered in watches, made him aware of the time. Alice would be just arriving. Plucking up the courage to move, he sidled up to the watch seller.

'Could you tell me the way to the Upper Barrakka Gardens?'

He pointed across the square. 'There's a big map on the street over there, it'll be easier than trying to explain.'

Studying it carefully, Tom made the surprising discovery that he was actually standing on the Triq-il-Merkanti. He traced the route to the Upper Barrakka Gardens. Not far at all. For a moment he was tempted to make a detour via the Auberge d'Italie, but Alice would be waiting impatiently. They could come back here once he'd collected her. She deserved to be present when they discovered what the second riddle revealed.

Tom's legs were aching badly as he climbed the steep Triq Sant Orsola to the Upper Barrakka Gardens, though it wasn't the physical discomfort that troubled him but an internal pain caused by the realisation that violence was no longer something that happened to other people. Today it had happened to him and he knew he would never be the same person again. How dramatic that sounded. He needed Alice to help him get life back into perspective. He saw her immediately.

She was leaning against the rail, laughing merrily with the two people flanking her. To her left stood Carlo. To her right, the girl from the plane.

15

Blind panic took over. Tom made a dart for the exit only to find his way barred by another Goliath, a hulking specimen with a coarse swarthy complexion and thick-lipped mouth curving into a sneering smile. He reminded Tom of a story book pirate.

'If you ever want to see your father alive again, you'll come quietly.'

Tourists were milling past, laughing and chattering. For a moment Tom was almost tempted to appeal for help, realising to his dismay that he daren't take the risk. Seething with rage, he allowed himself to be led forward.

Outside the gardens a horse-drawn carriage was waiting. The man sat next to Tom, keeping a tight hold on his arm. Alice faced them, flanked once again by Carlo and the girl from the plane. The laughter had gone, to be replaced by an anxious frown.

She leaned forward, putting her hand on his arm. 'It's alright, Tom.'

He snatched his arm away, turning his head sideways and deliberately ignoring her. He couldn't believe how much it hurt that she'd betrayed him. It was a physical pain, lodged sharply below his ribs, crushing his spirit. A terrible sensation seemed to be rising from deep in his stomach, through his chest and into the back of his throat. He felt sick, tasting it vile and sour in his mouth. She and her father had been in league with Alphonso all the time. What a fool he'd been.

Alice sat back, gazing at Tom unhappily. Serves her right, he thought bitterly. All those offers of help were nothing but a pretence, a trap so I could lead them to Dad. Well, at least that's one thing I can't do, thank goodness, however much they question me.

Out of the corner of his eye he saw the unknown girl put a comforting arm round Alice's shoulder. That hurt as well. He'd liked both of them, showed what a poor judgement of women he had. It was laughable really. At least, it would be if it didn't mean that he'd messed things up for Dad and Tommasso. Why hadn't he just stayed in the house as he'd been told? It was his own fault he'd been caught, nobody else's. His decision. His stubbornness.

The girl kept up a flow of conversation, as though this were nothing more than a social outing. She'd been a good talker on the plane, he remembered. She'd fooled him completely. Why had she said she was Alice? That still made no sense. He knew he should try and find out who she really was but he couldn't bring himself to speak to her. He was hurting too badly.

'Have you been in one of these carriages yet, Tom? It's called a *karrozzin* ; they've been in use on Malta since 1856. Rather a splendid way of travelling, don't you think?' Tom stared straight ahead, his face expressionless. 'Many of the carriages are treasured possessions, passed down through the generations. This one has been in our family for as long as I can remember.' She smiled at him pleasantly. 'Have you managed to see much of Malta?'

He remained stubbornly silent, furious with himself that he still found her attractive; that inside he felt a deep urge to respond to her friendliness. What on earth was the matter with him?

'You really going to stick to your vow of silence?'

'With you I am, yes.'

After that there was no further talk until they drew up before an imposing three-story house in a quiet street.

'Take them upstairs,' the girl ordered. 'Tom's clearly not in a mood to be cooperative. Hopefully, he'll come to his senses before too long.

Perhaps Alice can convince him of our good intentions.'

They were hustled into a small sitting room and left alone. Tom rounded on Alice, the pain spurting from him in a stream of anger.

'Go on, laugh! Don't mind me. Laugh all you want. You must think I'm a complete fool.'

She took a step back from the ferocity of his outburst. 'Tom, I know how it looks but if you'd just give me time to explain.'

'I'm sure you've got a really good explanation. Dream it up with your friends, did you? But then you're good at lying, we both know that. I just didn't realise you were lying to me. I thought you were the one person I could trust. You made a good job of pretending not to know the girl on the plane. You had me fooled completely. All those phone calls you supposedly made looking for another Alice Rogerson when you knew who she was all the time. And that acting at the tower yesterday; I didn't recognise it was for my benefit, not Carlo's.'

'Tom, I don't know what you're talking about.'

'Of course you'd say that. You're as bad as your father. You're two-faced crooks, both of you.'

Alice glared at him angrily. 'What's my father got to do with this?'

'Forget it.' Tom turned away, too miserable to sustain his anger. 'I wish I'd never met any of you. I wish I'd never set foot on Malta.'

'No!' Alice marched around to face him. 'You can't leave it like that. My father's got nothing to do with any of this.'

Tom shrugged. 'Have it your own way. Only don't expect me to believe you.'

'As for the girl on the plane,' Alice continued furiously. 'If that was her then she's Adriane Lorenzo, Tommasso's sister. You told me on the phone that he was on our side. I met her for the first time this morning when I was cycling to Valletta.'

'I thought you were coming in the car with your father? Or was that another of your lies?'

'No, it wasn't. By the time I got off the telephone he'd left. I knew you'd be worried if I didn't turn up so I biked to Attard but the bus had just left so I tried to bike here and had an accident.'

Tom looked at her closely for the first time. Her left knee was swollen and bruised, streaks of dried blood patterning her shin. There was a graze on her cheekbone and her clothes were covered with fine, grey dust. 'What happened?' he asked more gently.

'I hit a stone and ended flat on my face in the road. I'm fine, don't fuss, which is more than can be said for my bike.' She gave a shaky laugh. 'I tossed it into a ditch and I was walking to Valletta when this car stopped. Adriane was driving and she offered me a lift. Carlo was with her. I didn't know who she was, not at first, and I was petrified when I saw Carlo, but then she told me she was Tommasso's sister and I thought that was alright because you said Tommasso was trying to find your father. That's why I told her where I was meeting you. I certainly never realised she was the girl on the plane.'

'She just happened to be passing?' Tom raised his eyebrows in disbelief. 'I thought we didn't believe in coincidences?'

'She explained that. She said that she'd been looking for us because Tommasso has found your father. That's what he was trying to do, wasn't it? I thought you'd like to know straight away.'

Tom's spirits soared, though suspicion still lingered. 'And how did she explain away Carlo?'

'That's easy, he wasn't at Buskett Gardens to spy on us, as we thought, but to protect us.'

It made sense, Tom realised, especially if he'd been sent by Alice's father. He should have known that Mr Rogerson would be allied with Tommasso rather than with Alphonso. 'I'm sorry,' he said, 'I shouldn't have jumped to conclusions. These days I suspect everybody.'

Alice didn't look mollified. 'You've still got to explain what you meant about my father. Don't think you can say something like that and expect me to ignore it. What on earth made you suspect him?'

Tom flushed. 'It's nothing, I realise that now. When we got back to your place yesterday I was putting my rucksack in the cloakroom and your father was outside talking to Carlo.'

'So what? He was probably being polite, he's like that.'

'I know, it's just that they seemed very friendly, they were laughing together as though they were sharing a good joke, but when we went out to see Pietro off he introduced Carlo to your father and they both acted as if it was the first time they'd met. You saw them yourself. I still think that's strange.'

Her brow furrowed, though whether in irritation or surprise Tom couldn't tell. 'Not enough to suspect him, though.'

'Probably not, but then I got to wondering how Pietro found us at Busskett Gardens. The only ones who knew where we'd be were you, me, Pietro and your father.'

Alice frowned. 'You think Dad rang Carlo and told him?'

'It's the logical answer,' Tom said reluctantly. 'It wasn't me or you and Pietro wasn't out of our sight before Carlo arrived.'

Alice's face cleared. 'Even if he did,' she acknowledged, 'Carlo's on our side. We were wrong about him. Carlo's a friend of Tommasso, Adriane said so.'

'I hope that's true.' A new suspicion had formed in Tom's mind. 'Don't forget we saw him first in the church with Alphonso's servant, when they were hunting us. He can't be working for both sides, can he? And if Adriane is Tommasso's sister, then she's also Alphonso's.'

Alice went white. 'I'd forgotten that. The episode in the church feels such a long time ago and Adriane seemed so likeable that I believed her straightaway.'

'Don't worry,' Tom said, 'she fooled me just as easily. I don't suppose she explained that little charade on the plane when she pretended to be you? If she's Adriane Lorenzo, why did she pass herself off as Alice Rogerson?'

'I'd forgotten that, as well. Have I ruined everything?' Alice sank down on the couch.

Tom shrugged. The events of the last week had succeeded in making him mistrust everything and everyone. He wondered if he would recognise the truth if it was staring him in the face. 'No doubt we'll find out all too soon.'

As if on cue the door opened and into the room strode the first man they had met at the Casa Peralta, the one who'd pretended to be Tommasso, the one who'd turned out to be his brother Alphonso, who Tom now knew had staged the break-in at the library. He was smiling but the smile did not extend to his eyes. They were cold and grey like small hard pebbles.

'So we meet again.'

There was no threat in the tone but Tom's anger rose. After all he'd gone through today, this was the last straw. 'Don't waste your time pretending to be a friend.'

Alphonso laughed. 'Is there any point in my offering refreshments? You spurned them last time, if I remember correctly. Ran away after making such nuisances of yourselves to get in. Very rude I thought. I'm afraid you won't be able to make such a quick exit this time.'

'We don't want anything from you.' Even to his own ears, Tom's bravado sounded hollow and he could hear his voice shaking.

'No?' Alphonso settled himself comfortably in a chair, regarding them with amusement. 'That surprises me. Sure you don't want to hear about your father?'

The question caught Tom off-guard. Had Tommasso failed? Was

his father now in Alphonso's clutches?

'How about some lemonade? You look as though you need something to cool you down and then perhaps we can discuss this in a sensible manner.'

Tom's bitterness erupted. 'I've got nothing to discuss with you. Tommasso told me the truth so don't think you can fool us any more. You broke into the Bibliotheca, you and your friends, stole the book and killed the security guard. Then you let Dad take the blame. I can never forgive you for that.'

Alphonso seemed unmoved by the accusation, as though he found it highly amusing. 'I can see my brother's been up to his tricks again.' He leaned forward. 'Why don't you sit down?'

'I'll stand.' Tom's legs were aching badly but he wasn't about to give Alphonso the satisfaction of seeing his weakness.

'Tom.' Alice patted the couch at her side. He sat down, taking her hand and glaring at Alphonso.

'I suppose you're going to pretend that Tommasso told me a pack of lies? Well, you can save your breath.'

'I'm sure he didn't.' Alphonso's mouth curled in scorn. 'That's not my brother's way. He's stupid, yes, always has been, but with a certain cunning. My guess would be that he's rather bent the truth.'

Tom and Alice, in unspoken agreement, remained mute.

Alphonso gazed at them in exasperation. 'If you had only stayed at the Casa Peralta last Monday there wouldn't have been any of these complications. It could all have been sorted out there and then. Why did you make all that fuss at the gate and then run away?'

'We asked to see Tommasso. Why did you pretend to be him?'

'I didn't pretend. Did you hear me say I was Tommasso? I'd have introduced myself properly if you'd given me the chance, but you didn't. Your fault, not mine. And I'd be interested to hear how you learned I wasn't Tommasso.'

They stared at him sullenly.

'We'll come back to that later. Look, it's about time you started using your brains. Think about this for a start. Who was the one obsessed by the Farrigiani treasure? Was it me? What's the matter, are you afraid to answer the question?'

'Tommasso said. . .'

'Tommasso said . . .!' Alphonso mimicked. 'You sound like a parrot. Forget Tommasso for the moment and think it out for yourselves. Who spent their whole childhood in a quest for the treasure?'

'My Dad,' Tom said reluctantly, 'and Tommasso.'

'Exactly. Your father was fixated by the idea and he affected Tommasso with his enthusiasm. Nobody minded when they were boys but later it got so ridiculous that Luigi and my father joined forces and put a ban on any further investigating. That would have been enough for Tommasso, he's always been scared of my father. Trouble was, Beppe was by far the stronger character. He could twist Tommasso round his little finger. For a time they continued in secret and there was an almighty row when Luigi discovered what they were up to. Beppe left home and went to live with Ricardo. You see, he wasn't prepared to give up his dream. Does that make sense so far?'

It did, Tom thought with dismay, though Alphonso made it sound far more damaging to his father than Tommasso's version. 'Nothing wrong with pursuing a dream,' he muttered.

'Not until it gets out of hand.' Alphonso's voice was cold. 'As it did on the night they broke into the Bibliotheca.'

'No they didn't! That was you and your friends,' Tom growled. 'Don't try and wriggle out of it. My Dad isn't a thief or a murderer.'

'Think straight for once. I wasn't interested in the Farrigiani treasure. Not then, not now. Why would I have wanted the book? The robbery was organised by your precious father and my very stupid brother tagged along, as he'd always done ever since they were little kids. All they intended was to have a look at the book. They weren't even going to steal it. Trouble is, it went disastrously wrong. While Beppe was collecting the book a security guard discovered them. Tommasso panicked and hit him. He didn't mean to kill him but the guard caught his head on the edge of a step.'

'I don't believe you.' If Alice hadn't kept a tight grip on his arm Tom would have leapt at Alphonso. 'Tommasso was Dad's best friend. There's no way he'd have let him take the blame and go to prison for a murder he'd committed himself.'

'Then you don't know my brother. He's always been a weak character; he'd have been terrified my father would discover the truth. And if you think about it honestly then your Dad was equally guilty. The idea was his and he knew Tommasso well enough to realise he'd lose his nerve in a crisis.'

'If that's true, then surely the police suspected Tommasso along with Dad?'

'They were both questioned and naturally they both denied all knowledge of the incident, but Tommasso had our father's name behind him. That counts for a lot here on Malta, as Alice can tell you. It's the reason that Beppe was the only one arrested. In one way you should be proud of your father. Even when he was sentenced, he never implicated Tommasso. That takes some courage.'

Tom was lost for words. The more he found out, the less he understood.

'Did you know about this at the time?' Alice asked.

'I suspected what had happened. I knew Tommasso would never have let Beppe go to the Bibliotheca alone, yet I daren't say anything that would lead the authorities to my brother.'

'So how did you find out?' she demanded.

'After Beppe was sentenced, Tommasso sneaked the book from the Villa Magrino and brought it to the Casa Peralta. Indecisive as always, he hesitated about how to destroy it, finally deciding to burn it on a bonfire being held for my little sister's birthday. Foolishly, he put it with the rest of the rubbish to be burned, not knowing that my father had decided to supervise the bonfire personally. He recognised the book and tackled Tommasso. You know the rest. My father could not bring shame on our family name but he worked night and day to get Beppe acquitted.'

Tom was at a loss. He preferred Tommasso's version yet Alphonso's had a ring of truth. Except that he didn't like Alphonso. There was something too cold, too devious and arrogant about him.

Alice was beginning to recover her wits. 'Why are you searching for Tom's father now? And why were you hunting me and Tom?'

'Who says I was?'

'We saw your men at the church in Haz Zahra. They were talking about reporting back to you.'

'Fair enough. I had no choice. I thought you might lead me to Giuseppe. When he was released and left Malta we thought the affair was at an end, but over twenty years later this whole sorry mess has blown up in our faces.'

'How?' Alice insisted.

'I know how,' Tom told her. 'Tommasso found the book hidden on a ledge inside the chimney.'

'Almost true,' Alphonso admitted, 'except that I was the one to make the discovery.'

'While you were hiding presents for your son's birthday, I suppose?' Tom asked sarcastically.

Alphonso laughed. 'For my daughter's birthday, actually. Can you see how Tommasso has woven a fabrication around the truth? He's cleverer than I suspected. You believed him, of course.'

'I don't know which of you to believe,' Tom said helplessly. 'Why wasn't the book destroyed?'

'At the time, my father swore he had destroyed it. When I presented him with the evidence he admitted he couldn't bring himself to destroy a national treasure. He thought we were quite safe, our secret well and truly buried. He told me to replace the book and forget it ever existed. Which I did.'

'You didn't send it to my father?'

'Why would I do that? Even if I'd known where to send it, the last thing I wanted was to stir up old memories.'

Maybe Tommasso had sent it after all, Tom thought. The rest of his story could be true. He was quickly disillusioned.

'A few months ago,' Alphonso continued, 'a friend at the airport told me he had seen Giuseppe Farrigiani arrive on Malta. I tackled Tommasso but he knew nothing about it.' He stared at Tom. 'I can see that you think Tommasso was lying to me.'

Tom didn't know what he was thinking. Tommasso hadn't mentioned anything about his father coming to Malta a few months ago. He was beginning to panic that Tommasso had been lying to him again, or only telling him part of the truth. Not that he was about to admit that to Alphonso. The less Alphonso knew the better until he had time to work out which brother to trust. Confusingly, his head told him Alphonso; his heart insisted on Tommasso.

Alphonso grinned. 'I assure you I can tell when my brother is speaking the truth. The news worried him far more than it worried me. Remember that after Beppe's acquittal the murder of the security guard is an unsolved crime. Tommasso panicked even more when we discovered the book was missing.'

'Who took it?' Tom asked.

'Now that's where I thought you might be able to help us. I've no idea, neither has Tommasso. When nothing happened I relaxed, not realising that Tommasso had set about tracing Giuseppe. A week ago one of my servants relayed the news that he'd heard my brother on the phone, reporting to persons unknown that your father was arriving on Malta the following day. He was giving orders for him to be dealt with. I'll leave you to imagine how.'

Tom stared at him, horrified.

'I felt the same reaction as you, though to be honest I wasn't surprised. My brother is a murderer after all, even if he claims it was an accident. What was I to do? I couldn't let him be so irresponsible for a second time; it would destroy our family. That's why I arranged to have Beppe met at the airport. As you know, he failed to turn up. It's why I've been searching for him ever since, to protect him from my brother. Make no mistake, I don't particularly like your father, I never did. I always thought he had far too much influence over my brother, but I cannot allow Tommasso to place the family in jeopardy.'

'What will you do if you find him?'

'Ask why he has returned. See if he is any threat to my family. Advise him to return to England by the first available plane, taking you with him. I don't intend to harm him, if that's what's bothering you. Don't you think it's about time you cooperated?'

'I can't help you,' Tom said, 'even if I wanted to. I haven't seen my father for years.'

'What about the Farrigiani treasure? I know you've been following the clues.' Alphonso grinned suddenly. 'Thanks for sending us on a wild goose chase. Two of my men spent the morning searching every crevice of the Blue Grotto. Carlo suspected you were playing games but we couldn't take a chance.'

'I thought you weren't interested in the treasure,' Tom retorted.

'Not then, not now,' Alice added. 'That's what you said.'

'I'm not, though presumably your father still is. It's one of the ways we've been trying to track his whereabouts. If he finds the treasure he's welcome to it, as long as he leaves Malta.' He sat silent for a moment, staring into space. 'What to do with you two is a problem. I'd hate my brother to get his hands on you. I think you'd better stay here for now.'

'As prisoners?' Tom glared. 'You're as bad as your brother. There's nothing to choose between either of you.'

'It'll cause you more problems if you keep us here,' Alice said. 'My parents will kick up a fuss when we don't return.'

'We'll think up a plausible story for them, don't worry.' Alphonso rose. 'I'm afraid that I'm going to have to lock you in but you'll be comfortable enough. I'll even send you some refreshments. Whether you choose to partake of them is your choice.'

He left them sitting there. The door closed behind him and they heard the key turning in the lock.

16

For several minutes it was as though both Tom and Alice had been gagged. The silence hung in the room; a physical presence weighing down on them. Tom felt instinctively that it was impossible to judge between Alphonso's and Tommasso's versions of what had happened. There were too many loose ends, too many inconsistencies for him to ferret out the truth. Even considering that his father might be guilty seemed a sacrilege, yet he couldn't get away from the fact that his Dad had been the one obsessed by the treasure. Everyone agreed on that. Tom's head was spinning, his mind racing round in circles, frustrated that the pieces of the puzzle refused to slot into place. It could be because there were important pieces still missing, he decided. Pieces that could only be explained by his father. The one thing he was sure of was that he hadn't yet heard anything even approaching the truth.

Alice looked at him miserably. 'It's awful isn't it, not knowing who can be trusted? Are you still wondering about my Dad?'

Tom almost smiled. 'Actually, I was wondering about mine. I don't know him very well, but. . .' he shrugged helplessly. 'I know Alphonso made it sound believable but when it comes down to it, I can't bring myself to suspect him.'

'Then you should know how I feel. And I do know my Dad. He's completely honest; too honest for comfort, sometimes. There's no way he can be in league with Alphonso and Carlo.'

'So who told Carlo we were at the Busskett Gardens yesterday? Someone must have rung him with the information. It can't have been a coincidence that he just happened to be there.'

'I don't know, but whoever it was, it wasn't Dad.'

'What will he do when you don't turn up tonight?'

'Depends on what story Alphonso cooks up.' Alice recalled the moment she'd arrived at the Villa Magrino that morning to find Tom missing. 'Tommasso was clever. He slipped a note under Carmel's door, supposedly from Francesca, saying you'd all be away for a few days. Carmel had no suspicions. I didn't believe a word of it because I knew what'd been happening.' Her lip trembled. 'They're all clever in the Lorenzo family and they're all good liars. I know I've done quite a bit of lying recently but I'm not proud of that. Adriane fooled me completely. I was so happy when she said they'd found your father that I didn't think it out properly. I should have remembered seeing Carlo in church. I'm sorry, this is all my fault. We wouldn't be Alphonso's prisoners if I hadn't messed everything up.'

'You couldn't help it. We're no match for either Tommasso or Alphonso and we still don't know how Adriane fits into the picture. Neither of them implicated her in the robbery.'

'She was only nine at the time, I don't see how she could have had anything to do with it. Presumably she's helping Alphonso because he's trying to safeguard the family honour.'

'Or he says he is.' Tom stood up restlessly. 'We can't sit here doing nothing. At least at Tommasso's I had the run of the house.'

'Any suggestions?' Alice wasn't surprised at receiving no response. She watched Tom prowl around the room like a caged animal. 'What about the second clue? You said you'd solved the riddle.'

'I'd almost forgotten about that.' Tom sank down beside her on the couch. 'In Tommasso's house there was a book called the *City of the Knights*. I wasn't looking for anything in particular, just trying to pass the time, when I came across some photos of the Auberge d'Italie, where Claudio Farrigiani must have lived.'

'If he was a Knight,' Alice said sceptically. 'We're not even sure of that anymore. I don't see how he could possibly have been one which means this whole mess started out with a lie.'

'Not necessarily, I think I've solved this as well as the riddle, not that it's much help while we're stuck in here. The girl on the plane – I suppose I've got to call her Adriane now – and we're still no wiser why she said she was you. . .'

'Forget that for now,' Alice urged, 'What about Claudio Farrigiani and the second part of the riddle?'

'Adriane told me that by the end of their time on the island the Knights had become very lax about their vows of chastity. When they were banished from the island many of them left behind sons and daughters.'

'So that you think the Claudio Farrigiani who's buried in the churchyard at Haz Zahra must be the son of our Knight?'

'Makes sense,' Tom admitted. 'And that means the original Claudio would have been on the island when Napoleon invaded. He could easily have rescued some treasure, as Dad believed. If he'd become involved with a local girl and she'd been pregnant, she'd have given their son his father's name, and the clue to the treasure his father had left him. I bet Claudio never imagined it would remain unsolved for so long.'

'The treasure must have been something very precious for him to go to so much trouble.' Alice thought for a moment. 'Are we still on the track of a statue?'

'Unless you've any other ideas.'

She shook her head. 'A statue, a painting, it could be either. I can't think beyond the Angel Gabriel and that must be right because of the box you found at the Gabriel Tower. Well, put me out of my misery, where does the second clue lead?'

'Remember you thought it was something to do with time.' Tom pulled the riddle from his pocket and handed it to her. 'I'm sorry I was so nasty about your idea of the Pinto clock.'

'I wasn't right, I gather?'

'No, but that doesn't excuse me being so mean.'

She studied the riddle carefully. 'It was the years and days and minutes and seconds I was going by. That's why I thought of a clock. Was that part right?'

'In a way. Keep that in mind and look at the first two lines. When you add shadows and creation it becomes clear.'

Alice looked puzzled. 'I must be very dim but nothing's clear to me.'

'It's okay' Tom said kindly. 'You haven't seen the photograph. At the Auberge d'Italie there's a courtyard, surrounded by a beautiful garden...'

'Creation,' Alice said softly. 'The Garden of Eden.'

Tom nodded. 'That's what I thought, and in the centre of the courtyard is a sundial. How about that for time, shadows and creation? All the days and minutes and seconds calculated by the shadow of the sun.'

'Where's the Auberge d'Italie?' Alice asked excitedly.

'On the Triq-il-Merkanti, and I even know where that is, which isn't much use to us at the moment. We've got to find a way out of here.'

He began to prowl the room once more, pausing by the window. He'd had some luck with windows twice today already. Grasping the bottom catches he pushed upwards, stepping back startled as it slid open.

'We came up two flights of stairs,' Alice reminded him. 'That's not going to do us much good unless flying's on your list of tricks.' She jumped to her feet at the gloating triumph in Tom's eyes. 'What is it?'

'A tree. Right by the window. And climbable.'

Joining him, Alice viewed it with horror. 'You must be joking. Not by me, it's not. Tom, be sensible, you'll break your neck if you try and get down there and then you'll be no help to your father.'

'I'm no help to Dad as Alphonso's prisoner. I need to get back to Tommasso's to warn him and ask him to check out the Auberge d'Italie. If Dad solved the riddle, as Tommasso said, he might be hiding there.'

'Are you sure you can trust Tommasso?'

'That's a risk I'll have to take.' He turned back to the window. 'I've always been good at climbing trees. Come on, Alice, won't you give it a go? I'll help you.'

'No, sorry, there's no way I'd make it down there in one piece, but don't let me spoil your fun. And it's hardly right next to the window. The tree's several metres away so how on earth are you going to reach it?'

'Jump!'

Alice shuddered. 'You must be mad.'

'I should be able to catch hold of that branch and then it's plain sailing.'

'What if it won't hold your weight?'

'It should do, it looks sturdy enough. The thing is, I don't like leaving you here.'

'I'll be fine,' Alice said sturdily, pushing away the frightening thought of facing Alphonso's wrath alone. 'It's not me who's important to him, it's you he wants. If he ever finds your father, he'll be able to blackmail him through you. It's best if you go and get help, though I don't know who you'll turn to. I have my doubts about both Tommasso and Alphonso and we've no idea where Luigi and Francesca are. I'd suggest my Dad but I know you won't agree to that. Have we anyone left we can trust completely?'

'Perhaps I'll be able to get back in the house and let you out.'

'If you can I'd prefer that, just don't risk being caught.' Noting Tom's indecision she feigned a smile. 'If you're going you'd better hurry, don't forget those refreshments Alphonso promised us. He could be back at any moment.'

'Sure you'll be alright?'

'I've said so, haven't I?' She tried another smile. 'Don't worry, I'll eat your share for you. Go on, I'll shut the window after you, keep them guessing about your disappearing act.'

Third time lucky, Tom thought, perching on the sill. It was only a couple of hours ago since he'd negotiated Tommasso's kitchen window, and then there had been his exit from the police station, though they had both had the advantage of being at ground level. Was he being completely reckless? Time to find out.

After a moment's hesitation, Tom launched himself through the air, catching the branch with both hands. It creaked loudly but held firm. Kicking wildly with his legs, he found it much harder than he'd imagined making contact with the main body of the tree. His shoulders were already being wrenched from their sockets. Gasping for breath, he finally hauled himself into a cleft between two boughs, peering up through the leaves at Alice's white face above. He gave her a thumbs-up sign and she waved back, shutting the window.

Inch by inch Tom lowered himself downwards, every muscle aching with the effort; twigs like bony, malevolent hands scratched at his face and his hair and his clothes. At last he reached the bottom branch and peered down. It was a long way to the ground, much further than it had looked from the window. He couldn't risk a sprained ankle.

Tom rested for a moment before swinging down to hang by his

arms. Bend your knees as you land, he reminded himself. Taking a deep breath, he let go.

As he hurtled downwards, strong hands clasped him by the waist, holding him suspended in mid-air for a second before setting him on the ground.

Alice sank back into the couch as the door opened. She'd witnessed Tom's fiasco from the window, unable to warn him. She dreaded to think what kind of a mood he was going to be in now. He was ushered into the room by the hulking pirate, his face creased by a broad grin.

'Returning your friend,' he announced. 'I'll be in the garden if he fancies another try.'

Tom scowled blackly, making the man grin even more. 'Maybe see you, then.' He backed out and they heard the ominous turning of the key in the lock.

Alice wisely held her tongue as Tom plumped down in a chair and shut his eyes.

'Tom!' He felt a hand on his arm and his eyes shot open. How on earth had he managed to fall asleep? He looked across at Alice, who gestured at the doorway. 'I heard the key turn in the lock,' she whispered.

It opened slowly and Adriane entered, balancing a tray. 'Refreshments,' she announced brightly, setting them down on a table. 'I thought Tom might need some. I hear he fancied a little exercise.'

'You don't need to jeer,' Alice snapped. 'There's nothing to be proud of in the way you fooled me. At least, Tom and I aren't liars.' She flushed suddenly. 'Not unless there's a very good reason.'

'That's not the only lie she's told.' Tom found that anger was a powerful tool, his exhaustion vanishing miraculously as he faced her. 'What was all that pantomime on the plane? Why did you pretend to make friends with me and say you were Alice Rogerson?'

She gazed at him pityingly. 'Now you really are losing the plot. Been dreaming, have you? It's time to wake up.'

'Don't try and bluff your way out of it. You were on the plane from Gatwick to Malta. You know you were. You sat next to me and told me your name was Alice Rogerson. That you had a brother called Ewen.'

'I haven't left Malta for months. Check with my brother if you like. My brother Alphonso; not Ewen, I'm afraid.'

'Alphonso!' Tom sneered. 'That's a laugh. I'm supposed to take the word of a liar and a murderer? You're all the same, you and Alphonso and Tommasso. I don't think any of you are capable of even recognising the truth.'

Adriane stepped forward. 'You,' she said icily, 'are a stupid little boy. A stupid, very scruffy little boy. Have you seen yourself recently? You look like a scarecrow. I think you've brought half the tree inside with you. Believe me, if I ever had the misfortune to be placed next to you on a plane, I'd change seats hurriedly. Let's face it, even your own father has disowned you.'

She stormed out, slamming the door.

Tom was shaken by a flood of rage so intense that he had to dig his nails into his palms to control it. They were taking him for a ride, all of them, and he was powerless to stop them. He stared straight ahead, every muscle tense and rigid.

'Tom!'

He became aware of Alice shaking his arm. 'She's lying,' he gulped. 'She was on the plane. There's no way I could have imagined it.'

'Of course she was on the plane, but that's not important now. You made her so mad that I think she's forgotten to lock the door. I certainly didn't hear the key turn.'

Tom forced himself to relax, feeling the tension ease from his shoulders as he watched Alice walk slowly to the door. She put a tentative hand on the knob, turning gently. The door opened. She peered out before shutting it quickly and turning to Tom. 'There's no one outside. Dare we risk a look around?'

'We haven't anything to lose. We'll be no worse off if we're caught again, they'll just bring us back in here.'

Opening the door slightly, they listened carefully before edging their way out on to a wide landing. Looking over the banister, there was a clear view to the deserted hallway.

His heart racing, Tom signalled for Alice to follow him. They had just reached the top of the stairs when raised voices were followed by a loud slam.

'In here, quick.' Alice pushed open the door behind her and they tumbled into a small bedroom.

'Could you tell who it was?' Tom gasped.

She shook her head. 'No, but whoever it was they were clearly angry.'

Tom opened the door a fraction, listening closely. 'They don't seem to be around now. The slam sounded like the front door. I wish we knew if they'd gone out or come in. Shall we give them a couple of minutes and try again?'

There was no reply. Tom glanced round, and was alarmed by Alice's stunned expression. She was staring at him as though she'd seen a ghost. 'Alice, what is it? What's the matter?

'Look!' She pointed incredulously at a large photograph hanging on the wall.

Tom closed the door and moved to gaze up in utter disbelief at an image of himself, hair neatly brushed and a fixed smile on his face. He stared at it bleakly, his own eyes staring back at him from inside the photo frame.

'I know exactly when it was taken,' he said shakily. 'It was just before my sixteenth birthday. Every year since the divorce, Mum took me along to a studio in Manchester and got a photo done to send to Dad. How on earth did it end up here in Alphonso's house? You heard him say he'd never liked Dad, so why hang my picture on his wall?'

'I've given up expecting to understand anything.' Alice shivered. 'Let's get out of here, Tom, I hate this house. I want to go home.'

They reached the hallway without further trouble, only to find the front door heavily bolted.

'That means someone's still here,' Alice whispered. 'Hurry up, Tom.'

He drew back the bolts with shaking fingers, wincing at the harsh grating squeaks. Surely the noise could be heard all over the house? He expected Alphonso or Adriane to appear at any moment. Seizing the handle, he tugged sharply. The door was well and truly locked. Resting his head against the wood, exhaustion overwhelmed him, which was why he failed to take note of the loud click by his left ear, realising too late that the door had been unlocked from outside. It opened quickly, sending him lurching against the wall. A dark haired man stepped inside, locking the door behind him. He was somehow familiar, though Tom was convinced they'd never met.

Alice was standing frozen in the middle of the hallway, making no effort to hide. To Tom's horror she looked incredulously at the stranger.

'Ricardo! Ricardo, what are you doing here?'

June 1789

'Look, they're leaving!' Paolo pointed with delight at the ships that were turning away from Valletta. For a moment, for the briefest of moments, Claudio Farrigiani believed in his miracle.

'No, they're not.' An older Spaniard at their side dashed his hopes as he said, 'I should think they've decided that they cannot take Valletta from the sea. My guess is that they'll split up, there's enough of them, and take us from other angles.'

Even as he spoke, a flotilla of sails turned to the north-east, another moving away southwards.

Gianni's eyes followed the latter group. 'You know what that means? They'll probably land at Marsamuscatto or one of the other bays and march inland, which means that they'll hit us at Floriana.' He turned away abruptly. 'I'm going to round up my men.'

Although he was terrified of what was to come, Claudio Farrigiani almost wished that the French would hurry and put in an appearance. This waiting was nerve-wracking and he could feel his hands trembling as they rested on the stone walls of the fortifications. His rifle and sword felt like toy weapons in the face of what he knew the French would throw against them. News was filtering through, none of it good. The sky was red above the Island of Gozo, where fighting had already broken out. A few minutes ago, a scout had arrived to announce that the French had landed at St Julien's Bay and were already in command of Fort Riscoli. As for those that had sailed to the south, they were now marching steadily towards

Floriana. They would pass Haz Zahra and Claudio prayed that Maria and her parents were safely within the walls of her church. They were probably safer than the men around him. Paolo was positioned by one of the canons. Tullio had taken the other. Horses were tethered at posts in readiness for action. Claudio could see that Gianni had done his best: the few Knights with them were scattered between the ranks of the Maltese militia whose nerves were already frayed by the long wait. The heat was damp and stifling, pressing down on them and making it difficult to draw breath. Dark clouds were banked on the horizon, like angry purple bruises, threatening and ominous. A storm was brewing.

Claudio's eyes were drawn to a speck of dust rising from the plain.

'A horseman!' he shouted. 'Just one by the look of it.'

'He's ours.' Gianni ran down to open the gates.

The Portuguese rider shot through, his face grimy with dust and sweat. 'They're almost here,' he gasped. 'You'll see them in a few minutes. There are thousands of them.'

It was like a sea rolling towards them, wave after wave of dark blue coats, some marching rank after rank, others riding on fine horses. Most frightening of all were the riderless horses pulling carts on which rested huge field guns.

A shot broke out from the fortifications and Gianni turned to his horrified militia. 'Hold your fire. You won't hit anything until they're much closer. Wait until I give the word.' He turned to Paolo, shouting, 'Is that canon going to work?'

'I've got my fingers crossed. No doubt I'll find out one way or another before much longer.'

His grin was wiped away as a jagged fork of lightning tore the sky apart, followed by the low rumbling of thunder. All eyes were turned to the skies when a massive explosion hit the walls in front of them. The ground shook. Suddenly the air was raining sharp flints of stone that stung wherever they hit.

No one waited for Gianni's command. Firing broke out from the ranks of the militia; wild, panicky shots from terrified men.

For Claudio Farrigiani, the following twenty minutes were a nightmare. He seemed to be peering through a murky haze of powder smoke lit with flashes of flame and the blinding glare of lightning. His eyes were red and stinging painfully.

The noise was deafening: the crack of artillery and the roar of canon mingled with the shrill neighing of horses and the cries of frightened men. Worst of all, were the dull booms and the constant thud after thud against the walls of the fortifications, from which stones tumbled down in a deadly avalanche. Thunder crashed overhead, as though the heavens had joined battle with the world of men.

Claudio fired blindly, aware that he had little ammunition. What then? His sword was useless unless the French chose to scale the walls, which hardly seemed likely when they were finding them so easy to knock down.

Gianni moved briskly amongst his men, though the fighting force were pitifully few, clapping a hand on shoulders and offering encouragement, yet Claudio could hear that his voice was edged with despair. He could hear Paolo, too, cursing and swearing as his canon managed to fire off one shot in three. He crouched over it, coaxing and pleading with it to behave, as black and grimy as a chimney sweep.

Tullio had already abandoned his canon and, together with a number of the militia, he was hurling rocks that had broken away from the fortifications back over the walls that were still standing.

That just about sums us up, Claudio thought bitterly. The Knights of St John are reduced to throwing stones against the masters of Europe's battlefields. And the realisation came that all his boyhood dreams about the *romance of battle had been false; there was nothing glorious about war. Should the Order of St John survive this debacle, he knew it must reassess its future path. No longer were the Knights the brave fighters protecting the faith against the enemies of Christ. Today was Catholic fighting against Catholic? They needed a new way forward.*

A sudden commotion arose by the gateway and Claudio gazed down in alarm. Had the French broken through? A small cluster of men were gathered there, faces twisted anxiously backwards.

'No!' Claudio heard his own cry echoed by Tullio.

Gianni Correr, on his huge black horse, sabre raised on high, looked suddenly very much like the Knights of old.

'Now!' he yelled and, as the gates opened, he charged through and into the ranks of the startled French army and the gates shut behind him.

Claudio stumbled across fallen rocks to the gateway.

'Open it!' he commanded.

A frightened militiaman stammered nervously, 'Gianni said we weren't to open it for anyone, not until he returned.'

'He's not going to return. Have you seen what's out there? Open the gate, now.'

His last words were drowned out by the sound of bugles. They came from behind him, Claudio realised, not from the French. Someone was sounding the retreat.

Even as he wondered, two horsemen appeared, one carrying a large white flag. They were both from the German Langue, he noticed, of which Von Hompesch was commander.

The one with the flag leapt from his horse and mounted the fortifications, waving the flag wildly.

The other looked steadily at Claudio Farrigiani. 'I'm sorry; we are surrendering, on the Grand Master's orders. You are to pull back immediately.'

The gates were opened. A Frenchman stepped through, his dark blue jacket immaculate. It was difficult to believe he had been in a battle.

He raised a hand in salute. 'I bring you the regards of General Vaubois, acting on behalf of Napoleon Bonaparte. He accepts your surrender.'

As the gates were opened even wider to allow the French entry into Floriana, Claudio Farrigiani, accompanied by Tullio and Paolo, slipped through in the opposite direction.

The French were silent now, staring half in wonder and half in disbelief at the body of Gianni Correr lying motionless on the battlefield.

17

For Tom that was the last straw: his father's brother, the one person whose return he'd been longing for, had a key to Alphonso's house. What did that make him? One of the enemy? Suddenly, Tom knew he couldn't take any more. Feeling sick to the stomach, he stepped away from the wall, shaking in anger.

'Does Luigi know that you are . . .? Tom began harshly, but Ricardo raised a hand to hush him.

Past caring, Tom brushed the hand away. 'No wonder Dad stood no chance when even his own brother couldn't be trusted.'

'Shut up!' Ricardo scowled fiercely and Tom's protest died away.

Too late. At his raised tones a door to the left opened and Carlo emerged, staring in surprise at the three of them.

'Ricardo? What's going on? They should be locked upstairs.'

Ricardo drew him aside, whispering urgently. Tom strained to hear but all he could catch was the odd phrase; something to do with a mistake and a change of plans.

Carlo seemed unhappy at the news. 'OK, have it your own way, though Alphonso won't be pleased. He wants to use the brat to lure Giuseppe to the house. I'll leave you to explain why you've let them go.'

With a glare at Tom and Alice he returned, closing the door behind him.

'Keep quiet!' Ricardo barked as Tom opened his mouth. 'You've caused enough trouble by disobeying instructions. I should have told my father to send you straight back to England but I didn't want to miss the chance of seeing Beppe's kid. Come on, I'll take you out the back way.'

'There's a man on watch in the garden,' Tom said sullenly. 'I've already tried that and he didn't seem very keen for me to leave.'

Ricardo hesitated, withdrawing a key from his pocket.' Then we'll have to chance the front. If anyone sees us, keep silent and leave the talking to me.' Unlocking the door, he peered out into the street. 'All clear. Now go straight to Haz Zahra and just for once try and do as you're asked.'

'We haven't any transport,' Alice protested. 'Dad will have gone home ages ago.'

Ricardo's frown deepened. 'I'll arrange it, but you'll have to lose yourselves somewhere for an hour.' He glanced at his watch. 'Get to Valletta Bus Terminal, just inside the main gate, by six o'clock. I'll have someone meet you.'

'Who?' Tom persisted.

'You'll recognise him. Now go.' He shut the door firmly in their faces.

Alice set off at a sprint.

'Don't run,' Tom advised, 'it'll only make us look suspicious and Alphonso's men could be anywhere.' He shuddered at his memories of earlier. He hadn't told Alice about that yet, though it was perhaps best not to frighten her any more until they reached the safety of Haz Zahra.

'Let's walk quickly, then,' Alice urged. 'I hate that house. I want to get as far away from it as possible.'

Tom's spine tingled and he cast a wary eye over his shoulder, feeling unseen eyes watching them. 'You know how in stories heroes seem to have a sixth sense that they're being followed? I always thought that was stupid but now I'm not so sure. I don't think I'll ever feel easy walking down a street again. I'm rapidly developing the most enormous persecution complex. We've got an hour to kill, let's find the Auberge d'Italie and check out the second riddle. Do you know how to get to the Triq-il-Merkanti from here?'

'It's this way.' Alice stumbled, bumping against him, and he put out an arm to steady her.

'Are you alright?'

'I've had enough,' she admitted wearily. 'When I met you last Saturday it was exciting, with the riddle and the treasure and wondering who'd impersonated me. To be honest, Giuseppe Farrigiani didn't seem real, more like a romantic hero in a book; it was a thrill trying to unravel the mystery surrounding him. Even yesterday, once I'd got over my fright at seeing Carlo, I enjoyed outwitting him at the tower. It was all a big game. Today, ever since I got to the Villa Magrino and found you missing, it's not fun any longer. I hate all the deceit; I hate the fact that you suspected me and that you still suspect Dad.'

Tom was horrified to see her eyes were wet and she was using every ounce of her strength to stop herself from crying. He'd seen Alice excited, angry, frustrated, defiant, miserable, but he'd never seen her on the verge of tears.

'Now Ricardo's waltzed into the picture,' she continued, 'and suddenly someone I've always liked seems to have become a different person. I hardly recognised him he was so nasty. And we're no nearer than we were a week ago to finding your father.'

Tom could think of no reply that would comfort her. Slipping an arm round her shoulders, they went on in silence.

'I'm sorry,' Alice said finally. 'Everything's just got a bit too much for me. I don't want you to think I'm running away from the situation.'

'One thing I know for sure, you're not the running away type. If you were, you'd have given up on me days ago. I don't suppose it's any consolation but suspecting you, really hurt me. I hated myself more than I hated you. It's taught me one thing, though. I was totally wrong about you and I'm probably equally wrong about everyone else. In future, I'll reserve judgment until I have some hard and fast evidence.'

She nodded. 'Though when I get home the first thing I'm going to do is tackle Dad.'

Tom doubted the wisdom of that move but said nothing.

Ten minutes later, they stood in front of the Auberge d'Italie. A plaque on the wall pronounced that the coat of arms belonged to Grandmaster Gregorio Carafa.

'Perhaps Claudio Farrigiani knew him?' Tom wondered.

'I doubt it.' Alice hid a grin. 'Look at the dates: 1680-1690. If our Claudio was a Knight when Napoleon invaded in 1789, he wouldn't have been born in 1690, would he? Are we going in?'

'Let's try the archway first. It's the courtyard we want.'

They passed through a dim tunnel and out into a shadowy world of gold and green, carpeted with a richness of red and orange flowers. The sun, almost blinding in its intensity, pierced a maze of paths through the throbbing greenery to lie in glittering pools around an elaborately decorated sundial.

The beauty of the setting did nothing to calm Tom's instant frustration. 'Another dead end. There's nowhere to hide anything here.' He looked at the trees and bushes. 'Unless it's in a cleft of one of the branches, but with all these leaves it would take hours to search. Maybe it was winter when Claudio hid the treasure.'

Alice shook her head. 'You're not thinking. It was June when the Knights were banished from the island so the courtyard would have looked virtually like this. Anyway, it's the sundial the riddle pointed to, not the garden.' She walked round it carefully. 'You couldn't conceal anything here. The only thing that could be significant is this writing and that's in Latin again.'

Tom squatted down, struggling to make out the letters. 'Hic. . .ra. . . I can't even read it, let alone understand it.'

'Hic ratio tendandi aditus.'

The voice seemed to come from the middle of a large bush.

'Is anyone there?' Tom asked. For a brief moment, he wondered if the ghost of Claudio Farrigiani had just spoken to them. Alice was staring at the bush, her face white.

'Is anyone there?' Tom repeated more forcibly.

There came a deep chuckle, a rustling of leaves, and out through the foliage stepped a wizened figure, in his eighties at least, Tom guessed. His brown face was creased into a map of wrinkles, the skin around his eyes puckered up by long exposure to the sun, and he brandished a pair of gardening shears that seemed as ancient as himself. Despite the heat, he was dressed in well-worn overalls covered with patches.

'Give you a surprise, did I?'

'Do you work here?' Alice asked, rather unnecessarily Tom thought considering the shears and the overalls.

'Have done for over fifty years. Not that I'm much use now, though I can still manage a bit of pruning. *Hic ratio tendandi aditus.* That's what it says.'

Alice smiled. 'Thanks. We're neither of us much good at Latin.'

'And what does it mean?' Tom asked.

'Bit difficult that, you see it's mediaeval Latin, written by one of the Knights.'

'Do you know his name?' Alice's voice was breathless with

excitement.

'Might do.' They waited impatiently. 'Claudio he was called. Claudio something. . .' His eyes twinkled. 'It'll come to me in a minute. Farrigiani, that was it. Claudio Farrigiani. He used to live here once. That was long before my time, of course. All the Knights made a contribution to the auberge and Claudio Farrigiani provided the sundial.'

'Can you do a rough translation?' Alice urged.

'If it's rough you want,' he said, eyes twinkling even more, 'Then it's pointing you in the direction of the entrance way.'

Alice and Tom both turned to gaze at the entrance into the auberge.

'Where does it lead?' Alice could hear the excitement in Tom's voice.

'Not to the Farrigiani treasure, if that's what you were hoping.'

They stared at him incredulously.

Alice gave a shaky laugh. 'You know about that?'

'I should do, you're not the first to come seeking it, though the last time was way over twenty years ago. Mind you, sometimes it seems just like yesterday.'

Tom hardly dared to ask. 'Was that Giuseppe Farrigiani?'

'Beppe it was, with his young friend Tommasso trailing behind him. They must have been about your age. Perhaps a bit older. They searched every inch of the auberge and found nothing, so you can save yourselves the bother of looking.'

Tom's spirits fell. He'd been so sure that the sundial held the final clue.

Alice was more resilient. 'Do you know what they were looking for?'

'Should do. They wanted to know if I'd ever seen a statue of the

Archangel Gabriel in the auberge.'

'And had you?'

'No. That didn't stop them searching, though. Young Tommasso got bored pretty quickly, but Beppe was made of sterner stuff. Would have taken the archway apart stone by stone if I'd let him.'

His eyes were gazing way back into the past when a shutter seemed to come down over his face. 'That's enough of that,' he said abruptly, turning back to the garden. 'I've work to do.'

Tom moved swiftly to obstruct his way. 'What else can you tell us about Claudio Farrigiani?'

'If you know Beppe's story, then you'll know it ended in tragedy. I don't want a repeat of that, especially as I was to blame.'

'You?' Alice was shocked. 'You broke into the Bibliotheca?'

A faint smile crossed his face. 'I'd never be so stupid. Still, I did tell Beppe about the book. Wasn't really a book of course, more of a pamphlet, and at one time it belonged to this auberge. Written by one of Claudio's friends it was, in 1798; it gave a description of the Italian Knights living here at the time and chronicled their final months on Malta.'

'The time of Napoleon's invasion? Do tell us about it,' Alice urged.

'How much do you know?'

'Very little,' she admitted, 'except that Giuseppe thought Claudio Farrigiani had saved some treasure from falling into Napoleon's clutches.'

The old man hesitated, sitting down on the edge of a wheelbarrow that seemed as ancient as his shears. 'It was a difficult time for the Order of St John. During the French Revolution, you see, the Knights sided with Louis XVI when he attempted to regain the throne. It wasn't exactly a wise move. After Louis' death, that didn't make them very popular with the new French Assembly.

'Napoleon was building an empire based on Liberty, Equality and Fraternity and he believed the Order was composed of the sons of the privileged classes, which it was, of course. That was one of the reasons Napoleon attacked Malta and banished them from the island. In some ways you could say that was the end of the Knights. They were never the same force again.

'Beppe was probably right about the Farrigiani treasure. It's true that the French ransacked the churches and the property of the Order until they were in possession of an enormous collection of gold, silver, precious stones, statues, paintings and many other priceless items. The pamphlet said that Claudio Farrigiani was an idealist and a dreamer, always thinking back to the days when the Knights were a force to be reckoned with. He and his comrades tried to persuade the Grand Master of the time, a German called Von Hompesch, to organise resistance to Napoleon, but he was a weak leader and he left it too late. Claudio must have hated what was happening. It would have been like him to save some treasure. Do you know what Napoleon said when the Knights asked to take with them their most precious relic, the hand of John the Baptist?' They shook their heads. 'Napoleon replied, "You may keep the dead hand, but the ring on the finger looks better on mine." Then he slipped off the Baptist's ring and placed it on his own finger.'

The realisation that they'd had far more than the hour Ricardo had allotted them resulted in a sprint for the Bus Terminal. They slipped through the throng of people at the main gateway and stood uncertainly, glancing around. Tom half expected to find Alice's father waiting for them. Or Carlo. Could be anybody.

'Want a lift?' Behind them stood Marco Petroni, a frown on his face. 'I suppose it would have been too much to expect you to be here on time?'

Alice looked as startled as Tom. He followed her into the back seat of Marco's car, his mind racing. 'How long have you been involved with. . .?'

Marco shut him up swiftly. 'No questions. It was asking questions that got you into this mess in the first place. I did warn you.'

Alice slipped her hand into Tom's and for the rest of the journey they travelled in silence.

Marco dropped them at the end of the track to Trevisan, driving off without another word.

'I've had my fill of surprises,' Alice said mournfully. 'It really is time to tackle Dad, though I'm not sure I'll be happy with the answers. I'm even beginning to think you might be right about him after all. I mean, if Ricardo and Marco are involved. . .'

'Perhaps you should leave it till morning,' Tom suggested.

'I'd never be able to sleep tonight.'

Mrs Rogerson greeted them less than cheerfully. 'You're very late. I was about to send out a search party.'

'Sorry,' Alice mumbled. 'We lost track of time. Where's Dad?'

'In the village. It's the last band rehearsal before tomorrow's concert. He wasn't too happy about being late, especially as he made a fruitless trip to the police station in Valletta.'

Tom went bright scarlet. 'Sorry about that.' Out of the corner of his eye, he could see Alice staring at him in astonishment. 'Thanks for bailing me out. I know I owe you an explanation but it's an incredibly long, complicated story.'

'Which we haven't time for at the moment. Don't bother to sit down, either of you, you're going out again.'

'Where to?' Alice asked.

'Ricardo rang, he's back from Sicily. He's heard all about Tom and he asked me to send you straight over.'

'Over to where?' Tom stammered.

Mrs Rogerson looked at him as though he'd taken leave of his senses. 'To the Villa Magrino, of course, you didn't imagine I was going to send you back to Valletta, did you? Ricardo's come down to see his parents and they've kindly invited Alice over for dinner. He's promised to see her home safely afterwards. You'd better get a move on, Francesca won't be pleased if her food is spoiled and they usually eat much earlier than this.'

Outside once more, they hit an immediate problem.

'I've no bike here,' Tom said. 'What are we going to do? Walk?'

'We've no choice. It won't take long if we hurry.'

'Why don't you cycle, I know you're tired?'

'I'd have to ride so slowly that I might as well be walking. I don't intend to let you out of my sight in case you disappear again.' She gave a sudden squeal. 'I can't ride anyway, my bike's stuck in a ditch on the way to Valletta. Dad'll be mad when he finds out, though for the moment that's the least of my worries. What was all that about my Dad and a police station?'

'I should have told you earlier but being captured by Alphonso drove it from my mind.' He filled her in on the events from the moment he'd found himself staring up at Alphonso's skeleton servant. Thinking about the chase through the Valletta streets made him shudder. It wasn't an experience he wished to revisit, not even in his mind. He had never been so scared in his life.

'Why on earth did you say you were Ewen?'

'Goodness knows. I didn't want to say Tom Newton because it was obvious my captor didn't know my name and then I thought of you and before I realised what I was doing I said Ewen Rogerson. Then, in the police station I gave your address. I was horrified when they rang your Mum and as soon as they told me that your Dad was coming to collect me I knew I had to escape. I left by the window.'

'I can see how you found it difficult to explain all that to Mum.'

'I'll have to sometime, I know. She must think I'm an absolute idiot.'

The light was draining from the sky and huge purple clouds massed on the horizon. The heat was stifling and Tom felt his T-shirt sticking to his back.

'Going to be a storm,' Alice said. 'We get really dramatic ones.'

As if on cue, a streak of lighting shot across the sky towards them and the world darkened even more.

Tom was full of apprehension. 'I wish you'd stayed at home. We don't know that Luigi and Francesca have returned. And there's another strange thing. If Ricardo was coming out here why didn't he bring us himself instead of leaving it to Marco?'

'Maybe he had business to finish first and didn't know how long it would take.'

'With Carlo and Alphonso? He went back into Alphonso's house after showing us off the premises.'

Alice nodded unhappily. 'It feels awful to suspect Ricardo, though I can't see how we can do anything else. You heard him with Carlo. I've never known him to be so horrible and Marco wasn't much better. He's never spoken to me like that before. I've always got on with them really well because they're Dad's best friends.'

Not much of a reference, Tom thought. 'They were a threesome, weren't they? Your Dad, Ricardo and Marco? They all seem to be involved somehow.' She looked so wretched that he added quickly. 'But remember we've given up suspecting anyone without hard and fast evidence.'

'How come Ricardo had a key to Alphonso's house?'

'I'm wondering if it was Alphonso's,' Tom said slowly. 'Think about my photograph on the wall. The only person Dad would have sent it to is Ricardo or Tommasso and I know where Tommasso lives. His house is in Floriana.'

'You mean it might have been Ricardo's house?'

'Haven't you ever visited him?'

'No, I've only seen him when he comes to Haz Zahra. If it was Ricardo's, then what was Alphonso doing there?'

'Perhaps we got it wrong again. Perhaps Alphonso was telling the truth all along. Maybe he's trying to protect Dad from Tommasso, as he said he was, which makes sense of Ricardo helping him. It also explains your Dad and Marco being involved.'

'No!' Alice shook her head decisively. 'In some ways I'd prefer to believe that because of Dad, but I hated Alphonso. You heard Carlo say he was going to use you to lure Giuseppe to the house.'

'He'd still do that if he wanted to protect Dad. I didn't like Alphonso much myself, though the alternative is that Ricardo's in league with someone who's trying to harm his brother.'

'It's hard to know how everyone's linked,' Alice said slowly. 'There's Tommasso, he seems to be working on his own, then Alphonso, Adriane and Carlo, they're definitely a threesome, and now Marco and Ricardo have become involved which does make it likely that Dad's mixed up in it with them. They always do everything together. Maybe Ricardo will tell us what's going on. He must have invited us over for a purpose.'

'I doubt we're going to get any answers.' Tom gestured down the track towards the Villa Magrino. For the second night running, the house was cloaked in darkness. 'Doesn't look as though Luigi and Francesca are back, does it?'

Alice clutched his arm. 'Do you think we're walking into another trap? Anyone could have rung Mum and said they were Ricardo.'

'You stay here, I'll go and find out.'

'No.' She clutched his arm even tighter. 'From now on, we'll stick together.'

Tom hesitated by the back door. It was so much a repetition of the night before that he expected at any moment an arm would reach out to grab him. The farmyard appeared deserted, but he knew to his cost that appearances could be deceptive.

Thunder began to rumble overhead and a sheet of lightning lit the yard with the brilliance of a stage set.

He tried the handle. The door opened, the kitchen beyond dark and lifeless. Removing Alice's hand from his arm, he crept inside.

'At last. You took your time.'

A torch was switched on, a hand shielding the beam, and there stood Tommasso Lorenzo.

Tom's immediate impulse was to run, yet instinctively he knew that the time for running was long past.

Tommasso moved to the doorway. 'Are you coming in, Alice, or have you decided to wait outside?'

She marched in defiantly, determined to show no fear. 'Where's Ricardo?'

Tommasso closed the door before leading them forward. 'All in good time. It's nice to see you again,' he told Tom. 'Don't you ever do as you're told?'

'Not where the Lorenzo family are concerned,' Tom retorted. 'I've had enough of you all to last a lifetime.'

Tommasso paused by the door to the sitting room, switching off the torch. Tom realised with surprise that he'd never been in there; the life of the house, when Luigi and Francesca were present, revolved around the kitchen. He and Alice were escorted through the doorway. Heavy drapes curtained the windows, leaving the room in a total darkness through which they could hear the sound of someone breathing.

A lamp was switched on suddenly, casting a dim light on a figure sitting by the fireplace.

'Welcome,' he said.

The man's face was in shadow, but the voice was familiar.

'Dad!' Tom shouted, rushing forward.

June 1798

Extract from the book by Tullio Falcone.

The Sacra Infermeria was as quiet and hushed as usual, despite the constant arrival of the wounded who were placed in beds down each side of the long room. The Order had extended the courtesy to the French, but they had precious few injuries.

Paolo, Claudio and I carried out the duties we were given: heating water, rolling fresh bandages and cleaning the floor where blood lay in deep, red pools. We didn't need to speak to each other to know that our thoughts all lay with the surgeon who laboured over the body of Gianni Correr.

We had carried him here ourselves. Strangely, it was the French who had provided a plank of wood, helping us to strap his body securely. They gazed at him in admiration, or perhaps marvelling at his stupidity. Whatever the reason, we were grateful for their help.

'Tullio.' Paolo tugged at my sleeve.

I looked over to where Claudio was already making for the bedside from where the surgeon was signalling us. Surely his smile presaged good news.

'I've taken a bullet from his arm and another from his shoulder. The third, fortunately, simply grazed his scalp. I've heard about his exploit. What was he trying to do, take on the French army single handed?'

We shrugged. 'That's Gianni,' I murmured.

'He's going to wake up with a very sore head.' The surgeon smiled, gathering up his instruments. 'You can wait with him if you like, though he won't be in a pleasant mood. I can promise you that.'

We sat quietly without talking, the four of us who had become more than friends. The other three were like brothers to me, I knew them so well.

Gianni, brave and fearless, has been born centuries too late. I can picture him so easily, on his black horse, sword raised, charging along the road to Jerusalem. What fear he would have struck into the Turkish foe.

Paolo is our joker, always laughing, always chattering, but always loyal. No one can be depressed for long when Paolo is around.

As for Claudio Farrigiani. . .

18

Giuseppe Farrigiani hugged his son tightly, both seeming at a loss for words. Alice stood well back, hand raised to brush away the unexpected tears from her eyes. She swallowed hard and looked away. So this was Giuseppe, the romantic figure at the heart of the mystery. Except that as from today, Alice decided, the romance had vanished, buried deep beneath layers of deceit. She'd have recognised him anywhere as a Farrigiani: the lean, athletic build, the unruly black hair that was neither straight nor curly, wrinkly being the most apt description; the very deep brown eyes; Tom's eyes. She'd always thought them unusual with his fair hair. Giuseppe was a more serious version of Ricardo, though that hadn't always been the case, Alice recalled, remembering the photograph of the wildly grinning schoolboy. All the troubles he'd been through were clearly etched on his face.

Giuseppe pulled back from the embrace and turned to Tommasso. 'Will you check outside and make sure these two weren't followed. We can't be too careful.'

When Tommasso had left he held out a hand for Alice. She moved forward shyly.

'Thanks for helping Tom. Now listen, both of you, this is important. While Tommasso is with us I want you to be very careful what you say.'

'Don't you trust him?' Tom asked in dismay. Surely Alphonso's story wasn't going to turn out to be the correct one?

'Yes I do, but you've met his brother which can't have been a pleasant experience for either of you. Alphonso is a very dominant character. If it came to a battle of wits between them, Tommasso wouldn't stand a chance. He was never a match for his brother. What he doesn't know he can't be forced to tell. The last thing I want to do is put Tommasso in a difficult position, so don't ask awkward questions. In fact, keep your mouths shut as much as possible.'

Tom was hurt. 'You mean we're not going to find out what's been going on? After all we've been through? So far, we've heard a different story from everyone. I thought you'd be the one to tell us the truth.'

'I will, I promise, but not tonight. Hopefully, this whole mess will be over very shortly. I'll tell you as much as is safe for now, but do remember not to ask questions in front of Tommasso.'

On Tommasso's return, Giuseppe sat back in the chair, Alice and Tom taking the sofa. Tommasso hovered by the fireplace, clearly nervous and on edge. Giuseppe gave him a reassuring smile before turning to his son.

'There's some sandwiches and a bottle of home-made lemonade on the table. I haven't forgotten I invited you over for a meal, though I'm afraid it's hardly up to my mother's standard.'

'Then it was you who rang up Trevisan and pretended to be Ricardo?' Tom stopped short, recalling his father's ban on questions.

With a warning glance Giuseppe answered, 'Yes, that was me. I had to pretend to be my brother. I could hardly tell Alice's mother it was me, not that she'd have believed me if I had.' He smiled at Alice. 'The last time I saw your mother she was nineteen and she'd just got engaged to your father.' He turned to Tom. 'I thought it was safe to say I was Ricardo because he returns home today from Sicily. I hope it won't be long before you can meet him. It's about time you had an uncle.'

Tom refrained from admitting that they had already met, under rather strange circumstances. His father needed to be told, though perhaps not in front of Tommasso. And what could he say? Did you know that your brother seems to be on very good terms with your enemy? How likely was it that Dad would believe him? He turned to the safer subject of the sandwiches. 'These aren't bad. Much better than the ones you made for that picnic in Greece.'

Giuseppe returned his smile. 'Seems a long time ago, doesn't it?'

'A lifetime ago,' Tom said. 'I can't believe that I only arrived on Malta last Friday. This week has been the longest of my life.'

'I'm sorry about that. I know Tommasso has told you how all this originated.'

Tom nodded, relief washing over him. Thank goodness Tommasso's story had been true and his father hadn't planned the robbery. Guilt hit him for even considering Alphonso's version. He should have trusted Alice's judgment.

'When Tommasso sent me the book I read it from cover to cover. There was no mention of the Farrigiani treasure but a very revealing section about Claudio Farrigiani. The riddle that had puzzled us all this time was suddenly so obvious.'

Tom and Alice gazed at him expectantly, not daring to ask. Surely he could tell them that much?

At the sight of their eagerness, Tommasso gave a twisted smile. 'Don't worry, kids, he hasn't told me either. He has some strange notion that he's protecting us.'

For the first time Giuseppe looked ill at ease. 'It's not that I mistrust any of you, please don't think that. If everything had gone as planned. . . That's the problem, you see, nothing has. For over twenty years I've dreamed of returning to Malta. I never thought it would be like this. My intentions were simply to travel here with Tom, telling him the Farrigiani story on the plane, to collect the treasure together and then visit my parents. I knew they'd be overjoyed to meet their first grandson. I thought I could put the past behind me and start living again.' He was silent for a moment. 'Back in England it all seemed so simple.'

'And then I told you about Alphonso's welcoming party,' Tommasso prompted.

'I came out that afternoon instead, leaving a note for Tom at the British Airways Desk.' He looked unhappily at his son, seeing the question in his eyes. 'I honestly thought you'd be safe because by the time you reached Malta the treasure would be with the authorities and Alphonso would have no further cause to trouble us.'

What about the killing of the security guard? Tom wondered. Didn't Dad take into consideration that Alphonso was a murderer and would do anything to ensure that it never came to light? He contented himself with saying, 'Go on.'

'At the airport I recognised two of Alphonso's friends and realised they'd got wind of the new plan. I managed to avoid them and took a taxi to Ricardo's where I was due to meet Tommasso. Fortunately I got the taxi driver to drop me a few streets away, because Alphonso already had the house under surveillance. The strange car parked outside alerted me. I went straight into hiding, though I did manage to ring a friend in London with instructions to stop Tom from travelling. That was another plan of mine that went astray.'

'You didn't know I'd arrived here?'

'Not until Tommasso found me today. I thought you were safe in England; I imagined that your grandparents would be looking after you.'

'Even if I'd got your message they wouldn't have been much help. They're touring Scotland.'

'I messed things up all round, didn't I?'

'It doesn't matter, I'm fine now. What happened next?'

'I spent a frustrating week dodging Alphonso's men who seemed to be everywhere, including Haz Zahra, so there was no way I could get at the treasure.'

Tom looked stunned. 'The treasure's here in the village?'

'Has been all along. Ironic, isn't it?'

'It's something we should have thought of.' Alice spoke up for the first time. 'The village is old, it was here at the time of the Knights and it's where the Farrigianis have lived for centuries. I know because Dad told me. He was comparing your family to the Rogersons who've only been here since the Second World War. Presumably Claudio Farrigiani's girlfriend lived in Haz Zahra and when he had to leave Malta in a hurry he visited her to say goodbye and hid the treasure at the same time.'

She reddened as Giuseppe gazed at her admiringly. 'Why did we never think of that approach? The one place we never searched was Haz Zahra, apart from the festa time when we were eight and we scaled the steeple to examine the lighted angel.' He and Tommasso grinned at each other like two naughty little boys and Tom suddenly saw a side of his father that he'd never realised. 'My father was furious and we weren't very popular in the village for weeks afterwards.'

'I wouldn't have thought of it,' Alice admitted honestly, 'if you hadn't said the treasure was in the village.'

'Somewhere in the village.' Tom looked pointedly at his father. 'What else are we allowed to know?'

'Tommasso has told me about your exploits, plus the fact that you'd landed in Alphonso's clutches, despite all his attempts to keep you safe. You can imagine how worried I was. Tommasso went to visit his brother this afternoon, we decided we'd have to take that risk, only to find you'd escaped.'

'Something you make a habit of doing.' Tommasso was clearly less than pleased. 'How did you manage it?'

'I'm getting good at escapology,' Tom said vaguely, making no mention of Ricardo or Marco. 'If you will leave windows open you can't expect me not to take advantage of them. How did you know I was at Trevisan?'

'We didn't.' Tom heard the concern in his father's voice. 'It was a guess that you'd return there, we couldn't think of anywhere else you'd be likely to go. As it was, I had to leave a message with Alice's mother. And now that we've found you, reassured you that I'm alive and well, we're going to have to leave you again.'

'What about me and Alice? We can't stay here.'

'We'll take you back to Trevisan, you'll be safe enough there.'

Tom doubted that. 'You mean you're not including us in your plans?' he asked with more than a touch of resentment. To be sidelined at this stage, like a couple of kids, was insulting.

'Don't worry, you're at the centre of my plans. In a few minutes Tommasso and I must return to Valletta; it's far too dangerous for me to hang around here. We've got a car hidden in one of the empty barns. We'll drop you and Alice at Trevisan; you'll have to find an excuse for Tom to stay the night. Tomorrow I want Tom to go into the village and collect the treasure.'

'I don't know where it is or what it is.' Tom heard the rudeness in his voice but was past caring. 'And if you think I won't be recognised then you haven't been keeping up to date with what's been happening to me. I'm quite well known in the village. I helped with the preparations for the festa and I switched on the church lights.'

'You have got yourself involved.' Giuseppe looked at his son with pride.

'I'll also be recognised by Alphonso and his friends, and definitely by his sister.'

'Adriane?' Tommasso questioned. 'Was Adriane with Alphonso?'

Having blurted it out Tom could do nothing but nod, aware of his father's disapproving stare. I wouldn't put my foot in it, he thought irritably, if someone told me the rules of the game. For nearly a week his sole objective had been to find his father; now he had, there were too many questions left unanswered.

His father studied him anxiously. 'I know you've had a difficult time. If you don't feel you can do this, I'll understand.'

Tom bit back a retort. 'Of course I'll do it if someone will tell me how I can go into the village unrecognised. I don't want to be the one to mess things up at this stage and I haven't got a very good track record so far for getting things right.'

To his surprise, his father chuckled. 'I think Alice can tell you.'

'Don't worry,' she sympathised, smiling at Tom's disgruntled face. 'I haven't suddenly become much cleverer than you. It's simply that I know the village and the details of the festa.'

'What's that got to do with it?'

'Tomorrow is the start of the festa weekend. It always opens with a fete and all the young people will be in the most elaborate fancy dress.' She turned to Giuseppe. 'I suppose that's what you mean?'

'Exactly. We'll have to make sure Tom's so well disguised that none of Alphonso's friends recognise him.'

'I hate to mention this,' Tom said caustically, 'but I didn't think to bring any fancy dress from England. Stupid of me, I know. I would have, of course, if I'd known what I was letting myself in for.'

They all laughed, even Tommasso, and Giuseppe leapt up.

'There's a trunk full of costumes in the attic that belonged to me and Ricardo; my mother never threw anything like that away.' He pulled Tom to his feet. 'Come on, let's see what we can find.' He turned to Tommasso. 'Would you and Alice clear these things away. We don't want to leave a record of our visit.'

Tom recalled the previous time he had climbed into the dusty attic and learned the story of the Farrigiani heritage. 'I suppose you're going to tell me where to find the treasure, now you've neatly got rid of Tommasso and Alice. Do you really not trust him? I can vouch for Alice.'

'I'm sure you can and I've told you why I want Tommasso to know as little as possible. It's for his own good. I don't want you telling Alice. Is that understood? I think it's wise to keep this to ourselves until everything's concluded.'

'I'm surprised you're trusting me.' Tom heard the bitterness in his voice. 'You don't know me very well, do you?'

His father sighed. 'We've never had much time to spend with each other, have we? My fault, I know. When this is over I'll try and make it up to you.'

He looked so downcast that Tom asked gently, 'What about the treasure?'

'Let's get you a costume first. We'll have to hunt through all the trunks to find the right one.'

'It's over there.' Tom pointed to a shadowy corner, grinning at his father's surprise. 'I've been through them all looking for one of your school photographs. I found one eventually in your treasure chest. It was just like the one you bought me and I guessed it belonged to you when your birth date unlocked the combination. You can imagine my shock when I discovered that my father was probably Giuseppe Farrigiani. The inscription on the box was how we found Tommasso's name.'

'Very clever.'

'Alice's idea,' Tom admitted. 'She's been the brains. I lurched from one disaster to another. I insisted on barging into the Casa Peralta, blurting out your name, which is how we came to Alphonso's attention. Then I ran away from Tommasso and got caught by Alphonso. I hope tomorrow's not another of my catastrophes.'

'I've got faith in you.' His father patted his shoulder.

Tom wished he had the same confidence. Hurriedly changing the subject he said, 'I also found the riddle in your box which is why we've been trying to track you down by searching for the treasure.'

'I'm surprised they kept my box. I thought they'd have thrown away everything of mine long ago. That's what I deserved.'

'Tommasso said you broke Francesca's heart when you went away. He told me a lot of lies, I still don't understand why when he's your friend, but I think that was true.'

'It was. That's another thing I've got to put right.' Giuseppe looked over at Tom, the ghost of a smile on his face. 'I'm relying on you to help me there, as well. But first we have to deal with tomorrow.'

'What's the answer to the riddle? Alice and I have been trying to solve it all week. I'll need to know if I'm to collect the treasure for you.'

'Let's get you fixed up with an outfit, then.'

They settled, appropriately enough, on a Knight's costume, complete with chain mail and helmet.

'I made this.' Giuseppe ran his fingers lovingly over the silver sheen of the helmet. 'I must have been about your age. Mum did all the sewing. Such a long time ago it seems; before everything went wrong.'

'I'd love to hear about your childhood,' Tom said. 'But if we don't hurry Tommasso will come looking for us. Where do I find the treasure? And what is it? Alice and I came to the conclusion that it must be a statue of the Angel Gabriel.'

'You have done well. It took me and Tommasso years to reach that point. Trouble is, we were led astray by its description as a priceless relic. We imagined it being made of gold or silver. . .'

'Covered with jewels, that's what we thought.'

'When I read the book,' Giuseppe continued, 'though it wasn't really a book, more of a. . .'

'Pamphlet,' Tom supplied. 'I know. We also got as far as the Auberge d'Italie.'

'The old man's still there?' Giuseppe looked astonished. 'He seemed ancient when we met him and that was over twenty years ago.'

'He's still very much there and still brandishing his garden shears. He remembered you. Go on, sorry I interrupted.'

'The book was written by one of Claudio's friends, a Knight called Tullio Falcone. The passage about Claudio Farrigiani described him as a romantic young man, fascinated by the early tales and history of the Knights. He arrived on Malta in 1780, at the age of nineteen, with a burning determination to take up his sword against the enemies of Christ. That makes him twenty-eight when Napoleon invaded. Claudio's particular interest, according to Tullio Falcone, was the period in Jerusalem, long before the Order became rich and influential. He stated that for Claudio their greatest possession, after the hand of John the Baptist, was the small wooden statue of the Angel Gabriel carved in Palestine by Gerard de Saxo, the very first Grand Master, who was one of Claudio's heroes. Then I knew. . .'

Tom gave a sudden gasp. 'So do I. The dead tree is the wood it was carved from and the statue is in the church at Haz Zahra, on the ledge below the Rose Window.'

'Right under our noses all the time. Alice was right. When Claudio came to make his farewells he must have slipped into the church and placed it on the ledge. Their child was obviously a boy and the Farrigianis have lived here ever since.'

Tom was puzzled. 'I don't see how we were supposed to guess its location from the riddle. It didn't mention the village or the church. What was all that about summits and minutes and seconds?'

'We didn't look deeply enough. There were different layers to the clue that we missed. I won't enlighten you now; having got so far, try and work it out for yourself. You'll need both sections of the riddle. Will you be alright, tomorrow?'

'Collecting the treasure should be no problem now I've got this.' Tom patted the costume. 'What do I do then?'

'I'll be waiting for you outside the village. Once you've got the statue ask Alice to point you in the direction of the crossroads. I'll be there from eleven o'clock. Remember what I've said about keeping this to ourselves. Don't tell Alice anything about the treasure and don't bring her to the crossroads. We'll do this together, just you and me.'

Tom's mind was spinning and he failed to register Alice's silence as they walked down the now familiar track. The storm had ended and the moon hung low over the farm.

'I won't come in,' he said, making a sudden decision. 'Your mother would never believe that Luigi and Francesca would let me turn up on your doorstep at this time of night without an invitation.' What he didn't say was that he was wary of meeting her father. The less he saw of Mr Rogerson the better, especially if he was still cross about the police station episode. Tom knew there was no way he could explain that incident so that it made any sense.

He expected a protest but she took the news surprisingly calmly. 'You can sleep in the loft and don't worry, I won't say anything about finding your father. I know when to hold my tongue.'

The farmyard was deserted. Alice showed him into a stable, where two horses raised their heads inquiringly, pointing out a ladder at the far end. 'You'll be well hidden up there. When I've told Mum I'm back,

I'll slip out with a blanket for you.'

'Thanks.'

She avoided his eyes, leaving abruptly.

Tom realised to his dismay that she was upset and angry. After all they'd gone through together his father had excluded her, cut her out of his plans. I wouldn't be here now if it wasn't for Alice, he thought miserably, I'd be back in England and Dad would have to cope alone. I've hurt her once, I'm not going to do it again. I'm not going to become like Dad, not daring to trust anyone.

'Aren't you joining me for a few minutes?' he whispered as she perched halfway up the ladder, proffering a blanket.

'Why? It's late. You need to get some sleep before tomorrow.'

'Don't you want to hear the answer to the riddle?'

'Your father didn't want me to know. He made that obvious enough. I'm not to be trusted.'

'Dad doesn't know you like I do. Remember what you said earlier? "From now on we stick together." You're not going back on it, are you?'

She flushed. 'I thought. . .'

'We started this quest together and tomorrow we'll finish it together. Besides, you know what a mess I make of things on my own.'

He moved aside to let her clamber up.

'You don't have to do this, Tom.'

'Yes, I do. Like you I'm sick of all the deceit, of not knowing who to believe. Even my Dad is keeping things hidden from me, I can tell that. It's sad, but you're the only person I can trust. Anyway, I need your brains to solve the riddle.'

'I thought you'd got the answer?'

'The answer, yes, but not how it was reached. Dad said I had to work that out for myself.'

'Were we right about the statue?'

He filled her in with the details, enjoying her excitement, before asking, 'How were we supposed to come to that conclusion from the riddle?'

'Have you got a copy?'

'We need both, Dad said. They're a bit creased, I'm afraid.'

Smoothing them out, they began to read.

Age fades, observe aright.
Hill beckons.
Alight ashore at cavernous
Steepness auguring
Heavenly summit.
Angel adorns dead tree.
Starless shadowy years.
Creation counts as reckoned.
Minutes enduring into days,
Everlasting seconds.

Tom sighed. 'Dad said it would make sense now we know the answer but it's just as mystifying. What's all that about *alight ashore*? Haz Zahra is miles from the sea and the church is hardly on a summit, there's not a hill in sight, though I suppose the Rose Window is pretty high up. He did hint that there's a layer to the clue that we've missed.'

As he babbled on Alice sat back, lost in thought. The light of the moon through the skylight cast flickering shadows over the words so that they seemed to merge together, losing their individuality. She leaned forward suddenly. 'I can see *rose* – look, the letters are all there in the line *Creation counts as reckoned*. Maybe we should be concentrating on the letters as well as the words. Perhaps there's a pattern and. . .'

'*Everlasting seconds*,' Tom blurted out. 'The last line tells us. It was nothing to do with time. *Rose* comes from the second letter in each word.'

With trembling fingers, he pulled a pencil from his pocket and underlined the second letter of each word. There before them appeared the message left by Claudio Farrigiani all those centuries ago.

Gabriel statue under the rose in nave.

They fell silent. All that effort, Tom was thinking, all that dashing about the island and in the end it was so simple.

Alice roused herself to say, 'Now all you have to do is collect the statue.'

'All we have to do,' he corrected her. 'Have you got a fancy dress? They'll know who I am straightaway if I'm with you.'

'Plenty. I'll choose the one with the best disguise.' She got up reluctantly. 'I must go in, Dad's not back yet from the rehearsal and I don't want him to find me here. I'll come and fetch you in the morning when the coast's clear. You'll have to pretend you've just arrived. And thanks for sharing it with me.'

After she'd gone Tom sank down in the straw, discarding the blanket. The night was hot and clammy. After all the excitement he felt restless, too wound up to settle. Sleep, he told himself sternly, you'll need your wits about you tomorrow.

He was just drifting off when the roar of a car pierced his subconscious. Mr Rogerson was returning. Hopefully, he'd go straight to the house. Tom wriggled uncomfortably, the straw tickling his neck, freezing suddenly as footsteps sounded below him. What was he doing in the stable?

'Okay then?' The voice was gentle and calming.

The horses, Tom realised thankfully. He's come to check the horses. He hasn't a clue where I am. He lay back, careful to make no noise.

Mr Rogerson moved about quietly. There was the gurgling of water as he refilled a bucket and the soft rustling of hay.

Tom was just relaxing when a faint tinkling broke the silence. What was he doing now? It took a few seconds for Tom to realise that he was hearing a mobile phone.

The noise ceased as it was answered and Mr Rogerson's voice came floating through the silence. 'I can't think we'll have any problem as long as we're in position by the time the festa starts at ten o'clock.' Who was he talking to? 'There shouldn't be any difficulty in spotting Tom, he'll have Alice with him and I've given her instructions. She knows what to do.'

June 1798

The night belonged to the French as they looted shops and raced, in drunken, laughing mobs, throughout the streets, liquor dribbling from their mouths.

The ground was a shambles of broken wine casks.

The Standard of the Order, which had flown so proudly over Fort St Angelo, had been hauled down to be replaced by the French Tricolour.

Valletta's citizens huddled indoors, their houses barred and shuttered, or stood on balconies, calling to their saints for help. But no help came. Those who had come to Valletta for protection had already left, making their weary way back to their villages and farms.

The Knights, apart from those still wounded in the Sacra Infermeria, had been herded back to the auberges, to await the outcome of the meeting between Napoleon and Von Hompesch.

All but one. Claudio Farrigiani was a shadowy figure huddled in the dusky shelter of a bakery doorway. Normally it would be a scene of bright activity, the air full of the yeasty smells of dough being kneaded for the morning's baking. Tonight the shop was black and silent. Somewhere in the darkness a dog howled.

He peered out into the street. For the moment, it was deserted. Dodging between the shadows he made his way towards his destination.

He heard the crowds of French soldiers celebrating in the square before the Cathedral long before he reached them. They were clearly settled there for the night. The front entrance was blocked to him. Slipping into a narrow alley he made for the side door.

It opened easily and with beating heart he stepped into the darkness of the Cathedral.

19

Tom woke to blinding sunlight. The small skylight funnelled a laser beam of brightness into his eyes, stinging them painfully; he rolled over, the loft a blur of dancing colours. It took a few moments for his vision to settle and he lay still, his mind focusing on the enormity of the task ahead.

He had slept badly, Mr Rogerson's revelation about Alice making him sick to the stomach. Yesterday, when she'd explained about the bike accident and the meeting with Carlo and Adriane, he'd trusted her completely. Now, once again, he didn't know what to believe. Hard and fast evidence, he told himself, that's what you need. You said you wouldn't jump to conclusions anymore. Trouble was, hard and fast evidence wasn't exactly easy to come by.

He thought back to the meeting with his father. That should have solved everything, instead it had solved nothing. Dad's got Tommasso on his side, that's for certain, and Alphonso, Adriane and Carlo are the enemy. That leaves Ricardo, Mr Rogerson and Marco. I wish I could know for certain why they're involved. Who was Mr Rogerson talking to on the phone last night? And what instructions has he given Alice? Whatever they were, she kept them well hidden from me.

At the thought of Alice he panicked, sitting up so abruptly that the loft spun. Alice knows about the treasure, he thought miserably. I told her everything, despite Dad's warning. He said it more than once. "Don't tell Alice," and "Don't bring Alice with you to the crossroads." Does Dad know something I don't? Why on earth didn't he tell me why I shouldn't trust her? By now, Mr Rogerson could have collected the statue and taken it to Alphonso. But would he do that? Tom tried to work it out. Is it the treasure Alphonso wants or is it Dad? Or both? It's far more likely that he'll wait until I've got the statue and then follow when Alice leads me to Dad. I can't let that happen? I need to leave here quickly.

He glanced at his watch – almost 9 o'clock. What had happened to the time between dawn and now? He'd woken earlier, he remembered, to the continuous peeling of bells, a sound he would always associate with Malta. They were silent now. He peered down the wooden ladder into the barn. No sign of movement. Dare he risk making a dash for it? And what should he do about his disguise? His eyes fastened on the Knight's costume lying neatly where Alice had arranged it the night before. Was it worth bothering with now? Alice had probably given them details of his fancy dress, though in his own clothes he'd be immediately recognisable by everyone. The thought of another encounter with Alphonso's men terrified him.

Tom looked at the costume with distaste. He'd never been one for dressing up, not even as a kid; it always made him feel self-conscious and slightly foolish. Still, if he had to don a disguise this was the most appropriate. I can pretend I'm Claudio Farrigiani, he thought with a lifting of spirits, stealing into the church to hide the statue, except instead of hiding it I'm rescuing it from obscurity. His mind refused to dwell on the difficulties that might entail without Alice's help. For a moment, Tom conjured up an image of the young Knight creeping towards the church; the young Knight who was his ancestor. Had he been scared? Rescuing the treasure from Napoleon and the French had probably been the most frightening moment of all. It would have been evening, he decided, picturing the darkness and the figure who in his imagination looked very like Dad. It was so real that he almost felt as though he were with him. Pushing the thought away, he concentrated on the task at hand.

Reluctantly he began to dress, comforting himself that his father was safe, for the moment anyway, that was the main thing. The chain mail trousers were bulky and awkward over his shorts and the tunic scratched at his neck. Once he'd pulled the tabard over the top he was drenched in sweat. It would be best to leave the helmet for later.

'You ready?'

Tom's heart sank. Kneeling at the trapdoor, he peered down at a multicoloured clown, all red and yellow spots and a lurid green wig.

'Glad to see you found a disguise that wouldn't be noticeable.'

She failed to pick up on the sarcasm in his voice. 'Covers me completely, though, and I've got a T-shirt and shorts underneath in case we need to do a quick change. Are you coming down? Dad's just gone and Mum's finishing the washing up.'

Tom descended rather awkwardly, finding it difficult to bend his knees in the chain mail, and clutching the helmet under one arm. 'I'm not sure about my outfit. You haven't got anything else I could borrow?'

She examined him critically. 'It looks fine, what's the problem? Once you've put on the helmet and pulled down the visor no one will recognise you.'

Not much hope of that, Tom thought miserably, when your Dad's probably supplied the details to Alphonso's men. 'It's so hot,' he protested, wriggling uncomfortably.

'You'll be able to take it off once we've handed the statue to your father. Come on, don't be such a misery. I thought you'd be full of excitement today. you'll soon have your hands on the treasure that was rescued by your own ancestor.'

For how long? Tom wondered. How long before Alphonso and

your father take it from me?

He followed her into the farmyard. 'What about your face? Shouldn't you have painted it or something?'

She held up a grinning mask. 'I thought this was more practical. In the heat, face paints run and become all sticky. Mum used them last year on Ewen when he was a Red Indian and after an hour he just had a splodgy face. I'll let Mum know you've arrived and we'll set off.'

'She won't want to come down with us, will she? We'll be pretty obvious if we arrive in the village with your mother.'

'No, Dad's coming back for her. He just went to check something with Marco.'

Check what? Tom wondered. Perhaps it was best not to know.

'Let's hurry then.' The last thing he wanted at this stage was a meeting with Mr Rogerson.

Alice's mother looked startled at the sight of Tom. 'I remember that costume. Years ago it was, when we were all about your age. It was worn by. . .' She broke off, flustered. '. . . Ricardo, I think.'

She'd been about to say Giuseppe, Tom realised. Had Dad chosen it specially because it belonged to him? Didn't he remember how hot and uncomfortable it was? He felt a surge of resentment against his father. Would it matter so much if the statue remained in the church that had been its home for over two hundred years? Though that wouldn't solve the problem of Alphonso.

'We'll be off now,' Alice said, smiling at her mother. 'See you down there.'

'Biking?'

'No.' Alice caught Tom's eye and winked. With his bike at the Villa Magrino and hers stuck in a ditch on the road to Valletta, that was an impossibility. 'There's plenty of time to walk and we'll get a lift back this evening. Probably with Pietro, you know how he likes to show off his car.'

Tom doubted that. He had to get rid of Alice long before evening fell. If all went well, which seemed highly unlikely at this moment, by evening he'd be safe with his father and Tommasso.

By the time they reached the road to the village, he was even hotter and more irritable.

Alice looked at him in concern. 'You OK?'

'Never felt better.' Tom swallowed hard. The last thing he wanted was for her to guess his suspicions. 'Sorry, I'm a bit on edge. I didn't sleep too well last night.'

'I can imagine. You must have been so excited at finding your father. I bet you were beginning to wonder if you'd ever see him again.'

'Yes.' Tom could hardly tell her that Mr Rogerson's revelations about his daughter had swamped his feelings for his father. 'Is there another way into the village? Anyone watching for us will be stationed along this route.'

'We could cut through the field. It's a bit longer but you're right, it's probably safer.'

Tom watched her carefully as they crossed a large field, skirting another by the hedgerow. She seemed just as normal and he wondered, not for the first time, if he was misjudging her. Yet he couldn't forget how well she'd acted at the Gabriel Tower. Was she acting now? If so, she was giving a good performance. What instructions had Mr Rogerson given her? However much he wanted to believe in her innocence, he couldn't risk endangering Dad at this stage.

If Tom had thought it would be cooler away from the road, he was disappointed: there was little relief from the stifling warm air; the occasional tree stood motionless, branches and leaves unstirred by even the faintest breeze. Beneath their feet the dry grass crunched like egg shells.

Squeezing through another hedge, they arrived at the far side of the village.

Alice regarded Tom with mock outrage. 'I don't think the Grand Master would be pleased at your state of dress.' She detached the twigs that had snagged in the chain mail, removing leaves from hair that was more dishevelled than usual. 'Is this the latest fashion in England?' she asked, eyeing his long locks.

'No, it's what you'd call a teenage rebellion. I started to let it grow when Mum met the American she finally married. Seems stupid now. By the time of the wedding I was really pleased for them both. I'll get it cut once this mess is over. There and then he decided that if he managed to hand the statue to his father he'd go straight back to England and become a simple Manchester schoolboy again. And that couldn't be soon enough as far as he was concerned.

'Better put on your helmet, we're about to join the crowds.'

Tom groaned. 'I'm having enough difficulty breathing as it is. This must be the hottest day since I got here.' It was getting hard for Tom to remember what it felt like to be cool.

'It is a scorcher,' Alice admitted, 'but I don't see any other way of disguising you.'

'Point taken.' Tom grimaced, not having the strength to argue. 'I'll suffer a bit longer.' Putting on the helmet, he lowered the visor, feeling like a spaceman preparing for a moonwalk. 'Can you tell it's me?' His voice came out tinny and distorted.

'You could be anybody.'

Alice covered her face with the mask and together they marched forwards towards the houses and into a different world.

Every narrow, twisting street was festooned with vivid flags, hanging from flower-decked windows and draped across the roadway. Below them, a swirling mass of gaily clad figures, a multicoloured stream of bodies, flowed towards the heart of the village to the accompaniment of music blaring from loud speakers.

Tom stopped suddenly, pulling Alice to the side of the road and crouching down, pretending to tie his shoelace.

'What's the matter?

'You see the man on the opposite side of the road, a few metres down, watching the procession?'

'Tom, there are stacks of people watching the procession. How on earth am I to tell which one you mean?'

'You can't miss him, he's built like a giant. Stands head and shoulders above everyone else.'

Alice straightened and then bent back to Tom. 'OK, I see him.'

'It's the man who caught me in Valletta yesterday, when I was rescued by the police. It means Alphonso's got his men stationed in position to watch for me.'

'We knew he would, your Dad told us. That's why you're disguised. There's no way he's going to recognise you dressed like that. Come on, Tom, we can't hang around here or we certainly will draw attention to ourselves.'

Tom stood reluctantly. 'I can't help feeling vulnerable. I've already had one fight with him and if that policeman hadn't turned up I wouldn't have stood a chance.'

'Here's our solution.' Alice pointed to a large chain of people, holding hands and dancing a conga along the street.

Before Tom could protest, she grabbed his arm and ran to join the laughing line of people. They broke hands in the middle, accepting Tom and Alice into their midst.

'Dance, you idiot,' Alice hissed at him. 'You look really conspicuous just walking along like that. We're supposed to be enjoying ourselves.'

Tom had never felt less like enjoying himself. He hopped along as best he could, in the chain mail trousers that wouldn't bend at the knee and a helmet that bobbed up and down on his head, scratching his bare neck. He felt that he was rapidly losing control of the situation.

By the time they reached the grass in front of the church Tom's self-consciousness had vanished. He stared in amazement at the scene. 'Who are all these people?' The population of the village had increased tenfold during the night.

'Visitors. We always get them, comes with having our festa in August. We're one of Malta's major tourist attractions. Impressive, isn't it?'

'It's incredible.'

As they wandered around, Tom thought of the fetes he had seen in England; they were drab affairs compared to this ostentatious spectacle. Stalls were everywhere, laden with a vast variety of goods: fantastic glass - blown animals caught the sunlight, casting it out in a kaleidoscope of rainbow beams. Intricate lace held the delicate flimsiness of a spider's web. Stands heaped with pink and white nougat attracted hordes of children.

'It's called Qubbagit,' Alice told him, 'and it's one of the traditions of festa days. Mum made a great trayful and I'm sure Francesca added a contribution.'

Tom recognised mqaret, the deep-fried pastries stuffed with dates he'd first sampled in Mdina. He sniffed appreciatively. 'It smells like Christmas. Wish we could buy something,' he added, breakfast having been none existent, 'but my rucksack is. . .' He stopped in horror. 'I've no idea where my rucksack is. I last had it just before Tommasso's man knocked me out and I've not seen it since. It's got my wallet in it, plus my passport.'

'Tommasso probably picked it up. You'll have to get your Dad to ask him.' She glanced at her watch. 'I've just got time to buy some mqaret, we can't have you starving to death, and then we'll collect the statue.'

Tom held back as she pushed through the crowd. He hated what he was about to do. But I've no choice, he thought miserably. I can't run the risk that she's in the plot with her father. Let's hope she has to queue and then spends time looking for me among the sightseers. She'll probably just think I've wandered off.

Dodging round the stalls he hurried to the church, where the steps leading up to the porch way had become a resting place for tired feet. Tom hesitated. Trying to clamber over them was going to draw unwanted attention to himself.

Making his way cautiously round the side of the church, he cast a wary glance over his shoulder. As far as he could tell, no one was showing him any interest and more to the point there was no sign of Alice.

Set into the side wall was a small wooden door. To his surprise the handle turned easily, the door creaking open. Now that the moment was nearly here, Tom's pulse raced. He hoped that the sensation of faintness came from the heat and not from cowardice. He felt suddenly chilled, even on such a hot day.

The door led to a narrow passageway. Tom paused, realising how little he'd thought this out. What if the church was full of visitors? He couldn't simply walk off with the statue. And how was he supposed to reach the ledge? For a moment, he regretted that he had so successfully ditched Alice.

Not much point standing here, he told himself, and crept into the church. It was empty, thank goodness. Flowers perfumed the space with a fragrant odour mingling with the aromatic scent of incense and the Rose Window shaped the morning sun into shafts of fiery light that pierced the wooden pews and washed the floor in crimson pools.

Keeping close to the wall, Tom edged forwards until he stood below the Rose Window and looked upwards at the figure of John the Baptist, the sun turning him to a portrait in blood-red and gold.

The ledge beneath the window was empty.

20

'Where did you get to?' Alice plonked herself down in the pew at Tom's side. He didn't know how long he'd been sitting there, his mind refusing to function. Ignoring the question, he pointed at the empty ledge.

'I wonder how Alphonso beat me to it? The only ones to know about the statue were Dad, me and you.'

There was a moment's silence before Alice's response. 'It's my fault.'

Although it was exactly what he had been thinking, Tom was stunned. It was the last thing he'd wanted to hear. 'You admit it, then?'

'Admit what?'

'That it's your fault the statue's gone?'

'Not exactly.' She looked at him curiously. 'It's my fault that I didn't remember the statue wouldn't be here. Look!' She gestured around the church. 'No chalice. No silver plates. No candlesticks. Remember the day we were going to Marco's café and we saw lots of women coming in here? I said they were cleaning our relics ready for the festa and I told you they'd be put on display. That's where they are now, in the churchyard so everyone can pay their respects. Your Dad should have remembered that, it happens every year, though I suppose it's a long time since he's been to a festa. Come on, I'll show you.'

She seemed to have forgotten about Tom's unexplained disappearing act and he wasn't about to remind her. They left by the side door, continuing round into the churchyard.

Three long trestle tables had been erected, covered with a rich array of relics: silver crosses, candle sticks, small icons, a mediaeval crucifix, illuminated books and gold and silver platters. In the centre of the middle table Tom saw the small wooden statue of the Angel Gabriel, unassuming amidst all the pomp and glory. In full view but unobtainable.

At each side of the tables a line of people passed slowly by, several bowing their heads in respect.

'When are the relics put back in the church?'

'Not until this evening.'

'Well, that's it then. I can't wait that long. I may as well go straight to Dad and report my failure. Unless you've got a plan?'

'No, but we'd better join a queue, we look too conspicuous just standing here.'

What good would that do? Tom's mind reeled with possibilities. Could he snatch the statue and make a break for it? He wouldn't get very far, especially as he'd no idea how to get to the meeting place.

In the line across from him a group of boys jostled for position. Despite the fancy dress, Tom recognised a scarecrow as Ewen. This year his face looked as though it had been dipped in a barrel of dirt. Fortunately, he showed no interest in the knight and clown opposite.

Past the first table they moved, then onwards to the centre table and the statue. In front of him, Alice slowed, bowing her head, before moving on. Tom's bowed head was one of despair: he had lost all hope. The statue was so close, yet it might as well have been a million miles away. Why, just for once, couldn't something go right?

A commotion opposite startled him. The scarecrow, with an enormous yell, hurtled wildly into the table, arms flailing. There were gasps and startled screams from the crowd as the table tilted alarmingly in Tom's direction, its collection of relics raining down at his feet.

'Who pushed me?' Ewen wailed. 'Someone shoved me in the back.'

Tom righted the table, replacing the chalice. He had already seen the statue disappear into the voluminous sleeves of the clown.

'It wasn't my fault!' Ewen's wails increased in pitch, drawing every eye to him. 'I was just looking and someone gave me an enormous shove.'

'No harm done,' his father said comfortingly.

Where had he come from? Through his visor Tom stared hard at Mr Rogerson, but he was taking no interest in anyone but his son. Was he deliberately avoiding the knight and the clown? Surely he would be able to recognise his daughter?

On the other side of Ewen, Marco cheerfully rearranged the treasures. Had one of them pushed Ewen? In that case they knew about the treasure. They wanted Tom to get it. But whose side were they on?

Alice pulled him away. 'Hurry up, Tom! We don't want them to realise they're a treasure short.'

He stared at her sadly, all his suspicions aroused. 'Who helped us? It was no accident. That means that someone else knows all about. . .'

'Tom, come on. You're already late and you know your Dad won't want to hang around too long.'

Seeing no other course of action, Tom followed her towards the back of the churchyard.

'I never want to see another hedge again,' Tom groaned, as they squeezed through into a field. 'How far do we have to go?'

'Just across here, or round the edge would probably be safer.'

'Do you think we could get rid of our fancy dress?' He laughed a touch hysterically. 'A knight and a clown strolling round a field are pretty noticeable.' Perhaps that was her plan.

Alice removed her mask, smiling up at him. 'You've got no stamina. Just think if you'd been a Knight of St John fighting all day in the blazing sun.'

'I'd have melted away completely,' Tom declared.

Stripping off the tabard and chain mail he found it a relief to feel the air on his bare arms. 'I really pity Claudio Farrigiani if he had to dress like this all the time.'

'Here.' Alice handed him the statue. 'Your family heritage. Ready to take it to your father?'

'No!' The word came out as more of a shout than he'd intended.

She stopped, gazing at him strangely. 'What's the matter with you now? Tom what's happening, you've been odd all day?'

He took a deep breath. 'What are your instructions?'

'What?'

'Your instructions from your father?' She stared at him blankly. 'You don't need to pretend, I heard your Dad talking to someone on the phone last night. They were talking about watching out for me and he said it would be easy because he'd given you instructions; that you knew what to do. I want to know what they are. I'm not going to risk you leading Dad into a trap.'

Alice's face blazed with a sudden fury. 'So that's why you tried to lose me at the church. You did it deliberately. After all you've said, you didn't trust me.'

'What are your instructions?' Tom insisted. 'I'm not going anywhere till I know.'

'Alright, I'll tell you. Yes, Dad did give me instructions. And do you know why? Because he's kind and thoughtful, that's why. He was worried about you. He told me you needed a friend, one who'd stick by you even if you were moody and bad tempered and irritable half the time. It was after we came back from Mdina, when we heard about the murder of the security guard and about Giuseppe being in prison, and you were all depressed and cross and talking about going back to England. If you really want to know, I'd had enough of your moods, I was quite ready to give up on you. When Mum asked if we'd had a good day, I mumbled something about you being hard work and Dad jumped on me like a ton of bricks. He told me to imagine what I'd feel like if he suddenly disappeared and that I had to be patient with you and excuse your moods. That I had to stick by you. That's what being a friend is all about. He's told me that over and over again, everytime I've been in danger of losing my temper with you.' She swallowed hard. 'And I have tried to do what Dad said. I have tried to be a good friend, but I've obviously not been very successful. We almost quarrelled about it the other night and I hardly ever quarrel with Dad. It was after that awful meal when we'd just found the second clue, and Mum and Dad both knew something was wrong. I told Dad to leave me alone and I said I didn't know why he was so bothered about you, and he said he hoped that if I were ever in your position, on my own in a foreign country, then someone would be concerned about me.' She turned away abruptly. 'I'm going home now. Carry on down the edge of this field, through the hedge at the bottom, turn left at the road and you'll see the crossroads. I hope everything goes well for you and your Dad.'

She squeezed through the hedge and was gone.

Tom sat in the shade of the hedgerow staring blankly at the small statue, too miserable to move. His hands were clammy and his chest felt as though it were being squeezed by a tight rubber band. Every breath was painful. Hurting Alice like that was the worst thing he had ever done. He'd not felt as bad as this, not even when his father disappeared.

I didn't really know him, he thought wearily; not like I've got to know Alice. I should have realised she'd never let me down. You'd think I'd have learnt my lesson from Dad, but I'm as bad as him at not trusting people. Alice has treated me far better than Dad ever has. Searching for the treasure as a boy got him into trouble but he didn't learn from his mistake. Tom gazed at the statue with distaste. Dad's obsessed with you. When it came to a choice between you and my holiday, I didn't stand a chance. Dad abandoned me without a thought and you're nothing special, just a crude little wooden thing. You're not worth all this misery. Alice is worth more than you any day and now. . . The tears fell and he did nothing to wipe them away.

He glanced up as a shadow fell across him.

'I'm sorry,' Alice said simply. 'I'll see you safely to the crossroads before I go home. I'm not being followed, I promise you. I haven't said a word about the statue to anyone.'

She held out a handkerchief and he took it, wiping away the tears without embarrassment.

'It's me who should apologise,' he stammered. 'Your Dad was right, I did need a friend, but I didn't deserve such a good one as you.'

'Saint Alice! Doesn't sound quite right, does it?' She laughed weakly. 'Well, are we going to take the statue to your father?'

'Is it worth it?'

She sat down beside him. 'What's troubling you, now?'

'Nothing, I'm being silly that's all.'

'You wish it'd been gold or silver and covered with jewels like we imagined?'

Tom reddened. 'I can't keep anything from you, can I?'

Alice grinned. 'Mind reading's another of my skills. When I was lying in bed last night and I couldn't sleep, I was thinking about all the wonderful statues I've seen on display in Valletta and I was disappointed with this plain wooden one. I suppose it's understandable, the Knights are just history to us, yet if you think about it this was carved by Brother Gerard and without him there would never have been an Order of St John. Claudio Farrigiani would never have come to Malta and met his girlfriend, his descendents would never have lived on Malta and you would never have been born.'

'You mean I owe a big thank you to Brother Gerard?' He held up the statue. 'This came all the way from Jerusalem. It's been touched by my ancestor Claudio Farrigiani. That should be enough for me, shouldn't it?'

'I'll tell you what does puzzle me, though. Why the second part of the riddle?'

'We needed it to get all the letters for the clue.'

'Yes, but that was what your Dad called the second layer. The first part also gave us the statue, the angel and the dead tree, and Gabriel's Tower. Why did the second part lead us to the Auberge d'Italie when there was nothing to find. That doesn't make sense.'

Tom shrugged. 'It's something to think of for later. I suppose I'd better get this to Dad. Then we'll both go back to the festa and enjoy ourselves for the rest of the day.'

Hiding their costumes in the hedge, they trekked round the field, through the hedge and on to the road. Turning left, Tom saw the crossroads.

'You sure you want me to come any further?' Alice asked. 'I won't be offended if you'd rather I wait here.'

'No.' Tom took her arm. 'From now on, I'm doing things my way.'

At first sight, the crossroads appeared to be deserted. Tom experienced a familiar sinking feeling. 'Don't tell me Dad's not going to turn up for a third time?'

'We are awfully late.'

'If Dad doesn't appear, this statue is going straight back on the shelf below the Rose Window and I'm having nothing else to do with it.'

'No need for that.' Tommasso Lorenzo stepped out from a gap in the hedge. 'What happened to you? Was there trouble?'

'Nothing we couldn't handle,' Tom said nonchalantly. 'Where's Dad?'

'He decided it was too dangerous for him to be seen here. Alphonso has spies everywhere. I'm to take you to him.' He indicated a car parked behind the hedge. 'Get in, he'll be worried that something has happened to you.'

Tom stood aside to let Alice climb in first.

'Your father insisted you come alone.'

Alice flushed and Tom took her hand. 'Alice comes with me or we both stay here. I'm sick to death of being told what to do.'

Making no further comment, Tommasso settled in the driving seat. Once they were on their way, he glanced over his shoulder. 'You got it, then?'

Tom held up the statue.

Tommasso eyed it in disbelief. 'Is that what we spent all our youth searching for? Doesn't seem worth the effort.'

'It's priceless,' Tom said quietly, wishing he really believed that.

'How come?'

'You'll have to ask Dad. Where are we meeting him?'

'My house in Floriana. You've been there before, remember? Not that you stayed long.'

'What happens then?'

'You'll have to ask your father, I'm only the chauffeur.'

In the silence that followed Alice took Tom's hand, whispering, 'He's in a mood because he hasn't been put in the picture. I felt like that last night. He'll be fine when we get there and your Dad tells us the full story.'

The house was just as Tom recalled, though last time he'd been arriving under less auspicious circumstances. Before they left, he must remember to ask Tommasso about his rucksack.

Tommasso led them into the hallway, pointing to a door on the right. The room in which Tom's guard had watched a film.

'Go straight through.'

Opening the door the first thing Tom saw was his father sitting on a chair facing him, bound and gagged. At his side stood Alphonso, Adriane behind him.

21

Tom stopped in horror, fear skewering him to the spot. At that moment, he knew he had reached the end of his tether and was suddenly more tired than he had ever been in his life. He didn't think he could take anymore.

'Do come in.' Alphonso's smile was less than welcoming. Tom recoiled from the cruel amusement in those cold eyes. His legs felt heavy, wooden, as though it would be impossible to take another step.

Tommasso placed a hand on each of their backs, propelling them forward, before moving to stand on Giuseppe's other side.

A slam behind them and Tom swung round. Carlo lounged against the door, smiling pleasantly. 'Nice to see you again.'

'You know Carlo, I gather?' Alphonso queried.

'Oh yes, we're old friends,' Tom said bitterly. 'Spent a very interesting day together. In fact, I'm surrounded by old friends. You, Tommasso, Adriane, Carlo... Where are the others? What's happened to your servant who looks like a skeleton or the giant who tried to kidnap me yesterday? Where's Ri...?'

'Do we still need the gag?' Adriane interrupted. 'Tom's such a laugh and his father's reaction might be equally entertaining. Beppe was always amusing. They could do a double act. A comedy duo. Father and son. Loser and Loser. Come on, Alphonso, let's have a bit of fun.'

Tom wondered if he'd ever hated anyone as much as he did the Lorenzo family, aware that part of his anger stemmed from the fact that he'd finally made up his mind that Tommasso could be trusted. And despite everything she'd put him through, there was still something about Adriane that he found appealing. How stupid could he be?

A glance at Alice reassured him that she'd known nothing about what was happening. Her face was crumpled in shock.

Alphonso chuckled and removed the tape from Giuseppe's mouth, ripping it away painfully. Tom watched his father run his tongue over raw lips before gazing round with scorn. 'I should have known, shouldn't I? I've been so stupid. It's what I always feared but wouldn't let myself believe: I couldn't trust any of you. But we believe what we want to believe, don't we?'

Tommasso put a hand on his shoulder. 'Beppe, I didn't want it to end like this. I tried to persuade you to tell me where the treasure was. If you hadn't insisted that...'

'Don't make me laugh!' Alphonso's contempt for his brother was obvious. 'Let's have the truth for once. You've been waiting for this moment as avidly as the rest of us, don't pretend you haven't. More so, in fact. You were the one who kept tabs on your little pal during those treasure hunts. All those years of reporting back. Not that you ever had much to report. Quite a failure you were, but I'm surprised we expected anything else.' He grinned sadistically at Giuseppe. 'You didn't know that, did you? That your every movement was being monitored?'

'I thought he was my friend,' Giuseppe said quietly.

Tommasso flushed and turned away.

'The truth hurts, doesn't it?' Alphonso gloated. 'And now I think it's time we took possession of the Farrigiani treasure. We've waited long enough.'

'No!' Instinctively Tom pulled back, clutching the statue as though it were the only thing in the world he possessed.

'Oh, let him keep it for a few minutes.' Adriane smiled wickedly.

'He went to such a lot of trouble to retrieve it. Look at the poor boy, he's terrified. Can't you see him shaking with fear?'

He was shaking, Tom knew, but surprisingly not from fear. Feeling the rage building inside him, he wished his father would show some anger rather than sit there defeated, sunk deep into his chair, head bowed. All the fight seemed to have gone out of him.

Alphonso looked from one to the other. 'Not noted for their courage, the Farrigianis. As you said, like father, like son.'

A riptide of fury swept through Tom. 'Who are you to talk? All I've heard since I got to Malta is about your aristocratic family, how noble you are. That's a joke. What would the people of Malta say if they knew the truth? Would they admire you, then? They'd say you're a disgrace to your name, all of you. And they'd be right. You're nothing but a pack of liars and cheats with blood on your hands.'

'Enough!' All traces of humour vanished from Alphonso's face and his fist slammed down on the table at his side.

'Tom's far nobler than you,' Alice retorted. 'He's descended from a Knight who belonged to one of the greatest families in Europe. You're only a second rate noble.'

Alphonso's face grew even blacker as he stepped towards them.

'Can't take it, can you?' Tom mocked. 'So used to getting your own way. Well you don't scare me. Noble! You haven't a noble bone in your body, none of you. You're the lowest of the low.'

Tom saw the glint of Alphonso's ring just before he backhanded him across the face, sending him sprawling into the wall. He put a hand to his cheek, the fingers coming away red and sticky with blood.

There was an immediate onset of action.

Giuseppe struggled wildly in his chair, anger roused at last. 'Leave him alone! You've got what you wanted.'

Alice launched herself at Alphonso, fists flying, Carlo leaping forward to restrain her. 'Let go!' she yelled. 'Perhaps he'd like to hit me as well. I'm even smaller than Tom.' She broke away from Carlo's grasp to confront Alphonso, cheeks bright red and eyes glaring. 'Go on, hit me. I dare you. Liar! Cheat! Bully! Murderer!'

'Stop it.' Giuseppe's voice cut through her shrieks.

She swallowed hard and held out a hand to Tom, helping him to his feet. Taking a tissue from her pocket she pressed it gently to the cut on his cheek.

Tom saw tears glistening in her eyes and he tried to smile reassuringly, aware that he could offer no comfort. He gazed despairingly at his father, begging him silently to do something.

Giuseppe's tone was cold and threatening. 'You've got me, Alphonso, and the Farrigiani treasure. That's what you wanted so let the kids go.'

'And have them tell their story?' Alphonso looked at him pityingly. 'Do you think we're stupid? I'm afraid we're going to have to arrange a little accident.'

Tom listened in disbelief. This couldn't be happening. It was worse than any nightmare. This was real. There was a crazed look on Alphonso's face and with a sinking heart Tom realised that he was capable of anything.

'If you harm the kids I'll. . .'

'You'll what?' he sneered. 'You're hardly in a position to help them. Shame about the girl but she knows too much. We can't afford to let her go free.'

Tom tightened his hold on Alice's hand. She was white-faced but not trembling. How Tom wished he'd heeded his father's words and left her safely in the village. Every decision he'd made, however well meaning his intention, had been the wrong one.

Tommasso had so far been silent. Now Giuseppe turned to his

former friend. 'Tommasso, have you thought this out? That's my son standing there, named after you, and James Rogerson's daughter. Remember all the happy days we spent at their farm? Are you really going to let them be killed? I presume that's what Alphonso means by a little accident?'

Tom found he'd stopped breathing and exhaled slowly, feeling Alice's hand beginning to tremble. Things like this didn't happen to ordinary people.

'I tried to stop them interfering,' Tommasso blustered. 'I got them away from the Casa Peralta, tried to fob them off with only half the story and told them to keep out of sight. It's not my fault if they chose to ignore my warning. They've only themselves to blame.'

Giuseppe shook his head sadly. 'There's nothing you can possibly say that will justify your actions. You're talking about murder. The murder of two young people the same age as your own son and Alphonso's daughter. The murder of two young people whose fathers thought you were their friend. That's not the Tommasso I knew, or thought I knew.'

Tommasso shuffled uneasily. He was by far the weaker brother, Tom realised, Dad had been right about that. Could they persuade him to help them?

'You did try to get rid of us,' Tom agreed, 'so why are you siding with Alphonso now? It makes you as guilty as he is.'

'You still don't understand, do you?' Alphonso thrust his face close to Tom's. 'There's no point in listening to my brother, he can't get out of his unfortunate habit of telling lies. All that about trying to keep you out of sight! You've no idea how stupid you've been. Do I have to spell it out for you? You were bait. We used you all along, we both did, to lead us to your father and the treasure. I ordered Tommasso to tell you I was hunting Giuseppe because we hoped it would give you the impetus to speed up your search. The supposed rift between us was a complete fabrication, an attempt to get you to trust one side. Which worked perfectly but didn't matter when your father contacted Tommasso and said he intended to ask you to collect the treasure. Trouble is, by that stage Tommasso had lost you and Alice had so kindly told Adriane where we could pick you up. Suddenly we had prisoners we no longer wanted. That's why we let you escape; why Adriane so conveniently forgot to relock the door. You must have thought you were very clever, but you were so easy to fool. You've carried out our plan perfectly, you and your precious father.' He turned to Giuseppe. 'What's it like to be as gullible as your son? Shame you didn't trust Tommasso enough to tell him the whereabouts of the treasure. If you had, we'd have been able to leave the kids out of the equation.'

Giuseppe seemed to deflate, sinking even lower on the chair, and Tom's anger overcame his fear.

'It won't be the first time you've committed murder, will it? Or was that Tommasso? You may as well tell us the truth, now. Which one of you planned the robbery at the Bibliotheca?'

'Neither of them. I did.'

Standing in the doorway was a tall, elderly man who radiated power. Tom didn't need Giuseppe's startled cry of 'Taddeus!' to guess his identity. Taddeus Lorenzo had thick grey hair brushed back from a high forehead, his hawk-like nose reminding Tom of a Roman Emperor. He strolled into the room, straight-backed but completely at ease.

Giuseppe stared at him in bewilderment. 'You? I don't understand. You were the one who helped me; the one who financed my appeal.'

'Rather a nice touch, don't you think? I'm surprised you failed to realise that the robbery was my idea. Surely you didn't credit either of my sons with so much intelligence? I thought you knew them better than that. When Tommasso reported that the Bibliotheca refused to let you see the book, I knew there was no other solution. My sons were carrying out my commands, as they've always done. Both of them. The murder was unfortunate but we got what we wanted, not that it proved any help at the time.'

'Why?' Giuseppe burst out. 'You're rich. You've far more money than you can possibly need, what use was the Farrigiani treasure?'

'Money was never a factor. The treasure would have established our family name for posterity. It will establish our family name, once we hand it over to the authorities. Can't you imagine the plaque? *Relic of Order of St John restored to the nation by Taddeus Lorenzo.*'

'You'll never be able to explain how you found it.'

'We'll prepare a story, don't you fret. Admittedly, we were unable to decipher the riddle, even with the book in our possession, but before your little accident – as Alphonso so rightly termed it – one of you will tell us its meaning, won't you?'

It wasn't a question, Tom realised; Taddeus already knew the answer. How did he expect to extract the information? The thought made Tom shiver.

'What about my parents?' Giuseppe demanded.

'They're quite safe for the moment.' Taddeus regarded him steadily. 'You could say that they are enjoying the hospitality of the Casa Peralta, though perhaps enjoying is not exactly the right word. Hopefully, they will accept whatever story we concoct. If not. . .' He gazed at the statue clutched firmly in Tom's hands. 'Is that the treasure? A wooden statue?' His frown deepened as he turned to Tommasso. 'Are you sure we're not being duped? If we hand this over and it turns out to be worthless we'll be a laughing stock.'

'It's priceless,' Tommasso said quickly. 'Tom told me that in the car on the way here.'

'What makes it so special?'

Tommasso shrugged. 'We didn't get that far.'

Taddeus swung round on Tom who stared at him defiantly. No way would he provide the information.

Taddeus' gaze turned to Giuseppe. 'Which one of you is going to tell me the importance of the statue and the meaning of the riddle? You will talk, I can assure you of that, so why not make it easy for yourselves? Alice?'

'I haven't a clue,' she said untruthfully, glaring at him in defiance. 'Tommasso will tell you that he and I weren't given the information and I wouldn't tell you if I did know.'

A hostile silence descended on the room. Tom stared fiercely at the carpet. His cheek throbbed and he could feel the blood trickling down his face.

'I'm sorry, but you've brought this on yourselves.' There was a distinct chill in Taddeus' voice. He gestured to Alphonso. 'You know what to do.'

Before Tom could move, Alphonso seized Alice, pulling her towards him and twisting her arm viciously behind her back.

Pain tore through her shoulder and she gave an involuntary cry before clamping her mouth closed.

Tom cast an imploring glance at his father. Surely he wouldn't stand by and watch them hurt Alice?

'I'll tell you everything you want to know,' Giuseppe said, 'including the history of the treasure and the meaning of the riddle, as soon as Tom and Alice have safely left this house.'

'You're in no position to bargain.' Taddeus' steely gaze was that of a man used to getting what he wanted. 'You'll tell me now, or your son will. It's up to the pair of you how much we have to hurt the girl. Your choice. I'm sure neither of you want to put her through unnecessary suffering.'

There was another strangled cry from Alice and Alphonso laughed. 'Take your time, I'm enjoying myself.'

Tom could see her eyes were wet from holding back the tears. 'The statue is of the Angel Gabriel,' he blurted out, 'who announced the coming of John the Baptist. It was carved by Brother Gerard in Jerusalem when he founded the Order of St John. It was probably their very first treasure. That's why it's important.'

'And the riddle?'

Tom looked helplessly at his father. 'The dead tree is the wood that the angel was carved from and the heavenly summit was Gabriel's Tower on St John's Cliff.'

'We'd already got that far,' Tommasso said. 'How did your father find the location?'

Tom stared at him sullenly.

There was a gasp from Alice and another laugh from Alphonso.

'The second letter of each word spells out the message *Gabriel statue under the rose in nave*,' Tom snarled. 'It's been in the church at Haz Zahra, on the ledge under the Rose Window, ever since Claudio Farrigiani hid it there after rescuing it from Napoleon. Now let Alice go.'

Alphonso released her and she rubbed her arm fiercely. She almost buckled, dizzy from the pain, and Tom put out a hand to steady her.

'Now all that remains is to arrange your little accident.' There was a cruelty in Taddeus' eyes that frightened Tom more than his words. 'And of course Giuseppe's death will be particularly useful to us as I shall be able to report that he made a last minute confession confirming that he stole the book and killed the security guard. Case closed.'

Surprisingly, Alice was the first to speak. 'I was brought up to admire you,' she said, her voice catching in her throat. 'You have the respect of so many people on Malta because of your family name, but I don't know how you can respect yourself. You called the murder of the security guard "unfortunate" – is that how you think of the little accident you're arranging for us? Haven't you got any conscience?'

'Very noble!' Tom mocked. 'So honourable!'

Taddeus' face darkened with rage but Tom's own anger was once more stronger than his fear. 'Why don't you get your son to hit me again? How about the other cheek this time? Or perhaps he'd like to twist Alice's other arm. That's clearly the height of good breeding in your world. Alternatively, some might say you'd got two thugs for sons.'

For the first time Taddeus' mask of composure faltered. 'There's been enough talking. Take the statue and let's get this finished.'

Tom's bravado vanished as Alphonso stepped towards him, his face twisted in a sneer.

'No!' Adriane had been so quiet that Tom had forgotten her presence. She was standing calmly, gun in hand, pointing it straight at her father.

22

Taddeus laughed, moving towards his daughter, but she gestured him back.

'Don't make the mistake of thinking I won't use this. You taught me to shoot, remember, along with the boys. All those afternoons on the rifle range weren't wasted, I assure you. I think I was a better shot than either of them.'

Her father paused, a sudden wariness in his eyes. Arrogant he might be, stupid he wasn't. 'Hand me the gun, Adriane. Now!'

The last word was a barked command, but she did not even flinch.

'This is ridiculous!' Alphonso strode forward.

A loud retort shook the room and Alphonso gaped in disbelief at the seared carpet by his feet, raising his eyes to the doorway where Carlo stood. His nonchalant pose had vanished. His gun was firmly trained on Alphonso.

'That was a warning,' Carlo said pleasantly. 'Next time the bullet will be higher. Now listen to Adriane and don't be more of a fool than you already are.' He smiled at Tom and Alice and winked.

Suddenly the world seemed a brighter place to Tom. Adriane and Carlo? Had his first instincts been right all along?

'Very dramatic.' Taddeus had regained his composure. 'What exactly do you hope to gain by this, Adriane?'

'You'll find out soon enough. Tom, I think it's about time we released your father. Just keep out of Alphonso's reach, please. I don't trust him not to be stupid and I shouldn't like him to be the one to suffer a little accident. He is my brother, much as it pains me to admit the fact.'

Tom handed the statue to Alice, wincing as he unpeeled the tape from his father's hands.

'Just rip it,' Giuseppe advised. 'It'll be less painful that way.'

Once free, he moved over to take Carlo's gun, asking quietly, 'Did you manage. . .?'

'No problem.'

'Then you know what to do.'

With a wave to Tom and Alice, Carlo left the room.

'What was that about?' Taddeus gestured to the retreating Carlo and Tom could see that he was having trouble reining in his anger. It was probably the first time in his life he hadn't been in control of a situation and the experience was clearly not to his liking.

'You'll find out.' Adriane pointed to the couch. 'Sit there, the three of you.'

'If you think I'm. . .' Alphonso was brought up short by the sight of Giuseppe's gun raised in his direction.

'I was allowed to accompany Tommasso to the rifle range, remember?' Giuseppe said lightly. 'I didn't enjoy the experience but I became quite proficient. Certainly enough to stop you in your tracks if you're going to insist on being stupid.'

'Sit down!' Taddeus signalled his eldest son to obey. Tommasso slumped down on his father's other side, his face a study in misery.

Once seated, Taddeus stared hard at his daughter. 'I think it's about time you stopped all this silliness and told me what's worrying you.'

'What's worrying me?' She gave a hollow laugh. 'I'll tell you what worries me the most; that you even need to ask the question. Do you really not know? You intend to murder – and let's call it by its proper name, no more talk of little accidents – you intend to murder three innocent people, five if you count Luigi and Francesca, and you dare to ask what's worrying me?'

'Suddenly got scruples have you?' Alphonso sneered, his lip curling in contempt. 'You don't deserve to be a member of the family.'

Taddeus silenced him with a glare. 'We've been planning this for months. Why didn't you voice your objections earlier?'

'Because you didn't even think to include me when you were discussing your plans. And would you have bothered to listen if I'd said anything? You never have before, why should it be different this time? I'm the little sister, when have my opinions ever counted? It's all very well being an old family but as far as women are concerned you're living in the Middle Ages. Mum and I are just like wallpaper, decorative but not worth consulting on matters of importance.'

'You're exaggerating.'

'No, I'm not. Funny thing is, I'm not complaining, not about that anyway. It's what I've come to expect in the family, but I can't turn a blind eye to the way you're behaving. All my life you've trampled over anyone who stood in your way. You've made the decisions and Alphonso and Tommasso carried them out without once questioning whether they were right or wrong. I can remember an argument I had with Tommasso when I was a little kid about the way he was spying on Beppe for you, but I never expected to be able to change anything. In fact, if I remember rightly, Alphonso threatened me with murder if I didn't keep my mouth shut. He hasn't changed, has he? When I was older I created a new life for myself in the world outside and stood on my own two feet, which helped to ease my conscience. Believe me, I tried to love my family but you made it very hard work.'

'Then why are you doing this? Why turn against us now?'

'Because, for the last few months I've seen you as you really are and I can't let it continue. Tom and Alice were right, our family honour is a sham. I suppose I've always known that, even if I didn't like to admit the fact. I can't think why I didn't suspect you of being involved in the robbery and the death of the security guard. It's just the kind of thing you would do. When there's something you want you won't let anyone or anything stand in your way. You trade on your wealth, on our family name, and you don't care who gets hurt. Your sons are no better. They haven't even got minds of their own. But I'm not like Mum. I can't pretend it's not happening and I cannot sit back and let you commit murder for the second time. That's why I decided I had to do something to stop you.'

'Whatever you think, Adriane, you are a member of this family,' Taddeus said sternly.' 'Does that not count for anything?'

'Yes it does, which is why I cannot simply hand you over to the police as I ought to do. As I'd like to do. Believe me, the idea is very tempting. After what you've put Tom and Alice through in the last half hour I'd love to see the three of you in prison, but that would mean destroying Mum. She'd never survive the shame.'

With her confession, Taddeus visibly relaxed. 'Then what do you mean to do?'

'You'll hear soon enough. For now, we wait.'

'For what?'

Adriane ignored the question, turning to Tom and Alice. 'You must be tired, do you want to sit down?'

Tom shook his head. 'I'm fine. Can I ask a question?'

'Later,' his father said gently. 'Don't bother Adriane for the moment.'

There was a silence for several minutes and Tom studied the Lorenzo family. He could almost see Taddeus' mind ticking over, working out how he could rescue the situation. Alphonso was red with rage and frustration. Tommasso leaned against the arm of the couch looking drawn and exhausted. Tom could work up no sympathy for him.

Giuseppe and Adriane stood quietly, their guns never wavering.

Adriane looked strained and tired, Tom thought, very different from the lively girl on the plane who had so attracted him. For the first time, it dawned on him what a terrible experience this must be for her. He remembered how he'd felt when he'd considered the possibility that his father might be a murderer. For Adriane it was not just a possibility but the truth. He wondered what he'd have done if he'd been placed in the same position. Would he have been able to turn his father over to the police?

The silence was broken by the sound of a mobile phone. Adriane took it from her pocket, listened a second, smiled and nodded at Giuseppe before saying, 'Thanks. Yes, everything's fine here, they're behaving for the moment. We'll see you later.'

'Who was that?' Taddeus demanded.

He has a nerve, Tom thought, almost in admiration. He still hasn't accepted that he's beaten.

'That was Carlo, which is why I can now tell you our plan. You'll find it has an advantage over yours in that nobody gets hurt. Carlo was ringing to say that he has successfully completed the task we set him.'

'Which was?' Alphonso growled.

'To make a recording of everything that happened in this room after the arrival of Tom and Alice. Every word. Which means that we don't need these anymore.'

She and Giuseppe lowered their guns.

Alice shrieked as Alphonso launched himself forward, grabbing her and pulling her in front of him. She struggled frantically as Tom leapt forward to grab Alphonso's arm.

'Stop that!' Taddeus snarled. 'Let the girl go. For god's sake, Alphonso, use your wits for once.'

He released her reluctantly and she gave him a shove, saying scornfully, 'Even I can see you're beaten and it's what you deserve. I'd hit you if it didn't mean I was sinking to your level.'

'Alice!' Giuseppe was smiling as he gestured for her and Tom to move back. 'How about letting Alphonso sit down again?'

'I'll stand.'

Taddeus caught his son's arm in a pincer grip, yanking him down beside him. Looking at Adriane he asked, 'Where is the tape now?'

'Do you really think I'd tell you that? All you need to know is that it has been delivered to a person who also has as much influence here on Malta as you do. Carlo put it in a package with a covering note giving instructions that it be handed to the police if anything happens to Giuseppe, Tom, Alice, me or Carlo.' She smiled at her father. 'Of course we can retrieve the tape at any time so you'd better make sure that Alphonso understands the situation; he's shown very little intelligence so far.

'You won't get away with this,' Alphonso blustered.

'We've already got away with it.' Adriane looked wearily at Taddeus. 'Can't you knock some sense into your eldest son?'

'He'll behave.' Tom could see that Taddeus had finally accepted the bitter truth that for the first time in his life he'd been beaten.

'He'd better, because this time your wealth and position will be of no use: you condemned yourselves with your own words. Just think back over what you said. It's all there on the tape: how you planned the robbery. How Alphonso and Tommasso carried it out, which makes one of them a murderer. How you kidnapped Luigi and Francesca and were planning to kill Beppe, Tom and Alice. That would involve a lengthy prison sentence, though what you'd probably hate even more would be the trial when all the details of the tape were made public. Think how your precious society would react to your eldest son striking a sixteen year old boy or taking such delight in hurting a young girl. Your noble ancestry wouldn't be worth much then, would it?'

'I suppose it's too late,' Taddeus asked, 'to realise that the brains of the family were handed down to the daughter?'

'Far too late,' she said sadly, turning to Giuseppe. 'Can we go now, please?'

He took her hand and led her from the room, Tom and Alice following.

A car was waiting outside, Ricardo at the wheel. By now Tom was immune to surprises, not bothering to even comment on his uncle's presence. Adriane sat beside Ricardo, Giuseppe squeezing on to the back seat with his son and Alice, who handed him the statue.

Ricardo looked back at his younger brother. 'Everything go as planned? I saw Carlo come haring out and he gave me a wave.'

'Down to the last detail. It's all over.'

Tom could not believe what he was hearing. He stared angrily at his father. 'You knew this was going to happen? You knew Tommasso was in league with Alphonso and his father?'

'Adriane told me.'

'Then everything in that room,' Tom spluttered, 'when we thought we were about to die, all that was staged by you?'

His father flushed. 'I'm afraid so, but I'm not proud of what I've put you both through. I tried to keep Alice out of it. I asked you not to tell her about the treasure and I told Tommasso to leave her in the village. You were the one who insisted on bringing her along.'

That silenced Tom for a moment, before he muttered, 'What about me? I'm only your son. I suppose I don't count?'

'Of course you count. I tried to stop you travelling to Malta, remember? Once you'd arrived and come to the attention of the

Lorenzo family I had to include you in my plans. You left me no other choice.'

'Where were you hiding?'

Giuseppe sighed. 'It's all very complicated. Do you mind waiting just a little longer? We're on our way to Haz Zahra and I'm going to have to tell the full story to my parents. Yes, they're safe, you don't need to worry about them. I'll tell you the details when we're all together.'

Forty minutes later they reached Haz Zahra. Picnickers dotted the green, many in large family groups. Sunlight transformed the church lights to sparkling diamonds and high above the angel blazed forth in all its glory. Tom thought of the other angel, safe in his father's pocket; far less spectacular, but far more precious.

They circled the grass slowly, weaving in and out of excited tourists.

'We're never going to be able to park,' Alice said. 'You have to get here incredibly early for that.'

'No problem.' Ricardo smiled, gesturing at a waving figure.

Marco was waiting outside his café, a parking place reserved. Beside him was Alice's father. As they got out of the car, he hugged his daughter.

'What happened to your clown disguise?'

'Stuffed in a hedge. You knew it was me?

'I'd know you anywhere and I watched your mother make the outfit. The identity of the Knight didn't take much guessing. I've collected your bike from the ditch, by the way. Adriane told me where you'd dumped it. Your front wheel will never be the same again.'

Tom looked curiously between Marco and Mr Rogerson. 'It must have been one of you two. Who pushed Ewen into the table so that we could get the statue?'

Marco beamed. 'You might say it was a combined effort. James gave him a shove and I tipped the table.'

Mr Rogerson chuckled. 'Poor Ewen, he's never going to live it down.'

'Then you knew about the treasure. Both of you. You not only knew what it was but where it was.' Tom glared at his father. 'All that talk about secrecy. "It's best to keep it between you and me", that's what you said.'

'And who told Alice?'

Tom blushed. 'That's different.'

'It's alright, I'm only teasing. I've a lot of explaining to do, I know, but first I've got an important meeting.'

Mr Rogerson patted his shoulder. 'They're over the far side of the green, my wife's keeping them company.'

They made their way across the grass towards a picnic table under the shade of a large tree. Luigi and Francesca were sitting, backs to them, with Mrs Rogerson.

Giuseppe paused and Tom felt a sudden lump in his throat.

As if sensing their presence, Francesca looked round. The next moment she was flying across the grass towards her youngest son.

23

'Story!' Tom demanded. 'You can't put it off any longer. There's such a lot I don't understand.' He and Alice had worked their way through the contents of Francesca's large picnic hamper and then begun emptying Mrs Rogerson's. 'This is the first food I've had since yesterday evening,' Tom explained in way of justification, 'and that was only sandwiches. No wonder I'm hungry.'

'I did buy you some mqaret at the fete,' Alice teased, 'but you did a vanishing act on me.'

'One of my mistakes.' Tom reddened. 'One of my many mistakes. I was a disaster area.'

'It's alright, you're forgiven.'

He grinned and reached once more into the picnic hamper.

The adults watched them thankfully. At least the events of the day had not dimmed their appetites. They were gathered together, the Farrigianis, the Rogersons – minus Ewen who had wandered off with friends - Marco and Adriane.

'Well?' Tom looked across at his father, sitting between Francesca and Adriane. 'I'm beginning to suspect Alice and I were the only two who didn't know what was going on.'

Luigi patted his hand. 'Don't worry, Francesca and I were equally in the dark.'

'But you guessed I was your grandson, didn't you?'

'Eventually. Not at first. Then, when you started asking questions about Giuseppe I began to put two and two together. I went up to the attic to get his treasure chest and saw you'd managed the combination. That's what confirmed my suspicions. I was going to talk to you but left it too late.'

'Were you kidnapped by Tommasso? He told me you were somewhere safe but then Taddeus said that you were being held at the Casa Peralta.'

'Tom!' Giuseppe sighed. 'How about trying to let me explain, though it won't be easy. It's what you might call complicated and. . .'

'Don't worry, it couldn't be any more complicated than what I've experienced so far. It got to the stage where I was suspecting everyone.'

'Even me.' Alice smiled at him.

'Even you,' Tom acknowledged, 'which is something I'm not proud of. It started when I saw you with Adriane and Carlo and. . .' He turned to her accusingly. 'You've never explained that impersonation on the plane. Why on earth did you say you were Alice Rogerson?'

'Tom!' His father laughed. 'You're jumping right into the middle of the story.'

'Tommasso accused me of that.' He looked suddenly sad. 'I'm sorry about Tommasso. I liked him much better than Alphonso and he was your friend for a long time, even if he was spying on you. That must count for something.'

'He was my first friend, but right from the start I always knew if it came to a question of loyalty between me and his family they'd win every time. The Lorenzos were all brought up to revere the family name, which is why this has been so difficult for Adriane, and why we had to plan things the way we did.'

Marco clapped Tom on the shoulder. 'What have I told you about asking questions? Come on youngster, keep your mouth shut for a bit and let Beppe tell things his way. James and I have the band concert shortly.'

Alice leaned over and handed Tom a pasty. 'Fill your mouth with that. I don't know about you, but I'm bursting with curiosity.'

All eyes turned to Giuseppe, who took a deep breath. 'This will have to be a condensed version or we'll be here till midnight. You all know the first part, when Tommasso and I were kids, there's little point rehashing that. Dad was right, I had become obsessed with finding the treasure, I know that now. I just wish I'd heeded his warning. At the trial I'd no idea who was responsible for the robbery at the library, I just knew it hadn't been me, though after Taddeus offered to finance my appeal I had my suspicions that Alphonso might be involved.'

'You never suspected Tommasso?' Ricardo asked.

'No. He visited me in prison, was very upset about the whole situation and said he'd persuaded his father to help me. I should have realised at the time that Taddeus wasn't a man who yielded to persuasion. Even the money he gives to charity has the ulterior motive of enhancing the family name. Anyway, after I was acquitted I behaved abominably.' He glanced regretfully at his parents. 'I've no excuse to offer, except that I was a very confused young man. All I wanted was to get away from Malta as quickly as possible and leave the whole sordid mess behind me. I was running away; never a sensible option because the past has a nasty habit of trailing in your wake. I didn't want to think about the Farrigiani treasure ever again. I didn't even want to be a Farrigiani. That's why I changed my name from Giuseppe to Joseph and my surname to Newton because……'

'*Ton* is the Old English for a settlement,' Alice interrupted, 'and you were settling in a new place. Tom explained it,' she added, grinning at her father's raised eyebrows.

'Glad to see you were listening on those car journeys.'

'And I'm listening now. Go on.'

'It felt strange at first, as you can imagine. I'm not sure that

Joseph Newton ever really felt like me, but everything went well for a while. I studied history and got my degree, met your mother, married and had you.'

'And called me after Tommasso Lorenzo?'

'I still thought of him as my closest friend, even if we didn't correspond very often. Maybe one day, now this has been sorted out, we might be able to resume our friendship. It won't be the same, I know. One thing I've learned – the hard way – is that you can never totally put the past behind you. At least, I can't. It's why my marriage didn't work. Part of me was grasping with both hands at the new life I was carving out for myself in England; another part remained here on Malta. I couldn't forget what had happened and stupidly I bottled it all up inside. I should have told Tom and his mother the full story. They might have been able to knock some sense into me. If I had told them we'd probably be still together as a family, but it's too late for that now.'

Far too late, Tom thought, recalling the hulking American who had whisked his mother off to Montana.

'After the divorce I immersed myself in travelling, anywhere but to Malta which was the one place I was desperate to visit, and all the time I was becoming more and more frustrated with my life. Then, about a year ago, I met Adriane in London. She'd been a child of nine when I left Malta, yet I recognised her immediately. I'm ashamed to say that at first I didn't tell her who I was.'

'I made no connection between Joseph Newton and the Giuseppe Farrigiani who'd been a large part of my childhood,' Adriane said. 'It's not surprising; the Beppe I remembered was always laughing. I had a very clear memory of his grin.'

Alice nodded. 'I know. We saw the photograph.'

'Whereas Joe was a grave, rather serious man.'

'I can see that.' Francesca squeezed her son's hand, the hand she'd been holding ever since they'd sat down. 'How did you find out who he was?'

'He confessed eventually and we decided it would be best if I didn't mention him at home. Giuseppe seemed to have faded from our lives; I hadn't heard him mentioned for years, not even by Tommasso.'

'I'd virtually lost contact with him,' Giuseppe agreed, 'and we didn't know how they'd view our friendship. What happened next is Adriane's story, to start with anyway.'

Adriane swallowed hard and Alice looked at her with sympathy, knowing how difficult it must be to disown your family. She remembered the pain she'd felt when Tom accused her own father. For Adriane it was much worse.

'I'd returned to Malta,' Adriane said finally. 'I have a contract to do a certain number of lectures at the university. I'm another historian, I'm afraid, which is why Beppe and I found we had so much in common.

'I returned home early one day – a lecture was cancelled – and when I entered the drawing room father was standing at the fireplace, his back to me, gazing earnestly at a book. There was nothing strange about that, our house is full of books, and I was about to greet him when he slammed the book shut angrily, stooped and placed it up the chimney. It was so unexpected that I left hurriedly without him seeing me. Later, curiosity got the better of me and I went back and retrieved the book.'

'And found it was the one stolen from the Bibliotheca,' Tom declared. 'Both Tommasso and Alphonso claimed to have found it up there. Was either story true?'

'A pure fiction,' Adriane asserted. 'They knew it was there all along. The only one who hadn't known was me.'

'Did you tackle your father?'

'No. I might have done if I hadn't already met Beppe. I realised at once that the family had been involved in the robbery and murder, leaving Beppe to take the blame. It was something I couldn't forgive. I rang Beppe in England, told him what I'd found, and he came out secretly to Malta. We met at Ricardo's and I gave him the book. He took it back to England.'

Luigi and Francesca turned accusing faces to their eldest son. 'I'm sorry,' Ricardo protested, 'I couldn't tell you. Beppe wanted to do it his way. I argued with him but he felt he couldn't make peace with you until he'd proved beyond doubt that he wasn't a thief and a murderer.'

'Then you knew about me when I arrived here?' Tom alleged. 'When Grandfather rang you on Sicily and you pretended you'd never heard of Joseph or Tom Newton?'

'Afraid so, though I daren't admit it, which is why I told them to keep hold of you till I returned. If I hadn't been responsible for the school party I'd have dashed home straight away. I was worried about what had happened to Beppe.'

'Don't blame Ricardo,' Giuseppe begged. 'I had this fixed idea that I wanted to put things straight before I returned to the Villa Magrino, and I wanted to bring Tom with me. I reckoned that the book would help me find the treasure and prove I'd been right to believe in its existence.'

'And it did,' Alice stated.

'As soon as I read about Claudio's fascination with Brother Gerard and the wooden statue he'd carved of the Angel Gabriel, the riddle gave up its message fairly easily. I was all set to come out and retrieve the treasure when I had disturbing news from Adriane.'

'My father discovered the book was missing. He tackled my brothers, never thinking to question me, and I managed to hear most of their conversation. Half the time I don't think they even noticed I was present. Alphonso and Tommasso both denied removing the book, naturally. I don't know that my father believed either of them. Then he somehow found out that Beppe had been to Malta and that's when things began to get ugly. He warned my brothers of the danger if Beppe ever discovered the truth, yet at the same time he still wanted to get his hands on the treasure. I was horrified when I learned the full extent of their involvement and the fate they envisaged for Beppe. That they could discuss murder so calmly was frightening.'

Luigi sensed her pain. 'That's when you devised the plan to trap them?'

'Not immediately.' Giuseppe took up the tale. 'Adriane returned to England, very upset at what she'd learned. Before she left, she confided in a friend.'

'Carlo?' Alice guessed.

Adriane nodded. 'Carlo works in the gardens. We've always been close and I knew I could trust him. He offered to keep a watch on my father and brothers. Then they played right into our hands by recruiting him into their plan, not that they told him of their previous crime.'

'Just after she returned,' Giuseppe continued, 'I got a phone call out of the blue from Tommasso. He was very cagey, said he'd been thinking a lot about the past and was I any nearer to solving the riddle. I knew exactly what he was getting at. I had to think quickly so that I didn't implicate Adriane. I said that the stolen book had arrived mysteriously through the post from Malta and I'd no idea who sent it. Tommasso immediately claimed that it had been him, which I knew was a lie, of course. He told me a complete fabrication about Alphonso – the same story he presumably told Tom and Alice – though I had the advantage of knowing it was false. He urged me to come to Malta and I agreed, saying I would let him know date and time. I made no mention of bringing Tom and certainly had no intention of letting him know when I'd be arriving. I thought Tom and I could collect the treasure, hand it over to the authorities, and then there was nothing the Lorenzo family could do to interfere. You know how wrong I was.' He paused, clearly thinking of all the trouble that had ensued.

'If you don't get a move on,' Marco complained, 'James and I are going to miss the ending.'

'I arranged the holiday with Tom. The morning before we were due to travel, Tommasso phoned to say he'd heard Alphonso on the telephone and that his brother knew I was arriving the following day. I'd like to think that Tommasso was concerned about saving me from what Alphonso had planned, for the sake of our earlier friendship. I told him I'd come out that day instead - perhaps it was foolish but I was determined to give him every chance to redeem himself – and arranged to meet him at Ricardo's. I didn't realise he was away until I got there. I rang Tom to postpone the holiday but got no answer.'

'I was watching Mum get married,' Tom said dryly.

'I remembered as soon as I'd put down the phone, which is why I decided I couldn't disappoint you. Instead, I left a message at Gatwick for you to continue alone, thinking that by the time you got here everything would be over and I could meet you at the airport. Trouble was, I arrived to a reception committee. How Alphonso got wind of the change of plan I don't know, he could have heard Tommasso on the phone to me. Neither brother trusted the other. Fortunately, I recognised two of Alphonso's friends before they recognised me. I took a taxi to Ricardo's, found the house deserted and used my own key.

'While I was waiting for Tommasso I tried to ring Adriane in England. She was out so I left a message with her flat mate, asking Adriane to go to Gatwick and exchange the note I'd left for Tom with another telling him not to travel. I'd just put the phone down when two cars pulled up outside the house. The first contained Alphonso. As you can imagine, I didn't hang around. My only option left was to hide out with a friend.'

'Where did you go?' Tom asked. 'Tommasso looked for you everywhere.'

'So did Alphonso,' Alice added. 'You were very popular.'

'I came here to Haz Zahra.'

'Here?' Tom looked astounded. 'You were here all along?'

'He came to stay with me,' Marco said proudly. 'When Ricardo was not there to help him, who else should he turn to but Ricardo's best friends?'

'You and Dad!' Alice exclaimed. She turned accusingly to her father. 'Then Tom was right, you were involved all the time I was defending you.'

'I wasn't right at all,' Tom admitted. He looked sheepishly at Mr Rogerson. 'I thought you were in league with Alphonso. Sorry. It was when I saw you talking and laughing with Carlo and I thought Carlo was the enemy.' His words trailed away. 'What a muddle it all was. No wonder Alice and I got confused. And how come I ended up on Malta if Adriane was supposed to stop me travelling?'

'Because I didn't get the message in time. I was late home that night and my friend had gone to bed. When she remembered the next day I dashed to the airport, only to find that you'd collected the note. Giuseppe had left me his ticket and I was able to register it in my name. That's how I ended up sitting next to you on the plane.'

'Why didn't you tell me who you were?'

'How could I? You'd never heard of the Lorenzo family. You still thought your father was Joseph Newton, an Englishman. It was Beppe's place to tell you the truth, not mine.'

'I can see that but not why you said you were Alice Rogerson. It doesn't make sense.'

'It doesn't make any sense at all. I was in the middle of what you so rightly call a muddle. I'd no idea what I was going to do. All I could think of was that your father didn't want you on Malta and how I'd messed up his plans. You showed me the note, asking about Haz Zahra. My mind was stuck there when you suddenly asked my name. I started to say Adriane – got as far as the A – panicked and said Alice. After that, I couldn't think of any other surname but Rogerson. You see how bad I am at lying.'

'Don't worry.' Tom grinned at Alice's parents. 'I told the police I was Ewen Rogerson. I'm sorry about that, like Adriane I was in a bit of a panic at the time.'

'My one hope,' Adriane said, 'was that you'd never get as far as Haz Zahra.'

'You stole my note, didn't you?'

'Afraid so,' she apologised. 'I had this vague idea that you wouldn't remember the names and when no one met you at the airport, because I knew Beppe wasn't expecting you, the officials would send you to the Consulate and you'd end up back in England.'

'They tried to. They thought they were dealing with an idiot, especially when my supposed relations failed to acknowledge me. Where did you go? You dashed off pretty quickly.'

'I'd no idea where Beppe was so I went home to the Casa Peralta. Carlo told me that Beppe had escaped from Ricardo's and that Alphonso had broken in and set up headquarters there, hoping Beppe would return.'

'So it was your house.' Tom rolled his eyes at his Uncle. 'I saw my photo on the bedroom wall, which made me wonder. I didn't think I had the sort of relationship with Alphonso that he'd want my image staring down at him every night.'

'It was my house, but you're jumping ahead again. I'm as much in the dark as you about what happened. I was in Sicily, don't forget.' He smiled at his brother. 'If I'm clear so far, we left you with Marco, Adriane at the Casa Peralta, a bewildered Tom at the Villa Magrino and Alphonso staking out my house.'

'I realised things had gone wrong and Tom had arrived here after all when he and Alice came badgering Marco with questions about me. Yes,' he said, raising a hand to forestall Tom's protest, 'I was upstairs all the time you and Alice were tucking into ice creams. You put Marco in a difficult position. You see, I daren't acknowledge you for fear of putting you in greater danger. I was relieved to hear that Mum and Dad had taken you under their wing and I got Marco to phone Luigi to complain that you were asking questions about Giuseppe Farrigiani. I knew he'd be cross. James pretended to be angry with Alice. We mistakenly thought that might shut you up. How wrong could we be?'

Mr Rogerson glanced at his daughter. 'I gave Alice instructions to stick by Tom, so we had some idea of where they were and what they were up to.'

'I don't understand,' Luigi said. 'Why didn't Marco collect the treasure for you and put an end to the whole mess?'

'Because by that time,' Giuseppe explained, 'I could no longer be sure that retrieving the treasure would be sufficient. It was clear I was going to have to deal with the Lorenzo family and until I did the statue was safer in the church. Also, I had Adriane to consider. I couldn't simply denounce her family. I rang England from Marco's only to be told that Adriane had flown to Malta. I guessed she'd be at the Casa Peralta. I couldn't simply walk in there but James came to my rescue.'

'I paid one of my visits to Mdina,' Alice's father said, 'and managed to get a message to her via Carlo.'

'I came straight out to Marco's', Adriane continued, 'and that's when we devised the plan. We knew we had to find a way to trap my father and brothers into condemning themselves with their own words. It was the only way to ensure their good behaviour.'

'Trouble is,' Giuseppe said with a smile, 'we hadn't reckoned on Tom and Alice who came up with a few diversions of their own.'

'You ought to be grateful,' Alice responded. 'I think we kept Tommasso and Alphonso well and truly occupied.'

'You certainly did,' her father added. 'It was worrying but we gave you as much protection as we could.'

'Like ringing Carlo and telling him we were at the Busskett Gardens,' Tom accused. 'That was you, wasn't it?'

'Guilty, I'm afraid.'

'That's one of the things that made me suspect you.'

'For our plan to succeed,' Giuseppe told them, 'I needed to get myself captured, though unfortunately Tom kept beating me to it.'

Tom clearly remembered the first time, outside the Villa Magrino. He looked at Luigi and Francesca. 'What happened to you?'

'We were stupid,' Luigi answered. 'Tommasso came to the Villa Magrino. He told us Giuseppe had arrived on Malta and wanted to see us. He had a car waiting and he promised to remain at the farm to tell you where we'd gone. We were taken to the Casa Peralta and put under lock and key. Carlo released us this morning and drove us home.'

'Carlo and Adriane have been invaluable,' Giuseppe said quietly. 'Carlo has been completely loyal and Adriane kept me posted on developments at the Casa Peralta so I was always one step ahead of both Tommasso and Alphonso. The problems started when Tom escaped from Tommasso's house. I thought that was my opportunity and contacted Tommasso, ready to put our plan into action. I knew that once I'd got the statue he'd hand me over to Alphonso and that

Taddeus wouldn't be far away. We had Carlo prepared to record the situation.

'Then Alphonso gave Adriane and Carlo the job of picking up Alice. He must have been having her watched because he knew she was biking to Valletta. It would have looked too suspicious if they'd refused, so Tom and Alice ended up in Alphonso's clutches. That threw me into a panic. All I could think of was to tell Tommasso that I knew Tom was on Malta and he was the only one I would trust to collect the treasure. As I expected, they allowed Tom and Alice to escape.'

'That's where James and I nearly complicated matters,' Marco confessed. 'When Ricardo landed from Sicily we met him at the docks and put him in the picture as far as we knew it. His wife and daughters went to stay with friends. Not realising that Tom and Alice were being allowed to escape, Ricardo used his key to see what was happening.'

'Imagine my surprise when I opened the door to see Alice standing there. I recognised Tom immediately; your Dad says you've got your mother's hair but there's no mistaking the Farrigiani eyes. I'm sorry I was so harsh with you both. I was taking my lead from Carlo and as it was I nearly blew his cover.'

'That's why Marco just happened to be waiting for us at the Bus Terminal,' Alice said.

'You know all the rest.' Giuseppe looked at them apologetically. 'Having told Tommasso that Tom was to collect the treasure, I couldn't help but involve him. I did try to keep Alice out of it, though Tom had other ideas. I'm sorry you had to go through that scene with Taddeus, it must have been very frightening, but it was the only way we could get them to betray themselves. If it's any consolation, you were both incredibly brave.'

'Not inside,' Tom confessed.

'It was even harder for Adriane,' Alice said. 'You must have hated every minute.'

'There was no other way and it's over now. Dad realised that, and he'll keep Alphonso in check.'

'What about the statue?' Luigi asked. 'It might surprise you, but I also had a spell of searching for it when I was a boy.'

Giuseppe smiled, taking it from his pocket and handing it to his father. 'It will return to its rightful home with the Order of St John. Maybe it will be put with the other relics in the Cathedral and we'll be able to go and visit. It's taken over two centuries, but I like to think that Claudio Farrigiani is looking down and giving us his blessing.'

June 1798

The stables were dark yet they dare not risk a lamp. The moon, shimmering and ghostly, sent a beam of pallid light through a narrow window to illuminate the four figures standing motionless by one of the stalls.

'I wish you wouldn't do this.' Claudio heard the catch in Paolo's voice. There was not even the semblance of a smile on his face tonight.

'I'm sorry, it's something I've got to do. I haven't any choice.' He remembered the words of Ferdinando Rosato and said quietly, 'It's my turn to stand up and be counted.'

His thoughts went out to the older Knight who, during their time on Malta, had been like a father figure to him and his friends. Mdina had fallen to the French with the same ease as had Valletta. Ferdinando had arrived at the Auberge d'Italie that morning, angry and weary and saddened, but had enveloped Claudio in a comforting hug, before turning to embrace each of his companions. It was amazing the way they all felt so much better for his presence.

'The streets out there aren't safe.' Gianni's voice betrayed his anxiety. An unnaturally subdued Gianni he was, with a bandage round his head and his arm in a sling. 'The French are looting everywhere. They've stripped the Sacra Fermeria of all the silver plates, they're even boasting that they're going to smelt it down, and they're carrying crate loads of treasures from the cathedral.'

'Can't you tell us why this is so important to you?' Tullio pleaded. 'We're willing to come with you, you know that.'

'Of course I know that, but I'll be safer alone. Four of us together would be spotted far too easily. Don't worry about me, I'll keep to the back streets and I won't ride until I'm through Floriana. As for telling you why, I promise I will tomorrow, when we've left Malta. Once you know, you'll agree it is something I have to do.'

His words silenced them all. The thought of leaving the island they had grown to love weighed heavily on all their hearts

'I'm glad Ferdinando's coming with us.' Paolo sounded like a little boy and Tullio put a comforting arm across his shoulders.

'I'd better go.' Claudio led his favourite chestnut-brown mare from her stall for the last time and wrapped the dark woollen cloak more closely around him. 'I won't be recognised in this, so there's no cause for any of you to worry.'

Gianni eased the stable door open. 'We'll wait here for you.'

'No, go back to the auberge. You never know, the French may decide they want our horses as well as our treasures. I'll see you there as soon as possible.'

'You will come back, won't you?' Paolo clutched his cloak in desperation. 'You won't decide to stay on Malta and hide out at Haz Zahra?'

There was a moment's silence.

'I'll return, I promise.' Claudio looked at his friends. 'The only way the Order will survive this is if we stick together.'

It seemed a long way through the tangle of back alleys, but Claudio Farrigiani knew he had no other course. In the main streets he could hear the shouts and laughter of the French as they ransacked Valletta, mingling with the cries of women and the sobbing of a child. The sky glowed red with fires that rampaged through scenes of devastation.

Once he was beyond Floriana, he mounted his horse and cantered across the plain towards Haz Zahra. All was going to be well.

Tullio's book was hidden in the auberge and his precious bundle he clutched safely beneath his cloak.

The second clue was already lodged in the Tower of Gabriel. He hoped that one day someone would realise its significance.

Now only the final task remained.

24

The day was a feast of sound and colour, the festa drawing to a close with the big bang that Alice had promised. Tom could feel the heat from the bonfire, even from a distance. He'd drawn apart from the others, feeling the need for a few moments alone. It had been an action-packed day: early mass with Dad, his grandparents, Adriane and Ricardo - he supposed it was time he started calling him uncle. Then Ricardo's wife and daughters had arrived for lunch and there were cousins to meet. It was going to take some getting used to, being part of a large family.

The Rogersons, Marco and Carlo had joined them for the saint's procession through the streets and now they were gathered by the blazing fire. He could see Alice clinging to her father's arm and laughing. How could he ever have suspected him of being in league with Alphonso?

'Penny for your thoughts?' His father materialised at his side.

'Just thinking. It's been an eventful week.'

'Still cross with me?'

Tom looked steadily at his father, his words sending him spinning back to the previous evening. . .

He'd made his way to bed too wound up to settle, slumping back against the pillows and staring out into the darkness, until there was a gentle tap at the door.

It had opened to reveal Luigi. 'I guessed you were too restless to sleep.' He tiptoed in, shutting the door behind him. 'Perhaps it's time we had that little talk we were going to have before events overtook us.'

'That was only two nights ago. I can't believe such a lot has happened in just a couple of days.'

'For you, maybe. It seemed endless to me and Francesca.'

'Did they treat you badly?'

'Not at all, but they locked us in a bedroom and left us with our worries. We had no idea of what was happening, and the worries you imagine are often far worse than the reality.' Tom nodded in agreement. 'I was so thankful to see Carlo when he released us.'

'He didn't tell you anything?'

'Only that Tommasso had spoken the truth about Giuseppe being on Malta. You can imagine how we felt about that, after all these years. Carlo said that Beppe and Adriane were bringing events to a close and they would meet us at the festa later, bringing you and Alice with them. It seemed such a long time until you arrived.' He looked gravely at his grandson. 'Isn't it time you forgave your father?'

Tom flushed. 'Have you and Francesca forgiven him? He hurt you far more than he hurt me.'

'For Francesca there was nothing to forgive. She is a far more generous person than I am.'

'That's not true,' Tom protested. 'You've always been kind to me, even when you had no idea who I was. It can't have been easy for you when I descended out of nowhere, claiming to be a long lost relative. A very tearful one at that.'

'And now you are one, which makes me happy.'

'Me too,' Tom said shyly. 'Well, what about Dad? Have you forgiven him?'

'Yes I have, I couldn't do anything else. When Beppe was released from prison Francesca begged me to go to him and make my peace. Like a stupid fool, my pride prevented me until it was too late and my son had left the country. I've always regretted that. Don't make the same mistake that I did, Tom.'

'What I can't get over is that Dad didn't seem to learn his lesson. Despite all the suffering he'd caused, to himself, to you and Francesca, to me and Mum, as soon as Adriane gave him the book and he'd solved the riddle off he went treasure hunting again. The statue belongs in the past. Why couldn't it have stayed in the past?'

Luigi smiled. 'One thing you'll learn if you spend much time on Malta, and we all hope you will, is that the past is all around us. Wherever you look, the landscape or the buildings or the people, you'll see the past and the present are irretrievably linked. The statue is part of our heritage: yours, Beppe's, Ricardo's and mine. Claudio Farrigiani gave us our name which you may one day pass to your own sons. Don't you think we owe it to him to return his treasure to the Order he loved?'

'Will we ever find out what really happened to him?'

'Maybe, one day. I'd like that. And your father says that he will tell us all the details that Tullio Falcone wrote in his book. We can learn about Claudio's friends and what his life was like here on Malta. From what your father has said so far, Claudio Farrigiani seems a very idealistic young man. In fact, he sounds very like you. I'm sure he'd be proud of the way you've conducted yourself this week.'

'What will happen to the book? We can't keep it, can we? It doesn't belong to us.'

'When your father hands over the statue, he will take the book at the same time. He is going to say that it was posted to him from Malta, that he has no idea who sent it, but it enabled him to solve the riddle and retrieve the treasure.'

'Will they believe him?'

'Adriane will back him up. She will say she was there when the book arrived.'

'More lies?'

'Unfortunately yes, but he could not think of any other way of returning the book without implicating the Lorenzo family. Hopefully, those are the last lies that anyone will have to tell.'

Tom nodded, suddenly very tired.

'I'll let you sleep now.' Luigi patted his hand. 'And go easy on your Dad, he's had a hard time.'

Tom dragged his mind back to the present and smiled at his father. 'I was never cross with you, not really, but I don't want to go through anything like that again, especially not the moment I believed Alice and I were going to die. I'd like to pretend I was thinking of Alice, of the danger I'd dragged her into, but I know I was petrified for myself. It's something I'll never forget, however hard I try. I'm glad that the treasure has been found and that you've got your parents back. That I've gained a new family. I just don't like all the deceit.' He met his father's eyes. 'A deceit that started before I was even born. All those years I thought I knew you and really you were someone else, with a whole past I could never have guessed at. It hurts that you didn't trust Mum enough to confide in her.'

'I know, yet at the time I thought it was for the best. My life with you and your mother was a pretence; it didn't stand a chance of succeeding and the fault was all mine. You can't imagine the number of times I wanted to tell you both the truth, but once I'd said that my parents were dead there didn't seem any way back. I can't make things right with your mother, that's a past beyond my reach, but I hope I can make things right with you. I'd like to try.'

He looked so downcast that Tom said, 'Well, there's that holiday you promised me. I distinctly remember swimming and snorkelling being mentioned, and I've still to explore the City of the Knights. You can't count an hour's visit to the Grandmaster's Palace, can you? I'd like to learn more about Claudio Farrigiani, especially as he's my ancestor.'

'And after the holiday? Will you join your mother in America?'

Tom shook his head. 'I said right from the start that I didn't want to live in America, though I've promised to go for some holidays. I'll stay with my grandparents in Manchester until I've finished Sixth Form.'

'There is an alternative. I'm going to make my base on Malta and. . .' He faltered, looking suddenly embarrassed.

'. . . and marry Adriane,' Tom said, helping him out. 'It's OK, I guessed that, or rather Alice did. She's got far more brains than I have. Don't worry, I like Adriane. I always did, even when I thought she was the enemy. I liked Carlo, too, that's what made it so confusing.'

'Adriane and I hope you'll make your home with us. Any time we both had to be away, you could stay at the Villa Magrino. Your grandparents would love that.' Tom was silent. 'You could go to my old school in Mdina, with Tommasso's son Giuseppe Lorenzo. Maybe the two of you will be the ones to heal the rift between us. What do you say?'

Tom hesitated. 'I'll think about it.'

'Something else bothering you?'

'Nothing much.' He glanced up at his father. 'If you really want to know,' he continued, trying to be honest, 'I still feel a bit let down about the treasure. Silly, isn't it? Alice told me that without Brother Gerard there wouldn't have been any Knights of St John, so that makes the statue special, doesn't it?'

'Very special, but don't worry, I had the same initial reaction as you. Comes of spending my youth dreaming of gold and silver.'

'And precious jewels,' Tom added. 'That's what Alice and I thought. You're satisfied now, though?'

Giuseppe smiled. 'Very satisfied. That was a childish dream: this is reality. The statue was there at the very beginning of the Order; it travelled from Jerusalem to Cyprus, to Rhodes and finally here to Malta. It was valued by Claudio Farrigiani and he's been important to me ever since the riddle was passed down to me by Ricardo. That still doesn't satisfy you?'

Tom pulled a face. 'I can't help thinking of the security guard. He lost his life because of a small, wooden statue.'

'No,' his father said gently. 'He lost his life because of Taddeus' pride and Alphonso's greed. You can't blame his death on the statue.'

'I suppose not, but it still feels like an anticlimax.'

'There's something more troubling you, I can see that. You may as well tell me everything. No more secrets, we agreed.'

Tom looked over to where Alice was chattering away to her father. Catching Tom's eye, she came to join him.

'Is the festa as splendid as I told you?'

'Definitely. Especially the big bang. Dad and I have been talking about the future. There's one thing worrying me and I'm sure you've had the same thought.'

'If I'm guessing right, then yes I have.'

Giuseppe looked mystified. 'Whatever are you two talking about? Is it a secret code?'

Tom laughed. 'Alice is a mind reader, didn't you know that?'

'The tape,' Alice explained. 'You know how powerful and influential Taddeus is. What if he manages to find out who has the tape? I wouldn't put it past him. If he gets hold of it and destroys it then the danger will start all over again.'

Tom nodded. 'I know the statue will be beyond his reach, but

Taddeus could take revenge against you for fooling him. We'll none of us be safe.'

'He won't find the tape,' Giuseppe said confidently. 'It's too well hidden.'

'How can you be sure?'

'I am, don't worry. Can't you take my word for it?'

'We can't help worrying,' Tom persisted. 'We've seen what Taddeus is capable of. He won't give in easily.'

Giuseppe studied them thoughtfully. 'Look, this is just between us, OK? No telling anyone – and I mean it this time – not your grandparents, not Ricardo or Marco or Alice's parents. Not anyone. Is that understood?'

Tom grunted assent.

'I promise,' Alice added, 'and Tom will vouch that I can keep a secret.'

'Then put your minds at rest; Taddeus will never find the tape, I can assure you of that. Oh, he'll hunt for it, I've no doubts about that, but he'll never find it. You see, there isn't any tape. There never was any tape. It was all a gigantic bluff. He can search as long as he likes, the longer the better as far as I'm concerned, because there isn't anything for him to find. But as long as Taddeus believes the tape exists, he'll go on searching and we'll all be safe.'

Tom grinned. 'Devious to the end.'

'Afraid so.' Giuseppe put a hand on Tom's shoulder. 'Now, about that other matter we were discussing? I'm sure Alice would be interested in the answer.'

Tom looked across at her and winked. 'I've told you, I'll think about it.'

Reluctant to end the evening, Luigi and Francesca had invited everyone back for coffee. They sat in the front room, only the second time he'd been in there, Tom realised, missing the familiarity of the kitchen which already seemed like home. He'd stay on Malta, he knew that; he'd tell Alice but Dad could fret about his decision for a little longer. Tom still felt restless, as though there were unfinished business left to settle.

Seeing Alice staring at him, he nodded to the doorway. They slipped out unnoticed amidst the chatter of people who had twenty years of talking to make up for. Francesca, Tom noted, had never moved far from the side of her younger son.

'What's up?' Alice whispered as they made their escape.

'Questions that have no answers,' he mouthed back.

By common consent, they opened the front door and slipped into the garden. 'I came this way when I arrived,' Tom reflected. 'I've used the kitchen door ever since.'

'Tonight is a special occasion, though.'

Tom nodded, thinking of the glow on Luigi's face every time he looked at Giuseppe. He was far less demonstrative than Francesca yet his happiness was clear for all to see. It was the ending Tom had longed for, so why this restlessness?

'What's troubling you?' Alice asked. 'Is it the second part of the riddle?'

'Mind reading again?'

'That didn't take much brain power. The second part of the clue has never made any sense, has it? I know it gave us the letters to complete the message, but there must have been more to it than that. It's the one part of the puzzle we've never solved.'

'It led us to Claudio Farrigiani's home and the sundial that he gave to the auberge. I'm sure we were right about that. Dad and Tommasso thought so too, so why was there nothing to find?'

'There was nothing left to find. That's what's so strange. We already had all the letters leading to the statue as soon as we found the second riddle at the Gabriel Tower.'

Tom frowned. 'I can't believe that. He must have had a reason for sending us to the Auberge d'Italie; it was his home, his sundial, surely that must mean something?'

'Perhaps he expected us to find the statue as soon as we got the second riddle and the Auberge d'Italie was for something else.'

'An added message?'

'The only possibility was the Latin inscription,' Alice reflected. 'Something to do with pointing us to the entrance way.'

Their eyes locked, hope dawning. Slowly, almost fearfully, they looked upwards. Over the doorway were the words INTERIORA VIDE.

'Like the marble tablet in the graveyard,' Alice whispered. '*Interiora Vide*: the Farrigiani motto. I wonder if Claudio thought about the inscription on his sundial and devised the motto to fit the second clue. He must have asked his girlfriend to have it carved over the entrance to the house where his child would be born. Do you remember what it means?'

Tom's shining eyes told her that he remembered very well.

The adults were startled as Tom and Alice burst into the room.

'The statue!' Tom demanded. 'We need to see it.'

'Why. . .?' Giuseppe began, but Tom lifted it from the table where it had been taking centre stage and held it up to the light.

He nodded at Alice before confronting his father. 'When you and Tommasso were searching for the treasure, you got as far as the Auberge d'Italie, didn't you?'

'We examined every inch of the sundial and found nothing. I never understood that.'

'How about the Latin inscription?' Tom demanded impatiently. 'Didn't you consider that?'

'Pointing us to the entrance way?' Giuseppe smiled ruefully. 'We spent hours going through every room, much to the old man's amusement. Then we concentrated on the entrance way itself, tapping it all over for secret hiding places. We never found anything.'

'You'd never have found anything if you'd searched for years,' Tom declared, a note of triumph in his voice. 'You'd got the wrong entrance way.' He smiled at Luigi. 'The right one's not used very often, just for special occasions, like tonight, for example.'

'The family motto,' Alice said gently. 'The inscription on the sundial pointed to the motto over your front doorway. He must have presumed that by the time we reached the Auberge d'Italie we'd have collected the statue and he was giving us the clearest directions of what to do with it. *Interiora Vide*. Look within.'

Tom turned the statue upside down and handed it to his father. Giuseppe gazed at the circle cut into the wooden base. Luigi felt in his pocket and silently passed his son a penknife.

Tom could feel the tension as his father ran the knife gently round the crack, easing out a circular wooden disk to reveal the hollowed interior. Slipping a finger into the hole, he prised out a cylinder of thin parchment. Unrolling it carefully, there lay revealed a gold ring adorned with a glowing emerald.

The restlessness left Tom. He knew, without a shadow of a doubt, that his father's long search was finally over.

Taking the parchment, his face fell. 'It's not in English.'

'Of course not.' Giuseppe retrieved the parchment. 'We need to be careful how we handle this, it's very fragile. And it's in Italian, of course. Claudio Farrigiani was an Italian Knight.'

'The riddle was in English,' Tom protested.

'I translated it for Tommasso. The Farrigianis have always made it their business to learn Italian. Even before this incredible find, we were proud of our heritage. Perhaps I should put this away until you've mastered the language.'

'Don't tease him,' Luigi said quietly. 'Finish the story.'

Tom took Alice's hand as his father began to read.

12th June 1789

I wonder who will read this in the years, the centuries to come. I pray that Maria has a son so that, despite my leaving this island of honey in shameful failure, the Farrigiani line may thrive on Malta as witness to our once proud Order of St John. Maria's family are devout Catholics. I have enjoyed their simple faith, though they be but peasant farmers. Today I know that faith alone is not enough. The past few weeks have been the bitterest of my life. In desperation, I and my comrades sought in vain to sway Von Hompesch into action, urging him, "Where are our preparations for defence? What orders do we have?" Valletta, with its massive ramparts, should be adequate to withstand a siege for many months, yet battlements are only as strong as those who man them. And so it was that on the 9th June I stood on the walls of St Elmo gazing across the sea, glorious as hazy blue glass, and witnessed the approach of a fleet surely larger than even that of Suleiman the Great in 1565. On that occasion, under the leadership of Jean de la Valette, they repulsed the might of the Turkish force. We fell with disgraceful ease. The message that Bonaparte sent asking for permission for the whole fleet to enter the harbour was but a ruse. He knew it would be denied him. As I listened to his answer, "General Bonaparte is determined to take by force what ought to have been given freely under the rules of hospitality which govern your order," I knew I was hearing a declaration of war. We fought as best we could, I and my comrades, but with no organised resistance we were indecisive. The Order surrendered to the French army and Bonaparte entered Valletta. Then began a plundering of our treasures. I have saved what I was able. Our precious relic, the hand of John the Baptist, I knew would be too easily missed but I managed to exchange his ring for one of mine own. The Baptist's ring I have hidden inside the small statue of the Angel Gabriel, carved by our founder so long ago in Jerusalem. This evening, when I go to make my farewells to Maria and her family, I shall leave it in her church. Tomorrow, I and my comrades will be banished from this island I have grown to love. Throughout the last few days I have been devising a riddle setting out the identity and location of the treasure. The second part is already hidden in the Gabriel Tower. The first I will leave with Maria to be handed down to my descendants, until it reaches the one destined to recover the treasure and restore it to its rightful place in our Order. And to that person I, Claudio Farrigiani, Knight of St John of Jerusalem, Rhodes and Malta, send my grateful thanks.